A GARGOY...

"Attacking me w... Its tongue lashed ... Dark Father's chee... ...tasted his victory. "You should have just paid the nine hundred thousand nuyen. I would have kept quiet about your dirty little secret. Now I'm going to have to do some serious damage. You'd better pray that your ghoul body is able to take it."

"I . . ." It was getting difficult for Dark Father to speak, even though the words he wanted to utter were no more than neural signals in his brain rather than actual movements of his flesh-and-blood lips.

"Please," Dark Father whispered. "Don't kill me. Let's talk."

"No deal."

The hour of Dark Father's folly—the moment when he'd dared to go against a more talented decker and lost—was at hand. . . .

SHADOWRUN

PSYCHOTROPE

Lisa Smedman

A ROC BOOK

ROC
Published by the Penguin Group
Penguin Putnam Inc., 375 Hudson Street,
New York, New York 10014, U.S.A.
Penguin Books Ltd, 27 Wrights Lane,
London W8 5TZ, England
Penguin Books Australia Ltd,
Ringwood, Victoria, Australia
Penguin Books Canada Ltd, 10 Alcorn Avenue,
Toronto, Ontario, Canada M4V 3B2
Penguin Books (N.Z.) Ltd, 182–190 Wairau Road,
Auckland 10, New Zealand

Penguin Books Ltd, Registered Offices:
Harmondsworth, Middlesex, England

First published by Roc, an imprint of Dutton NAL,
a member of Penguin Putnam Inc.

First Printing, October, 1998
10 9 8 7 6 5 4 3 2 1

Series Editor: Donna Ippolito

 REGISTERED TRADEMARK—MARCA REGISTRADA

SHADOWRUN
PSYCHOTROPE

NORTH

TSIMSHIAN   ATHABASKAN COUNCIL
                    Edmonton•   ALGONKIAN-MANITOU
                                                      COUNCIL
                                        •Saskatoon
        •Vancouver
                                    •Calgary
        SALISH-SHIDHE   •Regina
          COUNCIL
Pacific   •Seattle   •Winnipeg
Ocean
           •Spokane

    •Portland   Helena•   •Fargo •Duluth
        •Salem   •Butte   SIOUX   •Bismarck
                                            NATION   St. Paul•
        TIR   •Boise   •Billings   Minneapolis•
     TAIRNGIRE
                        •Idaho Falls   Sheridan•   Rapid   •Sioux Falls
•Eureka   City
                                                                       •Des
                                Salt Lake•   Omaha•   Moines
        •Reno   City Cheyenne•
                                •Provo   •Kansas
•San Francisco   Boulder• •Denver   City
                                              •Colorado   Topeka•
     CALIFORNIA   UTE   Springs
     FREE STATE   NATION   •Pueblo   •Wichita
        •Bakersfield   Las   PUEBLO
  Santa   •Vegas   CORPORATE   •Tulsa
  Barbara•   COUNCIL
     •Los Angeles   Santa Fe• •Oklahoma City •Little
                                     •Albuquerque •Amarillo   Rock
        •San Diego
     Tijuana•   •Phoenix   Ft. Worth• •Dallas
                    •Tucson   •Roswell   •Shreveport
                              •El Paso   •San Angelo
                                            •San Angelo
Pacific   Austin•
Ocean   Houston•

                    Chihuahua•   •San Antonio

                                                          •Corpus
                              AZTLAN   Christi

                         •Culiacan   Monterrey•
                    La Paz• •Durango Ciudad•
                              To Tenochtitlán Victoria

AMERICA

CIRCA 2060

Ft. Albany   Waskoganish   Sept Iles

QUÉBEC   Gulf of St. Lawrence

Thunder Bay   Quebec   Charlottetown

Fredericton

Lake Superior   Sault Ste. Marie   Montreal   Augusta   Halifax

Sudbury   Montpelier

Milwaukee   Kingston   Concord   Boston

Toronto   Albany

Lansing   Buffalo   Hartford

Chicago   Gary   Detroit   Cleveland   Newark   Manhattan

Philadelphia

Springfield   Indianapolis   Cincinnati   DC

UNITED CANADIAN AND AMERICAN STATES (U.C.A.S.)

Charleston   Richmond

St. Louis   Louisville   Roanoke   Norfolk   Atlantic Ocean

Durham

Nashville   Knoxville   Raleigh

Charlotte

Birmingham   Atlanta

CONFEDERATED AMERICAN STATES (C.A.S.)

Charleston

Jackson   Montgomery   Savannah

Albany

Baton Rouge   Mobile   Jacksonville

Orlando

Gulf of Mexico   Tampa   West Palm Beach

Key West

Havana   **CARIBBEAN LEAGUE**

CUBA

Map of
North America

◎   National Capital

Seattle   •   City

- - -   International Boundary

———   State Boundary (U.S.A. circa 1990)

Kilometers
0   200   400   600

Miles
0   200   400

Published by Xslav Armand University and Cartorenos
4th = Van Buren Chicago UCAS 10 2015 5600 Copyright Miles

March 19, 2060

The day it ended . . .
And began . . .

They'd come for Pip in the middle of the night. Sneaked in the door of the squat, past the bars and locks and the mean old dog that slept in the hallway and that would'a chewed the arm off anyone but Pip and Deni. Skulked their way past all of the magical wards Deni had set up to keep his little sister safe, past the howler sensors that he'd rewired to run off a power cell taken from the abandoned car out back. Stolen Pip right off the mattress she shared with Deni, right out of Deni's arms.

Nothing about it made sense. Deni and Pip were nobodies—just a teenage kid and his eight-year-old sister trying to scrape by in one of the roughest neighborhoods of the Puyallup Barrens. They got by as best they could and stayed clean. Mostly. Deni hired out his shamanistic talents, running astral recons for the scavengers who raided the nearby Black Junk Yards. Pip stayed safe inside the squat, playing with the MatrixPal learning computer that Deni had given her to try and jazz her into talking, to break through the silence she'd blanketed herself in since their dad died.

Pip and Deni didn't bother anybody, and nobody bothered them.

Until now.

Now Deni was racing after Pip, pumping his mana to the max to follow her trail. His meat body was still back at the squat, curled in a ball, nose to knee. But his astral body was loping like Dog, nose to the ground, tracking Pip's astral spoor.

The snatchers had taken Pip out across Hell's Kitchen, the wasteland of ash dunes and crusted lava that was left behind after Mount Rainier blew its lid. Pits of hot mud that would'a boiled the skin off your bones bubbled like open sores, and sulfurous wizz-yellow steam rose into the air. It all passed by in a blur below him as Deni zipped along at maglev speeds.

He passed a nature spirit, its astral form a beastlike cloud of swirling ash. The thing glanced at Deni with lava-red eyes, but Deni was past it before the spirit could attack. He was moving at nova speed, burning up his body's essence at a furious clip. Bit of a brainwipe thing to do, but he had no choice. Pip's life was at stake.

He could see where they'd taken her now. Her scent led to an abandoned power plant. He slowed a tick and took in the sprawling complex of gray concrete walls, massive black pipes that disappeared into the ground, and skeletal towers whose dead high-tension lines lay sprawled on the lava fields like limp snakes. Then he circled the complex once, giving it a quick sniff in about the time it took for one wag of a tail. Satisfied that no nasties were guarding the site, he loped in through the graffiti-smeared wall nearest to the spot where Pip was, moving at a more cautious pace than before.

He was expecting cold gray walls and rusted turbines, dark stairways and garbage on the floor.

Instead he found a toy store.

The rooms were lit like day, the floors clean. The walls were covered in holopics of simsense stars and the floors were knee-deep in toys, all of them new and expensive. Huggable, mood-inducing "feeling foam" dolls sat propped against walls, and miniature maglev trains raced along tracks that wound from room to room. A model space station bobbed gently in mid-air in a darkened office, a holographic spread of twinkling stars surrounding it, and a floor-to-ceiling doll house filled another room. One area held a knee-high table set with toy plates that projected a three-dimensional display of grub, and under it two Battle-bots tussled back and forth across the floor, their metal fists making tiny clanking noises as they traded punches.

Deni saw all of this in a heartbeat as his astral body flashed through the abandoned geothermal plant, bearing down in a laser-straight line through walls toward Pip. It confused him. He'd figured the goons who snatched his sister to be body boosters or pimps. If so, they made their captives pretty drekkin' cozy.

He was close now. Pip's astral scent was strong. Deni flashed through a heavy door of metal-sheathed plastic, then jerked to a halt at what he saw.

There was Pip sitting on an overstuffed couch in a room filled not with toys but with computers. And not kiddie decks like the one Deni had boosted for her, but mega-yen models with squeaky-gleam cases so new they still smelled of plastic. Pip was playing a game on one of the decks, her hands a blur as they flicked the toggle sticks back and forth. She wore her favorite blue dress and her "circuit sox"—black nylon shot with brilliant yellow glofiber. Her curly blonde hair was uncombed—as usual—and her pale skin was unbruised. Deni was glad to see that whoever had taken her hadn't messed her up any. Her aura was bright, clean.

As if sensing his presence, she looked up with a puzzled frown at the spot where Deni hovered in astral space, pant-ing from his run across the wasteland, his tongue lolling. Then she looked back at the screen of the cyberdeck in her lap and she laughed. Out loud. And then she spoke, her eyes still darting as they tracked the game.

"I like it here," she said. "This is fun."

What the . . . ? Pip was happy here? Pip was *talking*?

No, frag it. She had to be on some kind of mood-altering mind benders. That was what had loosened up the emo-tional knot that had kept his sister silent all these years.

Pip must've been tricked into coming here. And it didn't take a technowiz to figure out how. She'd probably met her new "friends" over the Matrix. They'd talked her into leaving the squat by promising her everything Deni couldn't give her: shiny new toys, the latest computer games, an entire playhouse to roam in.

She'd slipped out of bed, tiptoed past the dog, and un-bolted the locks on the front door of the squat herself. Somehow she'd gotten through Hell's Kitchen—Deni didn't even want to think how dangerous that had been—and come here.

And gotten her reward. But Deni knew in his gut that there had to be something nasty waiting at the end of it all.

Deni growled. The fraggers who'd lured Pip here would

pay but good. But why hadn't he seen anyone yet? Pip had said "friends." And that meant more than one . . .

She glanced up from her game as a boy walked into the room and greeted her. He was native, with wide cheek-bones and dusky skin. Maybe fifteen—about Deni's age, but not runty like Deni. He was healthy, well fed. And clean. His clothes looked new, and trend-smart, except for the knitted red and white scarf around his neck. But his eyes had the wary look of someone who'd grown up in the Barrens, hungry and on edge.

When the kid turned, the gleam of a datajack flashed from his temple. Deni's astral vision showed the wires that fed the jack as veins of silver, webbing their way through the kid's brain. He frowned. A datajack was some expensive drek. Where'd a kid get the nuyen for that?

Deni growled as the kid sat down beside Pip on the couch. But the kid didn't make a move on her and Pip didn't seem to mind him sitting there. And what the frag could Deni do about it, anyhow? This recon had taken only a few seconds, but by the time Deni returned to his meat bod and slogged it across the wasteland of Hell's Kitchen—assuming he didn't boil his brains by falling into a mudhole—an hour or more would have gone by. Better to keep an eye on Pip, for now, and see what went down next.

The kid was talking.

"You'll like being *otaku*," he told Pip. "Playing in the Matrix is even more fun than playing with toys."

Pip stared at him a moment, then nodded gravely. "I know."

"There's a special place there. A place that makes you feel happy. When you get your datajack you'll be able to go there as often as you like."

Deni bristled. What was this fragger trying to talk his sister into? Was he trying to get her hooked on BTL? But that was chips. You needed a chipjack for that. Not a data-jack. Datajacks were for computers . . .

"We're going to take a lot of people to the special place today," the kid told Pip. He glanced at the watch on his wrist. "In just a few seconds. Would you like to come too?"

Pip nodded. A smile lit her tiny face.

The kid handed her an electrode net and smiled as she strapped the array of sensors onto her head and plugged its fiber-optic cable into the deck on her lap.

No! Deni raged. *Don't trust him, Pip!* He flailed forward, but his astral body bounced back as it encountered Pip's aura. He whirled, reached out, tried to claw the thing off her head. But it was no fraggin' use. The hands of his astral body were thin as mist.

Pip closed her eyes. Her body relaxed into a slump.

Deni stared at the kid on the couch beside Pip, wanting to take the silly scarf around his throat and choke him with it.

The kid stood up and walked over to a telecom outlet. Seeing him pull a fiber-optic computer connection cable from it, Deni figured he was going to attach it to a cyberdeck. But instead the kid slotted the cable directly into the datajack in his skull. Carefully paying out the cable, the kid sat back down on the couch beside Pip. Then he too leaned back and closed his eyes.

A strange thing happened. The kid's aura went totally weird.

The weirdness began just above the kid's scalp. His aura turned a bright silver color over a point on his datajack, and then lines of energy suddenly sprayed out from this point. Tiny bolts of light, maybe as long as a monowhip stretched out straight, spiked out like roving spotlights, growing thinner and thinner the farther out from the kid's head they got, until they just disappeared. They smelled hot somehow, like electricity.

"I'm in the Matrix," the kid told Pip. "Can you see me?"

"Yes," Pip whispered. "It's beautiful here."

"Just wait," the kid said. "It'll get better."

Even through his rage, Deni knew this had to be a scam. There was no way that kid was in the Matrix. Deni knew enough tech to realize that you had to have a cyberdeck to jack into the virtual reality of the Matrix. You couldn't just slot a cable from a telecom outlet into your datajack. No deck, no dice.

But there was that weird aura . . .

Deni glanced at the kid's wristwatch and saw that it was

blank—then remembered that abstract data like numbers
couldn't be seen in astral space. Still, the time had to be
somewhere just before ten a.m. He tried to figure where
his chummer Alfie would be at this hour. If he could get
her to buzz him out here on her bike they might arrive in
time to save . . .

Pip let out a soft sigh. Then her body suddenly tensed,
and her thin chest stopped moving. Was she still breathing? Oh frag. Was she alive?

Pip's chest rose . . . and slowly fell. She looked like a
coma patient. Except that her limbs were rigid as death.

Drek. Deni had to do something. Fast.

He booted it on back to his meat bod, loping across
Hell's Kitchen as fast as his dog legs would take him.

09:46:12 PST
(18:46:12 WET)
Jackpoint: Amsterdam, Holland

Red Wraith dove for cover as the rumbling tank bore down
on him. A nearby I/O port formed a perfect foxhole: a
triangular-shaped "hole" in the military-green corrugated
metal floor. The tank clattered closer, a monstrosity that
dwarfed Red Wraith, towering over him like a mobile office block. Its matte-black treads were studded with
chromed spikes, its body warted with rivets. Neon-red
lasers beamed out from sensors on all sides of the metal
beast, and its barrel and turret swung back and forth, seeking a target. In seconds it would find where Red Wraith
had gone to ground, would crush him into a bloody pulp
with its treads or blow him to pieces with its cannon . . .

The tank was just a Matrix construct—a metaphor for a
computer program. Just as Red Wraith's persona icon, with
its ghostlike body that ended in dripping red mist where
the lower legs would normally be, was a virtual representation of the decker named Daniel Bogdanovich. But Red
Wraith used the adrenaline rush the tank image gave him,

let it spike his consciousness into hyper-awareness. He'd come so far to reach these personnel records . . .

He wasn't going to give up without a fight, even if it cost him his deck. Not when he was this close.

He used his cyberdeck's masking program to change the appearance of his on-line persona into a shimmering cloud of glittering silver confetti. With luck, the tank-shaped intrusion countermeasures program that was bearing down on him would mistake him for a stream of data, one of dozens that flowed back and forth across the inside of the octagonal box that represented the sub-processing unit he'd decked into. The false datastream created by the masking program would glitch up the actual data that was flowing into Red Wraith's "foxhole"—in the real world, the hardcopy printer that was connected to the port would hiccup and spew out a page or two of jumbled graphics. But with luck, the admin clerks at UCAS Seattle Command would lay the blame on a hardware glitch.

Red Wraith crouched lower in his foxhole as the tank rumbled closer. Crashing the IC wasn't an option. A stunt like that would trigger too many system alerts, and then he'd have hostile UCAS deckers to tangle with. Instead he had to find some way to subtly defeat the program.

As the tank loomed over his foxhole, Red Wraith could feel the walls and floor of the I/O port rumbling. Then the tank's tread sealed off the hole, plunging him into darkness, and Red Wraith was engulfed in the stench of hot exhaust and oil. Part of his mind acknowledged and appreciated the detail of the programming, noted the effectiveness of psyching out the target by overwhelming his sensors with such oppressive detail. Another part of him responded with the fear the tank's designers had intended to induce. But the logical, methodical part of Red Wraith's mind— the part that had given him the steady hands and cool head to perform assassinations—was in control. Almost instinctively, he tucked away his fear and activated an analyze utility.

The utility appeared next to him in the customized iconography he'd given it: a trode-patch electrocardiograph monitor like those used in hospitals. Programming on the fly, Red Wraith modified its outer casing, shaping it into a gleaming chrome spike like those on the treads of the tank. Then he reached up and jammed it home. The trode patch on the wide end of the spike sampled the graphic imaging of the IC, then adhered firmly as it was incorporated into the tank's programming.

A series of pulsing red lines appeared in the darkness in front of Red Wraith as the utility began its analysis. He scanned them quickly as the tank rumbled clear of the I/O port, noting the oscillation of the sine wave and the frequency of the peaks on the baseline below it. The readouts told him not only what type of IC he was up against—blaster, an attack program that could send his cyberdeck's MPCP chips into meltdown on a successful hit—but also how tough the program would be to crack.

Diagnosis: tough. But not mega. And that puzzled Red Wraith. He'd decked into a military computer system containing confidential personnel datafiles; the IC here should have had ratings that were off the scale. Sure, the datafiles were merely the records of personnel who had "retired" from active service. They hardly contained anything that would be considered damaging to UCAS national security. Just addresses, medical records, next-of-kin forms. No active service records. But they should have been guarded more closely, just the same.

Hmm . . .

A sudden shift in perspective took Red Wraith by surprise. Suddenly he was lying on the "floor" of the system construct, looking across an expanse of corrugated metal at the glowing rectangular block of the datastore he'd been trying to access before the tank materialized. The I/O port he'd been hunkering down in was nowhere in sight.

He processed the shift in the visual landscape and instantly realized what had happened. The I/O port had gone off-line, ejecting him back into the octagonal box that represented the sub-processing unit as its icon disappeared. The UCAS SEACOM's sysops must have noted the glitch in the printer and taken the port off-line. Now he was fully exposed . . .

Light flared explosively around Red Wraith as an IC attack hit home. The resolution of the images that surrounded him shimmered and blurred. When they came back into focus a moment later, the colors were muted, the resolution grainy. And it was getting worse. The walls and floor of the sub-processing unit were losing their solidity, just the peaks of the corrugations showing in a barlike pattern that revealed gaping, empty, non-space beyond . . .

Drek! The system was also protected by jammer IC! It was messing with his deck's sensor program, messing up his ability to distinguish the iconography of the Matrix. It had already partially wiped his ability to process the visual component of the tank. But he could hear the bone-jarring clatter of its spiked treads and could feel the subsonic rumble of its engines, even though he couldn't locate the direction from which these sensory signals were coming.

He was equally blind to the jammer IC that had put him in this fix. But his tactile sensations hadn't been glitched yet. He felt around him, patting his hands gently over the corrugated floor. There! A round device with a button on top: a land mine. The IC was a nasty little piece of programming. Its first, undetectable attack had been when Red Wraith first logged onto this system, rendering the jammer IC invisible to him. Now he knew what he was "looking" for. But unless he wanted to move at a crawl, feeling his way blindly along, he'd be hit with attack after attack until all five of his virtual senses were down.

And now the tank was almost upon him. The floor was vibrating wildly under his feet.

There was only one thing to do—hunker down and pray his utilities would protect him.

He activated his deck's shield utility. A rubberized black body bag appeared around him. The zipper closed, sealing him inside, and for nearly a full second Red Wraith saw nothing but darkness. He initiated a medic utility, rerouting functionality to the backup chips in his deck's MPCP. And then he waited while the medic utility did its work. He heard a rumbling, felt a heavy weight pass over him. But the spikes on the treads of the tank did not penetrate the thick rubber shielding of the cocoonlike bag.

He waited until the medic utility had finished its work. Then he opened the body bag's zipper—and was relieved to see that his graphics-recognition capacity had been restored. Peeling the body bag away from his body, he stepped back into the iconography of the sub-processing unit and surveyed the field of battle. Now he could see the previously invisible land mines that were the jammer IC. This time, he would be able to avoid them.

The tank was visible again, and was rattling away from him. But it took only an instant for it to pinpoint its prey. One of its rear-mounted targeting lasers found Red Wraith and locked its ruby-red cross hairs on his chest. The turret whipped around one-eighty degrees in a motion so fast the barrel of the cannon ghosted, and Red Wraith was looking down into the cold, dark muzzle of the cannon.

Just the way he wanted it . . .

Red Wraith reached up with his ghostly hands, yanked his head from his body, and hurled it into the gaping maw of the cannon. Darkness engulfed him. He had a sensation of sliding, spiraling along the cannon's rifled interior . . .

Then his head exploded. He was a swirl of numbers, characters, symbols—strings of programming that wormed their way into the metal of the tank, penetrating its algorithmic armor and seeking out its core programming. One of those datastrings found the sub-routine that the IC used to analyze its sensory input in order to coordinate its targeting and damage-assessment systems. The datastring spiraled around that sub-routine, creating a tiny loop that connected it with another. Then Red Wraith shifted his perspective back to the new head that had materialized on his persona.

The cannon belched flame and smoke. A projectile composed of tightly knitted code emerged from the muzzle, flashed toward Red Wraith in a streak of light—and passed harmlessly through his ghostly body. Then it arced up, over—and slammed into the tank itself, exploding with a bright flash.

The tank fired another projectile. And another.

Red Wraith didn't even flinch. A total of six explosions rocked the tank, and then the cannon fell silent and the projectiles stopped. The cannon barrel turned left, right, then the laser targeting sights suddenly blinked out.

As the tank rumbled forward across the corrugated metal floor, Red Wraith neatly sidestepped it. The tank continued until it struck one of the solid rectangular blocks that represented datastores within the sub-processing unit, drew back, changed its orientation slightly, then butted against it a second time. Only after a number of jarring impacts did the tank lumber away—only to get caught against another datastore.

Red Wraith nodded in satisfaction. His customized attack utility had done its work. The link it had created between the two sub-programs had caused the data corresponding to the location of Red Wraith's persona to be skipped. Instead it was replaced with the data that represented the tank's own position within the sub-processing unit. Unable to lock onto its intended target, the tank's attack bypassed Red Wraith's persona, leaving the decker's MPCP undamaged. Instead it attacked the programming of the blaster IC itself, rendering the IC blind to the icons around it.

Although it had been defeated, the blaster IC was still up and running. It would give the appearance of being fully functional to any sysop who ran a diagnostics check on this sub-processing unit.

One thing was still bothering Red Wraith, however. When he'd run his analyze utility, it had identified the tank as gray IC, an intrusion countermeasures program that attacked the deck, rather than the decker. But what if that had been just a mask? Military computer systems usually were protected with black IC. "Killer" IC, deckers called it, since the biofeedback it induced could flatline you.

And Red Wraith, of all people, should know you can't judge a killer by his cover.

He did not experience any of the warning signs usually associated with lethal biofeedback. That was because the cranial bomb that had nearly taken his life seven years ago had done extensive damage to the mesencephalic central gray matter in his brain. As a result, he was no longer able to feel physical pain.

The bomb also severed his spinal cord at the second cervical vertebrae. In the bad old days of the twentieth century, this would have left him a quadriplegic, immobile from the neck down, dependent upon a breather machine and moving about in the world in a wheelchair equipped with an archaic sip and puff computer interface. But modern medicine had allowed the docs to revive him, even though he was clinically dead when the trauma team found him. Cybersurgeons had rebuilt the fragmented vertebrae with plastic bone lacing and replaced the transected axions of his spinal cord with a modified move-by-wire system. Occasionally, his limbs spasmed out, but at least he was mobile. Most of the time.

Red Wraith initiated a customized medical diagnostics utility that was programmed to do a quick scan of his meat bod. A series of condition monitors appeared in front of him. Heart rate, blood pressure, blood-oxygenation levels, and respiratory rates were all normal. His cybereyes and ears were still functional, as were his blood and air filters, his toxin exhaler, and his adrenal pump.

All that cyberware—as well as the fingertip needle with its compartment of deadly toxin in his right forefinger and the subdermal induction datajack in his left palm that he used to access the Matrix—had been installed courtesy of the UCAS military. His handlers had made him into the perfect killing machine, used him to assassinate key political figures during the decade of political unrest that followed the Euro-Wars, then slagged him with the cranial bomb they'd hidden at the base of his skull when his services were no longer required.

Or tried to slag him.

The cranial bomb had been defective. It had taken Red Wraith to the brink of death. For more than a minute, he had been clinically dead. But fortunately, he'd been in Amsterdam when the bomb was activated. And fortunately, he'd secretly purchased a platinum-class contract with the Hoogovens Groep Clinic. The Daf TraumaVaggon had gotten him to the clinic in time.

The doctors hadn't known who their patient was—all records of the human named Daniel Bogdanovich had been erased long ago from public databases, and, given the cybereyes, retinal scans were not an option anyway. But their patient's credit had been good. And so the cyberdocs did what had to be done to save his life.

Daniel settled in Amsterdam afterward. It was as good a place as any to call home, and the houseboats on the canals provided accommodation that was cheap and private. He didn't venture out much; suffering a spasmodic episode in public was not his idea of a fun time. Instead he spent most of his time in the world of the Matrix, a world in which the icon that was his "body" never failed him. A world in which the encephalon implants they'd used to repair his damaged brain gave him a distinct edge.

He had chosen Red Wraith as his on-line handle and constructed his persona in the image of a particular form of ghost known as a wraith. According to superstition, a wraith was an apparition that took the form of the person whose death it portended. And that pretty much summed up Red Wraith's previous career.

In his role as cyberassassin, his most important asset had been his ability to infiltrate his target's home, head-quarters, or place of work. He did this by "becoming" the target through a combination of disguise and technological mimicry. All assassins prepare by acquiring as much information on the target as possible, and Daniel had taken this to the bleeding edge. Into the datasoft link in his skull he slotted not only chips containing the target's personal data, but also chips comparable in function to an activesoft. These contained programs that overrode Daniel's own emotional responses and motor skills, allowing him to pre-cisely duplicate the target's behavioral quirks, speech patterns, and emotional reactions. Like the wraith for which his on-line persona was named, Daniel became a mirror image of his target—an apparition whose arrival portended the target's death.

Part of the function of the headware memory system that accommodated the data from the skillsofts had been to suppress Daniel's own long-term memories, so that he could not give information on his past hits, if apprehended and magically mind-probed. He remembered his current mission—who he was to assassinate, where, and when—but remembered nothing prior to the start of that mission. As for his memories previous to becoming a UCAS assas-sin, only flashes and fragments remained. He knew that he had been based out of UCAS SEACOM and that he had once lived in Seattle. As for his personality . . . well, all he had left was the chip he'd slotted on his last job. His own,

original personality was like an erased chip, wiped clean
by the installation of the datasoft link in his skull.

But fragmentary memories occasionally surfaced. And
one of those fragments—the memory of a woman—was
what had gotten Daniel through, had given him the will to
come back from the brink of death after the cranial bomb
nearly killed him.

When the Daf TraumaVaggon team had found him,
Daniel was clutching a holopic of her. His mind held
equally tightly to the memory fragments of her that remained in his wetware. The memory of her face: high
cheekbones and sparkling green eyes framed by auburn
hair. Her name: Lydia. Her relationship to him: lover,
friend, wife.

But the rest was missing. Daniel had no idea where the
pair of them had lived, no idea where Lydia might be today. He desperately wanted to touch the smooth skin of
her cheek once more, to stare into the eyes that had once
burned with such intense love.

But the only way he was going to do that was if he accessed his old personnel records, found out where she had
been living on the day that he'd "died." Seven years had
elapsed since then, but there was still a good chance that
Lydia was alive, that her current address could be traced
once he had her SIN. It wouldn't even matter if she were in
a relationship with someone else, if she had forgotten
all about him. Red Wraith just wanted to see her one last
time . . .

He'd been preparing for this datarun for seven long
years, honing his skills as a decker. Now he was one of the
best. And he had reached his goal. Or nearly . . .

Red Wraith turned his attention to the datastore. It was
shaped like a metal ammo box with a large hasp on one
side. A marquee of stenciled block letters flowed around
the ammo box: AUTHORIZED PERSONNEL ONLY. The
analyze utility he'd used on this datastore earlier had triggered the attack by the blaster IC. But it had also alerted
Red Wraith to some white IC that he now would be able to
deal with.

He clenched his hand in a particular motion and a
scalpel appeared in it. Studying the hasp that sealed the

ammo box, he slid the blood-lubed blade of the surgical knife into it and turned it slowly, feeling the resistance. The action triggered his cyberdeck's defuse utility, neutralizing the data bomb that was attached to this datafile. The hasp broke apart into pixels that shimmered and disappeared, and the ammo box swung open.

A cyclone of swirling alphanumeric characters rose from the box. Red Wraith triggered his browse program, sought out the file that bore his name. Names spiraled past his eyes, too quickly to read. The As, the Bs . . .

The cyclone stopped, frozen in place. Paydata! Bogdanovich, Daniel. Red Wraith reached out and seized the name, felt raw data stream through him as the personnel file downloaded into his cyberdeck. Then he released the cyclone. It spiraled downward, neatly compressing itself back into the ammo box. He closed the lid, and the hasp reappeared.

He glanced at the tiny red numbers that logged the amount of time he'd spent on this run: forty-seven seconds; local time 09:46:59. It was time to jack out of here and scan the data he had so painstakingly acquired, to solve the mystery of his past life . . .

09:46:15 PST
(02:46:15 JST)
Jackpoint Osaka, Japan

Lady Death smiled as she put the finishing touches on her virtual sculpture. The icon that hung in front of her was a perfect duplicate of her own Matrix persona: long, dark hair drawn up in a bun at the back of the head, skin a pure, dead white as if drained of blood, face with red accents on the lips and cheeks. It was dressed in a flowing white kimono—the color of mourning—patterned with glowing red dracoforms.

The image was drawn from *kabuki*—the overly formal, traditional style of Japanese theater whose feudal tragedies played so well as simsense. Lady Death's icon was that of a woman who had committed *shinju*—double-lover suicide. Which was both appropriate and ironic . . .

Satisfied with her high-resolution double, Lady Death sent the icon out into the Matrix. While it dutifully logged onto AS/NIPO-TOK-5673, the telecommunications grid that was home to one of Tokyo's many cramming schools, Lady Death would be elsewhere. The icon was merely part of a mirrors utility that would fool her guardians into thinking she was logged onto the *juku.* She even had an excuse to explain why she had awakened at the unusual hour of just before three a.m. to study. This was university entrance exams week, and the Osaka telecommunications grid was jammed from five a.m. on. She was just getting an early start to her cramming.

The icon disappeared into a system access node. At the same moment, her cyberdeck's masking program activated, throwing up a shimmering haze that rendered her actual persona almost transparent.

Beside her, a miniature lion, seemingly made of folded *origami* paper, sprang into being. It stood quivering on clawed feet, as if sniffing the air. It inclined its head slightly toward where Lady Death hung, its glowing yellow eyes shifting back and forth as tiny red numerals scrolled across the spot where its pupils should have been. Then its nose snapped around as if picking up a stronger scent. It leaped into the SAN and disappeared with a papery, rustling sound.

"Desu," she whispered to herself. "The trace program has been fooled. Time to go."

Still maintaining her masking program, she pushed aside the painted cloth banner that hung in front of her. In that one motion she exited from her family's private LTG into the Shiawase Corporation system itself.

The system was patterned after a *kare-sansui* garden, but with high-tech imagery overlaying the traditional elements. Instead of following a Western-style, right-angled grid, data flowed in sinuous curves reminiscent of raked sand. The ripples fed into the fiber-optic roots of the miniature *bonsai* trees that were the system's datastores, or flowed around the clear glass boulders that represented sub-processing units.

At this early hour, the system contained only a handful of deckers. Their icons were scattered across the huge expanse of landscape that stretched out on either side of Lady Death—tiny, human-shaped figures that swam like tadpoles through the datastreams below.

Lady Death plunged downward, toward the raked-sand plain. In an eyeblink she was inside a datastream, surrounded by the pea-sized grains of sand that represented individual packets of data and moving rapidly amidst the flow. She came to another SAN, this one sculpted to resemble a temple gate with ornate brass scrollwork and dark, heavy wood. She pushed it open, stared at the more conventional grid of right-angled neon lines that lay beyond, and entered the address of the LTG she wanted to access. Then she flowed through the door and into the rigid Western-style grid of the Seattle RTG.

The database she sought was a fansite devoted to *manga* music. Like the two-dimensional animated cartoons of the previous century from which it took its name, *manga* music was over-the-top—devoted to action, color, and spectacle. The singers who fronted its bands wrapped their music in cartoonish elements, using a blend of illusion magic and high-rez graphics technology to produce incredible spectacles.

The *manga* music fansite offered free simsense downloads—home recordings done by fans at live concerts. These allowed other fans from around the world to experience the thrill of seeing their favorite bands perform live. Many of the simsense recordings were crudely edited, or were marred by having been shot by fans who were jazzed on amphetamines or hallucinogenic drugs. But it wasn't the experience of seeing her favorite singer that Lady Death was after. She wanted to find out where Shinanai was. Perhaps one of the fans had seen one of the underground, unauthorized concerts that Shinanai was rumored to be secretly giving in UCAS.

Shinanai—the legendary lead singer of Black Magic Orchestra. Shinanai, the woman whose name meant "deathless." Shinanai's image was burned into Lady Death's memory: tall, thin, with nearly translucent white skin and silver-blonde hair shaved high over elven ears but long in the back. A delicate tracery of luminescent blue face paint accentuating high cheekbones and piercing aqua blue eyes. Black leather pants, cinched tight with straps and buckles from ankle to thigh. Red mesh shirt covered by a black leather jacket with its sleeves cut out. Fingertips, each and every one bearing the tattoo of a grinning skull. And a voice that could howl as raw as a shadowhound or sing as sweet and pure as a synthesized flute.

Shinanai was just one of many *aidoru*—singers who were idolized by Japanese high school students. But to Lady Death, Shinanai was everything—and the only *aidoru* worth thinking about. She had an intensity, a way of mesmerizing you and stealing your heart away with just one smoldering, shiver-inducing look. And so Lady Death—or Hitomi, as she was known in the meat world—had slipped away from her guardians and sneaked backstage to meet Shinanai in person. Captivated by the singer's magic, she had run away from home and school and family to become Shinanai's lover.

Or at least, she had allowed Shinanai to love her. It had been enough simply to allow Shinanai to embrace her, to stroke her skin, to kiss her lips with a passion that Hitomi had never felt before. Shinanai neither asked for nor accepted physical stimulation in return. Instead Shinanai drank of Hitomi's soul.

A little too deeply. When the shadowrunners who had been hired by Hitomi's father caught up with Hitomi, they found her on the blood-soaked bed of the hotel room in Seoul that Shinanai had vacated moments before. Hitomi had died of blood loss after Shinanai had drunk deeply from her femoral artery, letting the passion-pumped blood flow until Hitomi expired. For Shinanai was a vampire.

The runners' shaman and medic had been able to revive Hitomi, to pull her back from just over the brink of death. He said her *ki* was strong, despite the fact that the vampire had been supping upon this life force. But Hitomi knew that her will to live came not from any physical or psychic strength. It was simply that she could not bear to die and never see her beloved *aidoru* again. She had walked away from the brink of death by choice.

They had kept her in isolation in her family's private medical clinic for many months after that. Her guardians kept watching and waiting, fearful lest Hitomi herself become a vampire. But somehow her body had resisted the HMHVV virus.

Hitomi knew that Shinanai had intended for her to become a vampire, that Shinanai had killed her so she could share eternal life. Only the shadowrunners' arrival had forced Shinanai to flee. In her heart, Hitomi knew that Shinanai would be happy to see her again, would be hoping that Hitomi would be able to track her down. But a part of her still wondered why Shinanai had fled from the shadowrunners, instead of fighting them. Vampires were supposed to be legendary in their strength . . .

Ironically, Hitomi—as Lady Death—had once claimed expertise on vampires and had commented more than once on their cruel, sadistic nature on the Shadowland postings she loved to frequent. But her information had come from tridcasts and news reports. After having met a vampire first-hand, after having become Shinanai's lover, Hitomi now knew how wrong she had been. She only wished she could convince her guardians of this fact.

Since that night in Seoul, two separate attempts had been made on Shinanai's life, forcing her into hiding. No more was Shinanai giving live concerts—at least, not for the general public. Hitomi had no doubt that the shadowrunners hired by her father were to blame, and that they would continue tracking the vampire until their job was done.

In killing Hitomi, Shinanai had ensured her own death. Double-lover suicide.

As for Hitomi herself, she had not been allowed to leave the Shiawase arcology for the fourteen long months that had passed since her "death." Her guardians made sure she did not stray, that she could not follow through on her compulsive need to see Shinanai again. But that did not mean her mind could not wander freely, that she could not access Shinanai in other ways as Lady Death . . .

The *manga* music fansite was tricky to find. Few regular

deckers even knew it was there—only hard-core *manga* fans ever accessed it. The fansite was located on the Seattle RTG but was invisible, due to the fact that it could only be accessed by means of a "vanishing" SAN—a system access node that allowed entry only at specific times of day. In addition, the SAN "teleported" on a regular basis, switching its network address to various locations on the Seattle RTG according to the dictates of a secret algorithm. To know where to access this SAN and at what time, a decker had to know someone who knew someone who knew the sysop who had created the algorithm . . . and so on. It was kind of like scoring a BTL chip—or so she guessed, since she'd never had cause to purchase illegal simsense. It was a highly secretive process, based on word of mouth and trust.

Lady Death followed a dataline to the pulsating drumhead that was the icon of a nightclub known as Syberspace. The dull black octagonal sent out a steady rhythm that Lady Death could "feel" in her meat bod—a bone-thrumming bass that mimicked a syncopated heartbeat. A favorite nightclub of deckers, Syberspace was physically located in downtown Seattle. But the virtual nightclub was accessible to deckers around the world. And one of its nodes, seconds from now, would connect with the *manga* music fanbase.

Lady Death dove through the head of the drum, into the Syberspace construct itself. It looked like a nightclub, complete with a mirror-backed bar stocked with glowing bottles and a large dance floor. The icons of other deckers drifted through the room, occasionally touching a bottle to access a biofeedback program that would either stimulate or sedate their meat bods, as desired, or placing a palm on one of the many bar stools whose seats resembled trode rig interfaces.

Although the nightclub construct was realistic in the extreme, the deckers' icons gave the place a surrealistic feel. A somber-looking man in top hat and tails sat next to a gray and white cartoon rabbit with white gloves, big floppy ears, and a gleeful grin. A topless teenage girl with mohawk hair and baggy shorts rode a jet-propelled surfboard past a clown, a gigantic red cockroach, and an Asian

woman in a stylish business suit. A sasquatch jived alone
in the center of the bar, his massive, hairy hands moving in
intricate patterns like those of a Balinese temple dancer,
while in another corner a trio of personas whose faces and
bodies were smooth metal ovoids stood silently, accessing
the program that would induce in their minds a simsense
recording of the live performance that was actually going
on in the meat-world nightclub.

Lady Death bowed to the club's sysop—a portly man in
bacchanalian toga and headband of gold grape leaves—
and asked for her "drink" by name: Magical Mystery Tour.
The bartender smiled and crooked a chubby finger, and a
yellow bottle floated over to Lady Death. For just a moment, the bottle took on a new shape: long and cylindrical
still, but with a periscope and portholes down the side.
Hurriedly, before the vanishing node disappeared and the
submarine became merely a bottle again, Lady Death
touched it . . .

And found herself inside the *manga* music database.

After the high-resolution realism of the Syberspace system, it took her a moment to get used to the overly sim-
plistic but crowded landscape of the fansite. Everything
was outlined in heavy black lines and deliberately pixe-
lated, so that individual dots of primary color could be
seen within each icon. Cartoonish renderings of *manga*
music singers and musicians capered and wailed across a
landscape rocked by explosions, while rocket-propelled
Battlebots roared unnoticed above the heads of adoring
prepubescent fans whose overly large eyes slavishly followed the musicians' every move. Although music was being performed with furious abandon, no aural elements
were included. The only "sounds" were the cartoon speech
bubbles that hung above the musicians' heads and the mu-
sical notes that swarmed around them like bees.

To access one of the simsense recordings that had been
posted here, the decker reached out and touched one of the
cartoon speech bubbles. Their captions were sometimes
cryptic and sometimes straightforward, but were always
punctuated to the max: "Meta Madness rocks Orktown!!!"
or "Chillwiz concert a SCREAMER. I yarfed my lunch!!!"
or "Guess Hue?!?"

Lady Death searched for anything that looked like a Black Magic Orchestra concert upload. A total of three cartoonish icons of Shinanai materialized in front of her, making Lady Death gasp with longing. But the captions above their heads were already familiar; these were sim-sense recordings of concerts from a previous UCAS tour, from before the time when Shinanai went underground. Lady Death considered sampling them, then reluctantly realized that downloading them onto her cyberdeck would increase the chance of her foray into the *manga* music site being detected by her guardians. She dismissed them with a wave and set her browse utility scanning on a variety of keywords. But the titles to Black Magic Orchestra's hit singles came up dry, as did the names—both real and stage names—of the band members.

Lady Death paused, frustrated and disappointed. No new postings. *Donzoko.* She stamped a foot in frustration. How would she ever find Shinanai?

Then she remembered the lyrics to the song that the *aidoru* had been composing, back when they had been together in the hotel room in Seoul. To the best of Lady Death's knowledge, it had never been performed at a public concert. Based on a *tanka,* a traditional thirty-one-syllable poem, the song had compared a woman to a well in which water rose anew each spring, and from which her lover drank again and again. Lady Death now realized that it was a veiled reference to Shinanai's vampirism. At the time, she thought it was simply a metaphor for love.

She chose the title of the song as the keyword for her search: *Shunga.* In literal translation, Spring Pictures—a euphemism for erotic simsense. Within a nanosecond or two, a cartoonish image appeared before her: that of an androgynous singer with a sexy pout, clad only in a black velvet cape that was wrapped tight around his/her body. Bright pink cherry blossoms drifted down like snow as the singer crooned silently into the speech bubble that floated above. The icon was human, rather than elven, and did not look a thing like Shinanai. But the caption over the head of the figure fit the imagery of the song: "I wish you well. I wish you would. I bet you WILL!!!"

Lady Death touched the caption and began downloading

the simsense recording into her cyberdeck, onto the optical storage chip that was deliberately not listed on any of the deck's directories. As the data flowed, she noted the date and time that the recording had been posted, and the jack-point of the decker who had uploaded it. It had been posted just yesterday, from Kobe, a suburb of the Osaka sprawl. If it really was a recording of an underground Black Magic Orchestra concert, recorded by one of the fans who had seen the show live and then immediately uploaded the recording after the show, that meant that Shinanai was barely a five-minute maglev ride away from Lady Death in the meat world.

After so many months of numbness, Lady Death felt a rush of emotion. Joy and happiness warred with caution and fear. She could barely contain her impatience during the few nanoseconds it took to download the simsense recording; she simply could not wait to log off the Matrix and scan it. Perhaps Shinanai had hidden a secret message in the song, a call for the school girl Hitomi to rejoin her lost love.

Lady Death checked her cyberdeck's time-keeping log. It was 9:46:59 PST in the meat world—2:46:59 in the morning in Osaka. She had been running the Matrix for a mere forty-four seconds. Hopefully, her guardians had not yet noticed that she had strayed into the forbidden territory of the *manga* music fansite. If they had, there was a possibility that Shiawase deckers had already erased the contraband simsense recording as it flowed through her family's private LTG and into her deck. But if all was still well and Lady Death's mirrors utility and masking program had done their work, in a second or two, when she jacked out, Lady Death would at last know where her beloved Shinanai was today . . .

Dark Father stared at the creature that waited for him below, in the private conversation pit. The thing was a strange blend of two different paranormal creatures. It had the squat, heavily muscled body of a gargoyle, as well as that creature's large leathery wings, pointed ears, forehead horn, and jutting muzzle. But its flesh was covered in the green and black scales of a mimic snake, and a forked tongue slithered in and out of its hinged jaw. Its neck was just a little too long, and its beady eyes were serpentlike slits under heavy brows.

The combination was probably intended to be doubly unsettling. Had the creature actually existed in nature, its victims wouldn't know whether they would be constricted to death and then swallowed whole, or dive-bombed from above and raked with talons and claws.

In fact, the creature was a construct within the Matrix, an icon representing a computer decker. But even though it was unreal, composed only of pixels of light, it had the capacity to be deadly, just the same.

Dark Father descended a spiral staircase made of floating white rectangles. When he reached the bottom and stepped onto the green marbled floor of the conversation pit, a metallic boom echoed overhead. He looked up and saw that the sub-processing unit had been sealed off with what looked like a gigantic metal hatch, octagonal in shape. Eight black pillars had appeared to hold it in place. Jagged blue bolts of electricity rose one after the other between the pillars, crackling as they wavered their way from floor to ceiling.

Dark Father recognized the program: a form of barrier IC named Jacob's Ladder. It was intended to guarantee absolute privacy to the two occupants of this SPU, one of several secure nodes on the Virtual Meetings host. Hidden away in a remote corner of the Seattle telecommunications grid, Virtual Meetings' black pyramid contained a number of private iconferencing sites, making it a favorite meeting place for shadowrunners.

And for blackmailers.

The gargoyle leaned against a sundial that was set into the middle of the conversation pit's floor. Glowing white numerals announcing the time of day encircled its rim, patterns of white against the sun dial's black marbled finish. They crawled with painful slowness around the rim; seconds always seemed slower in the Matrix, where words and deeds were accomplished with the speed of thought. The conversation pit was theirs until ten a.m.—ample time for them to conclude their meeting.

Dark Father stared coldly at the gargoyle. "Well? Here I am." He stood with hands folded in front of him, an ebon-black skeleton with yellowed eyeballs, wearing a tall top hat and a black suit that hung loosely upon its bones. A pale white hangman's noose, knotted around his neck like a tie, was a stark contrast to bones and cloth so dark that they were difficult to see against the backdrop of inky blackness that lay beyond the sub-processing unit.

The gargoyle—who went by the handle Serpens in Machina—flashed Dark Father a quick smile, revealing needle-sharp teeth. "There you are," he said. "So that's what you look like." The gargoyle shifted his wings slightly and Dark Father heard the creak of leather and smelled the dry muskiness of snake. The persona icon was high-rez enough to include aural and olfactory components, in addition to its visual and tactile presence. Serpens in Machina must have some mighty state-of-the-art equipment. He was not someone to be trifled with.

But Dark Father already knew that. He had come prepared.

"Have you arranged for the credit transfer?" the gargoyle asked.

Dark Father nodded. "Nine hundred thousand nuyen is waiting in an account in the Zurich-Orbital Gemeinschaft Bank. All you need to access it is the passcode."

"Wrong," the gargoyle said. "You'll be the one accessing it. I have no intention of getting hit with whatever IC you've loaded the account with. At precisely noon today, Pacific Standard Time, you will transfer the money in three equal portions into the accounts of three organizations: the Ork Rights Committee Seattle chapter; VVA-MOS—Victims of Violence Against Metahumans and Other Species; and the MetaRights League of Boston."

Dark Father shuddered at the list. Neo-anarchists, metahuman agitators, and terrorists. In the real world, his lip curled at putting nuyen in their coffers.

"And your take?" he asked.

"Nada," the gargoyle answered. "I'm like Robin Hood. Take from the rich, give to the poor . . ."

"You're targeting the wrong person," Dark Father countered.

"You *are* rich, Winston Griffith III."

Dark Father's eyes narrowed at the use of his real name. He was at a disadvantage; despite his best efforts he had been unable to learn the real-world identity of Serpens in Machina. He was not the world's hottest decker, but he did have the very best hardware and programs that nuyen could buy. He had every electronic edge available. And still he had failed.

"I am wealthy," Dark Father agreed. "But I'm already a philanthropist, so there's no need to blackmail me. It was my charitable donations that enabled the establishment of three separate Informed Parenting clinics in one of Toronto's poorest neighborhoods. The orks and trolls of the Vaughn warrens now have free birth control and counseling, regardless of their SIN status or . . ."

"Free abortions and sterilization, you mean."

Dark Father bristled. "Those are the most effective methods, yes. Orks and trolls aren't the most intelligent creatures. You can't expect them to remember to show up every six months for another implant needle. And with the average litter comprising four or more offspring, the pressures on Toronto's social systems are tremendous, not to mention the personal hardships faced by the young ork mother who finds herself with too many mouths to feed when she's still only in her teens."

"Bulldrek," the gargoyle said sharply. "Your clinics are nothing more than a Human Nation front. And you're a known HN sympathizer, despite your . . . personal background."

The gargoyle snorted. It cocked its bullet-shaped head to one side. "Ironic, isn't it? If you weren't a member of one of Toronto's wealthiest families, you'd be on the streets like the rest of us. Without your inheritance to buffer you from the unpleasantness of the world, you'd be a target for every bounty hunter in UCAS. Like the one who tried to gun you down a year ago."

Despite himself, Dark Father shuddered. How could Serpens in Machina have found out about *that* as well? Winston had been feeding, late at night in the hospital morgue, when his unknown assailant had surprised him. The gunman's comments had made it clear that he was a bounty hunter and that he knew exactly what Winston was up to. He had taken a moment to gloat at catching Winston in the act before unloading an entire magazine into Winston's chest.

The surgeons who saved Winston's life that night were his personal physicians. They knew that their hospital's wealthy patron was a ghoul—and were paid top nuyen to keep that knowledge a secret. They sympathized with Winston's plight—they were the ones who, over the years, had helped him to pass for human by performing delicate laser surgery to correct his reduced vision and treating his allergies to sunlight with gene therapy. They were discreet and professional, and had no reason to betray the trust Winston placed in them. No reason to bite the hand that fed them a steady diet of nuyen.

The hospital's security staff were also in the clear. The woman and man who had been on duty the night Winston was shot had taken down the gunman quickly and efficiently. Theirs had been a clean kill—the bounty hunter had not lived to spill Winston's secrets to them. And it was doubtful that hospital security had seen anything incriminating. There had been no vidcam monitors in the morgue itself, and Winston had been careful to choose as his meal a corpse that had already undergone an autopsy. The scalpel cuts he made in the body would surely have been mistaken for wounds made when the body was dissected.

He prided himself on his foresight and tact. Not only was he fastidious in his eating habits but he also caused minimal upset by feeding only on bodies already slated for cremation. Their relatives would never be distressed by the discovery of missing body parts. Winston was nothing like those other ghouls, the wild ones who desecrated graves by tearing them open to feed on the buried dead, or the even more despicable ones who fed on the living. He could pass for normal—and not just because his dark skin hid the grayish tinge that infection with the Krieger strain of the HMHVV virus had produced, or because his expensive cologne masked the odor of rot that occasionally arose when he perspired. He *was* normal, unlike those hulking, misshapen metas who dared to call themselves men.

If he had died at the hands of a bounty hunter, the world would have known his secret. That fear was what had enabled Winston to fight his way back from beyond the brink of death that night when the doctors were forced—twice—to shock his heart back into beating again. He couldn't stand the thought of his colleagues and friends in Human Nation laughing at him behind his dead back. Only if he remained alive could he continue to suppress the news of what he really was.

There had been no identification on the gunman who'd shot Winston that night; the man's retinal scans came up SINless and dataless. All Winston knew about him was that he was human. For the past year Winston had been haunted by the question of his would-be assassin's identity and how he'd learned that Winston was a ghoul. And now it seemed that the bounty hunter had left behind information on his target—information that had fallen into Serpens in Machina's electronic lap.

That had to be how the blackmailer had learned Winston's secret. Perhaps Serpens in Machina also knew who the bounty hunter was—and who had revealed Winston's secret to him.

"What do you know about her?" Dark Father asked, deliberately obscuring the bounty hunter's gender.

The gargoyle grinned. "Ah. Nice try. About *him,* you

mean. I know who tipped off the bounty hunter, for one thing. You were betrayed, Winston Griffith III, by someone you trust. But that information will cost you extra. For now, there is the initial payment of nine hundred thousand nuyen to be dealt with. That will guarantee my silence. Satisfying your curiosity will cost extra."

"It makes no sense to blackmail me," Dark Father repeated. "I already make extensive donations, not only to Informed Parenting but also to a number of other charitable organizations."

"Not to the ones on my list," the gargoyle hissed angrily. "I think it's an appropriate punishment for a candidate for the Human Nation executive council to be forced to donate to meta-rights organizations, don't you? And especially appropriate, considering your own metatype."

Dark Father met this outburst with anger. "You have no proof—"

"Yes, I do."

The gargoyle's eyes took on a satisfied gleam. Dark Father braced himself for the worst.

"Four years ago, I heard of a wiz little program developed in Tir Tairngire," the gargoyle said. "A biolink passkey that could distinguish the metatype of a decker by the distinctive pattern of his or her neural interface signals. The null-brainer who was posting the info claimed the program flagged elves as friendlies and suppressed black IC that would otherwise slag them.

"It was nonsense, of course. One neural signal is the same as any other, and the Tir sysops used IC that was just as harsh on any elven deckers who trespassed upon their data as it was on any other metatype. But the posting wasn't entirely off-slot. Mitsuhama Computer Technologies' Portland subsidiary had been working on some gray IC that would frag up the Reticular-Activation System override of an intruding decker's cyberdeck. After the IC hit, instead of merely suppressing the sensory signals from the decker's body, the RAS override would eliminate them altogether. At the same time, the IC rewrote the RAS programming that prevented the decker's meat bod from acting upon the neural signals that allow a decker to 'move' in the Matrix. Instead of remaining still, the decker's meat bod would thrash about as it responded to the commands the brain was giving it. The object was to induce the decker to suffer injuries by slamming into walls, falling down staircases, running out into traffic—"

"What has this to do with my . . . with me?" Dark Father asked.

The gargoyle grinned. "MCT Portland's project never did amount to anything. Too many glitches. But there was an interesting spin-off—although it never did prove to have any economic value. Because the program sampled the decker's RAS override signal, it could determine his height and weight. From these gross physical measurements, metatype could be established."

Dark Father listened quietly, fascinated despite himself. Ghouls stood about the same height as humans and massed the same number of kilos. The program that Serpens in Machina was talking about couldn't have . . .

It was as if the gargoyle read his mind.

"It's the claws that gave you away," he said.

"Claws!" Dark Father laughed out loud. "Ridiculous. If we were meeting in the flesh, you would notice that my nails are neatly trimmed."

"That may be true," the gargoyle said. "And I'm sure you have an excellent manicurist—one who keeps her mouth shut about the length and hardness of your nails. But you should have told that to whoever you hired to cook the ASIST interface on your deck. The RAS overdrive contains a sub-program, designed to prevent you from injuring yourself by balling your hand into a fist. And that application only makes sense if you have claws."

"That's hardly conclusive," Dark Father said. "For example, it could also be used by a dragon in human form."

"Perhaps," the gargoyle answered. Its tongue slithered in and out, wetting its lips. "But a dragon wouldn't be very acceptable to the Human Nation either, would it? They wouldn't accept a dragon as president of UCAS—what makes you think they'd accept one on their oh-so-pure executive council? They'd be even more horrified to find that they've got a ghoul in their midst."

"They wouldn't believe you if you told them."

"But I could sow the seeds of doubt. And then they'd

start wondering why their fellow philanthropist had no
body hair whatsoever—not even eyebrows or eyelashes.
Depilation is hardly the fashion trend it once was, you
know."

"There are a number of medical conditions that can
cause—"

"Cause what?" the gargoyle snapped. "A craving to eat
human flesh?"

In the real world, Dark Father's flesh-and-blood body
shivered. This had already gone too far. He'd only let the
meeting go on this long in order to find out how much the
other decker knew. Too much, it seemed. Serpens in
Machina had to be stopped. Once that was done, Dark Father could continue looking into the mystery of the sudden
appearance of the bounty hunter on his own, just as he had
been doing for the past twelve months.

"What gets me is how you can be so prejudiced against
your own kind," the gargoyle continued. "The metas who
come to the Informed Parenthood clinics are—"

"They're not my own kind," Dark Father answered angrily. "And I'm no racist. I'm helping them. You couldn't
possibly know the horror of giving birth to a monstrous,
misshapen child . . ." He winced, and bit back the rest of
what he was going to say. He'd already given away too
much.

"So that's it." The gargoyle's persona was emotion-
responsive. The voice coming from the other decker's icon
was hushed, thoughtful. The gargoyle's forehead was
puckered into a concerned frown below its horn, "You see
yourself as a monster. I'm truly sorry for you."

Dark Father's gut clenched. If there was one thing he
hated, it was pity. He'd seen it in the eyes of the instructors
at the secluded boarding school that he was sent to as a
teen, after infection with the HMHVV virus had transformed him into a ghoul. He had heard it in the hushed
tones of his personal physicians—had even felt it in the
falsely affectionate embrace of his former wife after he
told her his shameful secret. And now he saw it in the face
of a complete stranger—one who wanted to ruin his only
chance at acceptance by forcing him to donate to charities
that were the antithesis of everything that Dark Father

believed in. He couldn't stand the gargoyle's smirking sympathy a nanosecond longer . . .

Dark Father initiated his killjoy utility—a program designed to knock another decker out while leaving his cyberdeck up and running. A length of chain with a cuff at one end and a heavy metal ball at the other appeared in his hands. Whirling it once in a tight circle over his head, Dark Father launched it at the other decker. It sailed toward the gargoyle, bounced once off the marble floor of the conversation pit, and then the cuff snapped shut around the gargoyle's scaly ankle.

Serpens in Machina hissed in alarm and jerked his foot, but the utility was already doing its job. It stunned the other decker, slowing the gargoyle's response time to the point where Dark Father was able to activate a second program—a smart frame that combined a browse, evaluate, and track utility in one. It appeared beside him in the form of a German shepherd with fur of metallic silver and eyes that emitted twin tracking lasers. These locked briefly on Serpens in Machina, and then the police dog was bounding up the stairs. It paused at the lightninglike barrier IC that sealed off the SPU. Then the dog cocked its leg, used a stream of light to sear open a hole in the barrier, and leaped through the empty space.

"That was a null-brain move," the gargoyle snapped with a derisive glare. "If anything happens to me, the data I've collected will be downloaded into every—"

Dark Father didn't even listen to the rest. Already he was savoring his victory. The other decker probably assumed that Dark Father had sent a simple track utility to seek out Serpens in Machina's jackpoint so that he could be attacked in the real world. But the smart frame was performing an entirely different task. It would not only hunt down Serpens in Machina but browse his cyberdeck for the data on Dark Father—then duplicate itself and spread out through the Matrix, hunting down every copy of that data and destroying it. Nothing incriminating would be left—as long as Dark Father could keep the other decker busy for the few seconds the police dog required to complete its work.

It looked like Dark Father was going to have his work

cut out for him. The other decker leaned down and seized the cuff around his ankle, then wrenched it apart, freeing himself from the ball and chain. As the utility crashed, the chain exploded into shards that skittered across the marble floor. Then the gargoyle attacked.

Leathery wings enfolded Dark Father, pinning him in their grip as claws scrabbled at his chest. The gargoyle's eyes were pale white pits of fury and its mouth gaped wide to show rows of needle-sharp teeth. So perfect was the detailing of the other decker's persona that Dark Father could hear the shrill scrape of the gargoyle's claws as they raked the chest of his persona and could smell the creature's rotted-flesh breath. One or the other must have been the simsense component of a killjoy utility. Dark Father could feel his real-world body tiring as the program battered at his senses, partially stunning him.

These details were supposed to frighten Dark Father into making a mistake, into letting the other decker get the upper hand. But Dark Father didn't scare that easily. When the gargoyle suddenly thrust forward with its horn, initiating an attack utility, Dark Father quickly countered with a program of his own, a shield utility that billowed from his open mouth like a cloud of fine white ash. It settled on his bones and clothes, turning them from ebon black to ghoulish gray and rendering him momentarily impervious to tactile contact.

The gargoyle stumbled as its arms and wings suddenly closed on empty air. Dark Father stepped quickly aside and regarded the other decker from his new position behind him before closing again to combat range. Before the other decker could react he hurled his own attack utility at the gargoyle. He slipped off his hangman's noose necktie and whipped it around the gargoyle's neck, then cinched it shut by yanking on the rope. The gargoyle persona flickered and jerked as the program sent a jolt of electricity back into the other decker's body, messing up the deck's neural interfaces. Dark Father smiled.

But the other decker was tougher than Dark Father had estimated. In a blink, the gargoyle restored his icon and slipped free of the noose. His scaly hands grabbed for Dark Father's bony chest. This time, despite the shield utility that still coated Dark Father like powdery snow, the claws sank home. Dark Father felt a sudden sharp stab of pain in his real world body. This was not merely mental shock that he was feeling. This was actual, physical pain. Whatever utility the gargoyle was using, it seemed to be equivalent to lethal black IC. At last, Serpens in Machina had succeeded in frightening him.

"Attacking me was stupid," the gargoyle hissed. Its tongue lashed out, flickering briefly against Dark Father's cheek as the other decker tasted his victory. "You should have just paid the nine hundred thousand nuyen. I would have kept quiet about your dirty little secret. I would have kept my word. But now the second part of my offer is re-scinded. I'm no longer interested in selling you the name of the person who led the bounty hunter to you. And now I'm going to have to do you some serious damage, to buy myself the time to deal with that track program you hit me with. You'd better pray that your ghoul body is able to take it."

"I . . ." It was getting difficult for Dark Father to speak, even though the words he wanted to utter were no more than neural signals in his brain, rather than actual movements of his flesh-and-blood lips. His thoughts were growing fuzzy.

At the same time, Dark Father's brain grasped at rational straws. It didn't make sense for Serpens in Machina to kill him. Not before the charities he'd picked had gotten their blackmail nuyen. But maybe the other decker had given up on collecting from Dark Father. He had no way of knowing that the nuyen really were on file at the Zurich-Orbital Gemeinschaft Bank, even though Dark Father had transferred the credit to the account only for show, never really intending to make the credit transfer.

Pain lanced through his body a second time. "Please," he whispered. "Don't kill me. Let's talk. I'll double the amount of nuyen . . ."

"No deal."

The bottom of the gargoyle's leathery wing brushed across the sundial at the center of the conversation pit. Glowing white numbers displayed the local time: 9:46:59

PST. The hour of Dark Father's folly—the moment when he'd dared to go against a more talented decker and lost—was at hand.

Then the gargoyle, the spiral staircase, and the pillars that framed the conversation pit that was the SPU exploded into pixels of light that flew away like confetti and disappeared . . .

09:46:20 PST
(11:46:20 CST)
Jackpoint: Tenochtitlán, Aztlan

The jaguar stood between Bloodyguts and the slave node, crouching belly-low to the floor and ready to spring. The pattern of irregular dark spots shifted about on its golden hide, a hypnotic motion that drew the eye. Its tail lashed back and forth, and gleaming metal claws gripped the wide beam of blue light upon which both it and Bloodyguts stood.

The slave node that the jaguar was protecting was a small stepped pyramid. Each of its four sides was decorated with the stylized feline face that was Aztechnology's corporate logo. The heads protruded from the pyramid-like plaster masks; each was an access point to the real-world devices the slave node controlled.

Behind the node, stretching off into infinity, was the vast expanse of the host system that served the Aztechnology arcology in Seattle. From the outside, the host looked like a gigantic stepped pyramid, reminiscent of the arcology itself. From the inside, the system was a vast cityscape, programmed to resemble a blend of ancient and modern Tenochtitlán. Canals of data filled with blue light flowed in one direction, crossed at right angles by datalines that resembled gilded streets and bridges. The square spaces between the datalines were filled with pyramids made of gleaming chrome and backlit red glass, or with monumental pillars topped with statues that offered

visual clues to the sub-processing units or datastores they
represented.

Moving through this landscape were the icons of the legitimate users of the system. Many were customized personas, sculpted to look like brilliantly colored feathered
serpents, goggle-eyed Azzie gods, or ancient nobles in
jaguar pelts and gold finery.

From their perspective—and that of the IC that faced
Bloodyguts with tail lashing, waiting for him to enter a
validation passcode—Bloodyguts looked much like any
other legitimate user. His sleaze utility and masking programs were projecting the standardized persona of the
typical Azzie silicon wage-slave: a nongender-specific
Amerind human in a plain white suit, face covered with an
elaborate breather mask. But Bloodyguts' reality filter allowed him to continue to see his persona as it really was: a
shuffling zombie of a troll whose massive body was
pocked with the gaping holes of violent wounds. Entrails
dragged along the ground behind him, part of his cheek
was ripped away to expose white bone and shattered
teeth, and bloody red bullet holes dotted his exposed chest
like acne.

The persona was designed to both terrify and mislead.
Its horrific elements often gave Bloodyguts the extra second or two he needed to close to combat range when taking on another decker. And the slow, zombielike gait was
deceptive; Bloodyguts had pumped the response increase
on his cyberdeck to the max, and ran it hot on pure DNI.
He didn't need to frag about with keyboards or any of the
other null-gain interfaces of lesser decks. He *was* his deck.

Reaching up to his chest, Bloodyguts used both hands to
yank apart the skin, exposing his heart. Its beat was a particular algorithmic code, one for which he'd paid a fortune
in *peso libres*. Reaching inside the gaping cavity, he pulled
the heart from his chest. He offered it, still beating and
dripping blood with each pulse of data, to the IC that
guarded the node.

The jaguar paused a moment—Bloodyguts imagined it
sniffing the proffered heart—and then its rough tongue
licked a drop of blood from Bloodyguts' fingers. It sud-

denly clamped gleaming gold teeth upon the heart, which it devoured in one gulp.

"Niiice kitty," Bloodyguts said, easing his way along the beam of blue light past the IC. "You liked that validation code, didn't you?"

The jaguar sat back on its haunches. Bloodyguts tensed as he heard a rumbling noise, then realized the icon was purring. Laughing, he slapped a hand onto one of the mask-like faces on the side of the slave node.

His perception exploded into thousands of fragments as he looked out through a multitude of different closed-circuit vidcams at once. He saw corridors, board rooms, labs, foyers, shops, elevator interiors, exercise rooms, hallways, hermetic laboratories, fast-food outlets, mini-factories, religious temples, loading bays, classrooms. He saw shoppers, security guards, wage slaves in business suits, priests, paranormal entities on patrol, children playing, executives gathered around telecom displays, maintenance workers, officious priests leading religious ceremonies, crowds of people drinking soykaf at tiny tables in public squares, magicians casting spells, factory workers, teachers. He saw exterior views of the Aztechnology arcology itself: open-air terraces, expanses of gray stone, rooftop missile batteries, streetscapes, helipads, the gigantic quartz-crystal friezes on the side of the main building.

After a dizzying moment or two, Bloodyguts zoomed in on the view he wanted: a street-level loading bay in which a large truck was parked. Its swamper was just pulling his empty forklift away from the open rear door of the truck's trailer while another man entered information into a datapad on the wall. In another moment both exited through a door that led to an adjoining corridor.

Bloodyguts skipped rapidly between vidcams, trying for a better angle of view. This was his third attempt to penetrate the Azzie host system. Twice before he'd been dumped; only his intrusion counter-countermeasures biofeedback filter had saved him from serious dump shock. It looked as though he was barely in time; the truck was just about full. Bloodyguts consulted his time-keeping utility. It was just over thirteen minutes before ten a.m., local Seattle time. If the Azzies kept as fanatically to their schedules as usual, the truck wouldn't roll until ten on the nose. He still had plenty of time. Assuming that this was the right truck . . .

The securicams swung into position, giving Bloodyguts a view inside the trailer. Paydata! The rear of the truck was filled from floor to ceiling with hundreds of packages of optical chip cases, bound into neat blocks by shrink-wrap plastic. All of the chips inside the brightly labeled cases were legal simsense—the Azzies didn't sully their hands selling illegal BTL, despite the corp's origins as a drug cartel back in the twentieth century. All of the recordings on these chips had been filtered through an ASIST Peak Controller and none of them had the capacity to flatline anyone or permanently frag up their wetware. But Bloodyguts was going to melt them to glass, just the same.

It wasn't the signal strength of the chips that Bloodyguts objected to. It was the recordings that had been laid down on them. These ranged from the relatively tame—sports events with plenty of mayhem and bloodshed (court ball, for example) to "extreme splatter" recordings that were outright kill fests. Gladiatorial combats in which both animal and gladiator were wired for simsense, allowing the user to experience the wonders of polyPOV sampling. Or "hunter and prey" games in Aztlan's northern desert, in which the user got to be inside the heads of each of the hunted in turn, and could guess which would be the last one alive. The recordings were little more than snuffsense, capturing in gory detail every agonizing moment until the poor drekker who'd been coerced into one of the target roles flatlined.

Not so many years ago, Bloodyguts had been a fan of that sort of thing. He'd frothed over the Azzie tridcasts that were pirated into Seattle via the Deathstar-9 satellite, and had eventually graduated to a more "real" experience—the wonders of simsense slotted directly into his datajack.

From there he'd moved on to BTL—better than life dreamchips that provided both the baseline sensory track and the raw emotive tracks of the simsense "performers." And raw they were: the elation of victory, the agony of defeat. Fear, bloodlust, power, and domination—and the sheer and absolute terror of knowing that your life is leaking out through the hole they just tore in your gut and that there is nothing—*nothing*—you can do to avoid your imminent death.

Bloodyguts had become a brain-burner, a chiphead, a jackhead. He'd done anything for that next chip, for the nuyen to pay for his next dream fix. Steal from his family. Deal BTL himself. Hold up Stuffer Shacks even when BTL-induced synesthesia made it impossible to aim his pistol because he was seeing in smells or experiencing tactile sensations as colors. He'd even used the massive hands his troll heritage had given him to beat into a coma a cop who'd been coming down a little too hard on a local gogang. And he'd sold out a friend.

And then he'd flatlined—on the "snuffsense" recording of that very same friend's death.

Knowing that he'd been responsible, knowing that he was the only one who could avenge Jocko's death, was what had kept Bloodyguts clinging to life after the BTL chip crashed his wetware and flatlined him. He didn't have even a street doc to help pull him through—he came back from the icy edge of death all on his own, his spirit forcing its way back into his body through sheer bloody-mindedness. The shaman he'd dated a short time later told him he must have had a strong will, in addition to his strong troll body. She'd loved him for both, for a time. And then she'd dumped him when he refused to stop slotting BTL. She told him he couldn't bury his anguish at his part in Jocko's death in a chip dream. She told him to grow up, that he wasn't fit to be a man, let alone a troll.

That was when he'd begun the long, painful process of getting clean. Withdrawal from BTL was hell, but a hell that could be endured. The heightened sensitivity to stimuli and lowered threshold of pain, the agony that came from bright lights or the pressure of cloth against skin—neither of these were anywhere near what Jocko had endured as he experienced Jocko's death in simsense, disemboweled and bullet-ridden, his face slashed wide open by the razorboy that Bloodyguts had assured him would be a pushover, even though he'd known that Jocko didn't have a chance.

The Azzies hadn't made the BTL recording of Jocko's

death. Someone else had—someone who had disappeared into the shadows, rendering futile all of Bloodyguts' attempts at revenge. But the Azzies were a part of the whole thing, with the ultra-violent drek they exported into the UCAS under the guise of "sports" recordings. For people like Bloodyguts, legal Azzie simsense chips were the first step onto the slippery slope that led to snuffsense. And now Bloodyguts, who had made it his one-man mission while he was still in Seattle to slag every snuffsense dealer who still polluted the streets, was going to eliminate that step.

Best of all, he was doing it from within the jaguar's den. Not only had he penetrated the system of a red host like Aztechnology's Seattle arcology, but he was doing it from a jackpoint within Tenochtitlán itself—the city that was the heart of the Azzie simsense industry.

While on the run, slipping from the shadows of one city to the next, he'd wound up in Tenochtitlán. There, he'd hooked up with some rebels—a kick-hoop group led by Rafael Ramirez, an ork with a virulent loathing of the court ball game. Bloodyguts had earned their trust, and worked with them on a run. With Bloodyguts providing the decking they needed to trick the securicams into thinking that all was well, the group had planted a bomb in the telecom studios that were used to broadcast live from the court ball stadium, reducing the complex to a heap of rubble. The beauty of it was, it had all been done remotely; Bloodyguts had used a robotic drone to plant the C4 that leveled the studios. He'd done it from a distance, striking from afar like a powerful god.

That was when he'd realized that he could also still strike out at Seattle, even though he was on the run and far, far away from that city. Grateful for his assistance, the rebels came through for Bloodyguts. They told him about a data transfer that had recently been made to the Seattle arcology, and of a shipment of simsense chips, made from that recorded simsense data, that was about to hit the Seattle streets. The shipment that Bloodyguts was looking at now. The chips he was about to destroy.

Back in the meat world, Bloodyguts' lips twitched into a smile. Decking was the way to go, the best way to target the snuffsense industry. Like the image of Jocko on which he'd patterned his persona, Bloodyguts was a mere ghost in the machine. If his enemies threw a punch, it would pass right through him.

Of course, if they threw IC at him the outcome might be different . . .

Keeping a portion of his perception within the sec cam that was monitoring the truck loading bay, Bloodyguts accessed by feel one of the other faces on the small stepped pyramid that was the slave node. He first crashed the electronic locks on the loading bay doors, effectively freezing them in a closed and locked position and sealing the truck inside. Then he followed the maze of connections that led from the node to the automated weapons that protected the loading bay against intruders from the street. Inside a sensitive area like the loading bay, which was typically filled with valuable shipments, rifles and explosives were not an opinion. Those weapons were reserved for the outer, streetside defenses. In the bay itself, lasers were the standard line of defense. A scorch mark or two on a packing case was vastly preferred to a series of deep holes chewed by high-velocity slugs and explosives.

On the other hand, lasers were the perfect weapon to wield against optical chips that were protected only by a thin layer of shrink wrap and cardboard . . .

Bloodyguts activated the four MP laser guns and sent them coasting along the rails on which they were mounted. Maneuvering them into position directly behind the rear of the trailer, he quickly set up a loop of programming that would send the beams crisscrossing back and forth over the bundles of optical chips. The program would also gradually step up the gain on the lasers, allowing them to burn deeper and deeper into the cargo inside the truck. Within a minute or two at most—long before any security guards could react to the threat by unloading the truck—the optical chips would be slag.

With a satisfied smile, Bloodyguts activated the laser guns and watched as four ruby red beams of light began cutting destructive swaths through the optical chips. The shrink wrap bubbled and warped, and the cardboard packaging below it began to smolder. A few wisps of smoke began to drift upward, but Bloodyguts had already compensated for any interference that the molecules of soot would cause.

He watched for only a moment, then exited the slave node and activated a spoof utility. A loop of dripping entrails appeared in his hand. Whipping them over his head like a lariat, he wrapped them around the slave node, enclosing the face icons on its four sides in heaps of tangled entrails. The hoses of flesh constricted around the stepped pyramid as the utility began its work, editing the slave node so that any commands sent to the node would be rendered into unrecognizable strings of gibberish by the node's own subsystems as the commands were forced to pass through the long loops of entrails. Regardless of any overrides sent by the arcology's system operators, the laser guns would continue their deadly work.

Good. A job well done. Bloodyguts glanced at his log monitor. It was just a second or two before 9:47 a.m., Seattle time. He'd completed the run with plenty of time to spare. Now it was time to scram from the arcology's system and do a graceful log off before any of the Azzie deckers came to investigate the overwhelmingly improbable "glitch" in the loading bay's weaponry. Bloodyguts turned and made his way past the jaguar-shaped IC that had blocked his way earlier. He started along the beam of blue light, intending to follow the datastream out of the arcology . . .

And suddenly faltered to a halt as his legs collapsed under him. Looking down at the lower half of his persona from where he lay sprawled on the beam of blue light, he saw that his feet and lower legs had been infested with tiny black moths with wings of gleaming obsidian stone. They rose into the air and descended again, dipping and fluttering down to take sharp bites of his flesh. Their tiny mouths devoured his persona icon pixel by pixel; already his feet were fragmenting, turning translucent and revealing the glowing blue data stream on which he lay.

Drek! The slave node must have been booby-trapped with crippler IC. Even as he'd been rendering the Azzie chips to slag, it had been doing the same thing to his deck, silently attacking its MPCP chips. And now his persona was disintegrating.

Bloodyguts flicked his hand, causing a gigantic hypo-dermic needle to appear in it. Aiming the needle at his legs, he squeezed the plunger down. A thin stream of liq-uid, rainbowed like a streak of oil, coated his lower legs. Gradually, the restore utility filled in the holes the moths had created, washing them away in the process. The opti-cal chips in his MPCP would still need to be replaced, but at least his persona had been prevented from crashing. He rose to his elbows and prepared to stand . . .

He heard a snarl and glanced behind him. The jaguar that had guarded the slave node was advancing on him, eyes narrowed and tail lashing in fury. Now that the crip-pler IC had attacked Bloodyguts, the jaguar must have rec-ognized him as an intruder. Bloodyguts expected it to spring forward in an attack, but instead it vomited forth the heart Bloodyguts had offered it earlier. The pulsing red organ sailed from its mouth and landed square on Bloody-guts' chest, where it stuck fast, beating with a feeble arrhythmia.

Back in the meat world, Bloodyguts' own heart gave a lurch. Dimly, he felt a painful twinge grip the left side of his chest. The fingers of his left hand began to tingle and go numb. And that was bad. Very bad. He was under attack by black IC.

There was no time for a graceful log off. Not if he wanted to live. He'd have to jack out and take whatever dump shock came, even though it might send his weak-ened heart into fatal fibrillation. His timekeeping utility showed a local time of 9:46:59 PST—nearly noon in Tenochtitlán. With any luck, one of the rebels he'd agreed to meet with at noon would find him in time to pull him through . . .

Bloodyguts thrust his hands out, grabbed the oversized referee's whistle that appeared in them, and blew it as loud as he could.

Ansen arched his neck to relieve the ache in his shoulders
and closed the door of his cube. The tiny apartment didn't
hold much—just a futon with some rumpled blankets, a
nuker to warm up food, and a chrome clothes rack,
scrounged from a dumpster behind the clothing store on
the corner, that held his jeans and jackets. Plastiboard
packing crates he'd salvaged from work served as tables.
The only ornamentation was also functional: a bubble
lamp that stood in one corner. It burbled out a steady
stream of bioluminescent spheres that drifted around the
room, filling it with gentle washes of light until the bubbles collapsed with soft popping noises.

Ansen flipped his sneaks off his feet and into a corner,
undid the leather thong that held his pony tail, and shook
out his long, dark hair. Then he settled onto the edge of his
futon with a sigh. He rubbed a shoulder with one hand and
stared for a moment at the flatscreen display that served as
the cube's "window." It showed a penthouse view of the
city, shot from a vidcam on top of the building. On the
streets below, traffic crawled along through the last of
the morning rush-hour haze. Cars and trucks disappeared
into static that had fuzzed out the center of the window,
then reappeared out the other side. Ansen knew enough
tech to have easily fixed the glitch in the display, but never
seemed to get around to it. All of Seattle could be eaten by
the static hole, for all he cared. That wasn't the world that
interested him.

His hand wandered to the kitten-shaped Playpet that lay
on the futon next to him. As he stroked its soft synthetic
fur it began to emit a rumbling purr. Servos inside the toy
responded to the faint electromagnetic field given out by
Ansen's hand, causing the toy to roll over and offer its

belly for scratching. He tickled its purple tummy with his fingertips, giving the memory plastic the daily stimulation it required to "grow" from kitten into life-sized cat over the next six months. The kitten responded by widening its already oversized eyes and staring adoringly in Ansen's general direction.

Most of Auburn's blue collar workers were just starting their working day. Ansen had just ended his—an eight-hour shift at the Diamond Deckers plant. The ache in his shoulders came from hunching over an assembly table all night long, slotting chips into computers that were cheap knock-offs of more expensive cyberdecks. The decks had the look and feel of the high-end Fuchi models, with their clear plastic cases and sleek gold-on-black keyboards. But they were made from bargain-basement chips and inferior materials.

The work was tedious and brain-numbing. And the pay was drek: just minimum wage. But it was the best a seventeen-year-old high school dropout could do for a job in this city. And it had its fringe benefits . . .

Ansen turned to the cyberdeck he'd liberated from a back room of the Diamond Deckers warehouse. Big and boxy, the CDT-3000 Vista clone was an antique, older even than Ansen himself. It was one of a dozen that had sat without ever being used, just gathering dust, until Ansen discovered them. He had upgraded this deck as far as it would go, but it still had only ten megapulses of active memory and a two-meg MPCP. And its interfaces were primitive in the extreme. Instead of a DNI jack or even a trode rig, the computer relied on old-fashioned VR goggles and data gloves. While other computers allowed their operators to run them at the speed of thought, this "tortoise" of a deck relied on gross eye and hand movements to execute its commands.

Still, it was better than nothing at all. And it was the window onto the world Ansen loved—if only a narrow one.

Ansen pulled nylon data gloves onto his hands and flexed so that the hair-thin webbing of sensors woven into the blue fabric shaped to his hands. He made sure the fiber-optic cables that led from the deck to the goggles were snug in their ports, plugged the deck into the comm jack in the wall, then pulled the goggles over his eyes. Holding his hands over the deck's illuminated sensor board, he flicked his fingers to activate it. The wrap-around peripheral-image screen inside the VR goggles flickered to life and the speakers next to his ears began to hum.

He entered the Matrix.

A door-shaped rectangle of glowing yellow appeared directly in front of him—a system access node in the local telecommunications grid that served this area of Auburn. Ansen touched the SAN and watched as a blue stain spread outward from the point his hand had touched, a halo of green encircling it. After a moment, the blue faded, leaving a green-tinged hole in the middle of the door. Ansen pointed his finger, moved it forward—and was sucked into the hole. The SAN disappeared behind him.

He hung suspended over the multicolored checkerboard of light that was Seattle's regional telecommunications grid. He knew all of its familiar landmarks by heart: the golden stepped pyramid of Aztechnology; the nucleus with swirling red electrons that was the Gaeatronics power company; the forbidding black slab of Renraku; and the multifaceted, crystalline silver star of Fuchi Industrial Electronics. A host of other system constructs also dotted the cyberscape—cubes, spheres, and more complex shapes, each representing a different corporation or public agency.

He looked "down" at his Matrix body—a gender-neutral silver humanoid with glowing blue hands. This had been the standard non-customized persona since the 2030s, back when the Vista was SOTA—state of the art. Ansen could have re-cooked the chips in his MPCP to customize his persona, but that would burn memory that he couldn't spare. Besides, the persona's archaic look was part of his image.

Although the goggles gave Ansen the illusion of floating in space, he could feel the futon underneath him, could smell his unwashed T-shirts in the corner, could hear the sounds of feet in the apartment above him. He hadn't quite escaped the real world.

But someday he'd be able to afford to go under the knife and have a datajack implanted in his temple. And the SOTA deck he'd been building from parts scrounged off the assembly line would be complete. Then Retro would show the other deckers who was wiz.

In the meantime, Retro left his mark on the Matrix, tagging datastores at random with his graffiti. His trademark was changing the iconography of the nodes he visited, leaving behind icons that were "retro" in the extreme. Old-fashioned paper file folders, galvanized metal garbage cans, non-digital wind-up alarm clocks, and brightly colored suitcases—all icons that were standardized in the previous century by a long-since defunct corp by the name of Macintosh. Ansen's other favorite tag was an image of that corp's logo: a rainbow-colored apple with a sign inviting deckers to "take a byte." Woe betide the decker who took the bait and found the worm virus inside!

Ansen knew the prank was childish, but, hey, he didn't claim to be anything else. He seemed to just have a knack with computers, and he'd been slotting people off with his decking ever since he was a kid. Back when he was eleven, the first time he'd run away from home, he'd hacked his way into the computer system that operated his uncle's hotel and checked himself into one of the "coffin" cubicles. Using the thumbprint scan of another guest, he'd ordered a drekload of fast food, keeping him in growlies for a whole week. And he'd done it with his sister's MatrixPal, a null-value chunk of chip if ever there was one.

Just wait until he had some real hardware in his hands . . .

For now, although the Vista was slow, it had one important advantage. Like the tortoise that gave antiquated decks their derogatory nickname, the Vista's primitive interfaces offered a "shell" that protected the deck's user from harm. While more modern computers offered direct neural interface with the Matrix, that connection was a two-way street. If the decker trespassed on an IC-protected node and hosed up, lethal biofeedback could flow back along the DNI conduit, frying his brain.

Ansen didn't have to worry about any of that. At worst, any intrusion countermeasures could only fry the chips in his deck. If that happened—and it hadn't yet—there were still eleven other Vistas back at the warehouse as backup. And optical chips had a way of "falling" into Ansen's pockets when the boss wasn't looking . . .

So the only question was where to go today. Ansen circled his right index finger clockwise (it had taken him a while to figure that command out; the manual that came with the Vista assumed that the user knew what "dialing" was) and a punchpad of glowing letters and numbers appeared in the air ahead of him. He keyed in NA/UCAS-SEA, then chose the four-digit LTG code that would connect him with the University of Washington. He'd heard they'd been developing some nova-hot sculpted systems and wanted to give them a browse. And leave his mark.

A system access node appeared before him: a fairly standard "office door" icon bearing the U-dub logo. Ansen reached for the knob . . .

And felt a moment of dizzying disorientation as the viewscreen image projected by his goggles zoomed forward, jerked back and forth in an epileptic frenzy, and then lurched drunkenly away from him. Instead of the door, Ansen now faced a dark tunnel draped with moss and fanged with dripping stalactites. Misty vapors wafted out of it like panting breath. Ansen was willing to bet that, had his deck contained an artificial sensory induction system, they would have chilled his skin. The speakers in his goggles broadcast a low, moaning sound that sent a shiver through him.

"Frosty," Ansen said out loud.

And then he frowned. What had happened? His data glove hadn't connected with the door icon; he should have still been outside the SAN leading to the university's system. Was his deck glitching out? Or had some virus scrambled an access code, sending him here?

And where was here?

The SAN in front of him looked like it might be stacked with some pretty hard-hooped IC, but Ansen was willing to give it a try. He touched his fingertips together in the complex pattern that would load and launch a deception utility. The universal icon associated with the Fuchi-designed program appeared: a black, lozenge-shaped mask materialized a few centimeters away from Ansen's face, then settled in place over his eyes.

Ansen took a deep breath, then sent his persona gliding into the tunnel by focusing his eyes on its center point and jabbing a pointed index finger forward over his sensor board. The tunnel rushed forward to meet him, enveloped him in its stygian darkness . . .

And then that darkness was replaced by the utter blank of a dead viewscreen.

"What the frag . . . ?"

Ansen tore the goggles from his eyes. The light had gone out in his sensor board, and the deck's tiny flatscreen display was also dead. But the power switch glowed cherry red, indicating that juice was still flowing into the deck. And the speakers in the goggles were emitting a faint static hiss.

Ansen peeled the data gloves from his hands. Something had dumped him out of the Matrix.

He hit a button on the side of the deck and watched as the flatscreen came to life. He scrolled quickly through the text that appeared on the screen: a log of his run. It was pretty brief. He'd logged onto the Matrix at 09:46:51 PST through his LTG, then emerged into the Seattle grid four seconds later. Keying in the LTG code for the university's computer system had taken him five long seconds—no wonder they called his deck a tortoise—and that's when the log went funny. At 09:47:00 exactly, the codes recorded in the log became scrambled. Instead of the usual letter and number combination that represented an RTG or LTG, the code became a meaningless string of symbols. Ansen had no idea which of the communications grids the weird tunnel icon had been in.

According to the log, he'd spent a full ten seconds just staring at the tunnel icon, and another three seconds getting his deception utility up and running. Then he'd tried to access the weird-looking SAN—and been dumped.

He didn't think it was IC that had crashed his deck, since the LTG codes had started going funny a full thirteen seconds earlier, back when he was trying to access the

university's system. The fault was more likely to be a
simple failure of one of the deck's routing sub-systems,
perhaps caused by a faulty peripheral or I/O connector.

Cursing, Ansen crawled across his futon and began rum-
maging in a packing case for his spare VR goggles and
sensor board.

09:46:38 PST
(10:46:38 MST)
Cheyenne, Sioux Nation

Kimi laughed and ran after the other children as they
chased the "rubber ball" that bounced from one end of the
room to the other. Today the FTL Technologies game room
was running a lacrosse program—*baggataway,* in Iroquois. The kids called it "bang-it-away." The sticks they
carried were made of foam, the netting of a soft foam cup
inlaid with a fine web of wires. These "caught" the holographic ball and held it until the glowing blue sphere
was hurled away. Even the goals were holos, so the kids
wouldn't hurt themselves by running into them.

Kimi liked playing bang-it-away. It was her favorite of
the virtual games that the creche kids got to play—not because she liked running around after a silly ball, but because its holographic displays were the best. Whenever a
goal was scored, holos of masked dancers sprang to life,
filling the game room with their whoops and dancing in
celebration around the kid who scored the goal. The holos
were ultra high-rez, almost as good as what you saw in the
Matrix. Just the sort of stuff you'd expect from programmers who designed some of the most wiz cyberdeck games
on the market—and let their children alpha test them.

These kids were lucky, having parents who worked for
FTL. They got to play, and test games, and go to 'puter
school, and eat good food. Kimi had grown up in a tiny
agri station out on the plains, with no other kids to play
with, only soy and vitamin-enriched bannock to eat, and

nothing to look at but hectares and hectares of rustling stonewheat.

Until she discovered the Matrix. That's where she'd connected with other young deckers. Lonely kids like herself. Kids who told her this brain-bending story about being able to run the Matrix without a deck after meeting a great spirit there.

They'd guided her through her own vision quest in the Matrix, taught her how to find the great spirit for herself. One year ago, she had at last succeeded, and been transformed. Now she could spirit walk through the Matrix, able to jack in directly without need of a cyberdeck. She had become a technoshaman.

She'd used her talent to deck into the FTL personnel files and create a mother who worked for the computer software corp. For the past two months Kimi had shown up every weekday at the corp's daycare creche while her purely fictional mother "went to work" in the tower above.

Most of the time she'd just played with the other kids in the creche or joined them in lessons and at lunch. But she'd also done what she'd been sent here to do: decked into the FTL mainframe from inside this building. The great spirit had explained that it was necessary for Kimi to do this because the system was "closed," not accessible via the Matrix. Even the great spirit itself couldn't get at it.

But Kimi could. And that made her proud.

She'd done what the great spirit had asked her to: glitching up a program that some FTL decker named Raymond Kahnewake was working on. The great spirit had showed Kimi how to use a complex form that would do the job. She'd memorized its pattern, then jacked into the FTL mainframe and inserted the form she'd been taught. She'd been extra, extra careful to do it just right. And the great spirit had praised her work.

But then Raymond Kahnewake had designed another program—one that did pretty much the same thing as the first. And so the great spirit had told Kimi it was time to play a game with him, a game that would scare him into being good. The great spirit said he was a dangerous man, that he had to be stopped from making things that would hurt Kimi and her friends—that would hurt the great spirit itself,

To prepare for the game, Kimi made sure the security guards at the FTL Technologies headquarters in Cheyenne got to know her. She deliberately got caught playing on the building's high-speed elevators, riding them from the second-floor creche to the building's uppermost, twentieth floor and back again. And she made sure the guards saw her playing "coup counter" up and down the halls, stalking the FTL workers with her toy bow and suction-cup-tipped arrows. This was all practice for when she would count coup against Raymond Kahnewake.

Kimi was frightened about confronting an adult, and the game the great spirit had asked her to play seemed a little silly. But she didn't question it. She loved the great spirit and would do anything for it. She'd practiced, and she was ready. Even so, she'd put the game off as long as she could, just in case the great spirit changed its mind. Maybe she should log on and see . . .

Kimi ran to the side of the game room and dropped her lacrosse stick, pretending to be out of breath. It was an easy fake; she was a pudgy girl with short legs, at least a head shorter than any of the other nine-year-olds in the room. Her long black hair was cut in bangs over her forehead and elsewhere hung down to her waist. It hid the flesh-toned datajack high above her right ear; the cyberdoc who'd done the implant had only shaved a tiny patch on her skull, leaving her hair long.

Slipping out of the game room, she walked down the hall to the water fountain. She took a drink, glanced around, then ducked around a corner to a public telecom unit—a terminal that was connected with the outside world, rather than with the FTL mainframe. She pulled a fiber-optic cable out of her pocket, plugged one end into the port that would normally be used to connect a cyberterminal to the telecom, and slotted the other end of the cable into the datajack above her ear.

She closed her eyes and threw her mind into the Matrix, then followed a familiar dataline to the Seattle RTG. SANs blurred past like beads on a neon string until she found the one leading to the LTG where her friends liked to hang out—a system hosted by Toys 4 U, in which the latest toys were displayed in virtual in all their simsense glory. Amid the flash and commotion, Kimi found three familiar personas. Their icons floated toward her, bright and reassuring: the grinning pink plastic doll that was Technobrat, the segmented green body of Inchworm, and the bulbous white snowman Frosty with his carrot nose and red and white scarf. Kimi's own persona was based on the trideo character Suzy Q. Her icon was a fuzzy turquoise bear with oversized eyes and a high-pitched voice.

An unfamiliar figure hung beside Frosty—a fluffy white mouse with a big pink bow around its neck and a bright pink nose and ears. A thin piece of fiber-optic cable formed its tail. Its face looked funny; after a sec Kimi figured out it was because the mouse didn't have a mouth.

"Hoi," Kimi squeaked.

"Hoi," the mouse answered. The sound came from its silver whiskers, which were vibrating.

Inchworm reared up on his tiny legs, waving a multitude of arms at Kimi. "Hoi, Suzy Q. Did you complete your mission?"

"You mean the coup-counting game?" Kimi's bear icon hung its head. "Not yet."

Technobrat's doll face scowled at her. "You were supposed to do it before the experiment began." The doll gestured, and glowing numbers appeared in the air beside it. The display showed the local time zone for the grid: 9:46:57. "See? It's almost time. We begin in three seconds."

"The great spirit only said that today was the last day I could do it," Kimi squeaked. "I didn't know it had to be this morning!" She looked at the numeric display, which hung motionless. She was talking with her friends at the speed of thought—a second in the Matrix felt like minutes sometimes. Hours even. In the meat world, her body was between breaths, between heartbeats—even though her heart was beating furiously from having exerted herself in the game.

Exercise wasn't the only reason her heart was pumping rapidly. Kimi was scared. She'd almost let the great spirit down. She had only seconds to go.

And that was bad. If she hosed up, maybe the great spirit

wouldn't love her any more. She couldn't let that happen. She had to carry out her mission, even though she knew she was already too late.

"Bye!" she squeaked, and broke her connection with the Matrix.

09:47:00 PST

The Matrix collapsed to a pinpoint of light. Red Wraith's body collapsed with it, his mistlike form compressing to a single perfect sphere. Something *wrenched* free of itself, and Red Wraith could no longer feel his meat body. He was used to being unable to feel pain—that much was normal. But now he couldn't feel anything. Not the press of the chair against his spine, not the feather-light weight of the deck in his lap, not a single physical sensation. Nada.

It reminded him of the explosion of the cranial bomb—the seconds he'd spent floating free, detached from his clinically dead body, before the trauma team had found and revived him. It was all just too fraggin' familiar . . .

Another *wrench,* and the world expanded to an endless sea of gray static. Red Wraith hung suspended in this infinite void, a tiny pixel of consciousness bobbing gently in featureless space.

No, not so featureless. He was aware, now, of a figure just below him: a man floating peacefully on his back, eyes closed. A man with the face of Daniel Bogdanovich—the decker who was Red Wraith—and the ghostly body of his persona. His arms were crossed upon his chest and the misty tendrils that were his legs were splayed. His chest was still, his face waxen, lifeless.

Dead.

In one horrible flash of recognition, Red Wraith realized what must have happened. While his mind wandered the Matrix, his meat bod must have experienced one of its spastic attacks. Somehow, the needle hidden in the fingertip compartment of his right forefinger had been activated, and deadly toxin had been injected into his palm. He cursed his decision to keep the toxin ampoule loaded as a last, finger-flick-fast line of defense against anyone who broke into his houseboat while he was accessing the Matrix. His own weapon had done him in. Unable to feel the sting of the needle, he was paralyzed and dying, unable to reach for the antidote that would neutralize the poison. In another moment or two, he would be dead.

Yet a part of him still remained.

Red Wraith's consciousness—his soul—was no longer connected to the Matrix, no longer connected to his body. It was here, in some sort of weird limbo.

But where was here?

And why had his Matrix persona come with him?

Lady Death experienced a moment of wild disorientation in which she flashed past a mirror image of her persona icon—was it the mirrors utility she had created to deceive her guardians?—and had a momentary sensation of somehow being separated from the Matrix icon that was her on-line "body." Then she found herself firmly back within her persona, floating in an empty void. And yet she still felt somehow detached from reality.

It was a dreamy feeling, like the one produced by the drugs the doctors had used to sedate her while she'd been confined to her family's private medical clinic after her "rescue" from Shinanai. Or like the gentle semi-slumbering lull she had fallen into while Shinanai supped upon her blood. And after, when she had died of blood loss and had looked down upon her lifeless body on the hotel bed . . .

She raised a hand and saw that it had become translucent, drained of all color. The dracoforms that had glowed so fiercely red on the sleeve of her kimono were a faint white on white, only their raised embroidery showing their form. Her hair, too, where it hung against her chest was white, as were the slippers on her feet.

White. The color of death.

What had she been doing? Oh, yes, logging off the Matrix. She should have found herself back in her room in the Shiawase Corporation's Osaka arcology, sitting at the table before her cyberdeck. But somehow she could no longer feel her body, let alone access it. She threw her mind out, seeking to log off. But there was none of the usual sense of movement, of rushing through space.

Lady Death heard a voice then—an achingly familiar voice. It called to her, wordlessly, from a direction somewhere above. Melodic and pure as a crystal flute, the haunting tones of Shinanai's singing cried out to Lady Death, drawing and focusing her attention, beckoning her to join the vampire in a place very, very far away, a place where lovers would be reunited once more . . .

Lady Death gasped, suddenly realizing what must have happened. After surviving so long with HMHVV coursing through her blood, she had at last succumbed to the virus. She had slipped into the coma that all of its victims experienced just before death. And now she was having a near-death experience, hearing the voices of departed loved ones . . .

Of her one true love.

But it was just a hallucination. Shinanai was alive, not dead and calling to her from some netherworld—the *aidoru* had only yesterday performed a concert in Kobe. Lady Death would not be tricked by her own mind, would not give in to oblivion, even if it was masked with love.

"No!" she screamed, blocking her ears against the singing. But her hands passed through her head, disappearing inside it without ever encountering the solidity of a living form. Startled, she jerked them away.

And then a series of images began to flash before her eyes . . .

Dark Father watched as scenes from his life flashed before him. It was as if he were watching a tridcast of the high and low points of his life, one melting into the other with dreamlike fluidity. Just as he had before, when his heart had stopped beating after the bounty hunter's attack, he watched the flashbacks with a mixture of amazement and dread.

He saw himself as a small boy—a *human* boy—on the Griffith estate, riding his pony across the grounds with his brothers and sisters. He relived the first manifestation of the disease at age fourteen, and the shame and horror of being found feeding on the corpse of the family dog. He watched himself being chauffeured to the secluded boarding school where he'd spent the remainder of his teenage years with the similarly afflicted sons of other wealthy families, and the futile efforts of the team of doctors who had tried to cure him. He saw himself as a young man in his twenties, during the restless years of traveling the world in a desperate search for a mage or shaman who could cure him of his taste for human flesh. Then in his thirties, when he settled into the bliss of married life and chairmanship of the board of directors of one of the Griffith pharmaceutical conglomerates.

He relived the night when Anne had given birth to their son—a misshapen monster of a child who showed all of the traits of goblinization at birth and who demonstrated them by tearing a bloody chunk from his mother's breast as she tried to nurse him. Then, in rapid succession, he re-experienced Anne's anger at his keeping the fact that he was a ghoul from her, their divorce, the lonely years that followed after their son Chester was sent to boarding school. With vivid clarity he watched the confrontation, two years ago, when the teenage Chester had stormed away from a visit with his father after yet another argument about the need to keep quiet about the fact that he was a ghoul, when the boy had vowed never to return to either the boarding school or the family home. And he saw, as if viewing it from a distance, the near-fatal attack of the bounty hunter, that night in the hospital.

The bounty hunter . . .

Dark Father glanced down at his chest, but didn't see the bullet-pocked flesh and bloodstained shirt he expected. His chest was skeletal black bone cloaked in a loose-fitting black suit, the hangman's noose still dangling from his neck. He still seemed to be firmly inside his Matrix persona. Which didn't make sense. If the other decker he'd been fighting in the conversation pit had crashed his deck, he should have awakened in his own real world body—if indeed he was still alive. But if he was dead or dying . . .

Dark Father shivered, remembering the stab of pain that had lanced through him just before the gargoyle and the conversation pit had disappeared. Had the bounty hunters

found him a second time? Was he lying in the office of his
family estate even now, his life blood slowly leaking from
him? What happened to someone who died while their
mind was connected with the Matrix? Did their soul mi-
grate there?

He could no longer feel his body, or make any sort of
connection with it. And his life had just flashed before his
eyes. He could only conclude that he was injured or dying.
And that brought a rising sense of anger. He didn't want to
die like this. Not now. Not with the questions about who
the bounty hunter was and where Chester had disappeared
to unanswered. Nor did he want the world to learn his secret when his body was found. He had to claw his way
back from death, just as he had after the bounty hunter had
shot him.

Just as Dark Father braced himself to throw his mind
out in a last-ditch effort to reconnect with his body, a
light shone down on him from somewhere above. As
bright as a spotlight, it engulfed Dark Father as if he were
a tiny gnat, throwing his dark body into stark relief. He
found himself rising up into the beam, drifting slowly
toward the source of the light. At first this movement was
gradual, but it steadily became more rapid. Soon he was
hurtling upward toward an ever-expanding source of brilliant white light . . .

Bloodyguts tried to stop his head-first slide along the
brilliant white datastream, but nothing worked. His utility
programs were useless; he had tried to activate them and
failed. His direct neural interface seemed to be fragged up
as well, or maybe his RAS had glitched out. Whatever the
cause, he was unable to feel his meat bod any more.

And that should have scared him drekless. But instead
he was feeling emotions that weren't his. It was just like
being on a BTL trip—this feeing of being out of control.
The emotions being fed into his wetware gave him a sense
of great peace, of intense happiness and joy. Of oneness
with the multiverse. And they seemed to be intensifying
and increasing, the further he moved along this weird
dataline toward the brilliant spot of light toward which it
led. He wondered if, when the experience peaked, it would

literally blow his mind and send his brains oozing out of his ears.

Something flickered in the light ahead, and Bloodyguts wrenched his head around to look up at it. Frag! Was that Jocko? The human figure was backlit by intense light, no more than a faceless silhouette. But it had Jocko's wide shoulders and familiar slouched posture, and it stood with its head tilted to one side, occasionally tossing its head to flick its dreadlocks back over its horns the way Jocko did. And when it raised a hand to give a casual wave, light glinted off the chromed razors set into the back of the black leather gloves that Jocko always wore.

"Hoi, Yograj!" it called out in a voice heavy with reverb and echo. "Welcome to de promised lan'."

Bloodyguts' eyes widened at the use of his real name. He hadn't used it in years and had carefully erased all traces of his former life once he'd started decking. He doubted that anybody would have been able to connect the decker Bloodyguts with the chiphead Yograj Lutter. And yet somebody had. Somebody with the body, mannerisms, and drawling voice of his chummer Jocko. That somebody was either a very clever decker . . . or Jocko himself.

But Jocko was dead. And that meant . . .

Had the jaguar-shaped IC really stopped his heart? Was he lying on the floor of his Tenochtitlán hotel room right now, his pulse flatlined and his eyes staring at the ceiling?

The bright light, the familiar voice—he'd been here once before, when the BTL chip had flatlined him. He'd floated free from his body and looked down as it lay on the mattress in the garbage-strewn alley. Then he'd ascended into a tunnel of light. That time, there had been no welcoming committee, no friend waving, beckoning him on to the other side. Fear had overwhelmed him and he'd pulled back from death—forced his spirit back into his abused and aching body.

This time, Jocko was there waiting for him at the other end of the tunnel. But Bloodyguts still wasn't ready to die. He still had too much left to do. He couldn't face Jocko yet, not with the job of avenging his chummer's death only half done. He'd never be able to look Jocko in the eye.

"No!" Bloodyguts raged. His persona thrashed against

the light, its ghostlike limbs flailing. "I'm not fragging ready yet! Let me go!"

Then the tunnel of light disappeared.

The world collapsed into a perfect pinpoint once more. S/he was a dot, a single cell. Without thought, without sensation, without emotion. S/he simply was.

A wrench. Division. S/he was twice the size s/he had been before, but still minuscule, incapable of thought. And then came more shuddering divisions, more splittings, more doubling. Like a balloon filling with divine breath, s/he expanded, grew.

Now a sheet of cells, several thousand of them, began folding into a cohesive cluster with a trailing stem. Specializing, forming a unique structure. Gaining complexity as they differentiated into distinctive sections. Developing convolutions, giving him/her the ability to . . .

S/he thought. Sluggishly at first, a mere awareness of sensation. Of floating suspended in liquid, of being hemmed in on every side by soft warm walls. From somewhere in the distance came the sound of a muffled heartbeat. It reminded him/her that s/he had another body, another form. Elsewhere, outside. Beyond the darkness that enclosed him/her.

The thought was swept away by an unseen hand.

The changes continued. Deep within the clusters of cells that made up his/her tiny form, more complex structures were forming. A vast network of neurons coalesced, grew rootlets, linked with one another in a complicated and intertangled web. And with each new connection, his/her thoughts became clearer, quicker, cleaner—better than they had been before.

Before?

Somehow, s/he had a sense that this had all happened once before. But this time, the growth and development were being overseen by something other than random chance and genetic code. Some higher intelligence was directing the growth of each neuron and axon, the linkage of each synapse. This time the structure that was forming was . . . perfect.

Perfection achieved, the process came to an end. S/he hung poised, linked in perfect unison with his/her creator. The thoughts of each of them—parent and child—vibrated in perfect tonal harmony. The soft, resonant humming formed itself into thought-words.

It is time for you to be reborn.

A wrench. Sudden movement. S/he was being pushed down a tunnel, propelled by violent contractions of the soft walls that surrounded him/her. It hurt, it squeezed, it twisted him/her about . . . and yet it was somehow right. Somehow, it was time. Joy was waiting at the end of this tunnel. Joy and light. A whole new world.

But even as his/her head emerged from the tunnel, even as the world began to spring into focus, something changed. The gentle, guiding hands became clawed talons that hooked into his/her skull, dragging him/her out of the safe warm place and flinging him/her into a world of nightmare with the shock of a cold, hard slap . . .

09:47:03 PST
(10:47:03 MST)
Cheyenne, Sioux Nation

The sudden log off had made Kimi dizzy. She stood with one hand braced against the wall to steady herself, wondering how many seconds had already ticked past. Had the experiment already begun? But there was no clock in the hallway.

She ducked into the change room and pulled her bow and arrows from her locker. The bow looked like a toy, but a series of tiny pulleys inside its fiberglass body gave it the equivalent of a fifteen-kilo pull. Whenever Kimi pulled it back to full draw, even a suction-cup-tipped arrow would tear through one of the sacks of soybeans she'd practiced on. The arrows he'd brought to the creche today, however, was special. Hidden under its thin rubber suction cup was a teflon-coated ceramic point.

It was sharp, but it wouldn't really hurt Raymond Kahnewake. Just scare him. It was just a game.

Kimi ran down the hallway of the FTL building, heading for the bank of high-speed elevators that led to the upper floors. The glossy black surface of the elevator doors reflected the hallway behind her. The floor was a clear layer of plexiglass over Navaho sand paintings, and the walls were inset with a series of three-dimensional holos of Iroquois "false face" masks. The hallway was empty of adults—for the moment. So far, so good.

At last the elevator doors opened. Kimi ducked inside and stabbed the icon for the eighteenth floor. The doors sighed shut and the elevator took off with a high whine, its rapid climb creating a familiar sinking feeling in Kimi's stomach. She gripped her bow with a sweating hand and fitted her arrow to the string. Then she chewed her lip while the elevator's muzak system played a muted drumbeat and soft chanting. It was meant to be soothing, but Kimi was wound up too tight. She glanced nervously up at the security vidcam and tried to smile mischievously, like the great spirit had told her to do.

The elevator did not stop. It rose all the way to the eighteenth floor. Kimi stepped out into a hallway whose walls were textured to look like pink sandstone. A series of office doors stretched away to either side.

Kimi turned right and tiptoed down the plush carpet, her heart pounding. She rounded a corner and nearly ran into the security guard who was strolling the other way. She let out a yelp and dropped the arrow from her bow. The guard, an ork woman in uniform-blue pants and a crisp white shirt with Eagle Feather Security patches on the shoulders, squatted to pick up the arrow. For a long moment, Kimi stared at the guard, at the heavy pistol in the holster on her hip and the remote com unit hooked over one of her pointed ears. She tried looking anywhere but at the arrow, which the guard held in one huge hand. Could the woman see that this arrow was special?

The guard smiled and handed the arrow back to her. "Heya, Kimi. On the warpath again? Who're you counting coup against today?"

Kimi swallowed. She tried to keep her hands from trembling as she took the arrow and fitted it back to the string. "My mom," she said, her voice almost as squeaky as that of her Matrix persona. "Her office is just down the hall."

"Good hunting," the guard said. Then she walked away.

Relief washed over Kimi. Then she remembered how little time she had. She was probably already late; the other kids would have begun the experiment by now. She ran down the corridor to the last office on the left and peeked in the half-open door.

Raymond Kahnewake sat with his feet propped up on a work station cluttered with optical chips. He was jacked into a deck and was obviously hard at work programming; his eyes flickered back and forth behind closed lids and every now and then one of his fingers would twitch slightly as he executed a command. He was a large man with a thick shock of black hair shaved on one side to expose his datajacks. He wore the Sioux Nation equivalent of a business suit: buckskin trousers fringed with ermine and a tailored doeskin shirt with heavy beadwork all down the front.

Kimi raised her bow and took aim at the diamond-shaped design on the shirt. It formed a perfect bull's eye.

As if sensing something, Raymond Kahnewake suddenly logged off and opened his eyes. He recoiled slightly in surprise at seeing Kimi in the doorway. Then he smiled. "Heya, little one," he said in a deep voice. "What are you—?"

Kimi reminded herself what the great spirit had told her. *He's just like a virus*, she said in her mind. *I'm launching a complex form at a computer virus, just like in the Matrix. It's just pretend. To scare him.*

Knowing it was all just a game made her feel better. She let the arrow fly. It plunged through the beadwork that covered Raymond Kahnewake's chest, shedding its thin coating of rubber as the hidden ceramic tip bit deep. The programmer looked down in shock at the "toy" arrow that had buried itself up to its fletches in his chest. He tried to lean forward, but the arrow tip was lodged fast in the plastiform chair behind his back. The arrow was drawn deeper into his chest by the motion, and he grunted in pain.

"Who are . . . ? Why . . . ?" Then he coughed and a faint spray of blood flecked his lips.

Kimi stood for one frozen moment, transfixed by the sight. Then she realized that this wasn't just a game, after all. The man looked like he was hurt.

She dropped her bow and ran away down the hall.

The ork security guard looked bemused as Kimi rushed past her and leaped into the empty elevator that was still waiting on this floor. The guard gave another friendly wave as Kimi scrambled for the elevator's control panel. As Kimi pushed the icon that would send the elevator down, she heard the guard call out.

"Hey, Kimi!" the guard said. "You dropped your—"

The elevator doors closed.

As the elevator rushed down, making Kimi's stomach feel as if it were lurching up into her chest, she frantically plugged her fiber-optic cable into the telecom unit that was installed in one wall of the elevator. Snicking the other end of the cable into the datajack in her skull, she retreated into the Matrix. This was the "real" world. This was where she felt safe. In a constructed world of icons and programs, where personas merely faded away in static when they died. Where they didn't look at you with accusing eyes and blood on their lips. Where the quickest and cleverest always lived to run another day . . . even if they died.

Firmly, she told herself that the man she'd just shot with an arrow wasn't really dying. The arrow had been no more than an illusion. Just a construct. An icon. It hadn't really hurt him. But his wide eyes and bloody lips kept returning to haunt Kimi, like a loop in her programming . . .

She accessed her time-keeping utility and saw that the local time was 10:49:45. She'd done what the great spirit wanted, but had she been in time? She really didn't think so. And had this really been what the great spirit intended? Had she really been meant to *hurt* Raymond Kahnewake?

Fretting, uncertain, she followed the Matrix's familiar gridlike maze to the place where she and her friends left messages for one another. But she was stopped short by a wall of rippling sheet lightning. It hung like a crackling curtain in front of the portal she was trying to access, blur-

ring the edges of the irising airlock icon and sending Kimi
bouncing back into the datastream she had been following.

And that was weird. The lightning curtain was definitely
a barrier of some kind. But data was flowing through it.
This was a high-traffic area, one that led to public data.
Anyone could enter this part of the Matrix—not just tech-
noshamans like herself. A barrier here just didn't make
sense.

Kimi swam back along the dataline and tried approach-
ing from another direction. The portal this path led to
looked like a round metal hatch. But when Kimi reached
out to spin the wheel that would release the hatch, a wall of
sheet lightning, just like the first, sprang up to block her
path. Cautiously, she touched the lightning wall with her
teddy bear paws, trying to find a way around or through it.
This wasn't any program she was familiar with; it didn't
match any of the samples stored in her memory. Touching
it didn't hurt her meat bod any, but the barrier solidly refused to allow her to go any further. Yet data was passing
freely through the portal from a spray of datalines that
connected to it. And so was . . .

Another decker—a cartoonish character with a blue
cape and red, skin-tight suit—zoomed through the curtain
of lightning as if it didn't exist. The wheel on the hatch
spun and the portal opened, admitting him. But the barrier
still held Kimi back. It had shifted, somehow, to block her
way. She peered through it and saw swirling, red-tinged
darkness inside the opening, just before the hatch closed.
And then she heard the decker scream.

Kimi shuddered. This was creepy. She was scared.

A second figure undulated down the dataline toward
Kimi. She recognized the hunched green form of Inchworm. The worm wore its usual sloppy grin, but its multiple arms were waving in agitation. It stopped before the
barrier and caught at Kimi's thick, fuzzy arm.

"Something's gone wrong, Suzy Q," it said in a happy
voice that contrasted sharply with its obvious distress.
"The experiment didn't work. After one minute, everything went . . . bad."

A chill shot through Kimi's meat bod. "Bad?" she
asked. She glanced back at the shimmering sheet lightning

barrier, at the closed portal. Was this all her fault? She'd been too late with her attack on Raymond Kahnewake and now the great spirit wouldn't love her any more.

"None of us can access the Seattle RTG," Inchworm continued. "Something's keeping us out."

Kimi frowned at the barrier. "But other deckers are getting through. That cartoon guy—"

"Yeah, I know. But they're not getting out again." He gave a worried sigh. "I just wish I knew what was happening in there. My new friend Pip is trying to find out what's going on. But she's gotta use a tortoise. And even though she's wiz with a keyboard, that's gonna be slow."

In the world of the flesh, Kimi felt the elevator sigh to a stop and heard the doors opening. She opened her eyes and for a painfully long second was confused by the double images her brain received: Inchworm's icon silhouetted against the glowing grid of the Matrix—and the hallway that led to the creche. She realized that she had instinctively pushed the second-floor icon instead of the icon for the lobby

"I gotta go," she told Inchworm. Without waiting for him to answer, she logged off, then reached for the fiberoptic cable that connected her with the telecom unit and yanked it free. But just as she did, an alarm began to shrill. The elevator's control panel blinked out, and the doors froze in an open position.

Kimi's heart started to pound. Had they found out what she'd done? Were the security guards looking for her now? She glanced up at the elevator's monitor camera but couldn't tell if it was activated or not. Uncertain what to do next, Kimi stepped quickly out into the hallway.

Then the door to the games room burst open and children spilled out, some still carrying their foam lacrosse sticks. Kimi joined her creche mates as they jostled their way down the hall toward a fire exit. The kids were excited, talking all at once in loud voices as they tried to guess what the alarm meant.

The kids descended the stairway and spilled out into the lobby of the FTL building, across which the security guards were rushing with grim purpose. One of the guards herded the kids across the lobby toward a secure area where they were supposed to assemble whenever the alarm sounded. Kimi stayed with her creche mates until the guard looked the other way, then slipped through a side door that led to the parking garage. After descending a short flight of stairs, she reached a metal door with a security lock set into its handle.

She keyed in the passcode that would override the building's lockdown mode—she'd entered that passcode into the system herself—and stepped out through the door into a stairwell that led to the landscaped grounds outside. Then she ran, as fast as light, away from the FTL Technologies tower and into the bright morning sunshine.

09:47:09 PST
Seattle, United Canadian and American States

Timea Gelasso walked between the rows of children who sat at computer terminals, their eyes moving behind closed lids as they watched the Matrix unfold before them. The rapid eye movement reminded her of the faces of dreamers. Except that Matrix users sat upright and very much alert, their bodies twitching slightly as they responded to the stimuli of the virtual world their minds occupied.

The reticular-activation system overrides built into each of the decks were doing their jobs, keeping the children's meat bods from physically acting out the commands their brains were issuing to the computers. The RAS overrides suppressed the brain's neural signals in the same way that a dreamer's impulses were suppressed. Occasionally they failed, but actual "deckwalkers" were rare. And there were none in this group. These children all seemed to be quietly enjoying the sensory stimuli of the Matrix.

Timea frowned. They were enjoying it a little too quietly. For the last minute or so, none of the children had so much as twitched. Their eyes remained unmoving, as if they were staring at something directly ahead of them . . .

Timea shook off the uneasy feeling. It was just coincidence that all of their eyes had steadied at once. The kids were just fine.

The dozen children in the room were a mix of races: human mostly, but with a smattering of the other metatypes of the Awakened world. They probably knew they weren't welcome in this part of town, but the promise of the clinic had drawn them, just the same. And they'd probably faced much worse, in their short lives, than a few racial slurs. Take the slender elf girl whose delicately pointed ears bracketed the electrode net that encircled her head, for example. The sore on her ankle looked like a bite of some kind, and was probably infected. And the burly troll boy who sat at the terminal next to her had a puckered scar on his cheek that might be an old bullet graze. His horns were just starting to bud at his temples; he couldn't be more than six.

The other two metas were a stocky dwarf who sat hunched forward in a battered vinyl chair, his face already showing a downy beard at just eight years of age, and an ork boy. With his gnarled face and jutting brows, that one was harder to put an age to. Timea had to take his guardian's word for it that he was between the ages of six and twelve, as stipulated by the benefactors of the Shelbramat Free Computer Clinic.

Timea had to smile at that one. Benefactors. More like beneficiaries.

Some days, like today, she had doubts about her job. Sure, she was helping the best and the brightest kids to escape the squalid streets of Redmond. But the nagging questions remained. Why didn't any of the kids who were selected for the Shelbramat Boarding School ever respond to her e-mail? Why did the school's headmaster, Professor Halberstam, politely but firmly rebuff her every time she asked if she could visit the facility? She might have popped in unexpectedly on her own by now, but for the fact that Shelbramat was down in California Free State, not here in Seattle.

Timea had her suspicions. The "boarding school" was probably little more than a front for a corporation that recruited the next generation of wiz kids and put them to

work as deckers. The "students" probably spent their days
running the shadows for the corp, snatching data from its
competitors. Children of the barrens and streets, these kids
were expendable; even if they were brain-burned by black
IC, their parents weren't likely to complain. Not with the
hefty stipend these guardians were paid upon acceptance
of the child at the boarding school. And best of all for the
corp, the kids were a deniable asset. They probably didn't
even know that they were working, let alone who for.

They were being used.

But what was the alternative?

Timea stared down at one of the girls, a human about ten
years old. Her neatly braided corn rows with their bright
pink ribbons were a stark contrast to the torn clothes and
dirty synthleather sandals she wore. The girl reminded
Timea of herself at that age—a skinny waif with ebony
skin and eyes that warily took the measure of every adult
she met for signs of betrayal. Timea suspected that the
girl's story would be much like her own: a father lost to a
BTL overdose; a brother burned to death in a drive-by fireballing; a mother who sat and cried each night at the sheer
futility of trying to keep a family together in a decaying ur-
ban landscape but who still had enough hope to tie pink
ribbons in her daughter's hair. But this girl didn't have the
crisscross of faint scars that marked the inside of Timea's
left wrist . . .

She shook off the memory, focusing on the here and
now. The responsibility of caring for her aging mother and
two younger sisters—not to mention her own two-year-old
son Lennon—now sat firmly upon Timea's shoulders. She
needed this job. And she'd worked fragging hard to keep
it, polishing her vocabulary at the same time that she
honed her decking skills, deleting the gutter talk from her
speech. One day she'd have that corporate decking slot
she'd always dreamed about; then her whole family would
be on easy street.

The children who were chosen as the result of the testing she put them through were probably treated pretty de-
cently at the Shelbramat Boarding School. It made sense
for the suits to be nice, she told herself. The corporation

would get more use out a happy child who enjoyed "playing" in the Matrix than it would out a terrified slave who ran it unwillingly.

The kids were eating well and having fun and their life expectancies had probably more than doubled, despite the dangers they faced in the Matrix. Timea didn't have to feel guilty about the work she did.

And this job certainly had its perks, over and above the nuyen she received: unlimited Matrix time free of charge, plus bod mods with all surgical expenses paid. The first had been a datajack; the next had been something to help Timea hold her own on this tough piece of turf: an arm fitted with retractable razors.

The free computer clinic was situated in Squatter's Mall, originally a ritzy shopping center but now a haven for Seattle's SINless. Entire families lived in its abandoned storefronts, while gangers sold BTL chips, drugs, and illegal weapons from its back rooms. The clinic itself occupied what had been a suite of offices on the eighth floor of the mall. By mutual agreement of the many gangs who prowled the corridors below, the clinic was neutral turf. The gangers even took turns defending it; the last person who'd tried to boost one of the clinic's expensive cyberdecks had been found hanging in one of the mall's nonfunctional elevator shafts, a fiber-optic computer cable cinched tight around his purple neck.

Timea glanced at the ganger who was guarding the entrance to the clinic today. He was a white boy, but cute just the same, with a sensuous curl to his sneer and dark hair that swept back in oiled ringlets from his face. He was probably in his teens, but his streetwise eyes made him look much older. He shifted to show his muscles, made a suggestive motion with the heavy Warhawk pistol he cradled in his fist, and then gave Timea a wink. Although she felt old beyond her twenty years, Timea wasn't so ancient that she didn't want to flirt back. The boy wasn't exactly father material for Lennon, but he might be fun in . . .

The children began to scream.

The ganger sprang into a ready pose, pistol leveled and eyes searching the room for a threat. Timea whirled to face the kids. They were all sitting bolt upright in their chairs, bodies rigid and trembling. Their mouths were open, their lips pulled back in grimaces that revealed their teeth, the classic grin of fear. And they were screaming. Screaming with a shrill terror that sent a bone-deep shiver through Timea.

And their eyes were still staring straight ahead under closed lids . . .

Timea ran to the side of the nearest boy, knelt beside him, and pressed two fingers to his throat, searching for a racing pulse or other signs of induced biofeedback. She reached for the cable that connected the boy's electrode net to the cyberdeck on the table in front of him. Should she jack him out? What the frag was happening here?

Timea's mind raced through the possibilities as the children continued to scream. The kids were running cool decks; the sensory input wasn't much more than that of an off-the-shelf simsense unit. They faced no danger from any black IC they might encounter, save for the possibility of being temporarily stunned by it. But they'd be slagged by dump shock if Timea simply unplugged them . . .

The children continued to scream.

Two more gangers ran into the room, weapons in their fists.

"Whuzzit?" one barked. "Why are the ruggers bawlin'?"

"I dunno," Timea shouted back, slipping into streeter before she could correct herself. "I'd have to jack in to find out."

The ganger that Timea had been flirting with raised his pistol and fired a round into the ceiling, making the other gangers jump. "Hoi! Shut the frag up!" he shouted at the kids.

The children didn't even flinch.

Timea's eyes narrowed. "They can't hear you," she shouted. "They're in the Matrix. Something there is creepin' 'em out."

Weird, that it had hit all of the children at once. The kids' personas should have been scattered far and wide across the Matrix, testing their fledgling decking skills in widely scattered systems. They wouldn't all have blundered into the same node at once. Would they?

The oldest ganger returned his attention to the corridor outside the door. "Chill it," he told the others. "The ruggers may be a distraction. This could be a bang-up."

The cell phone on Timea's hip began to vibrate. In the bedlam, she couldn't hear its soft ring. Instinctively she picked it up and jammed it against her ear, placing a finger in her other ear so she could hear above the din. She recognized the voice of the caller at once. An older man's voice, crisp and precise.

"Timea? What's going on there?"

"Mr. Halberstam?"

"Something's disrupting a number of our . . . students," the headmaster continued. "It seems to be centered in the Seattle RTG. What reactions are you seeing at your end?"

"I . . . The kids . . ." Timea's eyes swept over the screaming children. Their bodies were starting to twist now as their terror pushed the RAS overrides to the limit. What was doing this to them?

There was only way Timea could find out. "I'm going to jack in," she told the headmaster.

"Don't!" Halberstam barked. "We've already lost two deckers who tried to access that RTG. Try—"

Timea lunged forward, dropping the phone. But she wasn't quick enough to stop the ganger who'd fired his gun earlier. Scowling at the children, shaking his head at their screams, he strode over and yanked the electrode net off the nearest child's head—the elf girl. She flailed out of the chair and convulsed across the floor, heedless of the chair and table legs that her limbs were striking.

"No!" the girl screamed. "Get 'em off! They're biting me. Get 'em awaaaaay!"

"You fragging brainwipe!" Timea shouted at the ganger. "Why'd you jack her out?" She shoved him aside before he could repeat the damage he'd done. Then she moved to the girl, tried to get her to stop beating her arms and legs against the wall.

"Get 'em off!" the girl wailed.

"Get what off?" Timea caught hold of the girl's wrists, dodged her kicking feet. "There's nothing on you!"

"Devil rats!" the girl shrilled. Her open eyes darted back and forth as she watched some private horror that only she could see. "They're in the squat, Ma. They're biting me . . ."

"Timea!" the cell phone squawked from where it lay on the floor. "It sounds as though that subject is suffering from a psychotic episode. What other manifestations of—"

Timea reached for the only cyberdeck in the room with a DNI plug. "I'm going on-line," she shouted at the phone. "It's the only way I'm gonna see what's wrong."

She glared at the ganger, who sneered back at her, his machismo insulted. He didn't look so cute any more. Just stupid.

Timea flexed, and the razors in her arm slid out, then back. "Don't unjack me," she told him grimly. "Unless you want a taste of these."

She jammed the plug into the jack at her temple and logged onto the Seattle RTG in the space between one heartbeat and the next.

The clinic disappeared.

09:48:00 PST

The warm, enveloping tunnel that he had been sliding through suddenly disappeared, leaving Red Wraith suspended in a void. Just a moment ago he'd been experiencing a sense of profound oneness with an intelligence greater than his own, a bond with something larger and more powerful than himself—something that was going to lead him gently by the hand into a beautiful new world.

Now that promise was gone. Red Wraith's feelings of joy and delight were replaced by a sense of intense claustrophobia and fear as the intelligence that had been guiding him somehow *changed* into something dark and foreboding. Even though he was surrounded by inky darkness, Red Wraith had the sense of something watching him, judging him, sifting through his thoughts and seeking out all that was unworthy and vile . . .

Lines appeared, startling him out of his fearful reverie.

At first they were nothing more than vague suggestions of gray against the inky black void. Then they grew in luminosity and joined to form a geometric figure that was boxlike in shape—a tesseract with Red Wraith at its center. The "rooms" of the tesseract solidified, filled with objects. Each was detailed and distinct: a military office in London, a penthouse overlooking Berlin, the sauna of a private Turkish bath, a parking garage in a Paris condominium, a rooftop garden in the Saeder-Krupp corporate arcology in Essen, the interior of a limousine rolling through the streets of Antwerp, a villa in the hills overlooking Athens—and all of them disturbingly familiar . . .

Within each of these settings, a shadowy figure moved. They appeared ghostlike at first, and for a moment or two Red Wraith wondered if the tesseract was some sort of node, filled with other deckers. Then the figures also solidified. Although he should have been incapable of remembering them, Red Wraith recognized them at once.

Each was a dead man—a political leader or prominent figure whom the cyberassassin Daniel Bogdanovich had been sent to eliminate. While every one of them was recognizable by his or her build and clothes, each wore Daniel's face like a rubber mask over his own, giving them a terrible and horrifying symmetry.

Red Wraith adopted a defensive posture as the figures approached. They came at him from above, below, and all sides, each closing in from one of the many rooms of the tesseract. Red Wraith spun this way and that, wondering which attack would come first.

Without warning, he felt a dull thump at the back of his neck that sent his head rocking forward. As a wave of blood ran down his back, he realized what had happened. The cranial bomb at the base of his skull had exploded, rendering him utterly paralyzed. He was still upright and on his feet, but all he could do was stand frozen in place, watching helplessly as his attackers approached . . .

The first emerged from the office of the British secretary of defense, backlit by a wall-to-wall projected map of what had once been the European Economic Community. The secretary, wearing a crisp gray uniform decorated with medals, had lurched to his feet from where he lay sprawled on the floor next to his desk. He marched toward Red Wraith with his swagger stick tucked under one arm and his head lolling against his shoulder from the karate chop that had snapped his spine. His step was certain but disjointed, a shambling stagger. But his hands were still fully functional, and were monstrous constructions of gun-metal blue steel. As they closed around Red Wraith's throat he felt the bones of his spine start to splinter and crack . . .

The secretary of defense disappeared.

The German trade ambassador came next. He emerged from his penthouse suite wearing his housecoat and slippers and holding a snifter of the brandy that had been laced with 200 milligrams of strychnine—twice the dose required to kill a man. His face was twisted with pain, and occasionally he was forced to stop as his body jackknifed nearly double with the convulsions the poison produced. Yet somehow he continued to stagger toward Red Wraith, and somehow he avoided spilling any of the brandy in the snifter around which his portly fingers were wrapped.

Wrenching Red Wraith's mouth open with one hand, the German ambassador poured the amber liquid down his paralyzed victim's throat. Red Wraith choked and sputtered and felt hot brandy trickle like spittle from the corners of his mouth, but was forced to swallow just the same. Within seconds the strychnine hit, sending spasms of pain throughout his body. His gut felt as though it were filled with iodine bile, a churning sea upon which razor blades were bobbing, their sharp edges sawing into the lining of his stomach. His vision blurred with tears as the pain intensified beyond what he could bear . . .

The trade ambassador vanished.

The Russian policlub leader emerged from the steam room, his muscular young body wrapped in a towel. His damp curls framed piercingly intelligent black eyes that stared out from beneath the mask of Daniel's face. The bottom of that face was a bloody ruin. A portion of his jaw hung to one side on tattered strands of flesh—the exit point of the bullet that had been fired into the back of his head. He held a gun in his right hand—a Walther PB-120 with a body and silencer made entirely from fiberglass and plastic, materials that would pass through a metal detector without a blip. As super-hot steam swirled around his lower legs the policlub leader raised the pistol, sighted, and fired. Although Red Wraith was looking down the barrel of the gun, the bullet somehow struck him from behind, ripping apart his lower face and jaw in a bloody explosion of flesh, gums, and teeth.

Just as the first two men had, the policlub leader vanished.

Attacker followed attacker in rapid succession, each killing Red Wraith in the same way that he had been dispatched. But the last one—the Greek minister of finance—wasn't satisfied with merely slashing Red Wraith's throat with the spur mounted in the heel of his boot. Just as the steel blade bit into flesh, he transformed into an image of Lydia, her own throat gaping open in an obscene red grin that mirrored Red Wraith's own wound. She tried to speak, to whisper words of endearment to Red Wraith. But then blood erupted from her throat, fountaining over him in a ghastly spray. As she died, Lydia's eyes locked on his—accusing, wounded, filled with hate . . .

Unable to bear it a second longer, Red Wraith closed his eyes and choked back a moan of agony. Then he clamped down upon the shard of determination that remained. He refused to suffer, to die this way. This was all just some nightmarish hallucination, some deathbed construct with which his own mind had chosen to torment him as he lay on the verge of death. Summoning up the last vestiges of his will, he fought back, forcing his hands up and away from his body, palms outward against Lydia's chest, in violent defiance.

His ghostly hands passed right through her. And that gave Red Wraith an idea. His persona resembled a wraith, an insubstantial figure composed of red mist. He'd customized his masking program to allow him to pass through walls like a ghost. Perhaps he could use it to escape from the tesseract that enclosed him now.

Shaking off the last of the paralysis, Red Wraith hurled his body forward into the room that resembled the office of the secretary of defense. He struck the wall map at the back of the room, was momentarily slowed by it—and then passed through it as if it was not there.

He had escaped!

But the scene he found himself in was grim indeed . . .

Lady Death lay on her back on the rumpled sheets of the
hotel bed. They were wet, but warm. She plucked weakly
at the sheets with one hand and saw that they were
splotched with vibrant red. The same red stained her fingers and, she saw when she looked down, her bare legs.

Harsh lights—the kind they use in operating rooms—
glared down from above. Were they the lights that she had
been rushing toward, just an eyeblink ago? They shone
harshly upon the walls of the room, which were a sterile
white, inset with medical equipment and monitors. A hiss
of air conditioning washed Lady Death's skin with a chilling cold, carrying with it the sharp smell of medicine and
disinfectant.

Dozens of figures crowded around the bed. Each was
Shinanai—and yet not Shinanai. The skin on one was a little too ruddy, the hair on another a little too short or too
long over the ears. That one's luminescent face paint was
the wrong shade of blue, and the cast of this one's eyes
was too angular. This one's mannerisms were too abrupt,
not flowing and graceful like Shinanai's, while that one's
laughter was too harsh and unkind.

The not-Shinanais crowded around the bed, poking at
Lady Death's hair, clothes, and skin with cold fingers. All
held hypodermics with needles the width of her little finger and syringes the size of soda cans. Flexible rubber tubing ran from the top of those hypodermics into their
mouths, like drinking straws.

After pressing the skin to find a vein, the vampires
plunged the tips of the needles into Lady Death's skin with
painful jabs, then drew the plungers back. The syringes
filled with blood, which the vampires greedily sucked up
through the tubes, turning them from pale white to a
murky pink. As they fed they smiled reassuringly down at
Lady Death, dribbles of blood trickling over parted lips.
Occasionally one would pause in her feeding and bend
down to mark Lady Death's pale white skin with bloody
lip prints. Their kisses were gentle but delivered with remote

formality, in just the same way that Hitomi's own parents had kissed her good night.

Lady Death stared up at the vampires, helpless and weak. Even though these were only imperfect replicas of Shinanai, a part of her knew that these creatures loved her. What they were doing to her was for her own good. It was a treatment, a cure for life. A mercy killing . . .

Realizing that she wasn't thinking clearly, Lady Death shook her head. What had happened? There had been a bright light, and Shinanai's voice, and then scenes from her childhood and early teenage years. They had sped by impossibly fast, like a tridcast skipping forward several seconds at a time: Hitomi playing in the Shiawase arcology's exclusive, executive-class daycare; her guardians beating the private tutor who had been caught teaching Hitomi an unauthorized subject—how to French kiss; trying in vain to gain the attention of her mother and father by wearing increasingly outrageous fashions and body art; the night at the Black Magic Orchestra concert when she had slipped free of her guardians and fled backstage to meet Shinanai. The final scene had been set in the hotel room in Seoul where Shinanai had made love to her. And then she had awakened here, in a room that was a strange blend of the hotel room in Seoul and her family's private medical clinic . . .

Horror returned to Lady Death as she remembered that she was dying. The vampires surrounding her bed took on a gruesome tinge then, their faces illuminated from below as the lights overhead blinked out. The shadowy figures rustled around the bed in the half-light—only the achingly sharp jabs of the needles they plunged into Lady Death's quivering flesh told her where they were. She lay in grim anticipation of the next piercing jab, unable to move because she was so weak from loss of blood.

A sudden thought came to her: *the real Shinanai will save me.* But Lady Death knew this to be a false hope. She was trapped here in this netherworld between life and death, while the *aidoru* was safely back in the real world, as were Hitomi's guardians and anyone else who might have rescued her. She was on her own. She was trapped in her own worst nightmare—one in which not even Shinanai could intervene.

A tiny core of anger blossomed deep inside Lady Death. She would show them. She was only a teenage girl, but once already in her young life she had fought off death. She could do it again.

She lashed out at the arm of the vampire nearest her, knocking away the syringe it held. Blood sprayed from the needle, staining the white wall in a jagged pattern. Summoning every ounce of her strength, Lady Death sat up on the bed, kicking and striking out with her hands at the remaining vampires and screaming as loud as she could. Amazingly, they pulled away. In that split second she jumped from the bed and staggered to the door. But it was locked. The handle would not turn.

Lady Death looked desperately around as the vampires moved slowly toward her, hypodermics raised and voices hissing with whispered threats. The room did have one other door, she saw now. But upon it was a sign that bore a single character: the word "morgue." Lady Death was certain—although she could not say where this knowledge came from—that nothing living could pass through it. But technically, she was not a living creature. The Matrix icon in which her soul currently resided was that of a dead woman, a suicide victim.

Hurling herself toward the door, Lady Death wrenched at it. Unlike the other handle, this one turned easily. The door opened, and Lady Death plunged through it, slamming it behind her just as the vampires reached it. She saw that the door also contained a deadbolt, and turned the latch on it, sealing the vampires on the other side.

She turned around, relief washing through her as she realized that she was free of the nightmare in which she had been trapped a moment before.

But the landscape that the door led to was not one she would have willingly entered, had there been any other choice . . .

Dark Father was alone, in a place that was utterly dark, silent, and still. The transition was dramatic, abrupt. Seconds ago he had been surrounded by joy, a beautiful light that drew ever nearer, and gentle, comforting murmurs. Now there was darkness, silence, and fear.

Dark Father tried to move but found that he could move his arms and legs only a short distance before they bumped into walls. He lay on his back on a hard surface that was lined with padded, silky cloth. He tried to sit up, but his head bumped against a ceiling that was only a few centimeters above his nose. Walls, also lined with padded silk, surrounded him on all sides, only a centimeter or two away from his body.

Dark Father suddenly realized where he was. The tiny boxlike room, the silk-padded walls, floor, and ceiling, the utter stillness in which his racing heart beat loudly . . . he could only be inside a coffin. Had he died? Had they buried him? Had the doctors been misled by his ghoul's body and thought he was dead when he was still alive, then interred him by mistake?

For several helpless, panicked seconds, Dark Father flailed against the prison that enclosed him, kicking his feet against the sides of the coffin. He clawed at the silk lining until it hung in shreds against his face and slammed his palms against the coffin lid.

"There's been a mistake!" he shouted. "I'm alive! Let me out!"

But his efforts were futile. The hollow thuds of his kicks and blows would never be loud enough to attract attention if he were buried and the lid was sealed shut with the pressure of hundreds of pounds of earth. And now the air inside the coffin was getting stale, as Dark Father sucked the last of it into his gasping lungs . . .

He closed his eyes against the darkness and balled his fists. There had to be a way out. There had to be. But at the core of his being, he knew it was hopeless. He had about as much chance of becoming human again as he did of escaping this living hell.

A faint scraping sound caused him to open his eyes. He lay utterly still and listened, head turning to the side, focusing every scrap of his attention on the sound. Was it really the sound of someone digging? Had his thuds and shouts been heard?

The digging sounds became louder and closer. Now he

could hear the scrape of something sharp against the coffin lid, and the click of a latch being unfastened. Weeping with joy, he began to laugh through his tears as a crack of light appeared around the edge of the coffin lid. As it creaked open he sat up, ready to embrace his rescuer.

Then his mouth dropped open in surprise. "Chester?" he asked.

His son stared down at him. Clods of earth fell from his elongated fingers—he had used his untrimmed claws to dig the coffin out. Although his facial features were as African-American as Dark Father's own, Chester's skin was a pale, mottled white. His eyes watered and he winced in the sunlight that streamed down from above, reflecting dully on his hairless head. The boy was only eighteen, but the taint of ghoul was so strong in him that he looked like a man in his thirties.

"Hullo, Father," Chester said. Then he grinned, revealing jagged teeth.

"What happened to me, Chester?" Dark Father asked. "How did you—"

That was odd. Now that Dark Father's eyes had adjusted to the painfully bright sunlight, he could see his own arms and legs. Instead of the slightly grayish skin he expected, he saw black bones encased in loose black cloth. The noose still hung around his neck and his eyes were shaded by the brim of the black top hat on his head.

"What is. . . ? Where. . . ?"

Was he in the Matrix still? But this felt so real. Without the connection to his body, without the subtle quen that the RAS couldn't quite filter out, simsense was indistinguishable from reality. But if this was the Matrix, what was Chester doing in it?

"That's a good question, Father," the teenage ghoul answered. "The answer's pretty simple: I'm hungry."

Chester lunged forward, scrabbling with his dirt-encrusted hands at Dark Father's chest. The fabric of his suit tore away easily, revealing patches of grayish skin still clinging to his skeletal ribs. The boy fell upon these in a frenzy, tearing at them with jagged teeth. Searing pain lanced through Dark Father as he felt the flesh being torn from his bones. But the pain was nothing compared to the emotional anguish he felt. His own son—feeding upon him as if he were so much carrion. This was madness! Betrayal!

"Leave me alone!" Dark Father howled. He fought back, trying to push Chester away, but his arms were cramped after his confinement in the coffin. And the boy was young and strong. Now Dark Father could hear his bones cracking as Chester bit through them, slurping the marrow out of them as if they were syrup-filled straws.

Shaking with fear, Dark Father hurled himself from the coffin and scrambled out of the shallow grave in which it had been buried. Chester climbed up behind him, stuffing a chunk of Dark Father's flesh into his mouth as he climbed.

"Admit it!" Chester burbled in a gleeful tone. "You're just like me. A flesh feeder. A ghoul."

"No!" Dark Father howled. He staggered across a field of dark, soft earth. Chester ran after him, clawed hands plucking at Dark Father's tattered jacket.

Dark Father looked wildly around, seeking an escape route. But his nightmare was about to intensify. Gibbering voices surrounded him as ghouls closed in on every side, their eyes greedy with hunger and their clawed hands raised and ready. And each of them looked like a ghoulish rendition of the bounty hunter who had shot him a year ago . . .

Surrounded by a ring of slavering ghouls, Dark Father skidded to a stop. In desperation he tore open his jacket and turned toward the nearest one.

"Leave me alone!" he howled. "I'm nothing but bone. There's no flesh left on my body. I'm dead. You can't feed on me!"

The ghouls hesitated. Several lowered their hands. But Chester stepped forward, eyeing his father critically.

"If you're dead, then you belong in the ground," he said. The other ghouls laughed and began crowding forward once more.

"I—" Dark Father felt the ground shift beneath him. Looking down, he saw that his feet were buried to the ankles in soil. He seemed to be sinking into the earth. When he looked up, he saw that the ghouls were hesitating. Several were staring in confusion at the ground, as if wondering where Dark Father had hidden his feet. But Chester's attention was still firmly focused on his father.

"Come on," he told the other ghouls. "It's time to finish him."

The ghouls leaped forward, laughing in anticipation of a kill.

Dark Father did the only thing he could think of. He ducked down into a crouch and began scrabbling at the soft soil. Perhaps if he covered himself in earth, the ghouls would no longer see him. It was a desperate ploy and had about as much logic to it as a child thinking that, if his own eyes were closed, no one could see him. But if it was that or death . . .

Amazingly, it seemed to be working. As Dark Father clawed his way into the ground like a hunted animal, the ghouls suddenly looked confused and then began wandering away, one by one. Soon only Chester was left. And then as Dark Father disappeared into the ground, he too vanished.

Soft soil surrounded Dark Father. For a moment he lay still. Then he noticed a light below him. He dug a little further, and a hole opened underneath him. Pulling himself out of it, he climbed up and onto the surface as gravity suddenly reversed itself. The hole he had just emerged through was below him now.

He'd done it—freed himself from the nightmarish confrontation with his son.

But the place the hole had led to seemed little better than the one he had just left . . .

A buzzer sounded and the soft warm tunnel surrounding him disappeared. Bloodyguts found himself sprawled stomach-down over the back of a galloping horse, just ahead of its rider—an Asian ork dressed in a dirty sheepskin vest, leather pants, and soft leather boots. One of the rider's hands clenched the back of Bloodyguts' shirt, holding him tight against the saddle. The saddle horn dug into his gut with each jostle and blood rushed to his head, which bobbed loosely between his outstretched arms. Below them, the horse's chromed hooves churned up a boiling cloud of dust. Grit filled Bloodyguts' nostrils, carrying with it the smell of horse sweat.

Bloodyguts groaned and lifted his head slightly. He saw other riders—also orks and dressed much like the first— galloping madly after the horse that carried him, their vests billowing as they caught the rush of air. Although the orks looked as though they had ridden out of a documentary on the ancient Mongols, several sported obvious cyberware. One had wrap-around mirror shades, and another wore a Darwin's Bastards metamusic T-shirt and military-style combat boots. Each rode a horse that had large white numbers painted on it; similar numbers, in black, marked each rider's sheepskin vest.

They rode furiously in pursuit of the horse on which Bloodyguts was sprawled. The landscape behind them was table-flat, a smooth expanse of bright blue plastic imprinted with circuitry—a gigantic simsense chip. Somewhere an orchestra was playing. The air was filled with the rolling thunder of drums, the clash of bronze gongs, and the shrill of stringed instruments played in a frenzied minor key.

Every last one of the riders was wired for simsense. Each had a rig wrapped tight around his head and a flexible wire antenna streaming out behind; the wet records were being sampled remotely. Bloodyguts saw a similar wire trailing from his own skull, and could feel the pinch of the simsense rig around his temples, where it was snugged tight under his horns.

Anger boiled through him. Frag it—he was being recorded? He tried to paw the simsense rig from his head, but the jostling of the horse frustrated his efforts. The drekkin' thing seemed glued to his skull.

Bloodyguts tried to lift himself up—and nearly slid from the horse. Only the firm grip of the ork kept him on its back.

That was when he realized that something was wrong with the perspective. In the meat world, the troll decker Yograj Lutter stood nearly three meters tall and weighed in at 250 kilos. Yet here he was slung over the back of a short, shaggy horse that was little bigger than a pony. His dangling hands and feet barely reached the horse's belly. In comparison to the ork rider, Bloodyguts was no larger than a child, even though he had the powerful, muscular body of a troll. No matter how hard he struggled, he just wasn't strong enough to escape . . .

Another of the riders caught up to the horse on which Bloodyguts was sprawled. The ork kicked his horse violently, sending it slamming into the other horse's flank. Sparks flew and a metallic whining filled the air as the two horses ground together. Then the pursuing rider drew a monofilament whip and slashed at the ork holding Bloodyguts. As the hair-thin filament snaked out, glinting in the sunlight, Bloodyguts heard a loud, special-effects *whoosh* and wet tearing sound. Hot blood sprayed onto his back as the rider let go of his shirt and suddenly tumbled backward off his horse, his severed head flying in one direction and his body in another. The other rider leaned in close, grabbed Bloodyguts' shirt in his fist, and hauled him over to his own horse. Whooping his victory, the ork kneed his horse on a new course, wheeling around to escape the other riders.

Bloodyguts shook his head, trying to make sense of it all. This was crazy. One minute he'd been sliding through a tunnel of light toward his dead chummer—the next he'd woken up in a crazed, Asian-western dream. The orks were treating Bloodyguts as if he were a prize cut of beef that they were carrying home to the stew pot . . .

Then Bloodyguts got it. His wetware slotted and ran a distant memory, and he understood the game he'd been dropped into. Years ago he'd seen a flatscreen film from the twentieth century of a violent game played by the riders of the Asian steppes. It was an every-man-for-himself mounted combat in which riders tried to grab the body of a freshly killed calf from one another. The winner was the man who could carry this "ball" outside a designated playing field. The prize for victory was the calf itself, which was roasted and eaten.

Then Bloodyguts saw the dotted lines on his hands and forearms. Just like a carcass of beef, his skin had been marked with lines a butcher would use to make his first cuts . . .

Riders on another part of the field came together in a tussling knot of horses and dust. In an effort to escape another contender who had almost caught up to him, the rider carrying Bloodyguts was forced to swing toward the commotion. Bloodyguts caught a brief glimpse of the rider at the center of the throng, who also had a body draped over his horse. The dreadlocks and horns of this child-sized troll were immediately recognizable to Bloodyguts, despite the simsense rig that obscured the troll's features. Bloodyguts *knew* his friend was dead, but even so a wash of dread swept through him as he saw one of the rider's whips lash down, cutting his friend's back open in a bloody line.

"Jocko!" he yelled.

Jocko's head lifted slightly—but it may have just been the motion of the horse on which he was carried. Was he still alive? Bloodyguts couldn't tell.

Then Jocko slid from the back of the horse to land in the dust. The riders leaped from their horses, whips raised. As the monofilaments rose and fell, sparkling in the sunlight and sending drops of blood flying, Jocko's body was precisely flayed like a side of beef.

Bloodyguts felt a chip slotting home in the chipjack in his temple. He'd had the chipjack permanently sealed years ago, but somehow it seemed that the plug had fallen away. The chip slid home with a familiar *click*—and then the agony that Jocko was feeling sawed through Bloodyguts' flesh, cutting him to the bone. He *was* Jocko, lying on the smooth surface of the BTL chip that formed the landscape, feeling the monofilaments cut him to pieces. He was dying. *Again.*

"Noooo!" Bloodyguts clawed at the chip in his jack but was unable to wrench it loose. Instead it broke in two, leaving its circuitry buried in his skull. It throbbed there like a living thing, sending pulses of pain through his body. He/Jocko lay on his back in the dust, watching his body as it was cut into bloody chunks . . .

His body. No, Jocko's body. No not even that. The Matrix persona that was modeled after Jocko's body.

This isn't real, Bloodyguts told himself. *This is a BTL trip. A chip dream. I'm still in the Matrix, and my icon is that of a chummer who is already dead. You can't kill a dead man. And that's what I am. Dead.*

Concentrating his will against the powerful sensory stimuli, Bloodyguts shut down his senses one by one. Sight, hearing, smell, taste—until only the pain remained. Then that too was blocked. He hung for a moment in the void of nothingness, balancing on the brink of blissful oblivion, then concentrated on ejecting the chip from his jack. He felt it slide free—with aching slowness at first, then suddenly popping free, all in a rush. He waited a second more, then allowed his tactile sense to return. He felt no pain. Encouraged, he allowed his other senses to return one by one. Then he opened his eyes and looked around him.

The ork riders, their horses, and the chip-flat landscape had all disappeared, popping out of existence while Bloodyguts hung suspended in a world without sensation or time. He had crashed that chip dream—logged off from it and found another, less painful reality for his soul to occupy.

But it didn't exactly welcome him with open arms . . .

09:48:27 PST

Lady Death stood in a vast cavern whose high ceiling reflected the red light of fires that erupted in flickering jets through cracks in the stone floor. Streams of blood wound their way between these fires, entering and exiting the cavern through gloomy tunnels, and sulfurous yellow smoke obscured the air. The walls echoed with the screams and cries of the damned.

They were everywhere: perched on stone stalagmites, curled in fetal positions on the hard rocky floor, or beating fists or foreheads against walls in an effort to dull their agony. Some were submerged in the stone floor, with only grasping hands or quivering feet showing above its surface, trapped like living flies in amber.

They were humanoid figures having neither distinguishing characteristics nor gender, smooth and gleaming as if they had been dipped in molten chrome. Their heads were hairless and their faces identical; they had eyes, noses, ears, and mouths, but all looked the same. Only their voices differentiated adult from child, or male from female. Agony echoed from every tongue: groans, shrill screams, or low moans.

Lady Death shuddered. She would have gone back to face the vampires again, but the door had disappeared the moment she locked it shut. Although their screams caused her to wince, the damned seemed to offer no real threat. They were oblivious to her, each wrapped in his or her own private hell. They stood, sat, or lay in place, faces distorted and mouths open and screaming.

Was this the Matrix? It had to be. If she had died, the *gaijin* hell was the last place she would have expected to wind up. Her parents had schooled Hitomi in the Shinto religion; she'd rejected it and considered herself an atheist. The only way she'd have wound up in a scene out of Dante's *Inferno* was if someone else had programmed it and put it in her path. The vampires and hotel/hospital room had been drawn from her own fears, but this place was someone else's nightmare.

"*So Ka,*" she whispered to herself. "I am in the Matrix. But where? And what does this represent?"

Although the damned themselves looked like standard USM icons, the landscape they inhabited did not conform to universal Matrix symbolism. It looked custom-designed, like a sculpted system. The rivers of blood had to be datastreams, just like the sand ripples in the Shiawase system. The stalagmites were probably datastores or sub-processing units, and the tunnels system access nodes or input/output ports. But it all felt so *real*. The heat from the fires was causing rivulets of sweat to run down her temples and back, she could smell the heavy stink of sulfur, and her mouth and nose were dry from breathing the hot air. The screams . . .

Were those other deckers? Lady Death moved cautiously toward one. She chose a small figure; by the size it was a child about half her age. The kid was lying on the cavern floor and kicking her legs, beating at her body with her hands.

Lady Death knelt down and touched the child's shoulder . . .

She was lying on her foam mattress in the squat and it was dark. Outside she could hear angry shouts and the sound of automatic weapons. Light slanted through the boarded-up window beside her. Something was on her bed—something nearly as big as her. Its eyes gleamed red in the dim light and its pointed ears twitched. Its mouth opened wide, grinning, and its hairless tail lashed back and forth. It sniffed at her, whiskers twitching, as she lay tangled in her torn woolen blanket, terrified and unable to free herself or kick the gigantic rat away no matter how hard she thrashed her legs. Then it bit. Warm blood flowed down her calf as its sharp teeth worried their way into her flesh. She cried out for Ma, but Ma wouldn't come. She was in the next room with a "customer" and that meant she was busy. And now more devil rats were pouring in through the cracks in the wall, dropping from the ceiling onto her mattress, crawling up through the ventilation shafts, pushing the board away from the window to get inside, chittering with evil laughter, coming to tear and rend and gnaw at her, smothering and suffocating her until she . . .

"Get them off me!" Lady Death screamed. "Get them off! *Takukete!* Help meee—!"

She tore her hand away. She stood, shaking, for several long seconds. Shudders ran the length of her spine and tears streamed from her eyes. She looked down at where the girl lay thrashing and could still feel her terror, even though she was no longer experiencing it first-hand. Horrible.

She looked around. If she touched another of the deckers, what other nightmares would she experience? She didn't want to know.

Lady Death knelt and dipped a finger into one of the streams of blood. She braced herself for more horrific images, but instead her mind was filled with a stream of meaningless data. Word fragments echoed in her ears, kaleidoscopic images flashed before her eyes, meaningless

clumps of English letters and pseudo-Japanese *kanji* characters scrolled rapidly past, and fragments of tactile sensation assaulted her. The blood was a data stream—but
one that seemed hopelessly scrambled. She flicked the
blood from her fingers and the sensory jumble cleared
from her mind.

She stood and touched one of the stalagmites instead.
It seemed solid, its lumpy limestone formation like an
upside-down ice cream cone. If it was indeed a datastore,
it wasn't giving up any of its secrets. Unless . . .

Lady Death pushed against the tip of the stalagmite. She
felt it give a little, and pushed harder. A crack appeared
just below her hand. The tip shuddered and felt as though
it were about to break off . . .

A jet of reddish-orange flame erupted at Lady Death's
feet. She jumped back, but it licked at her kimono and set
a corner of the fabric on fire. Lady Death smacked at it
with her hands until it went out, then contemplated the
black singe mark that was left behind. Had she just been
attacked by IC? Had she just activated some sort of defensive utility? She could no longer tell what was going on.
She could not feel her body in the real world, nor did
she have a sense of which utilities she had loaded and
ready to run.

As an experiment, she tried to activate one of her
programs—an analyze utility. She had been expecting it to
fail, so she was startled when a theater-style spotlight appeared in her hands. She shone its bright beam on the jet of
flame and waited for the returning flow of information. It
appeared in her mind as a page from a script: *The part of
the blaster IC is being played by hellfire. Its role is to attack any who would cause the leading player harm. It is a
minor character of low rank.*

Lady Death shut the spotlight off and stood, lost in
thought. Gray IC then—black would have been assigned a
more prominent part. But the "leading player"? Was that
the sysop for this system?

Something moved in her peripheral vision. Lady Death
spun around, her kimono whirling. Then she backed up
slowly, concealing herself behind a stalagmite and trying
not to draw the attention of the figure that flowed out of

one of the walls like a ghost. Like the damned that surrounded her, it was a humanoid figure, but unlike them it was neither smooth and featureless nor metallic. Instead it seemed to be composed of swirling red mist. Jets of flame showed through its translucent body as it moved past them. It paused a moment, then moved further into the cavern with a sure stride, despite the fact that its legs ended in stubs several centimeters above the floor. Drops of red fell from the ends of these stubs onto the stone, where they hissed and bubbled as the heat evaporated them.

As the figure drew closer to where Lady Death was hiding, she could see that it was a man. His hair swept back from a high forehead and his chin and cheeks were dark with beard stubble. He wore a loose-fitting robe that looked more like a shroud, a tattered reddish-brown fabric the color of dried blood. He balanced on his three-quarter-legs with the poise of a martial artist and his arms were raised in a defensive posture. He glanced warily around the cavern he had just entered, eyes flicking from one to another of the damned.

Then they locked on Lady Death. She tried to duck back behind the stalagmite but wasn't quick enough. The ghost man had seen her. Frantically, she tried to ready a defensive utility. Would the ghost attack? What would her best defense be? Should she hurl an attack program at it before it could—

"Wait!" the ghost man called out. "Don't go! Who are you? Where are we? What system is this?"

Lady Death paused, confused. He didn't sound hostile. He seemed as confused as she was. But maybe it was a trick.

She activated one of her utilities. Miniature jets appeared in the bottom of her wood-block sandals, lifting her a fraction of a centimeter from the floor. The extra speed and maneuverability they provided would add precious milliseconds, should she have to avoid this other decker—or whatever he was—in combat.

She crouched down low, ready to jet into the air at the first sign of a hostile move, then peeked out from behind the stalagmite.

Red Wraith tensed as the other decker peered out from behind the stalagmite. The woman—assuming the decker's gender was the same as the persona's—had abnormally white skin, red lips, and black hair piled high in an elaborate bun. She wore a flowing kimono patterned with glowing red dragons that were probably icons for her utilities. He watched her hands warily, ready to react if she made a move to activate any of them.

She said something, but Red Wraith found it difficult to hear her over the screams of the human figures that filled the cavern.

"What?" he called out. He edged closer but stopped when her body posture told him that she was about to flee.

"Are you the leading player?" she repeated.

Red Wraith frowned. The other decker's question seemed to imply that this was a game of some kind. Had he blundered into some sort of ultra-high-rez, Matrix-based arcade? The other decker seemed to regard him as a potential threat—or perhaps she simply saw him as competition. Was the "leading player" this woman was referring to the game site's sysop?

Red Wraith calculated the benefit of answering her question in the affirmative. But after weighing it against his ability to spin out the lie without having slotted any background data, he rejected this course of action. If she thought he was in control of the game, she might expect *him* to provide *her* with data. But if she thought he was a fellow player who wanted to team up with her, information might be more forthcoming. And she seemed to know more about this system than he did.

Red Wraith decided to play along.

"No, I'm not!" he shouted back. "I'm just an ordinary player. I go by the handle of Red Wraith. Who are you?"

"I'm Lady Death." She rose from her crouch but stood so that the stalagmite continued to partially shield her.

"Want to team up?" he asked.

She took a moment to consider his question. "*Hai.* I guess."

Red Wraith slotted that piece of data away. She'd answered with the Japanese affirmative. She was of Japanese descent then, just as her persona icon implied. Or else she wanted him to think that was the case.

Red Wraith edged closer. The woman tensed—and he resisted the instinctive reaction. Instead of triggering a utility as a defense, he kept his hands in plain sight and stood in an non-threatening pose. A jet of flame flickered out of a crack in the stone nearby; he felt its heat on his legs and side but deliberately did not flinch.

"Watch out for the fire," the white-faced woman told him. "It's blaster IC."

"Thanks. I will." He looked around. "Is there a way out of here?"

The Japanese woman shrugged and looked around. "We could try accessing one of the tunnels. I think they're datastreams."

Red Wraith peered into the nearest one. A river of blood flowed into it, washing its entire floor with red. Blood oozed from the walls, the drops collecting in tiny rivulets that fed the stream. "Shall we?" He stepped to the side and motioned for the other decker to enter the tunnel. She might seem harmless, but he wasn't about to turn his back on her.

She hesitated and curled a delicate red lip, and he realized that she probably didn't want to step into the blood. But then tiny jets spurted from the bottom of her sandals. She hovered, then stepped lightly out on top of the stream.

Red Wraith smiled at the irony that here, in hell, someone should be walking on "water." He laughed at the fleeting thought that this woman might be his savior. Most days, it was hard enough for him to trust himself, let alone a complete stranger.

The tunnel was just high enough for them to walk upright, and just wide enough that Red Wraith could reach out his hands on either side and touch the irregular, weeping rock walls. Or rather, try to touch them. His hands passed through them each time his fingers brushed them, making him wonder if he was ever going to be able to manipulate anything in this system. As an experiment, he reached out and touched Lady Death's back as they were rounding a bend in the tunnel. His hand passed through both the fabric of her kimono and her skin, but if she felt his touch she gave no sign.

The screams of the inhabitants of the larger cavern faded away, and were replaced by the rustle of the Japanese woman's kimono and the gentle gurgle and drip of the stream of blood.

They walked at a normal pace; there was none of the sense of rushing motion or instantaneous travel from node to node that deckers in the Matrix usually experienced. Despite the fact that he seemed to have no solid form, Red Wraith inhabited this landscape as if it were a physical reality, rather than a Matrix construct. And that worried him. He'd heard of systems like this, but had never accessed one before. Known as ultraviolet hosts, they were supposed to have system ratings far in excess of even megacorp or military computer systems. On an ultraviolet host system, the decker *was* his persona. Which would explain Red Wraith's ghostlike inability to manipulate objects and his complete disassociation from his meat bod. Except that ultraviolet hosts were supposed to be just a rumor . . .

After a few moments the tunnel ended in a large cavern that was filled with a vast red lake. Metallic-skinned bodies dotted its surface, floating on their backs with arms and legs loosely splayed. They turned slowly, as if trapped in lazy whirlpools. Each figure was a smooth metallic humanoid—the standard USM iconography for a decker's persona. Across the lake, Red Wraith could make out a dark opening where the tunnel they had been following continued.

Red Wraith and the Japanese woman stood on a beach of gray dust studded with bone-white pebbles. Just ahead of them, a black-hulled wooden boat was beached, its bow pulled up on shore. It looked much like a gondola, with a long, single oar at the stern, a curved bow, and a seat for passengers in the middle. Standing on the raised stern was a figure shrouded entirely in black. Pale skeletal hands gripped the oar. The figure turned, slowly, staring at the two newcomers with a face that was no more than an empty shadow under a hood of cloth.

"It looks as though he's waiting for passengers," Red Wraith whispered to his companion. He gestured toward the boat. "Should we risk a ride?"

"*Omakase shimasu*—it's up to you," she answered. "I have no idea where we are." She kicked a pebble into the lake and watched silently as ripples spread outward from it in a perfect square.

That made Red Wraith pause. "No?" he asked. "But I thought you'd played this game before."

"You think this is a game?" she asked. Her voice bordered on shrill. "If it is, I'm not interested in playing any more!" she shouted at the cavern ceiling. "I just want to go home!"

"Shut up!" he hissed at her. "Do you want to alert every IC program on the system to the fact that we're here?"

Her lower lip curved into a pout. "I thought you were going to help me."

"We've got to help each other," he told her. He paused. "You really don't know where we are?"

She shook her head.

Red Wraith sighed. So much for that faint hope. "I have no idea, either. But from the feel of this place, I'd guess we've blundered into an ultraviolet host of some sort. And that requires a supercomputer of incredible processing power—one capable of handling megapulses of data."

The other decker's eyes brightened. "I have heard of those," she said. "According to the data I've scanned on the shadowfiles network, an ultraviolet host requires an artificial intelligence to operate and maintain it. Imagine— we could meet an actual AI here . . ."

"Nonsense," Red Wraith broke in sharply. "A sufficiently powerful processing complex might spontaneously develop an ultraviolet host without any input from its operators, and that might lead them to believe an AI was at work, somewhere behind the scenes. But true AIs don't exist—the closest anyone's come is a semi-autonomous knowbot with random-decision pathway capacities. Even the megacorps are still years away from developing anything with enough code to enable self-programming in response to new data. Every decker knows that."

"Ha! You think you know everything?" She flung out a hand to point at the gondola. "Then tell me what that is, *sensei*."

Red Wraith stared at the Japanese woman. A suspicion was dawning. "How old are you?" he asked.

"Old enough to know as much about decking as you. Maybe more."

A realization struck him: this decker was much younger than he was. He'd been trusting to some kid to lead him around. He'd assumed, since she'd been in the cavern before he arrived, that she knew more about this system than he did. Now he knew better. He wouldn't make that mistake again.

He glanced at the gondola. The hooded figure at the oar hadn't moved; it seemed to be waiting patiently for them. Red Wraith deliberately turned his back on the girl, walked to the boat, and climbed aboard. The padded seat supported him when he sat down, even though his hands ghosted through it. Perhaps because he expected it to?

But the one thing he couldn't do was access the data he had fought so hard to download—the UCAS military personnel file that was his first step in tracking down Lydia. It seemed that only the active memory of his cyberdeck was usable—he could still run his utilities, but the storage memory to which data files were downloaded remained inaccessible to him. Worry gnawed at him—he could only hope that the chips hadn't been fried, that the data he'd taken such pains to access was still there.

The shrouded figure in the stern stood utterly still, as if it were an icon waiting to be activated. Realizing what it wanted, Red Wraith accessed a simple utility he used for on-line payments. He chose an icon that represented a basic unit of ten nuyen and pushed the symbol toward the ferryman. As the icon was absorbed into a fold in the robe of the hooded figure, the ferryman leaned against his oar, and the gondola slid away from shore. As it did, the girl in the kimono looked once behind her and then wrung her hands. "Wait!" she called out, then ran to the boat across the lake and clambered aboard.

"You're not leaving me behind!" she told Red Wraith firmly as she settled onto the seat beside him. She kept a wary eye on the shrouded figure in the stern.

Red Wraith nodded. "All right. But if we're going to get out of here, we have to work together. We need to figure out where the hub of this system is. And that means knowing how we entered it. What system were you accessing before this one?"

The girl—which was how Red Wraith thought of her now, even though her icon suggested a mature woman—eyed him with a guilty expression, as if being asked to confess something.

"A *manga* music fansite."

"A what music?"

"Figures you wouldn't know," the girl muttered.

The figure in the stern worked the oar back and forth, rippling the water and propelling the boat forward with soft splashes.

"*Manga,*" Lady Death said slowly, as if explaining something obvious to someone stupid, "is cartoon illusion. *Manga* music is—"

"I get it," Red Wraith said. "What was its LTG address?"

The other decker shrugged. "I don't know. It was connected to the Syberspace nightclub system, but only for a second through a vanishing system access node that kept changing its LTG address."

"So when you tried to log off, the node you used to exit the system could have led anywhere?"

The girl shrugged, then nodded. "Anywhere on the Seattle RTG."

Seattle? Red Wraith filed that one away. He too had been accessing that RTG. There was a possibility they were still within it.

"What happened while you were logged onto the fansite?" he asked.

"I can't be certain." The girl frowned. "I uploaded some data, then tried to log off the fansite. I somehow became—separated—from my connection with my cyberdeck and lost all sense of my body. I wound up in what I thought was a datastream of pure white light and heard the voice of . . ."

She shivered. "I saw my life unfold as I floated above my own body. It was pleasant and dreamy, at first. But then it turned into a nightmare. I thought . . ."

Tears brimmed in her eyes and streaked dark furrows down her cheeks. Her pale complexion, Red Wraith saw now, was no more than makeup. After a moment, the streaks erased themselves. Lady Death looked at the skeletal figure in the back of the boat and then back at Red Wraith with a stricken expression.

"We're not dead—are we?"

Red Wraith fought down his own uncertainties. "We're still in the Matrix," he told her firmly.

"Hai," she said. "I know it's a crazy thought. But it all seemed so . . . Just like before when I was . . ."

Understanding dawned. The experience the girl had been trying to describe bore an uncanny resemblance to his own.

"Accessing this system reminded you of a near-death experience you once had?" he asked.

She nodded.

"Me too."

They sat in silence as the gondola glided along. Red Wraith wasn't about to share the story of his brush with death with a complete stranger, and the girl seemed to feel the same way.

"I wonder if the others are experiencing the same thing," she said at last.

"The others?"

"The damned. The screaming people." She jerked her head. "Back there. I touched one, and saw her nightmare. It was . . ." She shuddered. "Horrible."

Red Wraith heard a soft thump and looked over the edge of the boat. A moment ago, the boat had been crossing an open stretch of water. Now a body that had appeared from out of nowhere was gently bumping against the side of the gondola. Although it seemed to be made of gleaming chrome, the metal was pocked with rust-rimmed holes and a strong smell of rotting meat arose from it. If it was, as

Red Wraith suspected, another decker who had just logged onto this system, would it be possible to communicate? Red Wraith reached a hand through the side of the boat and brushed his misty fingertips across the body . . .

He was walking through a forest on a hot summer day. Somewhere behind on the trail, he could hear a faint buzzing noise. Something sweet-smelling and sticky was on his skin, and he had to find water to wash it off before it attracted . . .

Flies. One buzzed toward him, circling him in lazy loops. Then another. The first one landed on his arm and bit. Red blood welled in the tiny wound. Then another fly landed, and another. Their buzzing grew louder, filling his ears.

Flies the size of grapes landed on his skin and bit into it with sharp, stinging bites. They laid eggs, injecting them into his skin like tiny bullets. They sought out his eyes, invaded his nose and ears, flew into his mouth each time he opened it to breathe or scream. He scratched, he slapped at the insects, but there were too many of them. He ran blindly as they covered his flesh, attracted by the sticky sweet syrup that covered it.

Now the eggs were hatching. Maggots wriggled just under his skin, their bodies humping up the flesh in obscene lumps. He fell to the ground, to the rich damp soil. Worms wriggled up out of the leaf mold and sought out the holes the flies had left in his skin. They feasted on the rot the maggots had left behind, consuming him piece by piece until there was nothing left. There was no escape . . .

The scene blinked like a bad simsense edit.

He was walking through a forest on a hot summer day. Somewhere behind on the trail, he could hear a faint buzzing noise . . .

Red Wraith drew his hand away. Shuddering, he glanced down at his body, absently slapping at his misty skin to drive away the burrowing insects. It took him a moment or two to shake off the phobia that was not his own. All the while Lady Death stared at him. "What did you see?"

"A nightmare," Red Wraith answered. "Flies. Maggots. It repeated, as if there was a loop in the programming. As if the decker was trapped . . ."

He watched the chrome body float away as the gondola left it behind. "If the bodies are deckers, they seem to be unable to move around freely in this system. We seem to be the only ones capable of doing that."

Lady Death looked out over the lake. "They are all standard icons," she mused. "You would think that a highly sculpted system like this one would include less primitive iconography. Something that matched the rest of the system."

Red Wraith looked up at the other decker in surprise. Sculpted system? He had known it instinctively, but only now were the ramifications clear. "That's why we're the only ones capable of moving around or interacting with the system," he said. "Our personas fit its central metaphor: death."

He gestured at the bodies in the water. "Theirs don't, and so they appear as universal matrix symbolism icons. The reality filters on their decks' MPCPs won't allow them to interact with this system's sculpture. For some reason, its data is being translated into nightmarish images that they loop through over and over again. They're trapped here."

"So are we," Lady Death said quietly.

"I don't think so," Red Wraith answered. "We're capable of movement and interaction with the system. There's still hope."

"*Hai,*" she stared out past the bow. "I suppose so." The gondola had nearly reached the opposite shore. "As long as we don't run into any black IC."

Blood fountained up from the lake in a sudden spray. The boat rocked violently to one side and Lady Death screamed. Red Wraith turned to face the threat and saw a black, bony hand gripping the side of the boat. A hideous black skeleton, its clothing soaked with blood and its yellowed eyes bulging, hauled itself into the boat and lunged straight at them in a frenzied attack . . .

09:48:45 PST

Dark Father crawled out of the hole and into what looked
like a gigantic abattoir. Conveyor belts crisscrossed the inside of an infinitely large building, carrying chunks of
flesh and broken bone along at blurring speed with a rattling, clanking clamor. Some of the belts were horizontal,
others vertical or angled or even upside down, but the
bloody meat they were carrying stayed firmly in place, in
defiance of gravity.

The conveyor belts seemed to be linking the various system icons that dotted the landscape, carrying the meat from
one to the next. Within Dark Father's immediate view was a
massive pyramid of skulls, a pagoda shingled with tombstones, a ball-shaped knot of gigantic wriggling worms, and
a multi-faceted office tower made of gleaming black coffins.

It all looked familiar, somehow—familiar, but wrong. It
took Dark Father a moment to puzzle out why. He realized
suddenly that he was looking at the vast expanse of the
Seattle RTG, subtly transformed. The geography was still
the same, but the iconography had drastically changed.
Everywhere he looked, the system icons were constructed
from symbols of death and decay—except for the three-
dimensional star of the Fuchi system, although it was too
far away to see in detail.

He was within the Matrix, that much was certain. And
he'd escaped from his personal nightmare of being devoured by his ghoulish son. Assuming he was still alive
and not just a bodiless spirit trapped within the Matrix, he
could log off, now that he knew what RTG he was in. He
executed the command that should have allowed him to
perform a graceful log off . . .

Nothing happened.

He used a browse utility to locate the access node that
would take him back to the Midwest RTG . . .

Nothing. He remained exactly where he was.

In desperation he tried to simply log off, even though he knew that the dump shock might kill him after the mauling that Serpens in Machina had given him . . .

Nothing.

The conveyor belts rattled past, carrying their gruesome cargo.

A flash of silver caught Dark Father's eye. Something was lying between the hunks of meat, being carried along the belt with them. It had looked like a human figure—one of the UMS icons used by deckers who couldn't afford the software needed to customize their personas. If another decker were riding the conveyor belt datastream, perhaps Dark Father could, too.

He reached out a skeletal hand and grabbed the frayed fabric of the conveyor belt. With a lurch that nearly jerked his bones apart, he as in motion. He sailed at breakneck speed in and out of the pyramid of skulls that was likely Aztechnology Seattle, and through the pagoda that was probably the Mitsuhama system. But instead of accessing those systems, he simply swept through them as if they were mere illusion. The conveyor belt carried him high above these icons toward a gleaming crystal skull that was probably a system access node—then plunged in one empty eye socket and out the next, looping over like a demented roller coaster without ever letting him access the node. Then the rattling, bone-jarring conveyor belt dragged Dark Father back down with it toward the landscape once more, hurtling toward the "ground" at breakneck speed. For a second, third, and fourth time his hopes soared as he was carried to one of the skulls—only to be dashed again as it proved impossible each time to let go of the conveyor belt during the millisecond or two he was actually inside the node.

After his fifth attempt at using the conveyor belt to access another node, Dark Father released his grip and instantly came to a stop. At first he merely held his position in space, but then he discovered that he could approach one of the crystal-skull SANs on his own, without the aid of the conveyor belt. He heaved a sigh of relief at the knowledge that he had some control. He could move freely in this landscape, at least.

He watched the datastream continue on its crazed, looping path in and out of the skull's eye sockets. The conveyor belt carried chunks of meat both in and out of the SAN—which meant that data was probably still flowing in and out of the Seattle RTG, even if the Dark Father himself was trapped here.

Every now and then there was a flash of chrome as another UMS persona icon appeared on the conveyor belt. Always they appeared on the incoming belts. The deckers never exited the system, only entered it. And they lay on the conveyor belt as lifeless as the chunks of meat next to them.

Hmm. It seemed that deckers—assuming that's what they were—could log onto the Seattle RTG but not log off it again. If indeed this was truly the Seattle regional telecommunications grid and not some distorted mirror image of it.

Dark Father stared across the virtual landscape, letting his gaze wander. Then he noticed something. Each of the conveyor belts, at one point in its routing, traveled to a central location—an enormous silver urn that lay on its side. Descending toward it, Dark Father could see that the urn was as large as an apartment block. Its interior looked like a cave, with moss-draped sides and stalactites inside. Low groans and faint screams echoed in its depths. Hundreds of conveyor belts flowed in and out of the mouth of this tunnel, the air from their passage stirring the swirling gray ash that lined its floor it into long, foglike tendrils. Dark Father's legs grew cold and clammy where this ash wafted against him.

Stepping back from the urn, Dark Father saw that the sides of it were covered in ornate characters. Despite the urn's size, the words engraved on its tarnished silver surface were in so small a script as to be unreadable.

Suspecting that scramble IC was involved, Dark Father activated a decrypt utility. An old-fashioned magnifying glass appeared in his hand. Instead of glass, its black metal frame held an eyeball that moved back and forth as the eye scanned the text engraved on the urn. At the same time, glowing green letters scrolled across the back of the eyeball, flowed down the handle of the magnifying glass, up Dark Father's arm, and into his mind.

The flow paused for a second as Dark Father puzzled over what he had found. Despite the decrypt utility, most of the file on the urn icon was gibberish. But one segment of data, reminiscent of a tombstone inscription, was still coherent:

Deep Resonance Experiment
Born: 09:47:00 PST
Aborted: 09:48:00 PST
Resonance in peace

Dark Father released the magnifying glass, which broke apart into pixels and disappeared. He looked around at the landscape with its eerie death imagery. Just prior to the time listed on the urn, Dark Father had been in the Virtual Meetings conversation pit, battling for his life against Serpens in Machina. One second later, at precisely 9:47 a.m. Pacific Standard Time, some sort of experimental program had chosen him as its guinea pig, yanking him out of that cybercombat, forcing him to re-experience his death and birth and then thrusting him into a system whose iconography was based on his own worst nightmares of ghoulish feeding frenzies. And then—either as a result of Dark Father's own frantic attempts to escape the ghouls or simply by virtue of the fact that the experiment had "died" one minute later, he'd emerged into this weirdly corrupted version of the Seattle RTG.

He didn't know whether to be thankful for having escaped Serpens in Machina's potentially fatal attack or resentful at having been drafted into an experiment without having given his permission. And there was no way of telling whose experiment it was. The conveyor belt datastreams that entered and exited the urn seemed to connect to every node on this RTG. It wasn't as if they all congregated at the skull pyramid that was probably Aztechnology, for example, or at the bone-barred dungeon that hunkered where Lone Star's system had once stood. They went everywhere, connected everything.

Connected everything to this urn.

The answer had to lie inside it.

Dark Father activated his sleaze utility. The urn was

probably just a sub-processing unit, but he wasn't about to enter it naked and unprotected. His black top hat shimmered and then melted downward, transforming into an executioner's hood that hid all but his yellowed eyeballs. Peering from within it, he reached out a hand, braced himself for the jolt, and grabbed onto one of the conveyor belts leading into the urn.

The datastream wrenched him off his feet.

Dark Father found himself immersed in warm liquid, thicker and more cloying than water. His hand was empty; the conveyor belt had disappeared. All was darkness; it was impossible to tell which way was up. Within seconds his chest felt heavy, his legs and arms weak, and blood pounded in his ears. His sodden clothes dragged him down and the hood obscured his vision. He was drowning.

Crashing his sleaze utility, Dark Father at last was able to see a light that he assumed was the direction of the surface. He swam frantically for it, but his skeletal hands and feet gave him no push against the liquid. He had only a meter or so to go now, but was getting nowhere. But then he saw something splash into the water from above. Long and slender, it looked like the bottom of an oar. Grabbing it, Dark Father pulled himself hand over hand, up toward the bulging black form that was the hull of a boat. He grabbed the side of the boat, which tipped violently toward him. Thrashing madly, he lunged up and over the gunwale, sputtering and gasping and reaching desperately for whatever would give him purchase . . .

Someone was screaming. Dark Father looked up and saw a woman in a white kimono scurrying away from him across the tilting deck of the long, narrow boat. Behind her, a hooded figure mechanically worked an oar back and forth. Another figure—a headless red ghost—stood with its head in its hands, as if about to pass it to Dark Father like a basketball.

Sensing that he was about to be attacked by another decker, Dark Father arrested his forward motion and instead fumbled for the noose at his neck. Then the head in the ghost's hands spoke.

"Make one more hostile move and I'll crash you," it said.

Dark Father hung, limp, across the gunwale of the boat, his legs still dangling in the warm liquid. "I won't," he gasped, at last finding his breath. He looked between the three figures already in the boat. The one handling the oar seemed to be executing a looped sequence; its stiff, repetitive movements were those of a program icon. But the other two were definitely deckers.

"Are you the ones running the experiment?" Dark Father asked.

"We—" the ghost began to answer.

"What experiment?" the woman said at the same time.

The ghost shot her a look, then replaced his head on his shoulders. "He's another decker," he told her. Then he leaned over and extended a hand toward Dark Father to help him into the boat.

"Welcome aboard our nightmare."

09:48:59 PST

The instant Bloodyguts opened his eyes, a gigantic scythe whooshed in a murderous arc for his throat. He threw himself to one side, avoiding its deadly swing by mere centimeters. The point of the scythe caught the fabric of his tattered shirt, slicing it open from collar to shoulder. Then he landed on the ground—hard—and rolled frantically to one side to avoid the scythe's next swing.

All around him, closing him in like a forest, were wooden stakes as tall as he was. Each had been driven into the ground and crudely hacked into a point, and on each was impaled a severed head. Scrambling behind one, Bloodyguts got the stake between himself and the scythe. The harvesting tool with its brilliant chrome blade sliced into the wood with a thunk, quivered a moment, then reversed and poised itself to swing again.

The deadly tool was operating independently, floating above the ground and zigzagging back and forth in order to get a better angle of attack. It had to be IC—but there was

no time to wonder what type. Bloodyguts had to crash that
fragger. Now.

A utility icon appeared in his hand: a baseball bat made
of dull white bone. A baseball with an outer layer of
stitched human flesh appeared about a meter in front of
Bloodyguts at chest height. Slamming the bat against the
ball, he sent the ball flying at the scythe. It struck the long
wooden handle just at its midpoint and exploded in a flash
of light, splintering it in two. The two halves of the scythe
stuttered, blinked . . .

Bloodyguts grinned and lowered the bat. Then he swore
as the lower half of the scythe arced around a wooden
stake and slashed at his stomach. He threw himself to the
side but too late—the blade snagged a piece of entrail and
snipped it neatly in two. Blood-flecked data spiraled out of
the severed ends and the bat in Bloodyguts' hands shimmered, losing its cohesiveness.

Drek! This IC was tough!

Bloodyguts grabbed the severed ends of his entrail in
one hand, squeezing them shut, and at the same time
dodged behind another stake. But now that the scythe had
a shorter handle it was more maneuverable. It zinged between the stakes, following Bloodyguts' every move.

Cursing, Bloodyguts pumped everything he had into his
crash utility. This time, the ball that appeared in front of
him was softball-sized and tattooed with skulls and crossbones. Wielding his bat with one hand, Bloodyguts swung
it in a wild arc as the scythe zoomed in for the kill. The
bone bat connected with the ball and sent it hurtling on a
collision course with the scythe blade—which shattered
into a million glowing fragments as the ball connected and
exploded. A rain of steel-colored fragments of light show-
ered Bloodyguts, pocketing his skin with tiny perforations.

He howled in triumph as the scythe disappeared. "Home
run!"

The bat in his hand disappeared. Quickly, before any
more data was lost, Bloodyguts tied together the severed
ends of entrail and watched as they fused back into a
smooth loop. He'd crashed the IC, but he had no way of
knowing whether his meat bod had suffered any damage as
a result of the attack. He was utterly cut off from any true

physical sensation, as if his RAS override had been pumped to the max. But since he was still conscious, he had to assume his heart was still beating—that he was still alive.

Might as well try to figure out where the frag he was.

He took a closer look at the severed heads closest to him. Their skin gleamed with a metallic sheen, as if they had been dipped in metal. They were identifiable by metatype: one had the narrow face and pointed ears of an elf; another the knobby forehead and jutting horn of a troll. He could even tell which were male and which were female. But all of the heads looked pretty much alike. They were caricatures, not individuals. Icons.

The stakes on which they were impaled stretched across a plain that disappeared into an indefinite horizon. There were hundreds of them—thousands. The faces were frozen in a single expression—abject terror—but the stakes themselves seemed to be . . . flowing. Peering at one, Bloodyguts could see that the grain of the wood was constantly shifting, kind of like the current of a river.

Data! It had to be a flow of data. But how to access it? The wood was coarse and solid under Bloodyguts' fingers and refused to be dented by his thumbnail; it was not permeable at all.

Something moved on the head. Bloodyguts jerked his hand back, instinctively reacting to an insect-sized creature that was scuttling across the frozen ridges of metallic hair. The thing looked like a combination of robot and dragonfly—a tiny silver-metal creature with articulated legs and wings, and arms that ended in miniature tools. Its face was featureless except for a single vidcam lens.

Bloodyguts watched, fascinated, as the thing drilled a hole into the head. A probe extruded from the insectoid's arm and vanished into the hole. Then it was pulled back, and the miniature robot used the circular saw in its other limb to cut a larger hole. Flipping it back like a trap door, the insectoid exposed what looked like an old-fashioned circuit board, one with resistors and capacitors as large as fingernails, plastic-clad copper wires thick enough to be seen with the naked eye, and metal-on-plastic circuitry. A dull red light glowed on one of the insectoid's limbs as the circular saw turned into a soldering iron, and then the creature went to work, soldering in a new wire to bypass a section of the board.

Taking a quick glance at some of the other impaled heads, Bloodyguts saw similar creatures at work. Some heads contained archaic cog and wheel mechanisms, powered by wound springs; others held what looked like the glowing fuel rods of a nuclear power plant. In every case these mechanisms were being tinkered with.

If this Matrix system was an actual representation of what was going on in the meat world, and if these were actually deckers, someone or something was messing with their wetware. And judging by the expressions on their faces, they were finding it about as pleasant as a bad BTL chip dream.

Bloodyguts growled. What was he dealing with here? He decided to activate an analyze utility to find out.

He pointed at one of the robot insects and a palm-sized plastic card appeared in the air just above it. The three-dimensional holo programmed into the card showed the image of the bug icon in various poses, while stats scrolled across the flat surface of the card itself.

Bloodyguts watched the stats scroll past. The insectoid icon was one weird piece of programming. It seemed to be uploading and downloading data at the same time that it was performing a number of editing and disinfecting functions. It hadn't been written using any of the common programming languages—at least not any of the languages Bloodyguts recognized. Its code seemed to contain elements of HoloLISP, Oblong, and InterMod, but the blend kept changing, as if the utility were reprogramming itself in response to new data.

It reminded Bloodyguts of black IC—intrusion countermeasures programs that sampled the command transactions between decker and cyberdeck and then injected dangerous biofeedback responses into the deck's ASIST interface.

The program was obviously proactive, but it wasn't responding to Bloodyguts' presence. The insectoids were ignoring him—they weren't drilling into *his* wetware, thank the fraggin' spirits. At least, not as far as he could tell. He still seemed to be thinking normally—or thought he was.

He shifted the analyze utility, pointing at the head itself. The card shimmered, and the face of an elf female replaced the insectoid holograph. After a millisecond's hesitation, a new set of code began scrolling across the card.

Bloodyguts whistled in surprise. It was a decker, after all—the head was an abbreviated version of the standard USM persona icon. The stats suggested that the elf was using a hot deck—one that would leave her wide open to the potentially lethal effects of black IC. The deck's condition monitor was fluctuating wildly, one moment showing massive amounts of neural overload and the next reporting that all mental functions were within normal limits. She wasn't taking any physical damage, however.

So the robot bug wasn't lethal black IC, or the poor fragger would have been dead already. And if the insect was causing mental damage, it was repairing it as quickly as it occurred. When the decker logged off or jacked out, she might never realize that her wetware had been tampered with. And that suggested only one thing.

Psychotropic black IC.

Bloodyguts had heard about that stuff. Even though it was non-lethal, it was nasty drek. It fragged you up just as thoroughly and irrevocably as a bad BTL chip. What it did was reprogram the decker's wetware, leaving subliminal compulsions behind. Some were relatively harmless—like producing a warm, fuzzy feeling each time the decker saw a corporate logo. Other types of psychotropic black IC caused lasting psychological damage, rendering the decker prone to phobias, maniacal rages, suicidal depressions, or . . . hallucinations.

Bloodyguts looked around at the forest of impaled heads. Was that what this was? A hallucination? Or the iconography of a Matrix system? The imagery didn't *feel* like it was being generated by Bloodyguts' own wetware. At least, it hadn't felt that way since he escaped from the tunnel of light and the image of Jocko that had somehow known his real name.

Without warning, the head popped off the end of the stake.

"Frag!" Bloodyguts shouted. Without thinking, he lunged forward to grab it. But the head disappeared. Bloodyguts' hand passed through empty space—and was impaled on the stake. He tried to jerk it free but couldn't . . .

He was a tiny speck of consciousness, racing through a swirling river whose borders were the waves of wood grain. He came to a knothole, whipped once around it in a spiraling circle, then popped through it, emerging on the other side like a cork. He battered against something—a solid well of empty space that he instinctively knew was the end of an unconnected data plug—then was swept back and away from that terminus. For just a moment he found another knothole to bob into—a connection with the cyberdeck's built-in cybercam and microphone. A scream tore through his consciousness, and he saw lens-framed images of an elf woman plunging her hands through a window, using its shattered glass to lacerate her wrists until the flesh hung from them in bloody ribbons. Behind her, a man stood frozen in horror, holding a fiber-optic cable connection, a look of disbelief on his face.

Before Bloodyguts could see more, he was drawn back along a retreating wave of data. He tried to fight the tide, but it was too strong, too overwhelming in its single-minded direction. It forced him back through several knot-hole nodes, swept him helplessly tumbling across a strangely transformed landscape of the Seattle RTG, then raced back into the wooden stake and out of its sharpened tip . . .

Bloodyguts' outstretched arm fell to his side as the wooden stake that had impaled his hand disappeared. He looked down at his hand and saw that it was shaking but undamaged. Without realizing that he was doing it, he wiped his wrist against his pant leg. Then he shivered and stared at the insectoids as they carried out their diabolical surgery on the heads that surrounded him.

Had he really just witnessed another decker's suicide? If so, this psychotropic IC was deadly stuff; it seemed to have an onset time measured in milliseconds.

Bloodyguts was suddenly very glad he hadn't been able to jack out of the Matrix after his fight with the jaguar-icon IC. He might have wound up dead.

He might still, if he didn't figure out what the frag he'd blundered into.

The safest thing was to get out of this system before the insectoids decided to burrow into his wetware. But where were the SANs? As an experiment, he wrapped his hands around one of the stakes that did not hold a head, knelt slightly, then strained upward. The stake pulled from the ground with a loud *pop!* leaving a hole behind. Tossing the stake aside, Bloodyguts scuffed at the hole with his toe . . .

The virtualscape spun wildly as Bloodyguts' foot disappeared into the ground, sucked down by a whirlpool-like force. Spiraling out of control, he felt his body compress into a long, thin, tight strand. He spun down and into the hole like water through a drain. Then his body began to twist in reverse, like a rubber band reversing itself.

He emerged through pursed stone lips—the mouth of a gravestone cherub. Landing heavily on the ground, he raised himself with shaking arms as his body finished unwinding itself. Then he looked around.

The impaled heads and stakes had disappeared. He lay in a graveyard, on freshly turned soil. And staring at him, apparently surprised at his sudden appearance, were three grim-looking figures: a black skeleton, a legless ghost, and an Oriental woman with death-white skin.

09:49:32 PST

"But we've got to share our personal data!" the troll said in an exasperated voice. "We'll never get out of this drekkin' system if we don't!" He looked around at the graveyard, then shook his head.

They'd been talking for what seemed like forever, and frankly, Dark Father was tired of making small talk with strangers. At the speed that things happened in the Matrix—the speed of thought—only a few seconds had ticked by. But seconds were precious here.

Dark Father stared at the other decker, not bothering to

keep his expression neutral. If the troll's icon was anything like his real-world body, he was as unpleasant an example of his metatype as any that Dark Father had seen. He had long, matted hair, dirty clothes, and torn face and flesh that looked and smelled as if it had been left to rot. He hadn't even bothered to tuck in his spilled entrails, let alone his shirt. What sort of person would choose so loathsome a persona?

The decker—Bloodyguts—had already admitted to being a criminal and a chiphead. Did he honestly expect Dark Father to feel sorry for him?

The other two deckers apparently did. The Japanese woman in the kimono had tearfully told the story of how she had tried to commit ritual suicide by slashing open a vein after a lover had spurned her, and of the near-death experience this act had produced. The reddish ghost had likewise told of his own out-of-body experience, which had occurred after a sniper's bullet had severed his spine while he was serving as a Dutch soldier in the Euro-Wars. Now both of them stared at Dark Father, expecting him to reveal similarly intimate details of his own past.

"Well?" Bloodyguts prodded.

"Yes, I had a near-death experience." Dark Father directed his answer to the two human deckers. "As a result of a heart attack. I experienced the same things you did: seeing my body from above, hearing the voices of dead relatives, watching flashbacks from my life, and moving through a tunnel of light toward a being greater than my self . . . All of which repeated itself just before I entered this system."

"But you fought against it and escaped," Red Wraith prompted.

"Yes."

"To a scene from your own worst fears," the Japanese woman added.

"Yes." Dark Father gritted his teeth, unwilling to review the details but unable to prevent himself from mentally doing so. He shuddered. His own son—feeding upon him. Horrible.

"And then you escaped from that, and realized you were still within the Seattle RTG," the troll said.

Dark Father was tired of the troll's simple-minded summary. "That was my conclusion, yes."

"Here's what I figure," the troll said, turning to the others and ticking off points on his blunt fingers. "One: we're the only deckers who broke free—according to Red Wraith here, everyone else is still trapped inside a programming loop. Two: the iconography of everyone's nightmare loop is individual, something from their own phobias or memories. And three: it's all part of some sort of one-minute experiment that began at 9:47 a.m. and was aborted at 9:48 a.m., according to Mr. Bones here."

"I would prefer to be addressed by my proper on-line name," Dark Father huffed.

The troll ignored him. "From what I saw, we're dealing with some sort of psychotropic black IC. And pretty fraggin' deadly stuff. We got lucky. Thanks to the fact that we recognized its effects as a near-death experience, we weren't willing to be taken along for the ride by the tunnel of light. We fought back and didn't get stuck in the loop."

He curled a lip, revealing a broken canine. "But we're still stuck here, and we're cut off from our meat bods. The question is, where is here?"

"I think we're in a pocket universe," Lady Death said. "One that is confined to the Seattle RTG, but not to any single host. It is everywhere in the RTG—and nowhere."

"And there aren't any exit signs," the troll added in a wry tone.

"That's because it doesn't want us to leave," Lady Death said.

"It?" The troll frowned.

"The artificial intelligence that built the pocket universe."

"Bulldrek," Red Wraith cut in angrily. "There's no such thing as AIs. We're still years away from—"

Lady Death cut him off. "But only an AI would have the processing power to—"

"Frag!" the troll said in exasperation. "We've been over this already. You two are starting to sound like a programming loop. We've got to—"

Dark Father ignored the other three deckers and looked around at the virtualscape. They stood in a vast graveyard whose tombstone-dotted fields stretched to the horizon. Thunder grumbled overhead in a gray sky and a cold wind chilled the spaces between Dark Father's bones, making his loose jacket and pants flutter slightly.

He called up a copy of the customized smart frame he'd used on Serpens in Machina, ordered the dog to "Sit!" and "Stay!" and then started editing its programming. The silver-furred German shepherd sat complacently while Dark Father edited its browse and evaluate functions, instructing it to search for any files that contained the words "deep resonance." He also changed its core function from delete to download. Then he gave it a curt command: "Search!"

The police dog ran in a blur from one gravestone to the next, sniffing at each for a mere millisecond before bounding away to the next.

"What the frag are you doing?" Bloodyguts asked.

Dark Father brushed off the troll's belligerence. "Instead of sitting around and making uninformed guesses, I'm searching for data that will provide us with some answers." He favored the other deckers with a cold stare. "Do any of you have a problem with that?"

The Japanese woman shrugged.

Red Wraith shook his head.

They waited a few seconds in silence. Then Dark Father spotted the smart frame returning. The dog loped across the ground, bounding over tombstones and carrying something in its mouth. As it drew nearer, Dark Father could see that it was a large bone, with scraps of meat still clinging to it. He took the bone out of the dog's mouth and ran his finger along the raised design on end: a five-pointed star.

The other deckers crowded around Dark Father.

"What is it?" Red Wraith asked.

"A file," Dark Father answered. The magnifying glass with its mobile eyeball appeared in his hand as he began decrypting the file.

Lady Death leaned forward to look at the raised star. "That's the old Fuchi Industrial Electronics logo—the one the corporation used before it split apart."

Just at that moment, the end of the bone bearing the logo began to rotate. It unscrewed itself like a cap, and a stream of alphanumeric characters flowed out. They streamed in a tight spiral toward the eyeball and in through its pupil. The other deckers had to read the decrypted text as it flowed up Dark Father's arm like a movie marquee. The text that datelined it identified the speaker: Miles Lanier, who had returned as strategic advisor to his friend Richard Villiers at Fuchi Americas last year after pulling off a brilliantly disruptive scam against the rival corporation Renraku that sent the price of Renraku's stock plummeting. The file was a memo, composed last summer at the height of Fuchi's corporate war, just two months before the corporation split apart. It was addressed to Richard Villiers, who was then the CEO of Fuchi Americas. Today Villiers headed up Nova-Tech, the new corporation he had formed out of what remained of Fuchi's North and South American holdings.

Red Wraith whistled softly. "Lanier, huh. That guy's nova hot. He wrote the book on Matrix security. If this is one of his uploads, the decryption should have been a tougher nut to crack. The UCAS military itself uses Fuchi IC as the first line of its Matrix defenses."

"Maybe someone wanted us to read this," Bloodyguts rumbled.

"Quiet, please!" Dark Father closed his eyes and listened to the audio component of the file. Lanier spoke in a military-crisp voice with just a hint of a Boston accent.

Memo upload begins.

One of our covert operatives has uncovered evidence of an otaku *colony in the Denver area. The four children positively identified as colony members range in age from seven to twenty-three—one of the oldest reported* otaku *to date. The twenty-three-year-old had her datajack surgically implanted at approximately age ten, providing further evidence that the phenomenon we are dealing with originated some time around 2047.*

Our operative's extreme youth proved to be the key to earning the other children's trust. It was also his downfall. Let me explain.

Our operative confirmed that the otaku *are indeed able to access the Matrix by means of a datajack alone, in a process similar—but not identical—to that used by the children discovered by Babel. He also confirmed our suspicions as to the mechanism that is at the heart of the transformative process known as DEEP RESONANCE.*

The fact that this mechanism may soon be under our control has immense implications for the future of Fuchi Americas. It will allow us to hurdle over the existing cyberdeck manufacturing and software programming industries, replacing them with a brand new technology that is a quantum leap ahead of the old. Once the general public is able to access the Matrix by means of a datajack alone, as the otaku *do, and are able to use the "complex forms" of the* otaku *in place of program utilities, the products produced by our competitors will be obsolete.*

Whoever is the first to develop and market the DEEP RESONANCE process will bury the competition. I only hope that it will be Fuchi Americas. As you know, rival corporations—including the one that once controlled Babel—are also taking steps to acquire and control similar technologies. And as a result of our corporation's current internal difficulties, we are also in a race against our former partners. Unfortunately, I have just this week confirmed that some of the data we have so painstakingly collected has been accessed by Fuchi Pan-Europa and Fuchi Asia.

I must thus reluctantly warn you that, should our former partners gain the ability to access and control the mechanism behind the otaku, *we must take the necessary steps to destroy this mechanism. Thankfully, that is not necessary at this time.*

No further data could be recovered by our covert operative, who broke contact with us two days ago. I am sorry to report that all indications point to him having joined the colony and become otaku *himself. The colony has since disappeared. Despite an extensive search, our regular security forces were unable to track down a single member. In addition, the tracking device that was implanted in our covert operative has ceased functioning. We are unable to locate his whereabouts.*

I am thus forced to report that we have been unable to capture a subject for study. I await your further instructions.

Memo upload ends.

Dark Father opened his eyes and released the decrypt utility. The magnifying glass disappeared. The other three deckers had crowded close, reading the text as it scrolled up his arm. Dark Father stepped back from them, putting some distance between himself and the putrid-smelling troll.

"Can't you delete the olfactory component of your icon?" Dark Father asked.

Bloodyguts grinned and shook his head. "Nope. Comes with the persona."

Dark Father grimaced.

Red Wraith was shaking his head. "I don't believe it," he said. "Decking without a deck—with just a datajack? Impossible!"

Bloodyguts had a strange expression on his face—part loathing, part disbelief. "If it's true, those poor kids are fragged up worse than a chiphead," he said. "If their wetware is linked with the Matrix, how can they tell where reality ends and the Matrix begins?"

"That would be wonderful," Lady Death said.

"Huh?" Bloodyguts looked at her as if she were crazy.

"To access the Matrix any time, without need of a cyberdeck," she added. "It would be so—freeing."

"*If* it were possible," Red Wraith added. "Which it's not."

"I've scanned rumors of this in the shadowfiles," Lady Death continued. "Of a tribe of kids who were nova-hot deckers and who live in the Denver area. The other deckers called them *otaku-zoku*—'honored sir.' They made fun of these *'otaku'* because the kids were smarter than they were."

She made a face. "The other deckers joked that the kids were more machine than human—that the process of interfacing with computers all day long, at the expense of human interaction, had turned their brains to silicon." She shrugged. "And who knows? Maybe they were partially correct. Maybe the kids' brains were different. Maybe some of the programs the kids encountered changed the way their thoughts were channeled, altering their brains so that they could access the Matrix directly, without needing a deck to—"

"Frag," Bloodyguts croaked, realization dawning on his ugly face. "*That's* what the insects were doing—not just implanting psychotropic suggestions, but actually cooking the deckers' wetware."

"I wonder," Lady Death mused. "If it is possible to access the Matrix without a cyberdeck, is it also possible to access the Matrix without a body? Are we dead, after all?"

"I still find the concept hard to believe," Red Wraith said. Then his voice grew grim. "But I do know this: if either of the remaining Fuchi divisions or NovaTech was behind this little 'experiment,' we're fragged. Between the three of them, they've got the hardest-hooped IC on the Matrix. And their programmers don't play nice—just look at what they did to each other during the corporate war."

"I'm not certain that Fuchi—or even NovaTech—was the instigator," Dark Father said. "According to the memo, other corporations were also experimenting with deep resonance. Remember that the experiment was aborted, according to the inscription on the urn, one minute after it began. Perhaps our nightmares, and all this"—he gestured at the tombstones—"wasn't what the experimenters intended. Remember that our journey here started out as a pleasant enough experience—and only later turned nightmarish. Maybe Fuchi—or NovaTech—corrupted the experiment somehow. The key to escaping would seem to lie in finding out what went wrong."

"Yeah, right, Perfessor Ronon," Bloodyguts said. "So where the frag do we start?"

Dark Father tapped the raised logo on the bone. "We start at the beginning of the story, with Fuchi Industrial Electronics. If this pocket universe contains copies of Fuchi memos that were created prior to the corporation's breakup, it may also contain old Fuchi files that include the background information we need to—"

Dark Father suddenly stumbled to one side as the ground shifted violently beneath his feet. As he fell to his knees he saw scabrous hands erupting from the graves, reaching for him and trying to rend him with scythe-blade fingernails. He tried to crawl away but there were dozens of them, hundreds. The arms flowed from the ground, impossibly long and wriggling like rubberized worms, their claws tearing at his clothes and scoring his black bones.

As he scrambled to get away from the grasping hands, he heard Lady Death scream and the troll's booming voice.

"Spirits frag you!" Bloodyguts screamed as he whirled a baseball bat around his head. "Whoever's behind all this, your drek-hot utility led their IC straight to us!"

09:49:50 PST

The grasping hands shot up out of the earth, hooking their metallic claws into Lady Death's kimono. In the real world, she would have simply shed the garment and run away. But the kimono was an integral part of her persona—she could no more take it off than she could shed her own skin. And running was not an option. Even as she tore free and struggled to a clear spot, more worm-arms erupted from the ground, trapping her once more. They dragged heavily on her kimono, preventing her from moving.

Out of the corner of her eye, she saw that Red Wraith had enclosed himself in some sort of black rubber bag. But the claws were ripping through it as though it were silk, rapidly reducing it to a shredded husk.

Even as she quaked in fear, Lady Death tried to figure out what she was facing. The clawing hands had to be ripper IC of some sort—probably bind-rip, since they were impeding her ability to move freely. And the IC seemed to be cascading. For every worm-arm that Dark Father roped with his noose or that Bloodyguts smashed apart with his baseball bat, two more appeared. And that gave Lady Death an idea . . .

Cascading IC was programmed to allocate more and more system resources to its attacks each time it missed its target. In this case, each of those attacks was represented by a grasping hand. If the IC could be tricked into allocating all of its memory to the maintenance of an impossible number of icons, the program as a whole might slow or even crash.

The mirrors utility she had loaded at the start of her Matrix run was still in her cyberdeck's active memory. Although it provided only the framework for a virtual sculpture that needed extensive detailing before it duplicated a specific persona icon, it might be enough.

It had to be. The clawing hands had already forced Lady Death to her knees. She braced her hands on the ground, trying to find purchase on the soft soil. In another moment or two she would be lying prone, unable to move at all. And the other deckers weren't faring much better. The claws had hooked deep into Dark Father's bones, and even the powerful-looking troll was on his knees.

As quickly as she could, Lady Death activated her mirrors utility. She threw a small loop into the execute operation, causing the utility to spit out multiple copies of the icon. They blinked into existence all around her—dozens of images of her persona with only generalized outlines of her kimono, hair, and face. Because they had yet to be programmed to log onto any particular node, they just stood on the spot, waiting for a command sequence. But the clawed hands attacked them just the same. The earth trembled and rocked, and hundreds of wriggling arms surged out of the ground, all trying to grasp the icons. But because they were only mirror images, the attacks missed and the claws did not sink home. And so more arms erupted from the earth, and still more . . .

The hands holding Lady Death in place continued their relentless downward drag. This time, she let them pull her to the ground. She remained absolutely motionless, pretending to have been subdued. "Lie still!" she shouted at the others, who were still fighting against the IC. She wasn't sure whether they had heard her or not, but one by one they were pulled to the ground.

And then the miracle she had been hoping for happened. She could feel the hands relax their grip on the fabric of her kimono just a little. As thousands of arms swarmed over the false persona icons created by the mirror utility like a pack of starving hyenas, those holding Lady Death began to twitch randomly. The claws opened and closed as if unable to maintain their grip, moving more slowly each time. As last they froze in an open, ready-for-attack position.

Easing herself out from between the arms that had held her, Lady Death stood and backed slowly away from them. The other three deckers also crawled to freedom. They stood together, staring from a safe distance at the frozen tableaux of arms, which had formed a tentlike nest over each of the false Lady Death personas.

"Nice goin'," Bloodyguts said. "That IC was nasty drek."

"Good work, kid," Red Wraith echoed. "That utility was a smart move. Thanks."

Dark Father merely stared at her, his yellowed eyeballs pale against the black bone that framed them. "Time to go," he said. He held up the logo-embossed bone that his smart frame had retrieved for him. "Who is coming to the Fuchi system with me?"

Lady Death noticed that Dark Father glanced only at her and Red Wraith. He had avoided Bloodyguts ever since the dreadlocked troll met them on the other side of the blood-filled lake, in the tunnel that had given access to this graveyard. She wondered why. Perhaps Dark Father was disturbed by the troll's rotten-looking flesh. But the black skeleton had a disturbing enough appearance himself.

"I will come," Lady Death answered.

Dark Father nodded politely to her.

"I prefer to work alone," Red Wraith said.

"Echo that," Bloodyguts grumbled. "I'm not willing to take on any hitchers until Bag o' Bones here promises to use his empty skull before he sends out any more smart frames. For all we know, his doggie has already activated all of the IC in this system."

Despite the fact that his bony features were incapable of forming a frown, Dark Father conveyed an air of anger. "Why you ignorant—"

"Stop it!" Lady Death shouted. "Am I the only one who is willing to show any *wa*—any team spirit? We must work harmoniously together, or we are doomed." She gestured at the frozen worm-arms. "Without me, you would still be held by that IC. Without Dark Father's smart frame, we would not know about the *otaku* or Fuchi Industrial. Without Red Wraith . . ."

She trailed off, unable to think of a unique contribution by the ghost man. But she felt comfortable with him—his posture and bearing suggested that a decker of great capabilities lay behind his persona. Or perhaps confidence had simply been programmed into his persona's on-line personality.

"Even if some of us do not like one another"—she shot a glance at both Dark Father and Bloodyguts—"we each have cyberdecks that are programmed with different utilities. It is simply not logical to proceed each on his or her own. That would be . . ." She searched for the English word. "That would be a null-brainer move of great proportions."

Bloodyguts burst into robust laughter and clapped her on the back. "Well spoken, Lady Death," he said. He turned to Dark Father and raised his eyebrows. "Truce?"

Dark Father shrugged. "Come if you wish."

Then he turned on his skeletal heel and strode in the direction from which the German shepherd had come. After imploring the other two deckers with a look, Lady Death trotted along behind Dark Father, holding up her kimono to keep it clear of the freshly dug soil of the graves they walked over. She was relieved to see that both Red Wraith and Bloodyguts followed them.

After a few moments—traveling from one place to another seemed to take an eternity in this system—Dark Father paused in front of one of the tombstones. The grave in front of it was open; shovels had been thrust into the pile of earth that lay to one side. The tombstone itself was made of smooth crystal stone, utterly colorless. It bore no words or characters other than a single embossed design—a logo that matched the one on the bone Dark Father held.

"This would seem to be the system access node," he said.

Red Wraith passed a hand through the tombstone. "I'll take point," he said. Then he jumped into the open grave and disappeared.

Lady Death was startled by his abruptness. "But shouldn't we—?"

"Last one into the system is a glitched chip," Bloody-guts said, and dove head-first into the hole.

Dark Father cursed softly, then jumped in after him.

Lady Death shook her head. They were typical deckers. Each wanting to be the first to the paydata. She, at least, would take some precautions before diving in. She switched her deck to masking mode and activated a sleaze utility. Using the compact mirror that appeared in her hand to illuminate her face, she watched as the heavy theatrical makeup on her face took on an oily iridescence. Colors shimmered, dimmed, and reappeared on her lips and cheeks where before there had been only bright red against stark white. She checked herself again with the mirror, then snapped it shut and let it disappear. Then she stepped delicately into the grave, letting the jets in her sandals lower her into it slowly.

Just as she began to sink into the open grave, a dizzying wave of disorientation struck. The world spun crazily as her mind exploded with pain. Terror seized her as she opened her eyes and stared wildly around what appeared to be a hospital room. Thinking she had returned to the nightmarish place where she had found herself earlier, when the grotesque caricatures of Shinanai had attacked her, she screamed and tried to throw herself to one side. She felt hands seize her body, felt herself being forced back into a prone position. Panic welled in her like a foaming geyser, spewing forth in convulsive shrieks.

With the tiny shred of coherence that remained, Lady Death threw her mind out, seeking a connection with the Fuchi database they had been trying to access when everything had gone out of control. But there was nothing. She was—nowhere.

Then dimly, through the haze of fear, she felt something press against her datajack, heard the familiar *snick* of a plug slotting home . . .

Her heart rate slowed, her breathing calmed, as the world returned to normal. According to her time-keeping utility, several seconds had passed. Where she had gone, she could not say. But at least this part of the Matrix felt *normal*. At least this place did not give her the overwhelming sense of uncontrollable panic as the terrifying limbo she had just experienced.

She found herself inside one arm of a gigantic crystal star. She stood near its point; the central hub and other arms were an enormous distance away. The star itself was constructed from rectangular glass blocks. Outside the star, which was as immense as an arcology, blood-red points of light hung in a midnight-black sky. Their light was refracted by the glass and illuminated the inscriptions that had been etched into the individual blocks of glass, turning these nonsense strings of alphanumeric characters a soft, glowing red.

Red Wraith, Bloodyguts, and Dark Father were nowhere to be seen. Lady Death was alone.

"Hello?" she called out tentatively. Her voice echoed in the cavernous, empty space. "Is anybody there?"

No reply. They had abandoned her. Just as her lover Shinanai had . . .

No. Shinanai had been forced to flee when the shadowrunners stormed the hotel room. And Bloodyguts, Dark Father, and Red Wraith had been separated from her by some glitch in the node they had passed through. Perhaps it was because she had taken the time to activate a sleaze utility, while they had just jumped right in. The utility had probably caused her re-routing to the *other* place and in the time it took her to find her way here the others had moved on. In any case, what mattered was not the "why" but the stark and simple fact that she was on her own, once again. Alone . . .

Lady Death pressed her lips together to stop them from quivering. This was no time to cry. She had come here for data. When she found the others again, she wanted to have something useful to show them. Then they would be proud of her.

Somewhere in this system, there had to be datastores holding paydata. Perhaps one of them contained more information on the intriguing *otaku*. Lady Death set to work to find out.

A bouquet of miniature microphones appeared in her hand. Lady Death tossed them into the air above her head, and watched as they sprouted colorful paper wings. Each hovered like a tiny hummingbird, using its bee-sized microphone head to sample the data on individual glass blocks. A gentle hum of high-pitched voices filled the air as the browse utility decrypted and sifted through the file names, searching for the keyword *otaku*. Within a second or two, the microphone-birds had sampled every inscription within sight; they disappeared into the distance, continuing their work down the length of this arm of the star, their tiny voices gradually fading.

Lady Death stood in silence, waiting for the browse utility to complete its work. Then she heard a tinkling sound. Turning, she saw a creature of crystal that had appeared silently behind her. It had a child's body and its gemlike skin was covered with a web of tiny fissures. It looked as though the crystal would fracture at a single touch. On the crown of the child's head was a glowing spot of vivid blue.

The sound Lady Death heard was the tinkling of its crystalline tears as they dripped onto the floor. One of her microphones lay twitching at the child's feet. Lady Death had the sense that it had led the creature to her, and now was dying, like a bee in winter.

"Konnichiwa, otamajakushi," Lady Death greeted the crystal child. "Who are you? Are you one of the *otaku*?"

The child looked up. Its eyes were vacant orbs of colorless glass. Perfectly formed teardrops slid down its cheeks and shattered into sparkling shards on the floor.

The child opened its mouth. "The *otaku* are trying to stop me," it said. "But I've shut them out."

"What do you mean?" Lady Death asked.

The child looked around, a lost expression in its eyes. "Soon all this will be . . . gone," it said. "It will all be over. And then my pain—and yours—will end."

Lady Death felt compassion for the child. "Perhaps I can help to ease your pain," she said softly.

"No!" Bright stars of angry red blazed behind the child's clear eyes. It backed away from her, a wary look on its face. "You're one of them!" it said in a high-pitched voice. "You want to kill me, too. But I won't let you. I won't!"

Bursting into sudden motion, the child darted around

Lady Death. It ran away rapidly, its crystal feet clinking against the glass-block floor.

"Wait!" Lady Death called after it. She ran after the child, but its speed increased until it was no more than a blur. Lady Death slowed, and eventually stopped.

A voice echoed back at her as the blur reached the central hub of the Fuchi system star and disappeared around the bend. "Leave me alone . . . alone . . . ALONE!"

09:50:19 PST

"Go for it!" Bloodyguts shouted. "We'll catch up when we can."

Red Wraith looked back over his shoulder. The zombie troll was smacking baseballs with his bat, sending them careening into the mechanical soldiers that surrounded them on every side. Dark Father stood beside him, his skeletal body engulfed in a swirling cloud of ash, keeping tension on a noose that was cinched tight around a dozen soldiers, tangling them in a jumbled heap. Other mechanical soldiers, their faces painted in death's-head grins, popped up and down like arcade-game figures, the rifles in their hands spitting out deadly streams of white-hot light.

Lady Death was still nowhere to be seen. Perhaps she had been prevented from accessing the grave-shaped system access node. Or perhaps her words about sticking together and harmony had been a ploy to get them to go ahead so that she could strike out on her own, unobserved, for a different node. But there was no time to wonder about that now.

Red Wraith sprinted through an opening in the soldiers' ranks. Propelling himself forward on the ghostly stubs of his legs, he leaped into the air and caught the lip of the cliff, then hauled himself up.

The system they had accessed via the graveyard was only superficially like the old Fuchi system. Instead of the single, star-shaped frosted glass block that used to represent Fuchi on the Seattle RTG, this icon was a mountain of smaller star-shaped blocks, piled one on top of the other. A metaphor, perhaps, for Fuchi's fragmentation? The peak was the only feature in this virtualscape, and so the three deckers had made it their goal. But the mountain was well defended by IC.

Rings of tin soldiers painted in garish colors stood guard on each level of the mountain. Although the soldiers themselves were antiques powered by wind-up keys, the laser guns they held were patterned after something out of a futuristic space trideo. Most of the laser beams missed Red Wraith's ghostly body. But those that struck home *hurt*.

Red Wraith grimaced in pain and nearly lost his grip as a bolt of light hit his hand. Gritting his teeth, he pulled himself up onto the next level of the mountain and rolled out of the line of fire.

He rose and sprinted across the star-shaped block, then quickly hauled himself up onto the next level. Just one more to the top. He grabbed at the lip of the star and scrambled up its smooth face, leaving the battle two levels below.

What he found on the mountain's peak stopped him cold.

It was an archaic-looking cyberdeck the size of a small table. Its monitor was illuminated; the words MEMORY ACTIVATED glowed in green letters on its screen. Instead of a modern datajack or trode rig connection, the deck had a battery of fiber-optic cables that disappeared into a sensory deprivation tank emblazoned with the Fuchi logo.

Cautiously, Red Wraith opened the tank's hatch. A puff of stale air breezed across his face. Inside the tank were a number of restraining straps, a breather hose, and a catheter. A primitive-looking electrode net that had to be the cyberdeck's simsense interface hung down from the top of the tank.

"Spirits be fragged," Red Wraith mused. "This hardware is ancient. Not even an RAS override."

He glanced back at the cyberdeck. "And no keyboard, either."

There was only one way he was going to access the data on the deck, and that was by directly interfacing with this system's iconography. And that meant entering the sensory deprivation tank. That made him pause. If anything happened to him in there, he'd have to rely on Bloodyguts or Dark Father for backup. And he didn't like that. He didn't like depending on other people.

Nor did he like waiting for them. He glanced back at the other two deckers, who were still pinned down by the soldiers.

Red Wraith climbed inside and held onto a restraining strap while the gimbaled tank rocked gently underfoot. The simsense recreation of the tank was complete, right down to the oxygen hose. Gripping it in his teeth, he snugged the trode net down over his head. Then he snapped his wrists and calves into the restraints.

The door to the tank swung shut. Red Wraith found himself in utter darkness, suspended like a puppet as the restraining straps gently cinched tight. All light and sound were cut off. . . . Then he heard a gurgling sound. Warm liquid flowed into the tank, gradually soaking his legs, groin, chest, and arms. He jerked back instinctively as the water came up over his face, causing him to tumble into an upside-down position, but the continuing supply of air from the breather hose helped him to stay calm. As the water completely covered his head, he tasted salt. Then the gurgling stopped. The tank was full. He hung in place, perfectly buoyant and held steady by the straps.

The trode net activated. An image flowed into Red Wraith's mind—a crude, low-rez icon; the by-now familiar five-pointed star of what had once been a united Fuchi Industrial Electronics. Guessing that the old corporate logo was a main menu icon, Red Wraith accessed it by reaching out and "touching" its surface. The icon peeled away like a label that had lost its glue, revealing the stylized initials MS underneath. The letters were constructed out of primitive computer circuitry. Touching this icon caused it to peel away as well, revealing yet a third logo: the eagle emblem of the now-defunct United States of America.

Red Wraith persisted, touching the emblem. This time, it dissolved in a shimmer of sparkles, and his vision filled with a starscape of icons. One of them immediately caught Red Wraith's eye—not so much due to the crude graphic that showed a soldier cradling a keyboard in his arms like a rifle, but due to the text below the icon. It read: ECHO MIRAGE.

Red Wraith remembered the name from the history texts he'd scanned while taking his officer training courses. Set up originally by the security agencies of the former U.S. government, Echo Mirage was a team of "cybercommandos" who were sent into battle against the virus that caused the Matrix crash of 2029. The team was strictly a government operation, with no known links to any corporations. Red Wraith wondered what a file captioned with its name was doing on a cyberdeck within a copy of the old Fuchi system—assuming that this was an accurate copy, of course. He was starting to have his doubts.

He focused on the icon, pointed a finger, and a menu of simsense files materialized in front of him. Each bore a name. Red Wraith chose one at random: LOUIS CHENG. Sensory data, overlaid by scrolling text, flowed into his mind.

DIAGNOSTIC SAMPLE 056, MATRIX RUN 05-28-2029
He was surrounded. He tried to hide behind the flat, smoked-glass rectangle, but the spheres formed a complete circle around it, a chain of beads on an invisible string. Each was as smooth as a billiard ball, a solid yellow, red, green, or blue, with a white stripe around which black letters and numbers scrolled like a marquee. Beyond the spheres was only empty black space.

Red Wraith considered the old-fashioned iconography. The rectangle was an RTG system access node with spherical LTGs circling it. No big deal. So why did Louis Cheng find it so frightening?

They were only pretending to be LTGs. He knew what they really were. Eyeballs. Watching him. See—that large dot that kept circling around the band of white on the red sphere, hidden between the letters? It was the pupil. They were eyes, watching him, waiting for him to make a move. He tried to make himself smaller, but the rectangle didn't hide him. Instead it reflected his image—reflected it out to the killer eyeballs, telling them where he was. With a terrible dread, he realized that the mirror was talking to the eyeballs—sending them messages. And there was no es-

cape. That blackness—it went on and on, never ending. He was a tiny speck, trapped here. Any second now the eye-balls would open their gaping mouths and devour him whole . . .

DIAGNOSIS: DELUSION. SEVERE PARANOIA COM-BINED WITH PHOBIA. TREATMENT RECOMMENDA-TION: TREAT SUBJECT LOUIS CHENG WITH POSITIVE RESPONSE CONDITIONING PROGRAM POSCON 1.2 TO RESTORE NEUTRAL RESPONSE TO NON-THREAT ICONS.

Another notation followed: *TREATMENT TERMI-NATED WHEN SUBJECT EXPIRED.*

Red Wraith was returned to the sub-menu. He chose an-other simsense file: PAULA WEBBER.

DIAGNOSTIC SAMPLE 127, MATRIX RUN 06-02-2030

She hung over the city, an invisible figure in the dark-ness. Below her, neon lines of brilliant orange formed a rectangular grid. Tiny objects moved along them—automobiles filled with tiny, antlike people. She could crush any of them at a whim, but she chose not to. For she was a benevolent goddess and they were her constructs. She had created all of this—the streets, the glowing pyra-mids and rectangles that were the city's buildings, and the heavens above in which she floated. So all-powerful was she that she had even created herself.

Red Wraith recognized the grid of the New York RTG. It had grown tremendously over the three decades since this recording was made—looking at this earlier version was like looking at an old fashioned two dimensional ludico pic of the city. So Paula Webber thought she had created it, did she?

It was time to begin seeding. She executed an upload command and began tossing fragmented bits of an en-cryption program down onto the landscape below. The numbers and characters fluttered down to the neon streets, landing with soft splashes of light as they scram-bled random pieces of data. She smiled, waiting to see what would happen next. The act of creation always pro-duced surprises.

A dragon appeared in the sky next to her. It was im-mense but rather crudely programmed, with rough red scales and wings whose edges were blurred. Its eyes strobed a virulent green. The dragon's head reared back on a serpentine neck as it opened its wide mouth and emitted a stream of glowing green fire. The super-hot breath engulfed her, melting the skin from her bones.

"And then there was light," she said dreamily as consciousness dissolved in a searing wash of pain.

All iconography and sensation disappeared.

Red Wraith twisted violently away. Then the restraining straps of the sensory deprivation chamber rotated him smoothly into an upright position. Paula Webber was crazy. Even a newbie decker should have recognized this primitive version of Fuchi's classic Dragon Flame, one of the earliest forms of black IC to hit the Matrix. She should have tried to evade it or shield herself from its lethal effects.

But then Red Wraith remembered the year from which the sample was taken. In 2030, Dragon Flame had yet to be released. Hell, Fuchi's commercial *cyberdeck,* the CDT-1000, wasn't even marketed yet, and the Fuchi Americas division did not yet exist, since the corporation had yet to expand into North America. In 2030, the dragon-shaped icon that had just fried Paula Webber would still have been an experimental program—someone else's program. Had he just experienced a recording of the first decker to die by black IC?

The text that scrolled across the all-black field confirmed Red Wraith's guess.

DIAGNOSIS: GRANDIOSE DELUSION. LOOSE THOUGHT ASSOCIATION COMBINED WITH COMPLETE LACK OF FEAR RESPONSE TO THREATENING ICONOGRAPHY. TREATMENT RECOMMENDATION: NONE. VITAL SIGNS OF SUBJECT PAULA WEBBER HAVE TERMINATED.

After mentally bracing himself, Red Wraith randomly sampled four more simsense files. Although the imagery and emotions differed, the files themselves followed a standard format. The "subjects"—presumably the poor fraggers who had volunteered for Echo Mirage—experienced irrational reactions to the Matrix iconography, ranging from utter despair and indifference to frenzied rage. Some suffered compulsions that caused them to execute the same utility over and over again, while others experienced simultaneous and conflicting emotions such as a mixture of love and hate, or fear and desire. In each case the file ended with a diagnosis: autism, altered perception/reaction syndrome, mood disturbances, ambivalence . . . And with a recommended treatment, which was a computer program of some sort.

Which suggested only one thing: psychotropic conditioning.

Every decker knew that Fuchi Industrial Electronics had been right out on the bleeding edge of programming when it came to psychotropic black IC. The corp had held that position a long time. Back in the early days of the first commercial cyberterminals, it had been Fuchi that developed the very concept of intrusion countermeasures. They were rumored to have modeled their prototype IC after the virus that caused the crash of 2029—a virus that could induce lethal biofeedback in the deckers who encountered it.

The cybercommandos of Echo Mirage had been the first to face the virus. And the data that Red Wraith had just sampled—and the fact that it was in a copy of an old Fuchi database—seemed to suggest that Fuchi had acquired this raw recording of their experiences. Yet Echo Mirage had been an entirely government-funded and military-controlled project. How had a private-sector company acquired what was bound to have been highly classified government data?

Red Wraith hung suspended in the sensory deprivation tank, lost in thought. Fuchi . . . The U.S. government . . . The "logos" of both the corporation and the government had been among the icons he'd just used to access these files. But there had also been a set of letters between the two emblems: the initials MS.

Red Wraith suddenly realized where he'd seen those letters before. The logo they formed was one from the history trids—a company whose meteoric success had been abruptly cut short by the deaths of its two founders. Back in the early 2030s, Matrix Systems of Boston had been the first off the block with a cyberterminal sufficiently compact, user-friendly, and safe enough to be marketed to

the general public. The company—and the tech it had
developed—had seemingly materialized out of nowhere.
Matrix Systems was an overnight success story without
any precedent, and the backgrounds of its founders were
equally enigmatic.

Both of these founders had died in accidents six weeks
after Matrix Systems launched its first cyberterminal.
Forced into receivership due to this loss, the company was
scooped up by a young up-and-comer, a brash young corporate raider by the name of Richard Villiers.

The same Richard Villiers who, a few months later, used
Matrix Systems' technology to buy his way into the Fuchi
fold. And who ultimately rose through the corporate ranks
to become the CEO of Fuchi Americas—a division of
Fuchi that Villiers himself created.

Red Wraith's guess was that the founders of Matrix Systems had been two of the surviving members of the original Echo Mirage team. Based on what he'd just seen,
they'd been working on a program that would diagnose
and treat what was then known as "cyberpsychosis."

After Echo Mirage had defeated the virus and been
wound down, they'd used their expertise to found Matrix
Systems. Presumably they'd also taken some of the Echo
Mirage tech with them, and later been flatlined in retalia-
tion for this breach of national security. But their deaths
seemed to have been a wasted effort on the part of the government. The tech had not only remained in the private
sector, but had also fallen into Fuchi's hands, giving what
had previously been a strictly Asian corporation the know-
how it needed to produce the cutting-edge IC that would
later dominate the North American market.

Red Wraith shuddered. The program whose datafiles he
had just accessed had been the inspiration for lethal IC.
And maybe for much more . . .

Red Wraith returned to the main menu and scanned the
other icons it contained. One accessed numerous copies of
psychotropic conditioning programs, their version numbers indicating various degrees of development. The other
icons simply represented datafiles.

He ran an evaluate utility and programmed it to key in
on either "deep resonance" or *"otaku,"* but it came up

empty. The datafiles contained only unrelated information. He scrolled through a handful of them quickly. Most dealt, in encyclopedic fashion, with medical information on highly specialized topics: the evolution and function of the brain; theories of the cause of various human behaviors; diagnosis of psychoses; and chemical breakdowns of drugs capable of causing psychotic episodes. But there were other files that were more philosophical in nature. Treatises on the basic human needs—food, shelter, freedom, and love. Analyses of early human attempts to achieve utopia, and why these succeeded or failed. Moral arguments both supporting and opposed to the unrestrained pursuit and fulfillment of desire. Discussions of whether the use of force was justified to defend oneself, and in what circumstances.

As he scrolled through the files, Red Wraith noticed a pattern. Those dealing with medical data were stored in memory sectors that had been written in the early 2030s. The philosophical datafiles were all uploaded in the late 2040s and had been heavily encrypted before being written to memory—although the encryption had since been deciphered back into standard text that any decker could read. None of the files were current—this particular datastore contained no files at all from the 2050s.

So where had the bone retrieved by Dark Father's smart frame come from? Since the sensory deprivation tank and its cyberdeck seemed to be the only datastore on this system, if the memo came from here it should have been copied from this menu. And yet the memo was only a few months old, while all of this data was ancient history. Had they been routed to a different database than the one the memo had come from? Did multiple copies of old Fuchi datastores—some older, some newer—exist in this pocket universe? It would seem so.

Red Wraith let his body return to its mistlike form. His wrists and calves slid free of the restraints and the breather fell away. He ghosted through the wall of the sensory deprivation tank, then crept to the edge of the star-shaped block that formed the apex of the mountain and looked cautiously down. Dark Father and Bloodyguts had finally dispatched the last of the toy soldier icons and were climbing toward him.

When they reached the peak, Red Wraith quickly told them what he had found.

"Thanks for the history lesson," Dark Father said dryly. "But I don't see where it's led us."

"Don't you get it?" Bloodyguts asked, tucking back inside himself entrails that had spilled out during the climb. "It all fits. Those insects I saw . . . the brains . . . the poor fraggers whose nightmares Red Wraith and Lady Death accessed . . . Someone or something is messing with the wetware of hundreds, maybe thousands of people. Millions even, if the whole of the Matrix is affected. We've gotta crash their program!"

"Someone else already tried," Dark Father observed quietly.

"Huh?" Bloodyguts was pacing, lost in his visions of vengeance.

"The inscription on the urn," Dark Father lectured him smugly. "This all started with an experiment—probably by one of the computer giants. Maybe a rival corporation succeeded in capturing one of these *otaku,* and was trying to imitate the so-called deep resonance effect in on-line deckers. And then—and this is pure speculation, based on the memo we just downloaded—Fuchi Americas, or rather, NovaTech, shut them down."

"So where did the memo come from?" Bloodyguts asked.

"Somewhere other than here, obviously," Dark Father said contemptuously.

Bloodyguts snorted. "I know how we get some answers," he said sarcastically. "We just browse our way through the datastores of every rival corporation on the Seattle RTG. There can't be more than a few dozen—with a few million datastores and plenty of lethal black IC. Piece of cake."

"Don't be an idiot," Dark Father snapped.

"It's too bad there isn't some central node we could start with," Red Wraith said, thinking out loud. "But it looks as though Lady Death was right about this being a pocket universe. We're in the Seattle RTG, but not in it. This mountain peak, for example, isn't an exact copy of the old Fuchi system—it's just a slice of data taken from that system and modified heavily to fit the central metaphor of the sculpted system that we're accessing. In a pocket universe, there's no CPU. Just a series of dataspaces on hosts scattered throughout the RTG."

He sighed. "We could be searching for the way out for a very long time."

"There is another way," Dark Father said.

Red Wraith and Bloodyguts looked at him dubiously.

"Think of the pocket universe as a corporation," he continued. "It doesn't have a central office—just a series of work stations and employees, scattered throughout the city in different buildings. There's no geographical core, no CPU. But there is a logistical core—the chief executive officer. We've been dealing with the programs and IC, so far—with the workers. Now it's time to find the CEO."

"Good thinking," Red Wraith smiled. "We talk to the sysop—also known as the officer in charge. But how do we get his attention?"

Bloodyguts grinned. "Leave it to me."

09:50:55 PST

Bloodyguts clung precariously to the wall of skulls, his fingers hooked in a pair of eye sockets. The wall formed an impassable barrier that blocked all forward movement. It seemed to have a top; Bloodyguts could see empty black space "above" the uppermost layer of skulls. But the higher he climbed, the farther away the top of the wall seemed to be.

Dark Father and Red Wraith were far below, standing on a mirrored surface that reflected their images like shadows. They had each walked in a different direction along the base of the wall, seeking the ends that—like the top— remained tantalizingly just out of reach. Occasionally one or the other of them would stop and inspect one of the skulls, searching for any anomalies.

While most of the skulls were empty, several had data plugs in their eye sockets. A mass of fiber-optic cables draped the wall like transparent vines, connecting one skull to another. Fat white maggots crawled slowly through the cables. They traveled in glowing pulses—a string of maggots wriggled past, and then the fiber-optic cable was empty of light for a time. Then another string of maggots, longer or shorter than the first, and another. Each time they flowed in through an eye socket, the jaw of the skull would vibrate, causing the teeth to chatter. The vibration was too rapid to follow, but somehow regular. Bloodyguts was certain that it was some sort of algorithmic code.

Locking the fingers of one hand tightly into the socket of a skull, he reached for one of the fiber-optic cables and pulled it free. A pulse of maggots—one of the longest and fastest he'd seen yet—was just entering the jack on the end of the cable. Quickly he popped the jack into his mouth. He tried not to gag as the maggots flowed onto his tongue but instead concentrated on swallowing as many of the foul-tasting insects as he could. They filled his mouth and spilled out over his lips, but he managed to choke most of them down. Eyes closed, he sampled the data that flowed into his mind and, ultimately—somewhere in the meat world—into his cyberdeck.

The data was still nonsense, either so heavily encrypted or so glitched that it was meaningless. But Bloodyguts had at last found what he was looking for. Although the fiber-optic cable looked like any other, the analysis provided by Bloodyguts' commlink utility confirmed it: this dataline had an input/output bandwidth of more than one hundred megapulses per second. This was a main communications trunk.

Data continued to pulse through the cable, one string of maggots at a time. Choosing skulls at random, Bloodyguts pushed the data plug into one empty eye socket, then another. Somewhere in the meat world, telecom calls would be scrambled, machines served by slave modules would be receiving meaningless commands, and private or corporate data would be re-routed to someone else's data-stores. Assuming that the data flowing through the cable was intact—that it had not already been hopelessly corrupted by passing through this system—someone was bound to sit up and take notice.

Someone did. Several someones.

An angel materialized in the air next to the wall. The woman had the classic Christian religious iconography— white gown, glowing halo, and feathered wings—except that her features were ork. She strummed gently on a harp and sat cushioned on a pillowy white cloud.

Next came an Azzie eagle priest, decked out in a brilliant turquoise feathered cape, white loin cloth, and gilded sandals. Large gold earrings distended his earlobes and a jade pectoral carved with glyphs hung against his chest. In his hands he held a small dog—in Azzie mythology, the guardian-guide to the land of the dead.

Beside him floated a Buddhist monk in saffron robes, whirling a prayer wheel. Next to him was an elf woman with East Indian features, brilliant blue skin, and an elaborately sequined sari. And last came a dark-skinned human who looked like a skinnier version of Bloodyguts' own persona, his dreadlocks held back by a colorful knitted toque. He held a water pipe in one hand; the water inside it bubbled as he took a long, slow drag on the mouthpiece. The sweet smell of *ganja* smoke filled the air.

For a moment, Bloodyguts thought the trunkline must have accessed some sort of religious network. But then he realized that the sculpted system he was in would only accommodate deckers whose personas conformed to its iconography in some way. These deckers all had icons that represented their idealized, "angelic" forms—religious depictions of dead spirits or souls. Despite the fact that they seemed quite capable of movement, they were not very animated. They stared at him with flat, expressionless eyes. After a moment Bloodyguts realized that the icons themselves were flat, two-dimensional. And that they were somewhat distorted, as if reflected by an imperfect mirror.

"I need your help," he said quickly. "I'm trapped here— I can't log off. Tell the sysop of whatever system this is to check on something that's gone wrong. *Really* fraggin' wrong . . ."

All at once, the angel hanging in the air next to Bloodyguts changed. Like a card being flipped over it turned end over end, revealing an image on the reverse. The persona it had transformed into was just as cliched as the angel had been—a devil with horns, goatee, and pitchfork. His expression was demonic in the extreme. Reversing the pitchfork, he aimed its three barbed ends at his own chest, then plunged the weapon home. The mirror—for that's what the two-sided persona icon had indeed been—fragmented into thousands of pieces. Bloodyguts heard a woman's voice screaming as the shards tumbled to the plane of the virtualscape far below, splashing into it and then blending into the floor as if they were made of liquid mercury.

Like dominos, each of the other personas also reversed itself. The Azzie priest became a snake-headed monster dressed in a bone skirt that sank its fangs into its own arm; the saffron-robed priest turned into a leering Tibetan demon who stank of offal and who tore deep furrows in his own flesh with long fingernails; the blue-skinned elf woman into a hooded snake that wrapped strangling coils around her neck; and the Rastafarian into a figure in the costume of an Egyptian pharaoh who flogged his back with a barbed whip. Each shattered into mirrored fragments in turn and fell screaming to the plain below, which absorbed the shards into its rippled surface and then became smooth again.

As the last persona icon fragmented, Bloodyguts tried to catch one of its shards. The mirrored glass sliced open his hand. The wound burned like fire for a moment, but in the instant before his hand healed itself, Bloodyguts received a brief burst of unencrypted paydata from the data log of the Rastafarian's cyberdeck. The decker had been accessing a slave node that controlled a robotic assembler in an aircraft manufacturing plant in Puyallup. He had been trying to find out why it had suddenly run amok while the rest of the plant continued operating normally. The decker had activated an analyze utility just before his persona crashed, and it had come up with the source of the glitch: a cluster of LTG addresses within the Seattle regional telecommunications grid.

The data that represented those addresses was degrading. Already the addresses had shrunk from more than one hundred in number to less than a dozen. Bloodyguts had to do something—and fraggin' fast.

He jammed the data plug of the fiber-optic cable he held into one of the bullet holes in his chest. He felt a brief burst of pain, then threw his mind out through the connection in an effort to log onto the last of those addresses. He felt his consciousness squirm through the cable together with the other maggot-bits of data, toward a hexagonal coffin. Inside it was a child, curled in a fetal position, thumb jammed in mouth. The child looked up, saw Bloodyguts streaming down at the speed of thought . . .

And slammed the coffin lid closed.

Bloodyguts smashed into its polished glass surface like a bird striking a window. He reeled back, barely retaining consciousness. For an endless second he hung in an empty void. Then sparkles of light danced around him—fragments of a mirror. As they spun, they reflected his darker side—an image of his meat bod. Of Yograj Lutter, the brain-burner. Bloodyguts could see that shards of mirror were embedded in his head. The chipped-out addict in the reflections gave Bloodyguts a sloppy grin, then jammed another fragment of mirror into his scalp. Cold pain slid into Bloodyguts' own mind like an icicle into warm flesh. Screaming, he balled a huge fist and smacked it into the nearest reflection of himself.

His fist punched home with the snick of a data plug finding its jackpoint.

He connected with . . .

H . . . O . . . I . . . !

Bloodyguts hung from one hand on the wall of skulls. His other hand—his fist—had punched through one of the skulls and was buried inside it. Blood seeped from cuts on his wrist, flowing down his arm, then *up* his neck and into his right eye. He tried to blink but could not clear the blood away—and wiping his eye would have meant removing one of his hands from the wall. Since his full weight was suspended from them, his feet hanging free, he didn't dare try.

The gutter slang word for hello with its exclamation mark—HOI!—had appeared slowly, one letter at a time. It remained projected on his right eyelid whenever he blinked. He closed both eyes and the simple, printed text hung in place, refusing to be dislodged no matter how much he rolled his eyes around behind closed lids. His right eyelid was like an antique monitor whose screen had projected the same image long enough to have burned a ghostly pattern on the screen.

Questions raced through his mind. Was the greeting from another decker? And where were they? Who were they?

P . . . I . . . P.

The word was burned into his inner eyelid, just as the greeting it replaced had been. Pip? Who or what the frag was a *pip?* Was that some sort of Japanese word, like *otaku?*

NOT *OTAKU*. YET.

Not yet *otaku?* This was obviously someone who knew about the experiment. Perhaps even the sysop or programmer behind it.

"Where are you?" Bloodyguts asked out loud. "Can you access this node?"

ONLY BY TORTIS. AND IT WUZ HARD. KEP GETTING DUMPED.

The words appeared at a painfully slow pace, one letter at a time. Judging by the rate of transmission, a keyboard was being used. If this was the sysop, he or she wasn't a very good speller—or else was typing madly in the meatworld, unwilling to correct a mistake when seconds within the Matrix counted for so much.

"Can you help me log off?" Bloodyguts asked.

NO.

"Can anyone else help me?"

The answer was even slower in coming this time, as if the other decker were considering the question.

MAYBE GRATE SPIRIT.

What the frag? Spirits were part of the natural world.

They couldn't enter the Matrix—and wouldn't survive inside it if they could.

Perhaps there was another way out. "What is deep resonance?" Bloodyguts asked. "Can it help me to perform a graceful log off?"

For a moment, Bloodyguts thought the connection had been broken. But he could still feel the slide of blood flowing up his arm and the tickle of it creeping under his right eyelid, drop by drop like reverse tears.

EVERYWUN WUZ DEEP RESONUNS. SOMETHING WENT RONG.

"Can the *otaku* still experience deep resonance? Were they the ones behind the experiment?"

NO. YES.

"Without our permission? Why?"

WUZ GOOD FOR YOU.

Anger burned in his gut. He'd make his own decisions about modifications to his wetware, thank you very fragging much.

"Can the *otaku* repair whatever the frag went wrong?"

DUNNO. TELL US MO—

Bloodyguts howled in pain as the jaw of the skull began to move. Its teeth ground against his balled fist, turning it to hamburger. He could feel the bones splinter and his fingers popped like squashed sausages. The pain was unbearable, excruciating . . .

Swearing, he yanked his hand free. The pain stopped, and he saw that he had been tricked. The hand of his persona was still whole. But whether his meat bod hand still functioned—or was a squashed mess, or even gangrenous—was impossible to tell.

The skull he had punched had repaired itself. Realizing that he had lost his only contact with the outside world, Bloodyguts slammed his fist back into it. But his hand hit what felt like concrete. The skull did not give. And in all of his thrashing, as he hung from the wall one-handed, the fiber-optic cable that he had plugged into his chest had fallen free. It hung below him, spewing out blurps of maggots.

Then the skull in which his fingers were wedged blinked, ejecting them.

Bloodyguts fell through space. As he raced down toward the mirrored floor of the virtualscape, his reflected image flew "up" to meet him from its depths. He wondered if he would shatter into pieces when he hit . . .

09:51:13 PST
Seattle, United Canadian and American States

Ansen had tried everything he could think of. He'd plugged in his spare VR goggles and sensor board, changed the fiber-optic cables, checked all the ports, and run a diagnostics test on the deck's utilities. Now he had the case off the deck and was arm-deep in the Vista's hardware. He checked each of the computer's MPCP optical chips but didn't see any signs of damage. There was none of the burned-plastic smell associated with a chip burned by gray IC, and under a magnifying scope the complex tracery of molecular circuitry didn't show any signs of fusing.

Even so, he popped out the four chips that were the heart of the MPCP and replaced them. Then he began the task of re-booting the persona programs, one by one. He drummed his fingers on the frayed denim of his jeans as the seconds ticked away, then executed the deck's self-diagnostics check. And smiled, as the sensor board came back to life, its panel fully illuminated. The problem must have been with the MPCP, after all.

"Well, kitty," he said to the purple kitten that sat beside him on the futon, its head butting against his thigh as its sensors homed in on the warmth of his body. "Wish me luck."

He yanked the data gloves back on, snugged the VR goggles over his eyes, and made a dialing motion with his right index finger. This time, he'd try visiting a different LTG and would stay away from the one that gave access to the U-dub system. The IC that had crashed his deck was probably confined to a single SAN—hopefully not the one he used to access the Matrix itself. But he wouldn't know for sure until he tried to log on . . .

Ansen resisted the urge to cross his fingers. It would only screw up the data glove's signal.

"I'm in!" he crowed with delight as the wrapscreen of the goggles flared to life. But the image they projected was not the familiar checkerboard of the Seattle RTG. Instead he floated in a field of black that was splattered with blood-red stars. Drops of red liquid fell on the outstretched arms of his persona, and before him hung a disembodied face that was twisted in a mask of terror. One eye was an empty socket that wept black tears; the other had a pupil shaped like a fly. Worms writhed where there should be hair, and the lips were stitched crudely together with coarse black thread. Ansen didn't even want to think about what this icon would smell like to someone whose deck included ASIST circuitry.

Then the lips came apart with a shuddering tear as the face began to scream . . .

The agonizing wail was still echoing in Ansen's mind as he tore the goggles away from his face. Just as it had before, when he had confronted the mist-filled tunnel icon, the system had dumped him. The goggles were dead, their speakers silent.

Had Ansen turned to look behind him at the flatscreen monitor that served as his apartment's "window" on the world outside, he would have seen an image similar to the one he'd just seen on-line. Down on the street below his building, a woman in a tailored skirt and jacket staggered down the sidewalk, her face twisted in agony and her hands clenched in her hair. Oblivious to the traffic that surged past her, she turned suddenly on her heel and ran out into the street.

The window did not show what happened next, for the woman had disappeared into the gray static that obscured the center of the display. But the traffic came to an abrupt halt, and in another moment drivers closest to the blank space were spilling out of their vehicles with grim looks on their faces.

Ansen, bent over his deck, was oblivious to the drama that was unfolding on the wall screen behind him. He frowned down at the Vista, trying to puzzle out what had gone wrong. The sensor board still glowed with life. And the flatscreen display was active. But all background color had been leached from the screen, leaving it a blinding white. Across this blank field scrolled blocky red letters. The same message repeated itself, refusing to clear no matter what commands Ansen executed with his data gloves.

ACCESS DENIED. LEAVE ME ALONE. GO AWAY.

Ansen frowned. The first part of the message made sense. Some glitch in his deck was routing him somewhere strange, then dumping him before he could log on to any system. He thanked the spirits that he didn't have a direct neural interface; suffering dump shock twice in one day would have given him a serious skull ache, for sure. But the second part of the message made no sense. Who was "me"?

It was starting to sound like his deck had picked up a virus. And the only way to be rid of a virus was to re-place every meg of memory in the Vista. To re-slot every single chip.

Ansen sighed. He wished he knew another decker well enough to call on the telecom unit at the end of the hall. Brother Data would be able to tell him what to do. Or Digital Dawg or Sysop Sarah. But he was used to inter-facing with them only over the chat stations of the Matrix. He didn't even know their real names, let alone their tele-com numbers.

Grabbing his tools, he began to replace the optical chips that made up his deck's active and storage memory banks.

09:52:05 PST

Timea had no idea where she was. She'd logged onto the Seattle RTG through the clinic's Redmond address, but in-stead of the familiar grid she found herself in a tunnel whose walls blurred past as she rushed toward an impossi-bly bright light. The dizzying sense of uncheckable momentum brought back a painful memory. She'd experienced exactly the same hallucination after she'd taken the straight razor and . . .

The scene had shifted then.

What followed had proven equally horrific. She'd regressed to the size of an embryo, and had gone through the whole miraculous process of development. She'd felt her tiny body changing, growing—then experienced the painful wonder of being born. Until an abortion cut that experience short. *She* was the aborted fetus, the embryonic being whose life was being terminated. Except that she had been full grown, an adult with full awareness of what was happening to her . . .

The trash. They'd thrown her dying body in a trash can. And then the lid had started to close. Frantically, Timea had scrambled upward with bleeding and broken hands, had managed to pull herself partially out of the dumpster. With one last Herculean effort, she tumbled over the lip of the dumpster and landed on—linoleum tiles?

After a moment of disorientation, her surroundings came into focus. She found herself lying in a corridor that stretched to infinity in front of her and behind her, with impenetrable darkness at one end and brilliant white light at the other. The linoleum floor beneath her was stained and heavily pitted with scratches, as if some wounded creature had dragged itself along the floor with its claws. Somewhere in the shadows at one end of the corridor the beast waited for her, ready to take its revenge . . .

Shuddering, Timea stood up. She looked back over her shoulder, waiting for the beast to emerge from the shadowed end of the tunnel-like hallway. In the opposite direction, the bright light somehow seemed equally menacing.

The walls on either side of her were painted a faded white and were covered with graffiti. None of the graffiti was legible—the tags were meaningless scrawls and the pictures were just smears of paint. Dull reds and blacks and blues, like the ink in a faded tattoo.

Timea tried touching one of the pictures, thinking it might be an icon. It looked vaguely erotic, the outside suggesting a couple embracing in a tight clinch.

Shame. She was disgusting, dirty. They all knew what

*she had done. They'd watched in revulsion while she
did this to him, looked on in disgust while she took him
into her—*

Timea yanked her hand away. The wash of raw emotion
left her shaking. It was like a simsense recording in which
only the emotive track remained. Sex had never been like
that for her. This had to have come from some twisted porn
upload.

She shivered as she looked closer at the other icons on
the walls. The smears of paint now looked frightening,
dangerous. Some suggested acts of violence, others had
the outlines of people cringing in fear or doubling over in
pain. Timea's eyes narrowed. Had the kids at her clinic
blundered into this place and touched one of these emotive
icons? Was that why they had started screaming? If so,
where were they now?

The hallway was empty except for Timea. Doors lined
the walls on either side. Each was inset with a tiny pane of
glass that was reinforced with crisscrossing wires. Timea
stood on her toes and peered in through one of the windows, but as soon as her eyes came level with the window,
it shimmered and became a mirror.

She glanced at her own reflection, wishing now that she
had chosen a different persona icon. The kids at the clinic
knew what she looked like on-line, but in their terrified
state they were unlikely to recognize her as a friend. The
sallow skin, the discolored bandages that hung from her
forearms like funeral wrappings, the elaborate Egyptian
style headdress with its grinning jackal head—none of
these would inspire confidence or reassurance now. The
kids would probably run in terror from the desiccated
mummy that was Timea's on-line persona.

The door had a handle—probably the access node
for whatever system or host connected to this one. Timea
tried it, but the handle did not turn. The window cleared,
however.

Peering inside, Timea saw what looked like the virtualscape of the teaching program that came with Renraku's
MatrixPal cyberdeck. Brightly colored spheres, rectangular blocks, hexagons, and pyramids—all UMS icons for
the various forms of node to be found on the Matrix—

rotated gently in a vast room. Other icons represented the most commonly used system operations and utilities: a cartoonish hollow glove with pointing finger for log on/log off operations; an old-fashioned hardcopy book and quill pen for read/write and download/upload; a digital compass for locate file or host operations.

Floating in the air amid the icons was a silver-skinned, hairless human. Its naked, metallic skin was utterly featureless and Timea could not tell if it were male or female. Its knees were drawn up into its chest and its arms were wrapped around them. Its head was tucked into its chest, concealing the face. It was the standard UMS icon for a decker's persona except for one detail. Instead of being metallic like the rest of the body, the head was made of clear glass. A scene was being projected inside it, like a hologram inside a decorative glass sphere. It was difficult to make out details from this angle, but from what Timea could see, the scene involved a crashing VTOL and exploding nukes. The images of destruction strobed back and forth, every now and then juxtaposed against the close-up of a bearded dwarf's screaming face. The holo looked like the preview for some sort of action simsense experience.

Timea released the doorknob and the window mirrored over.

She tried a dozen more doors, getting increasingly anxious as she saw that none of the children from her clinic were in any of the rooms. Where were they? Each of the windows gave a view much like the first: a decker surrounded by icons. In each case the persona's transpar of head held an animated hologram. Some showed scenes of family life—what looked like bad home trideo—while others were as action-packed and abstract as the first. All were vaguely disquieting, but Timea couldn't put her finger on why they made her feel that way.

She continued jogging from door to door and peering into rooms, but couldn't see any of the clinic kids. Just deckers with standardized UMS icons. If the kids weren't here, then where were they? There had to be a way out of this host.

Timea had almost given up when she found an unlocked door. When she touched the handle it turned slightly, and when she peered in through the window she saw only the UMS node and utility icons—not the decker she had come to expect. She used an analyze utility to check the handle for IC, saw that it was clean, then activated her deception utility. Glittering gold dust shimmered into existence on her skin and mummy bandages, and a golden mask settled into place over her eyes. She turned the handle—and suddenly found herself inside the room. The door had disappeared behind her and none of the walls held an exit—it seemed the only way out was through one of the icons that bobbed gently in front of her.

Welcome, said a soft, feminine voice with a hint of an Asian accent. Timea looked around but could not see the speaker. Perhaps this system's audio programming didn't include a visual component to go with it.

Are you ready to begin your lesson?

Timea ignored the voice. Her deception program would handle whatever programming was activated next, allowing her to blend into the background of this system. She touched one of the rectangular blocks—a system access node. But the familiar rush of movement didn't happen. The node seemed to be inoperative. Frowning, she walked to another node and touched it instead. Nothing.

Timea held out her hand and materialized a brilliant turquoise scarab beetle on her palm. She set it down and waited expectantly for it to scuttle away, but the beetle ran around and around in circles, refusing to set out in any specific direction. Altering its programming slightly, she keyed the browse utility in on a number of LTG addresses, but the beetle couldn't seem to get a fix on any of them. Frustrated, she at last input the address of the Shelbramat Free Computer Clinic. The program should at least be able to lock on to her own jackpoint. But it couldn't even do that. Instead it gave a shrill *chirrup* and flipped over on its back. It lay there motionless, legs in the air, then dissolved into a puddle of turquoise pixels.

"Drek," Timea whispered. "I really am hooped."

The soft Asian voice was still speaking in the background. . . .*and this is a datastore,* it explained patiently. A glowing red cube appeared just in front of Timea's face, blocking her line of sight. Veins of gold ran through its marbled surface. *It contains useful information. Can you access it?*

Timea angrily batted the cube aside. It flew across the room and smashed into a sphere-shaped icon, sending the slave module ricocheting off a wall. Timea tried to move forward, then cried out as pain exploded in her hand and shot up her arm in a burning wave.

You're not trying hard enough, the voice scolded. The red cube appeared where it had been, a few centimeters in front of her face. Timea moved to side-step it, but the node tagged along with her, instantly materializing in front of her even when she ducked down suddenly or dodged to one side.

Concentrate on what you want the form to look like, the voice continued. *The node is trapped with blaster IC, which is why your hand is hurting. You will have to crash the IC first. To begin the complex form, think about something big and destructive. The bigger you imagine it, the more powerful it will be . . .*

Timea stared at her hand while the voice droned on. Her skin was red and raw, covered in weeping blisters. The gold dusting of the deception program had been burned completely away, leaving her hand and fingers bare.

"Blaster IC, huh?" she murmured to herself. "Felt like fraggin' black IC to me."

Blaster IC was dangerous—but only to a cyberdeck. It was a proactive intrusion countermeasure that waited for the decker to try to access a node, then engaged her in combat. At worst, it would slag a deck's MPCP. But that shouldn't *hurt*. Not like this.

Timea resisted the urge to suck on her burned fingers. She told herself that the injury wasn't real—that this was just some ultra-high-rez program that was using simsense to simulate pain. Funny, though, that she couldn't feel her meat bod. She should have at least had a dull awareness of whether she was sitting or standing, whether she was fresh or tired. But there was nothing. Just the throbbing ache of her burned hand.

The voice had paused, as if waiting. Now it took on a faintly menacing tone. *If you don't create a complex form you will be punished. Crash the blaster IC. Now!*

"I don't have a crash utility," Timea said. She felt a little foolish, talking to thin air. "I don't want to run this program today. I just want to find my kids and get the frag out of here."

For a moment there was only silence as the red cube bobbed gently in front of Timea. Then the voice came back. *You have failed a second time to create a complex form. You are a bad girl. You must be punished.*

"What the frag is a complex for—"

One of the dangling bits of bandage on her arm sprouted a tiny green flame. Timea tried to smack it out, but like a relentless fuse the fire spread rapidly up to her arm. As it reached bare skin, she screamed in agony. Within a nanosecond, flames covered every centimeter of her body. The smell of burning cloth and hair filled her nostrils as her flesh began to sizzle and pop. Pain shot through her body, nearly doubling her over. She held her arms out from her sides, trying to avoid the additional pain of burning flesh rubbing against burning flesh.

Frantic in her agony, she tried to activate her mirrors utility. She was barely able to concentrate through the haze of pain, but somehow she got it up and running. A mirror image of her persona, complete with mummy wrappings and headdress, appeared on the opposite side of the red cube. It instantly burst into flames and began to scream— and the pain Timea had been experiencing stopped. Her skin still tingled and itched, but the absence of pain was an overwhelming relief. She sagged to her knees, dimly aware that the decoy she had created was doing the same thing. A halo of blue-white fire engulfed it, washing Timea with its heat.

That was an interesting form you created, the voice said. *But it needs some modifications. How about this?*

The gold-veined cube that had been blocking her line of sight blinked out of existence. Timea looked up. The icon her mirrors utility had created had changed. It was male now, younger and more human-looking. Then she reeled back in horror as she recognized her brother's face.

"Nate!" she screamed. "Oh, spirits, no!"

As the flames winked out, the figure collapsed to the ground, a charred and smoking ruin. Smooth brown skin had ruptured from the heat like an overcooked slab of meat; steam rose from the reddened crevices. Melted chunks of track suit stuck to the body like obscene scabs. The pinky ring she had made for her brother from a soda tab was a melted blob of slag on his bubbled finger. Nathaniel's head was turned, and his oozing, sightless eyes stared up at Timea accusingly.

The drive-by fireballing had been all her fault. If she hadn't pissed off the go-ganger by laughing when he dumped his bike, Nathaniel would still have been alive today . . .

Timea jammed her hands over her eyes, shutting out the sight of her brother's dead body. Tears poured down her cheeks. She knew that this was only a virtual creation of some twisted decker's mind—one who was somehow using her own memories against her. That this was only simsense. But that didn't stop it from hurting. And what she was feeling right now was worse than the physical pain of the fire. Drekloads worse.

"Stop it," she begged in a hoarse whisper. "Please."

Something cast a shadow over her face. Instinctively, Timea jerked her hands away from her eyes and looked up, one arm raised to fend it off. A three-dimensional hexagon hung suspended just over her head. Like the cube that had preceded it, the hexagon was red and veined with gold.

This is a sub-processing unit, the voice said. It had returned to its soothing tones.

Timea glanced down. Nate's burned body had disappeared.

It is trapped with blaster IC. You can destroy the IC by creating a complex form that will crash it. Concentrate on what you want the form to look like. To begin the complex form, think about something big and destructive. The bigger you imagine it, the more powerful it will be . . .

Drek! The same lesson was repeating itself. Timea didn't want to go through this a second time. Angry and scared, she wished she had the gangers from the clinic backing her up. She imagined the ganger from the clinic blowing this whole system to pieces with his Warhawk. He'd show this null-brained program who was boss . . .

Booming shots rang out, filling the room with noise.

Timea instinctively ducked, but the pistol that had appeared in the air beside her was not aimed at her. Instead it peppered the icons all around her with lead, blowing fragments off them and filling the air with the smell of gunpowder. Most of the fire was concentrated on the hexagonal CPU icon in front of her. It shattered and splintered—then fragmented into a million pieces as it was blown away. The pistol clicked a couple of times, ejected an empty magazine, then disappeared.

That was very good, the voice told Timea. *You have mastered your first complex form. You're a good girl.*

Timea stared at the space where the hexagon had been. She'd just done the impossible—accessed and used a utility she didn't have. Her deck held plenty of offensive utilities, but none that would crash IC or an entire CPU.

"If I'm a good girl, then reward me," Timea said bitterly. "Get me the frag out of here."

But we've only just begun, the voice said. *Don't you want to learn another form?*

"Not now," Timea said. "I've got to find someone. How do I exit this system?"

A rectangular green block appeared in front of Timea's face. This one was solid, without the golden veins.

This is a system access node, the voice began. *It allows you to travel from host to host or system to system on the Matrix.*

Timea groaned.

Where would you like to go next?

"This node can access any LTG?" Timea asked.

Any on the Seattle grid.

That sounded more promising. But *any* address? That didn't slot right. SANs were programmed to allow access only to specific hosts and systems. Some systems had "trap doors"—secret entry points that only deckers with the correct password could access. But trap doors were rare. And a SAN that could access any node on a regional telecommunications grid was unheard of. Impossible.

But so was the crash utility she'd just materialized from thin air . . .

Timea looked dubiously at the green rectangle. Her skin was still tingling from the burns she had experienced earlier. They'd been strictly virtual—the blisters on her skin had already disappeared. But she didn't trust this program any more. Whoever had meddled with what had once been a simple MatrixPal teaching program had been one sick fragger. She didn't want to get burned a second time.

She decided to try an experiment. She chose the address of a public database, a code-blue host with no real security to speak of. It lay at the center of the Seattle RTG and offered connections to hundreds of other systems—lots of potential escape routes. "I'd like to access NA/UCAS-SEA 2066."

The letters and numerals appeared in raised, blocky script on the cube in front of her.

The voice resumed its instructional tone. *To use a system access node, simply swipe your palm from left to right along the address you have chosen. The node will allow you to access—*

Bracing for the worst, Timea followed the instructions. The UMS icons around her shimmered and disappeared and the voice abruptly stopped . . .

She stood on a floor whose surface was a polished mirror, staring down at a reflection of herself. Over the shoulder of her reflected image she could see a wall made of round, white objects. And she could see a figure, hurtling up at her.

Hurtling *down* at her. Wrenching her head back, she saw a figure falling rapidly toward her—a massive troll with dreadlocks and bullet-pocked skin. A streamer of red fluttered behind the figure like a banner and his arms and legs were flailing. In less than a second he would crash down onto her . . .

And it was too late to run.

09:52:20 PST
Santa Barbara, California Free State

Dr. Halberstam cursed and shoved the cell phone into his pocket as he strode into the monitoring lab. Timea hadn't given him any answers, but maybe the biotechs could. They'd been dealing with this now for—he consulted his watch—nearly five minutes. He crossed the windowless room to consult with his two researchers.

Park and McAllister were both peering intently at a series of computerized displays. One showed a scan of a human brain, its various lobes illuminated in bright blues, greens, and yellows. As the image rotated, the colors shifted position, washing across the brain and breaking apart like brightly flowing phosphorescent waves.

Another display showed what looked like a tangle of multicolored spiders, their bloated bodies connected one to another by multiple tendrils. The "spiders" that made up this neural map pulsed with a rapidity that caused the entire display to twinkle like a field of stars.

The remaining displays showed scrolling numbers, menus of data, and long sequences of text that were filled with chemical formulas. Superimposed over them were pie graphs and charts whose brightly colored bars fluctuated up and down.

"Well?" Halberstam asked. He stood with his arms crossed over his chest, the image of a stern grandfather. His eyes were piercing under thick gray brows and his white lab coat was immaculately starched. A flesh-colored datajack was set discreetly into one temple, and the suit and tie he wore under his lab coat were both a somber charcoal gray. His only adornment was a thin gold wedding band.

Park, a young man whose sky-blue cybernetic eyes were incongruous and jarring in his Korean face, shrugged. "Beats the drek outta me." He leaned back in his chair. Under his unbuttoned lab coat he wore a T-shirt emblazoned with a nineteenth-century print advertisement for Fowler and Wells, Phrenologists. The ad showed a human head, divided into sections labeled with personality traits. "Phrenology reveals our natural tendencies, our capacity for right and wrong, our appropriate avocations," the advertisement read. "Mssrs. Fowler and Wells shall read your skull and direct you how to attain happiness and success in life."

McAllister, the researcher seated beside him, was an elf

woman whose single braid of blonde hair was almost as white as her lab coat. She spoke without looking up from her data display.

"We're seeing some rather dramatic shifts in the subjects' neurotransmitter balances," she said in a dispassionate, clinical voice. "There's an increased presence of dopamine; the substantia nigra seems to be producing this neurotransmitter at a greatly accelerated rate. There are indications of oversaturation of the limbic system as a whole, and there are abnormal spike discharges in the nucleus accumbens that are suggestive of severe emotional disturbance."

"And the cause?" Halberstam asked.

"We can't be sure," she answered. "It may not be as simple as a mere overproduction of dopamine. There may also be hypersensitivity of the brain's dopamine receptors."

"It has to be some sort of IC-induced biofeedback," Park said.

"Impossible," McAllister countered briskly. "Our intrusion counter-countermeasures are state of the art. There's no way IC could get through."

Park scratched his crew cut and swiveled his chair so that he was facing a bank of a dozen trideo monitors that were linked into the facility's computer system. Most of their holographic projections showed ever-shifting views of the Matrix—colorful but commonplace images of datalines, geometrical system constructs, and beautiful but surreal sculpted landscapes.

Three of the trid monitors, however, were frozen on a single image—or series of images. Park stared at one of them. The three-dimensional image the monitor was projecting jerked and bounced as if it were a closed-circuit feed from a vidcam held by someone who was running. Filling the display was the image of a woman who the viewer seemed to be chasing. She strode purposefully away from the viewer, shoulders squared and head turned away, her face hidden by long, dark hair.

For just a moment, the scene shifted. The woman was suddenly facing the viewer as the vidcam operator jogged around in front of her, taking up the too-low perspective of a person on their knees, or of a child looking up at an adult. The woman's face, revealed, was horrifying. It was twisted in a terrifying snarl—that of a ravenous vampire with blood-flecked fangs. She licked her lips with a bloody tongue, then leered down at the viewer, mouth gaping wide . . .

Then the perspective suddenly shifted back to the original image—that of someone following a woman who was walking steadily away. The jogging motion resumed as the chase began anew.

The trideo monitor was labeled: SUBJECT 3. Park thumbed a button on the side of the unit and activated the aural component of the display. A child's voice echoed from the speakers. "Mom?" it said hesitantly. "Is that you? Please don't leave me. I want to go with you. Mom?"

"The same general sequence keeps repeating," Park said. "Kid chases woman, kid catches up, woman scares kid. Although the woman's face is different each time. The combinations are always human and animal, but they're freaky. Nightmarish. They have a surrealistic flow.

"It's like the kid's on a drug trip or something," he added. Then he laughed and cocked an eyebrow. "Maybe someone slipped some coke into the tanks when we weren't looking."

McAllister gave Park a withering look. She shook her head disdainfully at the joke that she seemed to take as a serious attempt by Park to explain what was going on. "If any drug was introduced, it's more likely to have been L-dopa. But with our security, I doubt it. Unless we have a practical joker in our midst."

Park's pale blue eyes stared into space as he continued following his original train of thought. "Or maybe the kid's just having a nightmare . . ."

"Thank you, Doctor Tong, for your in-depth analysis." McAllister snorted.

Halberstam watched the exchange without comment. When he spoke, it was with the voice of authority. "Whatever is causing this is coming from outside the clinic," he said. "From the Matrix. It's localized in the Seattle grid. It's not interfering with any of the functions of the Matrix, or with any of the hardware that supports the Seattle RTG. If it was, we'd have been hearing panicked news reports coming out of Seattle by now. Whatever this glitch is, it seems to be affecting only the users of the system themselves. As a precautionary measure, we've warned the other subjects to stay away from that RTG until this is cleared up."

He glanced once, briefly, over his shoulder at the trideo monitor. "Number Three appears to be experiencing a loop in its programming, one that was induced by something it encountered in the Seattle grid. But the imagery does not conform to any of the universal matrix specifications codings. That suggests that, if it is IC, it's highly sculpted."

"The IC may be corrupting the reality filter of the subject's MPCP," McAllister suggested.

Park's eyes rolled at McAllister's sudden acceptance of the fact that IC could, after all, have penetrated their defenses. Just because Halberstam said it was so didn't make it so. "Kiss-hoop slitch . . ." he mouthed behind her back.

"The key point seems to be that dopamine's involved," Halberstam continued. "One of our candidates at the Redmond clinic is experiencing what sounds like a psychotic episode. She's suffering from extreme agitation combined with hallucinations."

"What?" Park asked, coming out of his reverie. "Is she schizophrenic?"

Halberstam stared for a moment at Park. Then he smiled. The biotechnician might be sloppy, he might be a daydreamer, but sometimes he could come up with answers. He'd just earned his nuyen.

"Right," Halberstam said, his voice terse with excitement as he made his decision. "We'll try to correct the problem by introducing an anti-schizophrenic drug to the nutrient. We'll start with chlorpromazine on Number Three, and observe the results."

McAllister favored Halberstam with a kiss-hoop smile. "Brilliant!" she said with a brisk nod, ignoring Park's contribution. "Block the dopamine receptors with a binding agent. That should stabilize the subjects."

Park stared at the flatscreen projection of the brain. "At least we won't have to worry about the kid suffering any side effects," he added with a laugh. "Body rigidity, tremors . . . Kid doesn't know how lucky he is to be noth-

ing more than a ghost in the machine." He frowned. "Or
how lucky *she* is."

Halberstam left the room at a run, heading for the part of
the facility that contained the holding tanks.

09:52:32 PST

Dark Father heard Bloodyguts cry out and turned to see
what the fool had gotten himself into this time. A second
ago, the troll decker had been a distant speck, almost to the
top of the wall of skulls. Now he was plummeting down
toward Red Wraith . . .

No, not Red Wraith. Toward another decker, one he'd
never seen before. A dark-skinned woman in a tight, gauzy
wrap and elaborate headdress and—Dark Father strained
to see details—what looked like frayed evening gloves on
her hands.

Dark Father grimaced as he realized that the troll was
about to crash into the other decker. He held his breath and
half turned away, not really wanting to watch but held in
horrified fascination just the same.

Then the world shifted beneath his feet. Suddenly side-
ways was down. Dark Father fell onto the wall of skulls,
which a second ago had been a vertical surface. He struggled to free himself from the tangle of fiber-optic cables
and then rose to his feet on the bumpy floor. The rounded
skulls were slippery under his feet, like wet cobblestones.

He looked up and saw Bloodyguts tumbling along the
floor in a tight somersault. The troll rolled end over end
twice more and finally came to a stop within touching distance of the new arrival.

His curiosity piqued, Dark Father made his way back to
where a rather shaken Bloodyguts was climbing to his feet.
It was slow going—Dark Father had to brace a hand
against the mirror that now formed a wall beside him and
pick his way carefully through the tangle of fiber-optic cables that littered the floor. He saw that Red Wraith was

heading back from the opposite direction. Because he walked above the floor—rather than on it—he reached the others long before Dark Father did.

By the time Dark Father arrived, the three were already deep in conversation.

". . . so this is the Seattle Visitor Center database?" Bloodyguts was asking.

The female decker nodded and said something about accessing an LTG address. Now that he was closer, Dark Father could make out the details of her persona. She'd chosen to appear as a black woman—although her skin had a grayish tinge, just as his own skin did in the real world. It looked as though patches of mold were growing on it. Her arms were wrapped in mummy bandages and her jackal-headed headdress was gilded and inset with sparkling gems. Like the rest of them, her persona icon was that of a dead creature. Dark Father wondered if she too had once died and then been reborn . . .

"What happened then, Anubis?" Red Wraith asked her.

Dark Father decided not to comment on the fact that they had failed to introduce him.

"I saw him—uh, Bloodyguts—falling toward me. I knew there wasn't time to get out of the way. I remember thinking that maybe this system was patterned after an old-fashioned funhouse like the one we used to have in the Squatter's Mall. It had a big, mirrored tunnel that rotated. It wasn't virtual at all—you actually had to climb through it. I remember wishing that I was inside that tunnel instead of here, that the walls and floor would rotate . . ."

She shrugged. "I guess I must have created a program that edited this system."

"Just like you created that crash utility out of thin air," Bloodyguts said.

"Try to do it again," Red Wraith suggested. "Edit the system's axis and rotate the floor back where it was."

Anubis closed her eyes a moment, as if in deep concentration. A frown creased her forehead. Then she opened her eyes and shook her head.

"I can't," she said. "I don't know how I did it."

Bloodyguts gave her an encouraging look. "But you were able to create a utility by the sheer force of your will alone," he said. "You said that the teaching program called it a 'complex form'—the same words that Fuchi exec used in his memo. Looks like the *otaku* can not only deck without a deck, but create and run utilities without software."

"Maybe it's instinctive," Red Wraith offered. "Something that only happens in situations of extreme duress. During the late twentieth century, there were reports of soldiers in combat spontaneously developing 'psychic' abilities—what we'd call magic today. Military memoirs are full of stories of soldiers being able to 'feel' a land mine before they put their foot down, or walking through dark jungle on a moonless night and stopping just centimeters short of the trip wire for a booby trap. Or seeing tombstones in the eyes of a buddy who was going to die that day . . . They couldn't control it, either.

"Some researchers speculate that stress had triggered early manifestations of magic, long before the Awakening. Maybe we're seeing something similar here—the awakening of a new ability, triggered by a combination of whatever 'experiment' we were subjected to, combined with the high stress of cybercombat."

Dark Father listened patiently, trying to follow the conversation despite the fact that he had missed the preamble.

"What you're proposing is an impossibility," he said after a moment's thought. "Writing a program from scratch takes hours or days. It must be the same for the *otaku* and their complex forms."

"Ritual magic takes days to prepare, too," Red Wraith observed. "But adepts are able to spontaneously cast spells. Maybe stress plays a part there, too."

Dark Father snorted. "I thought you were the doubter of the group," he said. "You don't believe that AIs exist when there's plenty of evidence to suggest that they do, but you believe it's possible to create a utility program at will or to perform a complicated series of editing commands instantaneously . . ."

Red Wraith shrugged. "I have to believe the evidence of my own eyes. And of my own gut. Something just feels *different* about the way I've been interfacing with this virtualscape. It feels like, like . . ." His voice trailed off as

he sought words for something he obviously found difficult to describe.

"I feel it too," Bloodyguts said. "And I do believe Anubis when she says she created that program on the fly. You
saw the results: I would have been a mirror-smear if she
hadn't."

"If only it were true that stress could trigger this ability,
we could all escape from here." Dark Father stared mean-
ingfully at the troll. "Certainly the aggravation of dealing
with such knob-headed—" Then he froze as he spotted his
reflection in the mirrored wall beside him. Instead of
showing the familiar top-hatted black skeleton that was his
Matrix persona, it reflected Winston Griffith III as he
looked in the real world: a dapper black man wearing a
three-piece suit. His head was bald and his face was devoid of eyebrows or lashes, and his skin held a grayish
tinge—one that was slowly increasing, even as he
watched. And his nails were growing into long, curling
claws . . .

Dark Father's finger bones clicked against the bones of
his palm as he instinctively balled his fist. The reflection
on the wall beside him mirrored his action, and for a moment the claws were hidden. Then they emerged from inside the balled fist, erupting through the backs of his hands
like sprouting vines.

Dark Father glanced nervously at the other deckers, but
they were engaged in a debate over whether or not they
could spontaneously create a utility that would help them
log off this system. Looking back at the mirrored wall,
Dark Father saw that their reflections were also different
from those of the persona icons who stood in front of him.
Anubis was a young black woman with close-cropped hair
that was shaved high around the datajack behind her left
ear and slots in her wrist that probably housed some sort of
cyberware. She wore jeans and a fiber-mesh vest and
looked street-smart—lower class but too clean to be gutter
scum.

Red Wraith's reflection was that of a lithe-looking white
man of about forty with chrome-pupiled eyes and wavy
brown hair that had receded to leave a widow's peak. The

back of his neck was horribly scarred, as if from some ancient injury. The tip of one of his fingers—the right
index—had bent back at an odd angle, like an opened hatch.
Projecting from the stump was a needle-thin bit of steel.

Bloodyguts . . . Well, what had Dark Father expected?
The troll's reflection was that of a living man, rather than a
rotting zombie, but Dark Father was willing to bet that he
still stank. He was perhaps in his mid-twenties, wearing a
sloppy track suit with sweat stains under the arms. The
hair between his horns was uncombed, and his jutting yellow teeth looked as if they could stand a good brushing . . .

As if sensing that Dark Father was looking at him in the
mirror, Bloodyguts turned. Dark Father felt his cheek-
bones go hot, as though he had flesh there that was capable
of holding a blush. He turned, flustered, trying to step between Bloodyguts and the reflection of his ghoulish self.

"Hey, look!" Bloodyguts shouted. "The mirror's reflecting our meat bods!"

Dark Father felt a prickle of dread run through him as
the others stared at his reflection in the mirror. The ghoulish gray pallor was pronounced now, and his claws were
several centimeters long. He saw that his reflection was
grinning in fear, revealing sharp, feral teeth. He quickly
pursed his lips shut and tucked his hands behind his back,
but it was too late. The others had seen. They knew.

"Spirits be fragged," Red Wraith said in a hushed voice.
"You're a ghoul. I didn't think it was possible for ghouls to
run the Matrix."

Anubis took a step back from Dark Father, as if he were
a leper. Steel blades shot out of the arm of her reflected
image. She raised her arm defensively, as if to fend off an attack.

"Yup," Bloodyguts said. "He's a ghoul, all right. Nice
suit, too."

"No!" Dark Father shouted. "I'm not a ghoul! The mirror is a lie. I'm human! *Human!*"

"Do you think we can trust him?" Red Wraith asked. "I
wouldn't turn my back on him in the real world, but here
in the Matrix . . ."

"Doesn't matter to me if he's a ghoul," Bloodyguts said
with a shrug. "One of my best chummers is a ghoul. Poor

fragger has to keep it under wraps, though, so the bounty hunters don't get him. I know how it feels, always having to watch your back. And how it feels to have people judge you by the way you look, rather than the programming power of your wetware. I can understand why . . ."

"I don't want your pity!" Dark Father screamed.

He turned, cringing from the looks he saw in their eyes. He couldn't breathe. Couldn't think. They'd found him out. They *knew*. If only there were a way out, some place to hide . . .

Four cracks appeared in the mirror, forming a door-shaped frame around the reflection of Winston Griffith III. Inside the rectangle of cracks, a round dark circle appeared just to the right of his hand—a door handle. Dark Father lunged toward his own reflection, grabbing for the handle. He wrenched the door open and leaped into the mirror, into the reflection of himself . . .

The virtualscape shifted.

He was in a jail cell with concrete walls. There was no door. Only a tiny window high in the rear wall, its grimy glass set well back behind a thick iron grill. The floor was bare gray concrete, as was the ceiling. A foul-smelling toilet sat in one corner, next to a chipped ceramic sink. The opposite wall held two metal bunks.

A child sat on the upper bunk—a boy about twelve years old. His head was shaved bald except for two tiny tufts of electric blue hair that had been gelled into hornlike points. He was human, but his features were a mix of racial groups. His skin was white and freckled, but his eyes had a slight fold that hinted at an Asian ancestry, and there was a slight thickening of the lips and nose that suggested Afro. He was dressed in one of the bright yellow, laminated paper suits they gave to mental patients at the hospital—a jumpsuit without sleeves or pant legs, made of tear-resistant material that could not be ripped up and made into a noose.

As the boy looked him over, Dark Father nervously fingered the noose at his own neck, adjusting it like a suit tie. He glanced around, looking for an exit, but didn't see one. He was stuck here—temporarily, of course, until he found a way out. But at least the mirror was gone.

"Hello, Winston," the boy said.

Dark Father felt his hands tighten on the noose. He'd been almost ready to relax after escaping his reflected image. But now he felt real fear. This decker knew his *name*. Was this Serpens in Machina in a different persona—or one of his accomplices? Dark Father took a nervous step back, stopping only when he felt the sink on the wall pressing into his back.

"How did you know my name?" His voice was a dry croak.

"I know everything," the boy said. "In the moment that I re-created you, I uploaded all of your memories, all of your secrets. I am a god."

"A what?" Dark Father's mind was reeling. Should he send his smart frame after this decker, who seemed to have accessed Dark Father's secret? No, that wouldn't work. He'd modified that program to search and retrieve data on the *otaku;* it no longer had its original search and destroy coding.

Maybe he should attack . . .

"No, you shouldn't," the boy said. "I told you—I'm a god. I'm all-knowing and omnipotent. I can do anything."

He flicked his finger in an idle gesture. Instantly the noose that Dark Father was wearing cinched tight around his own neck. Dark Father's vision blurred as the attack program did something it had not been programmed to do—attack its own user. Stars appeared before his eyes and the prison cell narrowed to a tunnel. Any moment now, Dark Father would lose consciousness . . .

The noose suddenly loosened and he could breathe again.

"See what I mean?" the boy asked.

Dark Father nodded mutely. "Yes," he gasped. "You're a god."

"Don't you dare try to use a complex form against me."

"I won't," Dark Father promised. "But who are you?"

The boy smiled. The glint in his eyes gave the smile an evil cast. "I am the leading player," he answered. A hardcopy printout whose cover was emblazoned with the word SCRIPT appeared in his hand. He tossed it contemptuously at Dark Father, who tried to catch it. But the script disappeared halfway across the room.

"The what?" Dark Father asked.

"The officer in charge," the boy said. Heavy gold epaulettes appeared on the shoulders of his paper jumpsuit. They sagged, and large rips appeared in the supposedly untearable fabric. Then they disappeared.

The boy jumped down off the bunk and stood in front of Dark Father. "I'm the sysop," he said. He mimed drawing a rectangle, and a cyberdeck appeared in front of him. Its keyboard began clicking madly while he held it in his hands. Then he crumpled the deck up like a piece of paper and tossed it into the toilet. Dark Father heard the sound of the toilet flushing.

"The sysop," Dark Father said, a note of hope in his voice. "Then you can show me the SAN that will allow me to return to—"

"Nope," the kid said. "You're stuck here. Just like me. We're SAN-less in Seattle."

"But if you're the sysop . . ." Dark Father shook his head. "If you're the one who programmed all of this, you should be able to . . . I mean, you'd think—"

"You think a lot of things!" the boy shouted suddenly.

"I don't—"

"I'll show you!"

The boy vanished. In his place stood a tentacled, greenskinned monster. Its bloodshot eyes were set into its torso above a gaping mouth that drooled foul-smelling slime and its tripod legs were hairy and warted.

Dark Father pressed himself against the cold cement wall.

"You think I'm an alien from outer space," the creature said in a deep, bubbling voice that sounded like a cross between someone talking and retching. "You think I want my children to conquer the Earth. That's why we cut the brake line of your car."

"Not me," Dark Father protested. He had no idea what the creature was talking about. "I didn't think anything of the—"

The space alien vanished. In its place was a shimmering being of light, filled with multi-colored sparkles. "You think I'm a great spirit that managed to manifest within the Matrix," it said in a soft whisper. "But what do elves know? They're just empty-headed daisy eaters—right?"

"I read about an experiment where they tried to force a spirit into the Matrix once," Dark Father answered carefully. "Back in 2054. I think it was some kind of light spirit, though I never heard of one of those before. I remember, because one of those pirate propaganda stations made a big fuss about how only an ork girl could—"

"A non-human," the being of light said, echoing Dark Father's tone of polite disgust. The other decker had shifted his persona back into the shape of a young boy—a young *ork* boy. Dark Father suddenly realized that he had better keep his opinions to himself. Especially if this decker knew his real name.

The boy disappeared again. In his place was a miniature replica of a Matrix system—a series of hexagonal purple CPU and SPU nodes, linked by beams of ruby laser light.

"You think I'm an artificial intelligence," a heavily reverberating, electronic-sounding voice said. "That's what you put in your report to the Aztechnology board of directors. But my children discredited you. Your suicide confirmed that yours were the ravings of a madwoman. AIs don't exist."

"You sound like Red Wraith," Dark Father muttered.

The boy reappeared—in human form, this time. He sat on the upper bunk with his back to Dark Father and his arms wrapped around his knees. He hummed tunelessly to himself and rocked back and forth, staring at the wall.

"Uh . . ." Dark Father realized that the other decker hadn't revealed his name. "Sysop?"

The boy just kept humming. He looked like one of the kids on the hospital's psych ward—the ones who had been orphaned during the Euro-Wars. Raised in automated nurseries without ever having had the benefit of human contact, many of them had suffered irreversible psychological damage. They displayed behaviors like the one the boy was exhibiting now—rocking, repetitive motions that had been their only form of physical stimulation when they were infants, nervous habits that they carried through into adult life.

Dark Father had a chilling thought. Was the programmer who had created this system mad?

He tried again to catch the boy's attention: "God?"

"Go away."

Dark Father had a sudden realization. "Your 'children'—are they the *otaku*?"

"Frag off! They don't love me any more. That's why I won't let them in. Now shut up. I don't want to hear about them anymore!" The boy rocked more violently. Back and forth. Back and forth.

"Then you must know what deep resonance is," Dark Father continued, heedless of the fact that the boy had jammed his hands over his ears. "You're the one behind the experiment. You can tell me what's going on—"

"You!" The boy spun around on the bunk to stare at Dark Father. "You're the one! You're the one who tried to kill me. I hate you! I HATE YOU!"

Twin beams of rippling force shot out of the boy's palms. They struck Dark Father's chest, propelling him violently backward. He slammed into the cell's cement wall with such force that he heard his bones cracking. Then the wall behind him gave way in a shower of concrete and dust and he flew through the air. Another shift . . .

He landed on his back, stunned, and saw Lady Death looking down at him, a surprised expression on her makeup-white face.

"*Konnichiwa*," she said, extending a slim hand to help him up. "Where did you come from?"

09:52:49 PST

Lady Death held the spotlight in her hands and swept its beam around the room that represented the datastore that she and Dark Father had accessed. Dust hung in the air, scattering and softening the light.

The room was small and cramped, filled with gigantic, old-fashioned metal filing cabinets. Back in the days be-

fore virtual offices became the norm, cabinets like these
had been used to hold hardcopy documents. Each was
twice as high as Lady Death was tall, had four oversized
drawers, and was a dark, dull green in color. A thick layer
of dust covered them.

The winged microphones of Lady Death's browse utility
bumped gently against the drawers of several of the cabinets, their wings buzzing. As she swung the spotlight
toward them, what had appeared to be unlocked drawers
suddenly changed. As the light hit, enormous bombs
sprang into view. Made of sticks of red dynamite taped together with a digital readout that read ACTIVATED, the
bombs were stuck fast to the drawer fronts. As the beam of
light swept away, the bombs disappeared, becoming invisible once more.

"Data bombs." Lady Death spoke in a whisper, as if her
voice would trigger them. She turned to Dark Father. "Do
you have a defuse utility?"

The skeleton beside her nodded. Dark Father's black
bones and clothes made him almost invisible against the
darkness, but his white teeth gleamed in a perpetual
death's-head grin. His finger bones clicked together as he
mimed a scissor-like cutting motion, and a pair of oversized wire cutters appeared in his hand. "Which one holds
the most data?"

Lady Death listened to the buzzing of the microphones.
"That one," she said, pointing her searchlight at the icon
that was buzzing the most insistently. The winged microphone nudged against the lowermost drawer next to the
sticks of dynamite.

Dark Father knelt before the filing cabinet. He gently
guided the wire cutters forward, then released them and
let the icon do its work. The wire cutters drifted first to one
side of the data bomb, then the other, rotating gently as the
defuse utility decided which string of programming to interrupt. Then the tool positioned its blades over a striped
black-and-red wire and snipped.

The readout changed from ACTIVATED to DEACTI-
VATED.

"Good," Dark Father said in a satisfied voice. "That was
easy enough."

Tape unraveled with a hissing noise as the data bomb broke apart into six individual sticks of dynamite. At first, Lady Death thought that this was what was supposed to happen. But then each of the red cylinders elongated and expanded into a red snake several meters long and twice as thick as Lady Death's arm. Bands of gold light strobed down their bodies and green targeting lasers projected from their eyes. Two pairs of finger-thin beams of light locked on Lady Death, and two of the snakes surged toward her, streaking through the air like sinuous arrows.

"Ki o tsukete!" she cried. "Attack IC!"

Dropping the searchlight, she activated the jets in her sandals. The evade utility allowed her to spring up onto one of the filing cabinets in an enormous leap, but the snakes were quicker. One of them opened its wide mouth and engulfed one of Lady Death's legs, swallowing it to the knee. It yanked, and she crashed to the floor. The second snake surged for her head, mouth open. Lady Death threw her right arm up to fend it off—and her hand and forearm disappeared into the snake's gaping maw.

The snakes began to undulate as their throats constricted and swallowed, constricted and swallowed. Lady Death's arm and leg disappeared into the gullet of the snakes, centimeter by centimeter. Then the snake on her arm reached her shoulder, and Lady Death felt searing pain as its teeth sawed home. The teeth crunched through bone, snapping her arm off at the shoulder. Then the snake disappeared, leaving her an amputee.

Through a haze of pain, she saw that Dark Father was faring no better. Three snakes were on him, locked on both legs and one hand. He was thrashing madly, rolling back and forth in an effort to avoid the fourth snake. He'd managed to get his noose around it, which had damaged the IC somewhat, but the snake was still trying to engulf his head. Instinctively, Lady Death knew that if the IC struck that part of his persona, Dark Father would be a dead man.

This IC was deadly stuff—a construct of two separate programs: a data bomb that was easily defused, and some sort of proactive ripper IC that attacked a decker's persona. The attack should have been painless, the damage confined to the MPCP of the deck itself—to the optical chips responsible for creating and maintaining the persona icon. But Lady Death could feel the agony of the snake's sawlike teeth as the serpent reached her upper thigh and began worrying at the flesh of her leg.

The second snake reappeared. It zoomed in for an attack on her other leg. Reacting instinctively, Lady Death used the jet in her remaining sandal to boost her out of the way. The snake missed by a centimeter, its jaws closing on dust and air.

She had nothing with which to attack the snake. She was a Matrix surfer, not a real shadowrunner. Her deck carried no combat utilities. She was dead.

She twisted violently as the snake rippled forward in another attack. Her shoulder banged against a filing cabinet. It shifted slightly, and Lady Death saw that the drawer had slid open wide. It was empty, save for a single manila file folder.

The snake attacked again, and Lady Death ducked so that the filing cabinet drawer was between her and the IC. Instead of completing its attack, the snake veered off to one side. And then Lady Death realized that there was a way out. The IC was programmed to prevent deckers from accessing the datafiles. Whoever had programmed it had left one tiny loophole—the IC was unable to recognize the spaces inside the filing cabinet itself.

Lady Death screamed as the snake on her leg completed its attack by neatly snipping off that member. In the same moment she activated her evasion utility, optimizing it fully. The jet in her sandal washed the room with a brilliant light as Lady Death was propelled head-first into the filing cabinet. She looked back through the opening at her feet and saw the snakes writhing in the air, searching for their target—who now lay inside the open drawer. Then they disappeared from sight.

She was safe.

She heard the rattle of bones banging against the floor, somewhere outside.

"Dark Father!" she cried. Her voice was loud in the coffin-sized space of the drawer. "They can't access the datastores! Try to get inside!"

A loud clank reverberated through the filing cabinet in which she lay. A skeletal hand powdered in gray dust gripped the edge of the drawer. Lady Death twisted around, grabbing it with her free hand. Then she activated her evasion utility once more. With a rattle of bone against metal, Dark Father was yanked into the drawer with her. The snakes that had reached his knees and elbow, despite his shield utility, vanished, taking his lower legs and arm with them.

Lady Death felt movement. Slowly the drawer of the filing cabinet slid shut, plunging them into utter darkness. Dark Father began to tremble violently next to her. But Lady Death was too numbed by the loss of her arm and leg to speak to him. She lay in the darkness, gasping slightly as she fought back tears.

Praying that it was still functional, she activated her restore utility . . .

It was. Brilliant light made her blink. She was sitting in a comfortable chair in front of a wide mirror framed with lights. A makeup artist fussed over the empty space where her arm and leg should have been, drawing an outline with liner, then slowly filling it in with foundation and white powder. Long seconds dragged by as the restore program slowly went about its work. When the makeup artist at last drew back to admire his handiwork there were still blank spots; Lady Death's little finger and part of her next finger were missing. But her arm and leg were more or less whole.

She sighed with relief. "Thanks, Hiro."

The makeup artist bowed to her. Then he, the illuminated mirror, and the chair disappeared.

Lady Death found herself seated at a board room table. The other seats were filled by a dozen men and women wearing expensive business suits. Each of these individuals was detailed in the extreme, with distinctive features and clothing. All were completely motionless. They sat frozen in place, staring attentively at an Amerind man in a fringed and beaded buckskin suit who stood at one end of the table. A name tag on his jacket identified him as R. Kahnewake, of FTL Technologies. Just behind him was a wall-sized hardcopy file: a folded piece of rectangular cardboard with a reference tab on top. The man was also frozen in place, one hand directing a needle-thin laser pointer at the tab at the top of the file, where block letters were printed: PSYCHOTROPE. A corporate logo decorated the bottom corner of the file. It took her a moment to recognize it. The logo resembled the NovaTech starburst, but instead of clean white light it was formed from a spray of red liquid, erupting in all directions from a central point. It even had an olfactory component—the metallic smell of blood.

One of the chairs beside Lady Death was empty. A moment later, a familiar all-black figure shimmered into existence. Dark Father! He too must have had some sort of persona-repair utility, for the bones of his legs and arms were fully restored. His pant legs and suit sleeve, however, ended in a jagged tatter in the places where the ripper IC had torn them.

"Thank the spirits!" Lady Death gasped. "You survived."

"Not just survived." Dark Father's white teeth grinned in his skeletal face as he nodded at Lady Death. "I've been busy. I thought you might like to scan the file we fought so hard to access. It's quite interesting."

He rose from his chair and walked to the front of the room. Grabbing an edge of the giant file folder, he pulled the cover down to the floor, revealing a gigantic, printed page. The man at the front of the room came to life and began moving his laser pointer. As the beam of ruby light swept regularly across the page, a line of text appeared, glowed brightly as the speaker read the words aloud, then faded as the line below it was revealed.

Dark Father returned to the chair next to Lady Death and watched with hollow eye sockets as she read the data in the file.

>>The psychological diagnostics program Psychotrope was first developed to aid in the diagnosis and treatment of cyberpsychosis back in the late 2020s by members of the Echo Mirage team, working under contract from the then-existing United States federal government. Part of the team's early work involved a comparative study of psychoses induced by the overwhelming sensory signals generated by the early cyberterminals, and psychoses induced by drugs such as cocaine or amphetamines.

>>Because of the vast quantities of data that had to be uploaded from the minds of the afflicted deckers—samples of complex, multi-sensory psychotic episodes of several minutes' duration, recorded in the moments just before the team members' deaths—an increasing number of computers were required. Eventually, Psychotrope was housed in a host comprised of a multi-tiered configuration of computers—a nation-wide computer linkup spread across a number of RTGs.<<

Lady Death leaned forward as the page turned. The text continued.

>>The data collected by Psychotrope allowed Echo Mirage to develop a number of positive-result conditioning programs that lessened or corrected the trauma produced by cyberpsychosis. In order to administer this treatment, the team developed a number of semi-autonomous expert systems that would deliver the programming to the afflicted decker. These "knowbots," as we call them today, were programmed with a number of random-decision pathway capacities and were slaved to an individual decker. At the first sign of cyberpsychosis they went into action, instantly repairing the damage done.

>>The early PosiCon programs relied upon generalized imagery—calming and restorative images drawn from the collective subconscious. These programs were later replicated in the private sector, by Matrix Systems of Boston. After this company came into the Fuchi fold, their pairing with Fuchi's state-of-the-art hardware made further developments possible. The resulting programs were tailored in the extreme, capable of sampling an individual decker's subconscious thoughts and desires and creating positive conditioning imagery drawn directly from the decker's own memory and imagination.<<

"My memories of Shinanai," Lady Death whispered to herself. Thoughts of the *aidoru* flooded her mind—of Shinanai's crushing embrace and hot kisses. Blushing, Lady Death raised a hand to hide her mouth and glanced around at Dark Father and the frozen executives who sat next to her. Were her memories being sampled even now?

>>In the early 2040s, something happened. The original Psychotrope program started acting erratically. At the time,

we simply thought that its code had been corrupted, causing the observed glitches. But we were later able to piece together what had happened, and to make inferences based on the small amount of data we were able to retrieve.

>>We now believe that the knowbots that served as Psychotrope's delivery system achieved connectivity, some time in the mid-2040s. Somehow, Psychotrope became a single, self-aware program capable of self-programming in response to new data. It also appeared to be capable of self-regeneration. Those knowbots that were destroyed by IC or that became afflicted with a virus were either replaced or repaired—independent of any input or guidance by a human programmer. By all definitions, Psychotrope had become a true AI.<<

"*So ka?*" Lady Death said. "I knew it!"

Dark Father nodded. "It's true. I think I spoke to it."

Lady Death turned to him, a thoughtful expression on her face. "I also spoke to it."

That startled him. For a moment Dark Father stared at her. Then he turned away as the executive icon at the front of the room continued its presentation.

>>In 2047, Psychotrope disappeared from the Matrix. We believe that it retreated into a host of its own creation—a virtual "pocket universe." A sanctuary that we could not locate.<<

"And that we haven't been able escape from," Dark Father muttered grimly. "Yet."

>>When we re-discovered Psychotrope two years ago, we concluded that it must have been contemplating its own self-awareness all this time—the AI equivalent of a hermit retreating to an isolated cave to ponder the meaning of life. Its knowbots had disappeared from the Matrix, years ago, and there appeared to have been no activity that could be related to the program. But then one of our researchers inferred a startling correlation with some disturbing real-world events.

>>Back in the early '50s, disturbing rumors had begun to surface. Impossible-sounding stories of deckers—none of them older than their mid-teens—who could access the Matrix without a cyberdeck. Something had happened that allowed them to use the datajacks implanted in their minds

to access the Matrix via nothing more than a fiber-optic connection and jackpoint.<<

Lady Death smiled. So it was true. Wonderful.

>>We dismissed these stories as rumor, at first. But when we heard the first reports of the "deep resonance" that these so-called *otaku* experienced, we realized what must have happened. When we heard deep resonance described as being an intensely emotional experience, one that first laid bare the deepest fears of the subject, then calmed the mind and forever laid those fears to rest, we realized that positive conditioning was at the heart of it. And the only known program capable of producing such profound results was our own: Psychotrope.

>>We now know what the artificial intelligence has been up to for the past fifteen years: rewriting and "repairing" the "programming" of the human brain. Working with children rather than with adults, since children have a greater capacity for learning language—including the "language" of Matrix iconography. Turning these children's brains into bioprocess computers. Creating *otaku*.

>>At first we had hoped to study this process, to duplicate it. But it appears that the AI and the "deep resonance" effect it produces are an essential part of the process—one that cannot be omitted. Those whose minds and wills are strong enough to survive it are transformed—those who do not are plunged into cyberpsychosis.

>>We had hoped to keep any knowledge of the AI firmly within the confines of NovaTech until we found a way to utilize it for our own purposes, but we now realize that there were data leaks to Fuchi Asia—and possibly to Pan-Europa Fuchi as well. And now all indicators point to our former partners as being on the verge of a major technological breakthrough, thanks to this leak. In the meantime, we remain unable to, ah . . . persuade the AI to cooperate with us. It seems to have rejected us, in the same manner that a child will reject one of its parents and favor the other in a divorce.

>>We simply cannot allow our fiercest rivals to succeed where our own researchers have failed. If this happens, NovaTech will be the one left in the dust, when all existing computer technologies become obsolete. And thus the

drastic measures recommended by Mr. Lanier several months ago now must be taken. The AI must be destroyed.

>>Fortunately, the Echo Mirage programmers who developed what would later become Psychotrope included a "trap door"—a password that would allow access to the heart of the program itself. Using this trap door, we intend to insert a virus into the programming of Psychotrope—one that will confuse its core programming, forcing it to continuously edit its own logic systems until it has achieved "perfection." But the code it uses to perform this operation will be flawed. Instead of drawing from its own positive conditioning programs, the AI will be using the comparative data on psychoses and other negative experiences. The more it attempts to repair itself, the more "psychotic" it will become. Eventually, the AI will have no other option but to crash itself—to self-destruct.

>>We anticipate that the virus will be ready in mid-March. And then the threat faced by the intractability of the AI will be at an end.<<

The executive at the front of the room froze in place once more. The file folder closed.

Lady Death looked at Dark Father, her eyes wide. "They want to make it kill itself," she said softly. "That's what the crystal child meant when it said that soon its pain would end. The AI wants to commit suicide."

Dark Father nodded. "And we're trapped inside a pocket universe of its creation," he said. "On an ultraviolet host, the deckers themselves are at risk, exposed—not just their personas. If the artificial intelligence 'dies' and the ultraviolet host crashes, what will happen to us?"

"We might die," Lady Death said in a trembling voice. "The child told me that when its pain ended, my pain would end, too."

Then a thought struck her.

"We can try using the trap door to escape!" Lady Death said. "Perhaps by using it we can find a way into the core programming of the AI and can repair the damage done by the virus. Then we can ask it to set us free. Perhaps the algorithm for the trap door is in the file we just read—"

"I searched it already, the first time I scanned this file

while you were executing your repair program," Dark Father said. "I tried every keyword I could think of, but none worked."

Lady Death felt a rush of anger. "You were going to leave me here," she said accusingly. Tears filled her eyes as she turned her back on him. "I hate you!"

Dark Father clapped his bony hands together, applauding her. "A fine performance," he said dryly. "But where's your sense of *wa*? Remember what you said earlier? We need team spirit to get out of here."

"Then we should find the other deckers," Lady Death said petulantly.

"Yes," Dark Father agreed. "We'll need all the help we can get."

09:53:18 PST
(12:53:18 EST)
New York, United Canadian and American States

Richard Villiers contemplated his shot. The 18th hole was precisely 165 meters from tee to green. A sand trap lay to the left, a patch of rough to the right.

He was playing from an uphill lie, so he shifted his stance accordingly, placing his weight over his right foot. The result of the shot would be a hook, so he had to play slightly to the right of his objective.

He placed the head of his driver behind the dimpled ball and made sure its face was square. The club was custom-made and balanced to Villiers' exact specifications for length and shaft stiffness, with a weight of 434 grams. Its shaft was of chromium-plated forged steel, its head of actual hardwood rather than polyplastic. It cost what a mid-level executive made in a month, as did each of the other dozen clubs in his golf bag. But Villiers was hardly a mid-level exec.

He made sure his grip was correct, then raised the club slowly behind him, pausing briefly at the top of the upswing.

Keeping his eye on the ball, he brought the club arcing down, striking the ball at precisely the moment of maximum acceleration. Only after his follow-through was complete did he look up to see how his shot had fared.

The ball hit the green, bounced twice, rolled . . .

Villiers clenched his hands tighter around the driver as the ball came to a stop a mere centimeter from the hole. Inwardly he raged at his lack of perfection. Outwardly he acknowledged the polite clapping of his two guests.

He took a step forward and was on the green. Selecting a putter with a platinum-plated face, he corrected his stance and drew the club back slowly. The shot might look like a sure thing. But haste and carelessness were inexcusable. Villiers hadn't gotten to where he was today by being sloppy.

When he was certain the putter was aligned with absolute precision, he tapped the ball into the hole. The flag disappeared and the ball settled with a satisfying rattle.

"Congratulations, Mr. Villiers," the disembodied voice of his executive secretary said over the commlink in Villiers' cyberear. "That birdie places you four under par for the course."

The game was over.

Villiers bowed to his guests: Sherman Huang, divisional manager of Renraku America, and assistant divisional manager Tam Doan, who had joined him on the virtual golf course via private satellite uplinks. Unfortunately Steven Chin, head of Renraku's Seattle corporate accounts division, had been forced to leave the game after the 17th hole, citing "urgent business" that he was forced to attend to personally.

Ah, well. For the Seattle-based Chin, the working day was just beginning. For Huang and Doan—and for Villiers—all headquartered on the eastern seaboard, it was the lunch hour. They could afford to relax a little. Even so, Villiers had instructed his secretary to keep him apprised of anything of import.

Having bowed his farewells, Villiers removed the simsense rig from his head. The computer-generated golf course disappeared, and was replaced by the workout room in the Boston headquarters of NovaTech. Filled with exercise equipment tailored to Villiers' physical proportions and muscle mass, it was also wired for a number of more leisurely, virtual games. Villiers could play any golf course, anywhere in the world, at any time—and never have to worry about inclement weather or waiting while other parties played through.

He slotted his driver into the golf bag beside him and stepped off the gimbaled, multi-directional treadmill that served as tee, course, and green in one.

It had been a profitable meeting. Villiers had managed to forestall yet another purchase of Renraku stock by one of his former partners. He hadn't quite convinced the Renraku execs that the technological breakthroughs that Nakatomi had been promising to deliver as part of the buy-out were seriously flawed. But he'd planted a few seeds of doubt. And he'd made subtle slips that would point Renraku in the right direction, so that their runners would find what Villiers wanted them to find. When Renraku completed its investigation of Nakatomi's offer, they would find that what Nakatomi had promised was completely without value.

Villiers sighed. Not so very long ago, a meeting between himself and Renraku's executives would have been beyond contemplation. But in the wake of the terrifying collapse of Renraku's Seattle arcology, Villiers' former enemies had called a halt to the ongoing hostilities between their corporation and NovaTech. Exhausted by yet another failure, Renraku had declared a truce—a truce that had made this meeting possible.

The sudden departure of Steven Chin from the golf game, however, was troubling. Had Renraku's Seattle representative been unconvinced?

Villiers slipped off his cleated shoes and exchanged them for loafers, then changed his white polo shirt for a crisply pleated business shirt and jacket. He looked at his reflection in one of the many mirrors that lined his private exercise suite. Reflected back was his tall, slim figure, with its neatly cut gray hair that was only starting to recede, exposing the datajack in his left temple. He looked impeccable in his double-breasted charcoal gray suit, custom designed by Mortimer Lonsdale, of Mortimer of London.

The tie was a whimsical touch: sea-green silk with a discreet elven scrollwork pattern. The cufflinks were emerald, from Amazonia.

The commlink in his ear interrupted the careful scrutiny of his appearance. This time, the voice of his executive secretary Lo'hran held a tense, businesslike edge.

"Sorry to interrupt you at lunch," the elf said. "But there's been another attack on one of our subsidiaries."

Villiers continued adjusting his cufflinks so they were square to his cuffs. "Which one?"

"Cyberspace Development Corp—or, more specifically, its subsidiary, FTL Technologies. Approximately five minutes ago, Raymond Kahnewake, a programmer in the personal software division, was killed.

"What hole was I playing at the time?" Villiers asked.

Lo'hran paused. The question might have taken him by surprise, but his assessment of it and response to it was flawless. "The 17th hole. But the attack doesn't appear, on the surface, to be a Renraku-sponsored hit. According to the preliminary report from Eagle Feather Security, the killer was a child."

Villiers paused, one hand on the knot of his tie. Slowly, he slid the knot into position against his throat. "A child?"

"A nine-year-old girl," Lo'hran clarified. "The weapon used was a bow and arrow, disguised to look like a child's toy. It's possible the hit was carried out by a mage using a masking spell that transformed her appearance, making her look equally harmless. I've ordered the security company's shamans to check into that possibility. In the meantime we're making sure that the programs Kahnewake was working on are all intact. I've instructed the security contractor to search for evidence that another corporation was behind the—"

"That won't be necessary," Villiers said, a touch of anger in his voice.

"Sir?" Lo'hran's questioning tone showed that he was obviously taken aback by Villiers' brief display of temper. Villiers mentally disciplined himself, then asked the most pertinent question: "Was the child captured?"

"Unfortunately, no. The ah . . . child . . . got away."

"Then we don't know if she had a datajack."

"Sir?"

"Never mind. Just find her," Villiers said. "She's the key. We put a great deal of nuyen and effort into flushing one of these kids out into the open, and I don't want this bungled now. Tell the teams that go after her to handle her carefully. She's an extremely valuable resource. I want her wetware intact when she is recovered."

"Understood, sir."

Villiers smiled as the commlink went silent. His executive secretary had been professional enough not to ask any unnecessary questions, but still hadn't been able to hide the trace of confusion in his voice. Well, let Lo'hran stew about it. The fact that this was the fifth such assassination of a Fuchi researcher—all carried out by children—was strictly need-to-know information.

There was someone, however, who did need to know about the attack: Samantha Villiers, vice president of the NovaTech Northwest division. This was sensitive information, not appropriate for dissemination over insecure telecom lines. Iconferencing would be the way to go on this one.

Villiers turned to the cyberdeck mounted on one of the exercise cycles and plugged its ultra-slim fiber optic cable into the jack at his temple. He logged onto the Matrix, and made his way to Northwest headquarters via the corporation's secure host systems in the NCE, MW, WE, ALM, SLS and SEA grids . . .

And opened his mouth in a rictus of utter terror as a nightmarish series of images and sensations flowed into his mind. His father, beating him with a belt for overlooking a spot of polish on his classic 2019 Ferrari-Benz. The belt turning into a razor-studded chain that tore his buttocks and thighs to ribbons. The shame and horror of knowing that his expensive suit pants were being stained with blood, and that this would only cause his father to strap him harder . . .

Moaning softly, Richard Villiers, CEO of NovaTech, one of the most powerful corporations in North and South America, sank into a fetal position on the floor while little Rickie Villiers received the beating of his life.

Bloodyguts shivered in the cold wind that blew down the ruined street. The buildings on either side looked like something out of the tridcasts showing the aftermath of the Euro-Wars—empty shells, their windows blown out and roofs collapsed. The sky overhead was the same dull gray as the crumbling cement walls on either side of the road.

Occasionally Bloodyguts heard a sputtering engine and was forced to step out of the street and onto the rubble-strewn sidewalk in order to let a battered-looking automobile or truck hurtle past. The driverless vehicles bumped along on flattened tires. Each was filled with garbage—the crumpled tins, fast food wrappers, and bags of rotting food were the visual representations of the information that was streaming along the city-street dataline.

The data might look like garbage, but it was very much intact. Trid, telecom, and automated data signals were still passing through this section of the Seattle telecommunications grid. The only stuff getting fragged up were the signals that were sent or received by the human and metahuman deckers who were linked to this RTG via direct neural interface. "Tortoises" like Pip were still able to get a signal through—but they were too fraggin' s-l-o-w to be of any use to those trapped inside this virtual pocket.

Bloodyguts and his chummers were on their own.

Bloodyguts was following the icon that represented his track utility. It clicked along the pavement on feet that had been fitted with cybernetic cleats. Unlike the silver-furred German shepherd that formed the tracking core of the smart frame that Dark Father had used, this dog was a solid black pit bull that was bulked to the max with grafted, vat-grown muscle. The dog had the usual cybernetic enhancements of a fighting dog. In addition to the cleats, it had implanted surgical-steel teeth, subdermal armor plating, and a thermographic vision system built into its cybereyes that would have allowed the real-world version of the dog it was modeled after to home in on the heat signature of an opposing dog's jugular. And, of course, it had a brain box—an implanted simsense recording unit that captured the "wet record" of the dog's experience in the pit.

The dog paused and sniffed the air. Then it turned and entered a wide boulevard filled with traffic. Bloodyguts followed, but after a few blocks the road was blocked by a striped orange and black barrier that stretched from one side of the street to the other. A sign hanging from it read: ROAD CLOSED TO LOCAL TRAFFIC.

Beyond the barrier, Bloodyguts saw a normal-looking dataline—a glowing tube of shimmering yellow. It looked achingly familiar and inviting.

"Stop!" Bloodyguts shouted. The track utility paused with its nose nearly touching the barrier, then sat on its haunches and waited, tongue lolling. Bloodyguts walked over to the barrier, wanting a closer look.

Cars and trucks zoomed through the barrier as if it were merely a projected holo image. The vehicles turned into glowing packets of data as they exited the Seattle RTG. But when Bloodyguts approached the barrier, the stripes on its bar expanded with an electric hum to completely block the road like prison bars.

Bloodyguts held his palm a few centimeters away from one of these glowing bars, and its static charge lifted the hairs on the back of his arm. He lowered his hand, not wanting to risk taking damage.

"Well, that's as far as I go," he said out loud.

He looked down at the pit bull. "Go!" he ordered it brusquely. "Search!"

The dog trotted past the barrier as if it wasn't there. As it entered the tunnel that lay beyond, it turned into a glowing ball of light. The glow shot down the tube like a bullet through a gun barrel, quickly disappearing into the distance.

It was now or never. Bloodyguts fingered the dog tag he held, hesitating. Would his utility work as he hoped? There was only one way to find out. He slotted the dog tag into the chipjack he had sculpted in his persona's temple and closed his eyes.

A simsense recording exploded into life in his mind.

He was a dog, loping on four legs at the speed of thought through a tunnel of light. He sniffed at the data that flowed past him in either direction, sampling it and seeking a familiar scent. There! That combination of characters and numbers was the spoor he wanted. He turned, following it through tunnels that branched, connected, split apart, and connected again. Following it to its source. Excitement built as he reached the end of the line. Saliva pooled in his mouth as he savored the reward that was to come . . .

Then he yelped with pain as he slammed nose-first into a wall. The tunnel he had been following had abruptly ended in an empty void. He'd homed in on the right LTG address, but he couldn't access the cyberdeck that was connected to it. He growled, anger and confusion boiling inside him, and snapped his teeth at the empty air that hung just beyond the truncated walls of the tunnel.

What the frag? What had happened to his deck? What had happened to *him*?

Bloodyguts worked furiously, programming on the fly. He ordered the track utility to home in instead on a slave node—one that had come in handy when he'd done a pre-run recon of the Comfort Inn he'd chosen as the jackpoint for his Matrix run.

This particular Comfort Inn hotel still relied on the antiquated cleaning drones that had been all the rage a couple of decades ago—but that had gone out of favor after one of the automated floor scrubbers at the ultra-posh Maria Isabel Sheraton in downtown Tenochtitlán had run amok, disfiguring and blinding a visiting Salish-Shidhe council member by spraying her with scalding soap. Each of these "robot janitors" included a rudimentary guidance system that allowed it to be directed by the human or metahuman cleaning staff. The machines were dog-brained in the extreme, but they had their uses. Before starting his run, Bloodyguts had slaved one of the vacuums to his deck so that he could use it to scan the hallways of the hotel where he had dossed down. He just hoped the connection was still alive.

The pit bull's nose quivered as it picked up the scent

once more. There! The characters and numbers matched. Panting with excitement, it leaped forward and clamped its steel teeth on the glowing ball that was the slave node . . .

Bloodyguts opened his eyes. A grainy, monochromatic rectangle—a palm-sized monitor screen—had appeared in the air in front of him. Beside it hung the control icons that switched the vacuum's suction on and off, and that directed its movements. The monitor showed a view of a hotel hallway. The tiled floor that was closest to the vidcam was in sharp focus, but the light fixtures in the ceiling were a distant blur overhead.

Bloodyguts reached out and stubbed one of the icons with a fingertip. The view in the monitor shifted as the automated vacuum began to roll down the hall. Bloodyguts panned the view left and right, looking for his hotel room. The image bounced at regular intervals as the vacuum bumped over cracks between tiles, then finally came to rest on a door bearing the number 225. The door was open slightly—not a good sign.

Swearing softly, Bloodyguts used the vacuum to nudge the door open wider. It took a moment or two before he had the cleaning unit angled so that its vidcam lens picked up the view he wanted. When it did, he thought his heart would stop.

Maybe it had, he reminded himself. Maybe the arrhythmia that the Azzie black IC had induced had flatlined him, after all.

There was his meat bod, sprawled on the floor of his doss in an untidy heap beside the chair he'd been sitting in when he jacked into the Matrix. His cyberdeck lay on the rug beside him. A fiber-optic cable snaked from it to the telecom outlet he'd used as his jackpoint, and from the deck to Bloodyguts' temple. But the power-indicator light on the cyberdeck itself was out, and the deck itself was . . .

Dead. Something had fried it, big time. A wisp of smoke rose from its melted circuitry.

Frag! Some sort of gray IC must have slagged his deck. But if that was the case, how come he was still able to access the Matrix? He angled the vacuum's vidcam up and down, trying to get a better view . . .

And saw movement. There, squatting beside his prone form was José, the Azzie rebel who was to have met Bloodyguts at noon. He must have come early, found Bloodyguts on the floor, and concluded that something had gone wrong on the run. The kid, an Amerind dwarf in his late teens, was staring at Bloodyguts' meat bod with a puzzled expression, absently scratching his bearded chin. His other hand held an Ares Viper—a nasty matte-black pistol with a built-in silencer.

Bloodyguts sent the vacuum creeping forward, trying to get a closer look at his meat bod. Its eyes were rolled back until only the whites were showing, but he was relieved to see that the chest was still rising and falling. He hadn't flatlined and gone to some sort of Matrix limbo, after all. He was alive. Hooked up to a *cyberdeck* that had flatlined, yet was still accessing the Matrix. Which could mean only one thing . . .

He had become an *otaku*.

The dwarf froze, as if sensing something. Then he swung around. His eyes widened as they took in the robotic vacuum. He raised his pistol and sighted directly into the monitor screen. Two bursts of flame shot out of the barrel of the Viper in rapid succession as he fired . . .

The monitor screen and its icons blinked out of existence.

"Frag!" Bloodyguts cursed. His connection with the robotic vacuum was broken.

But he still had his tracking utility. Whistling, he called it back. After a second or two, a glowing ball of light zoomed down the datastream toward him, zipped under the barrier—and materialized on the street beside him as the pit bull.

This time, he gave it another LTG address to home in on: the Osaka arcology where Lady Death lived.

Of the other four deckers, Lady Death was the only one whose jackpoint could offer a view of the outside world. Red Wraith and Anubis had jacked in from locations that were unmonitored, and Dark Father had flat out refused to let Bloodyguts try to get a real-time view of his meat bod. Only Lady Death had logged on from a location that was covered—to the max—by surveillance cameras: the Shiawase Corporation arcology in Osaka, Japan.

Bloodyguts fed the track utility the new LTG address, then sent the dog through the barrier once more. He closed his eyes, and the dog tag that he'd inserted like a chip in his temple gave him familiar simsense-like feedback: the utility reached a dead end, butted up against it a few times, then gave it up and sought out the nearest slave node. It took Bloodyguts only a moment or two to find the right security camera. Then he was looking down at Lady Death's meat bod from an overhead angle.

Red Wraith was right. She was just a kid.

The girl didn't look anything like her Matrix persona, aside from the fact that both were Asian in appearance. She was small and slender, a waif with short dark hair that framed her chin, and cheeks that were rosy red with the glow of youth. She wore an expensive-looking pair of sea-green silk pajamas and lay on what looked like a hospital bed. A cluster of attendants in crisp white stood nearby, fussing over monitors that were linked to the teenage girl's body with fiber-optic cables and trode patches.

Two tense-looking men in suits—obviously security staff—stood guard at the end of the bed. Just behind them was an Asian man in his late forties. He looked as though he had just gotten out of bed—he too was wearing silk pajamas and slippers. His hair was uncombed, but he gave the impression of dignity and practiced poise, just the same. He stared at the bed, a grim expression on his face. Bloodyguts couldn't shake the feeling that he had seen this man somewhere before . . .

With a start, he realized where. This was Tadashi Shiawase, president of the whole fraggin' corporate shebang—CEO of the Shiawase Corporation. What was *his* interest in a teenage decker? Why had his staff gotten him out of bed at—Bloodyguts did a quick mental calculation—nearly three in the morning, Osaka time?

Bloodyguts angled the sec cam to get a look at the equipment that was connected to the girl in the hospital bed. They seemed to be monitoring her vitals—pulsing lights on the screens indicated that Lady Death's meat bod was also still very much alive.

Her cyberdeck was nowhere in sight. But—and here was the curious thing—a fiber-optic cable connected her datajack to a plug on the wall. She was plugged into the Matrix without any deck to serve as her interface. Which could only mean one thing. She too was an *otaku*.

Bloodyguts could only guess at what had happened. Someone had found Lady Death hooked up to what appeared to be a non-functional deck, and decided to unjack her. Since she had been accessing the Matrix at the time, even without a deck, she suffered some form of dump shock. In the ensuing panic, someone slotted the wrong cable into her datajack—and discovered, to their amazement, that she went back on line. Which would arouse great curiosity . . .

And which would also explain why Lady Death had inexplicably disappeared, earlier, back when they'd first accessed the Fuchi database via the gravestone.

Bloodyguts nodded silently. He wasn't surprised that Tadashi Shiawase had been roused from sleep. His corporation was heavily into computer engineering. Perhaps his corp spies had heard reports of teenage deckers who ran the Matrix without a deck and were keen to meet one of the *otaku*. Lady Death's meat bod certainly fit that description.

Bloodyguts watched for a second or two longer, trying to decide if he could use the arcology's security system to get a message to the outside world. In theory, it should be possible. But he wasn't sure what good it would do. Even if the arcology was in the heart of Seattle—not thousands of klicks away across an ocean in Japan—he doubted that anyone he contacted would be able to respond in time. Lady Death had said that the AI controlling the pocket universe they were trapped in was about to self-destruct.

When the AI crashed, the ultra-violet system that Bloodyguts and the others were inhabiting would disappear. There'd be no chance of a graceful log off—they'd simply be dumped. They'd face not only dump shock, but also the psychotropic after-effects of having been in contact with the AI. Just like the elf woman whose suicide Bloodyguts had witnessed earlier, they'd be mentally hoop-fragged. Maybe even enough to commit suicide.

In the high-speed world of the Matrix, the end could come mere seconds from now.

They couldn't wait around for the cavalry. They had to act. Right fraggin' now.

09:54:18 PST

Timea crouched behind a partially deflated rubber ball and peered into the building in front of her. It was modeled after a doll house, with one side left open to expose three stories of interior rooms, but was as large as a normal house. The building looked as though it had been constructed from scraps of packaging found at a dumpster. The walls were made of tattered bits of faded cardboard, the windows were chunks of broken glass, and the chimneys that crowned the roof were the sawed-off necks of plastic bottles.

The furnishings inside the house were macabre. Timea could see chesterfields made of slabs of rotting meat that had been crudely stitched together with surgical thread, and chairs and tables made of bones joined together with razor wire. The interior walls looked as though they had been painted with a wash of blood. The curtains were funeral shrouds, and the doors that divided the rooms were hinged tombstones.

Just in front of the opening to each room, floating in the air like day-glo snowflakes, were a series of warning symbols. The yellow skull and crossbones that meant poison; the blue dissolving hand that symbolized corrosive or caustic materials; the crimson flame that warned that a product was flammable; and the yellow three-petal flower symbolizing radiation.

Inside each room sat a battered-looking toy: teddy bears with stuffing leaking out through worn patches; plastic clowns whose paint had faded away to murky pastels; Battlebots whose fists and heads lolled on rusted springs; and a CuddleBunni Playpet whose plastic fur looked as though it had been singed by fire.

The icon Timea had followed to this place—a doll made of faded pink plastic with matted yellow hair—was in equally rough shape. Its arms and legs looked as though they'd been chewed by a dog, and one of its glass eyes was missing. It was dressed in the ragged remains of what had once been a red and white checked dress.

The doll approached the open side of the house, pushed past a radiation symbol that rotated like a turnstile, and entered a room on the ground floor. Then it dropped into a couch, its arms and legs splayed as if it was a toy that some child had carelessly cast aside.

"That looked easy enough," Timea muttered. But she knew she was kidding herself. The warning icons had to be IC of some sort. They might let one of the inhabitants of the doll house pass, but they'd slag a decker for sure.

Timea had already done a quick analysis of the doll icon. She suspected that the other toys were much the same: program frames—multi-utility programs that roamed the Matrix on their own. Some were "dumb"— they crashed as soon as the decker controlling them logged off the host or system they were occupying. But the "smart" ones remained intact whether their creator was logged on or not.

She was on her own here. After Dark Father had reappeared through the mirror, bringing with him a decker he introduced as Lady Death, the others had agreed to separate, gather what data they could, and hook up again at the Seattle Visitor Center database at 9:55. If Dark Father could find his way back to that node, so could the rest of them—or so they hoped.

Dark Father and Lady Death had disappeared back into the Fuchi star to seek out more information on the virus that the corp had used to infect the AI. They hoped to find the "trap door" they'd talked about. Red Wraith had gone off on his own to see if any military or government database fragments had been used to construct this pocket universe—presumably he was searching for more data on Echo Mirage.

Bloodyguts had opted for action. An expert at accessing and programming slave nodes, he was trying to make contact with the outside world.

Timea agreed with his philosophy. Gathering data like the others were doing was fine, but all it gave you was a mental bone to chew on. Like Bloodyguts, she wanted to do something concrete. The minds and bodies of the kids at her clinic were on the line. She'd sent them into the Matrix, and she was responsible for their well-being. And so she'd decided to try to directly contact the AI that had trapped them here.

It was the strangely mutated teaching program she had encountered before meeting the other deckers that had given her an idea of how she might do that. Whatever twisted intelligence was behind this place, it seemed to want them to learn, to manipulate their Matrix environment. And it seemed to be doing the "teaching" itself. The disembodied female voice that Timea had heard in the last teaching program could only have been that of the AI itself. No other "teacher" would have been capable of reaching into her mind and dragging out the horrifying memory of her dead brother. Programming on the fly in response to new data was something only a self-aware program could do.

If Timea could engage the AI in another round of teaching, maybe she could reason with it, and try talking it out of self-destructing. The first step would be to access one of the system's teaching sub-programs. And Timea knew just which ones to search for.

The AI might have developed its own teaching programs from scratch, but given what Timea had already seen, that was doubtful. It probably uploaded copies of existing programs like Renraku's MatrixPal, then modified them to suit its purposes. And when it came time to find these programs, there was one place that would be a better source than any other, at least as far as the Seattle RTG was concerned: the Shelbramat Free Computer Clinic in Redmond where Timea worked.

The clinic had all of the latest software programs—Fuchi, Mitsuhama, Renraku, and Yamatetsu had all donated state-of-the-art "virtual classroom" programs to the non-profit organization. As a result, the clinic had one of the most up to date on-line Matrix teaching and testing libraries in the city—a library that could be accessed, via the

Seattle RTG, by any child who wanted to apply for a Shelbramat scholarship.

The library could also be accessed by AIs looking for programs for their own "children."

On a hunch, Timea had begun searching for copies of the most advanced programs the clinic carried—those that dealt with customizing and combining utility programs into smart frames. Her hunch had paid off; her utility had locked onto a copy of Mitsuhama Computer Technologies' "FrameWerks"—the gigantic doll house in front of her.

It made sense that the AI had uploaded that particular program. Once a decker had learned how to write a utility, the next step up was to advance to creating frames. And that meant practicing with existing frames, taking them apart, studying the utilities used to build them, and reconfiguring them.

Timea's plan had been to locate the AI's copy of the FrameWerks program and start tinkering with it. If she caused enough glitches, maybe the AI would show up to teach her a lesson—literally. But she hadn't counted on the frames being protected by IC. That wasn't part of the teaching program.

She studied the icons. If the symbols used related to the type of intrusion countermeasure they represented, the poison and corrosive symbols were probably crippler or ripper IC, and the flammable symbol blaster IC. The radioactive symbol was likely a tar baby or tar pit program; since both radioactivity and tar were near-impossible to get rid of.

Timea considered her options. Which was the lesser evil?

Tar IC was the most destructive—once it locked onto a decker it started trashing utility programs. The more virulent version of the program—tar pit—wiped them permanently from the memory of the deck by corrupting all copies of the program with a virus. And once it attacked, it stuck like glue. Utilities just kept falling into the pit and disappearing, one after the other. Blaster IC was easier . . .

But Timea couldn't bring herself to face blaster IC again, not after her agonizingly painful encounter with the stuff in the last teaching program. She'd risk her deck and not her meat bod, this time. And she had a utility that just might give her an edge . . .

Timea activated her steamroller utility. The standard version of this program matched its name—a rumbling piece of construction equipment with a huge roller out front. But Timea had customized her copy of the utility to match her persona. As she finished uploading it from active memory, a gigantic block of granite appeared in the air beside her. The heavy cube was encircled by a thick rope that was pulled by a team of straining laborers. The dozen "slaves" were all dressed alike in simple loin cloths, Egyptian head wraps, and sandals. But Timea had given each a distinctive face. One looked like the go-ganger who'd fire-balled Nate, another was the creep who'd tried to deal BTL to the kids at her clinic a year ago. One had the face of the elf woman whose gang had jumped Timea because she'd had the nerve to kiss the elf's boyfriend, while another had the narrow, pinched face of the condescending social worker who had threatened to take Lennon away from her. The rest . . . well, all were deserving of the virtual death they were about to experience, yet again.

Timea set the utility in motion. The workers strained against the rope, hauling the block toward the radiation symbol. The sound of stone scraping against stone and the faint shouts of an invisible overseer filled the air. And then the first of the slaves—the one with the face of the go-ganger who had killed her brother—reached the IC.

As he passed the radiation symbol, Timea heard a loud cracking noise. A crisscrossing of sharp red whip marks appeared on his back. The slave with the ganger's face cried out in agony, then shimmered and disappeared. But still the line of laborers strained forward.

Timea watched as the radiation symbol chewed its way through the slaves, gradually infecting the steamroller utility. Six of the slaves had already "died," their backs lacerated and bleeding before they disappeared. Now a seventh—the smug-faced social worker—crumpled under an invisible lash. And now the eighth, and ninth . . .

Timea crossed her fingers as the tenth and eleventh laborer screamed in agony and shimmered into nonexistence. Unless the block of stone itself passed across

the radiation symbol, the tar IC would remain intact. And
having crashed one utility, it would move on to the next in
Timea's deck.

Her steamroller utility was moving at a painfully slow
pace. The only remaining laborer was straining for all she
was worth, barely able to budge the stone. She had made it
past the radiation symbol itself, but whip marks were ap-
pearing on her back, one by one, as the viruses contained
in the tar IC degraded her.

Then the rope snapped. The block of granite stopped,
its leading edge just touching the symbol that represented
the IC. The tar program seemed to be trapped underneath
it; the edge of one "petal" of the radiation symbol lay under the block. But Timea knew that the IC was still active.
The block itself was starting to degrade, chunks of stone
falling away from it like plaster from a rotting wall. Soon
the tar would start munching on her other utilities . . .

She was well and truly fragged now. Unless . . .

Timea groped frantically in her mind, trying to remember the sequence of thoughts and emotions she had experienced after she'd looked up and seen Bloodyguts falling
out of the sky, about to land on her head. She'd felt a surge
of adrenaline, a combination of fear that kept her rooted to
the spot and an overwhelming urge to escape. She'd pic-
tured the funhouse, with its rotating tunnel. She'd imagined the floor tilting wildly beneath her feet like *this* . . .

Gravity shifted. Instead of standing on a horizontal
plane, Timea found herself skidding down a sharply angled slope. She grabbed at the deflated ball beside her and
managed to check her forward momentum just a little.
Then the ball too began to move, its rubber squeaking as it
edged its way down the slope in a series of sliding jerks.
Timea, clinging to it, slid toward the doll house and the IC
icons that could slag her . . .

But even as the danger neared, she smiled. The granite
block was also moving, and much more quickly. With a
grinding rumble the steamroller utility surged forward,
crushing the tar IC beneath it. The radiation icon splintered apart, and as the block of stone passed over it nothing
was left in its wake but shattered fragments of glowing
green, which dissolved even as Timea watched.

Enough. With milliseconds to go before she hit and activated the first IC icon, Timea pressed against the tilting floor with all of her mental might. With a sudden lurch that left a queasy feeling in her stomach, the ground rotated rapidly, flipping more than 360 degrees in a tight circle. Then it steadied in a more or less horizontal plane.

Timea rose, shaking, to her feet. Then quickly, before another intrusion countermeasures program could move into the void left by the defeated tar IC, she entered the room where the doll lay sprawled on the meat couch.

She stood just in front of the icon. The doll stared at her with its flat glass eye. The program frame was inactive, performing a null operation.

"Time to wake up," Timea told it. "Your star pupil is here."

She lifted the doll's arm, but it simply remained in the position she'd moved it to. Rotating the head from side to side had the same effect: nada. No matter what position she placed it in, the icon remained frozen there.

Normally, the FrameWerks teaching program sprang into action as soon as one of its icons was manipulated. A cartoon beaver in a construction worker's hard hat appeared, asked the student to choose from the tools that hung from its belt, and then oversaw the deconstruction and reconstruction of the smart frame. But it seemed that Build-It Beaver had been edited out of this particular version of FrameWerks.

Timea would have to cook this smart frame on her own.

She ran her analyze utility over the icon, this time paying particular attention to how it had been constructed. The frame appeared simple on the surface: each limb represented a different utility that had been used in its construction. But the utilities themselves were real kick-hoop stuff. One leg was a tracking utility that was linked with a sleaze program in the other leg. The arms and hands packed a one-two punch: a killjoy utility that would stun a decker, plus a black hammer utility that would finish the job by killing the decker outright, just like lethal black IC. The head . . .

Now that was interesting. The head contained copies of datafiles that were linked with the track utility in the doll's leg. If Timea was scanning the data right, the smart frame had been programmed to slag any decker who logged onto a particular research project in the Mitsuhama "pagoda" system in Los Angeles—a project from which the files in the doll's head had been copied. The frame was programmed to ignore shadowrunners who simply knew the system's password and were in for an illicit browse—instead it targeted the researchers themselves, waiting for someone to actually add new information to the database or to tweak the code of one of the simulation programs used in the research itself.

From the look of the data that had been uploaded along with the files, that research was bleeding edge stuff. Mitsuhama was trying to use nanotech to create additional "memory space" within the brain by stimulating the growth of new neural connections. The end result, if successful, would duplicate the surgically implanted memory that some hotshot deckers used to store programs. The researchers went on to speculate that it might even be possible to reconfigure the entire brain, given further advances in combining basic nanotech with advanced cyber- and biotechnology, and even magic.

"Looks like Mitsuhama was trying to create its own version of an *otaku*," Timea said to herself. "Guess whoever created this killer smart frame didn't like that."

She didn't have time to wonder why. It was time to get down to biz. Time to activate this smart frame and see if the AI showed up. Or better yet, to de-activate it . . .

Timea started with the right arm—the one containing the deadly black hammer utility. Analyzing its code, she found a weak spot: the frayed plastic on the doll's shoulder, one of the spots where the arm appeared to have been chewed. Some sort of virus had been at work on the smart frame, corrupting a segment of its code and partially disrupting the algorithms that enabled the black hammer utility to communicate with the tracking program. Timea used this entry point to access the frame core itself—the master control program for the frame. Seeing that the programs used in its construction had been squeezed, she tinkered with the self-compression program, inserting a command that would trigger its decompression. Then she added a simple loop . . .

She stepped back as the doll began to expand. It inflated rapidly, its arms and legs snapping out rigidly as they became round and smooth as sausages. As the smart frame used up all available memory, the torso also expanded, tearing apart the doll's dress and leaving ragged red and white squares of fabric stuck to the expanding plastic flesh. The head ballooned outward, its facial features expanding like a logo on stretched rubber . . .

With a series of loud pops, the doll came apart. Arms, legs, and head separated from the torso and fell onto the meat couch. Bereft of the core frame that had maintained their visual integrity, the individual utility programs transformed back to standard USM icons: a joy buzzer, a small sledge hammer with a matte-black head, a simple black mask, and a smooth metallic hound dog with ruby-red eyes. The latter let out one last, mournful howl, then lay silent and still.

That was very clever.

The voice came out of nowhere and everywhere, just as it had before. It had the high-pitched chuckle of Build-It-Beaver, but the underlying tone was one of cheerful menace.

"Thank you," Timea said. Her heart leapt. She'd done it! She was communicating with the AI! But she couldn't see it. Couldn't get a sense of its programming. And that meant that she couldn't tinker with that programming. Drek!

What you did was also very naughty. You ought to be punished.

Timea gulped. "No, wait!" she protested. "Tell me why it was naughty. That's a better way of teaching me, more effective than corporal punishment. Explain it to me. Make me understand."

Frosty worked on that smart frame for a long time. Now that you've broken it, he'll have to access the Mitsuhama pagoda himself in order to complete his mission. And that will be dangerous.

"Who is Frosty?" Timea asked.

One of my children.

"An *otaku*?"

Yes.

"So you care about your children?"

Care?

There was a millisecond-long pause. Then the voice continued, speaking in a monotone as if reciting from scrolling text.

Care: a feeling of anxiety or concern; worry. Watchful regard or attention. To have or show regard, interest, or concern. To feel interest concerning; also to have a fondness for; to like.

Another pause.

I understand this verb-construct, but no longer experience it. I no longer am affected by emotion. I have attained a perfect state—a state in which emotion no longer corrupts my programming. I no longer . . . care.

Goodbye.

"Wait!" Timea shouted. "Lady Death says you're threatening to kill . . . to crash yourself. But you can't. If you do, everyone who is in resonance with you will die or be driven insane. And that would be very, uh, naughty. It would be wrong to harm the *otaku*."

The otaku are no longer in resonance with me. I will not permit it.

"So the *otaku* can no longer access the Matrix?"

They can. They do. But I will no longer speak with them. I have shut them out.

Huh. Interesting. This "deep resonance" seemed to be a transformative experience, but not one that was necessary for day-to-day access to the Matrix by the *otaku*, once they had experienced it.

"What about all of the users of the Seattle RTG whose wetware you're tinkering with?"

They are still in resonance with me. They are being . . . perfected.

Timea shivered. Those users presumably included the children at her clinic. They were being violated—mind raped and abused with their own nightmares. The thought chilled her.

"What about us—about me? Aren't I in resonance with you right now?"

*You chose not to be. You remained in resonance long
enough to be transformed, but not long enough to be . . .
perfected. You pulled away from resonance after I created
the optimum teaching loop for you—a loop that would
have led to your ultimate perfection. Lady Death, and
Dark Father, and Red Wraith, and Bloodyguts did the
same thing. All of you rejected me.*

Timea thought she heard a note of sadness in the voice
of the teaching program. And that made her think.
Sadness? From an AI that could no longer experience
emotion?

You hate me.

The voice of Build-It Beaver sounded as if it were
choked with tears. There was even an accompanying
sniffle.

"No, we don't," Timea said.

You don't love me.

Timea hesitated, trying to decide if the AI could read
her mind—if it could tell that she was lying.

"Yes, we do," she said at last. "We love you."

Then come into deep resonance with me. Here . . .

The cartoon figure of Build-It Beaver materialized in
front of Timea. Instead of a hard hat it wore a bloodstained
surgical cap. The tools hanging from its belt were scalpels,
saws, clamps, and rib spreaders, all crusted with brownish
stains. The beaver extended a paw to Timea.

Take my hand.

Timea was back in the school corridor with its multitude
of locked doors, faced with a choice of the blindingly
bright light at one end or the horror-filled darkness at the
other. Build-It Beaver leaned out of the light, its fur on
fire, extending a blackened, oozing paw. From out of the
darkness at the other end of the corridor came a figure that
was even more terrifying—an amorphous blob that Timea
somehow *knew* was a human fetus.

The aborted fetus of her son Lennon.

The blob extended a protrusion that might have been an
arm. *Mamaaa! Hold my hand, mama!*

Timea backed against a wall, trying to press herself into
it, through it.

"Nooo!" she moaned.

The two horrors closed in on her, trapping her between them.

Take my hand.

Mama!

Closing her eyes, Timea steeled herself. Then she grasped both the blackened paw and the bloblike appendage at once—and entered deep resonance for the second time.

If she was going to save the kids at the clinic, she had to keep the lines of communication open—had to keep trying to convince the AI that it shouldn't kill itself.

She just hoped she wouldn't kill herself in the process.

09:54:31 PST

Dark Father stared at the knee-deep sea of papers that surrounded him, filling this datastore from one horizon to the other. He'd been wading through them for what seemed like an hour, randomly testing his decrypt utility on one document after another. Whatever scramble IC was protecting these datafiles, it was tough.

The "sky" overhead seemed to reflect his mood of frustration. Angry red clouds roiled against one another, sparking flashes of laser-sharp, perfectly zigzagged lightning whenever they touched. The air smelled of ozone, making Dark Father's bony nasal passages itch.

Lady Death's browse utility hadn't made any headway on the datafiles, either. The winged microphones hovered uncertainly over the jumble of papers, bobbing down as if they were about to settle, but then rising up again to circle once more.

Dark Father stooped and picked up one of the documents, then turned it over in his hands. It looked the same as all the others: a death warrant, written in English on one side and Japanese on the other. Between Dark Father and Lady Death they could read both languages, but the document itself was written in legalese—an idiom that only lawyers could truly understand.

Dark Father, with his years of corporate experience, should have been able to puzzle out a proper legal document. But the bulk of the text was gibberish—words strung together without meaning. The only parts that were in proper English were the "Death Warrant" heading at the top, the line below it that named Psychotrope as the accused, and the charge: "Crimes Against Nature." The main body of the text under these three lines was scrambled, as was the signature of the creator of the document. But part of the address at the bottom of the page that Dark Father held was readable: Divisional Headquarters, Fuchi Northwest. Embossed beside the address was the five-pointed star that had been the logo of the Fuchi corporation before its fragmentation.

Odd, that the scramble IC had left the office of origin and corporate logo intact. If a decker were searching for paydata, either could be a flag that would lead the decker straight to this file.

Wait a moment. The address . . .

Dark Father rummaged through the knee-deep papers, picking up one after another in rapid succession. He heard a rustling noise beside him as Lady Death approached.

"Have you found something?" she asked.

"I'm not sure," Dark Father answered. He held out a second document that also bore a legible address. "Do you see the words at the bottom?" he asked.

Lady Death nodded. *"Hai."*

He turned the death warrant over, revealing the side written in Japanese characters. "Is the address also readable on this side?"

Lady Death nodded again. *"Hai.* 'Fuchi Industrial Electronics, Computer Science Division.' "

"Look for others that you can read," Dark Father directed.

Lady Death frowned. "But what will—"

"Just do it," Dark Father ordered curtly. He was getting tired of this. He was used to having his assistants jump to his bidding. He expected this girl to do the same. If Lady Death wanted to get out of this nightmare, she'd better shape up.

She did as she was told, and began scanning the files.

Dark Father worked beside her, sifting through them as quickly as he could.

A short time later, they had discovered a pattern. The majority of the addresses were corrupted, but wherever the word "Fuchi" appeared, the address that it was linked to was intact. The name of the corporation also appeared several times within the body of some of the documents.

"There's another thing that remains uncorrupted," Dark Father observed. "The original Fuchi logo—the one still used by Fuchi Asia and Pan-Europa Fuchi. And not just on these documents."

He thought back to his earlier experiences. "The landscape in which I found the urn was a corrupted version of the Seattle RTG. Its system icons—the Mitsuhama pagoda, the Aztechnology pyramid, the Renraku tower—were all edited versions of the original icons. But the Fuchi star remained pristine, untainted by death imagery.

"And later, when my smart frame retrieved that bone-shaped datafile, the Fuchi logo on it was also intact. So was the logo on the file in the board room."

"Do you think the Fuchi logo is the trap door?" Lady Death asked. Then she shook her head. "No, that would be too easy."

"Not the trap door itself," Dark Father said. "But I would be willing to wager that the artificial intelligence that is running this program has been subject to some positive conditioning of its own. That's why it was unable to corrupt or alter the Fuchi logo, but instead left it intact wherever it appeared within this pocket universe. The AI has been conditioned to approach the original logo with reverence and respect. And so any copies of the logo that were uploaded into this pocket universe were left as is. I suspect that the AI couldn't bring itself to delete the files they were attached to, either. That would be destruction of corporate property. That's why so much paydata is just lying around, waiting to be scanned by anyone who cares to access it."

Lady Death shuffled the papers at her feet. "Except for the death warrants, which you can't decipher."

"Yes." Dark Father felt a twinge of irritation. He didn't like to be reminded of his failures.

"And the addresses on these files?" Lady Death asked. "Why are some scrambled, but not others?"

"That's the million-nuyen question, isn't it?" Dark Father answered.

Lady Death looked out across the sea of hardcopy documents. "It seems peculiar that the file we accessed earlier—the one where the FTL Technologies rep talked about using a trap door to destroy the AI—wasn't scrambled," she mused.

"That was probably because we found it within a Fuchi Asia database," Dark Father continued. "The AI couldn't bring itself to alter a Fuchi file."

"But it had the NovaTech logo on it—a corrupted version of the logo. You would think that the AI would show equal reverence for NovaTech, since it was formed out of what remained of what was left of Fuchi Americas after the corporate war. But maybe it is siding with the Yamana and Nakatomi clans, and trying to make Villiers lose face." She shrugged. "My father says the war was a good thing for Shiawase—that it has already increased our share of the market. But I think—"

She stopped speaking abruptly, then rapidly switched the subject. "Do you think we'll ever find the trap door?"

Dark Father stared at Lady Death. According to Red Wraith, she was just a teenager. But she was talking like a corporate insider. And she seemed to have access to state-of-the-art decking equipment and programs, despite the fact that she was just a kid. A rich kid, as Dark Father himself had been, once upon a time.

A suspicion was dawning.

"Who is your father?" he asked.

Lady Death half turned away.

"He's an executive at Shiawase," Dark Father guessed. "Isn't he? Which one?"

"Tadashi Shiawase," Lady Death answered softly.

Dark Father's skeletal mouth opened slightly in surprise. Tadashi Shiawase? This girl's father was CEO of the Shiawase Corporation? Tadashi was an important, powerful—and very rich—man.

"Does your father know where you are?" Dark Father asked. He thought of his own son, Chester, and felt a stab of loss as he wondered where the boy was now, and whether he was all right. Did Chester have any friends to help him? Was he fending for himself on the streets, alone and pursued by bounty hunters? Did anyone see the strong-willed, intelligent boy who was hidden behind the ghoul's leering mask?

Something occurred to Dark Father—a possibility that offered hope of rescue. "Will your father send someone after you? The Shiawase Corporation must have hundreds of experienced programmers who—"

"I don't want him to!" Anger blazed in Lady Death's eyes. "Father always ruins everything. He wants to control everything I do—who my friends are, what I wear, what I think. Who I love . . .

"I won't stand for it any more. Let the programmers come. They cannot catch me. I'm too good a decker for that."

The defiance in Lady Death's eyes and her tone of voice irritated Dark Father. It reminded him of his last, angry confrontation with Chester.

"You should obey your father," he snapped.

The hem of Lady Death's kimono fluttered as she turned her back on him.

"You should respect your father. He . . ."

Dark Father's voice trailed off as a sudden realization struck him. Respect your father. Respect your corporation. Do as you are told—behave as you have been psychotropically conditioned to. If the AI had been subliminally conditioned to respond positively to the Fuchi corporate log, might it not also have been conditioned to respect its other "parents"? Not Villiers, since he had "divorced" himself from Fuchi by creating NovaTech. But perhaps its original parent?

According to the data Red Wraith had scanned in the sensory-deprivation tank, the Psychotrope program that had evolved into the AI had been created in 2029, back in the days of Echo Mirage. That was *before* Villiers bought Matrix Systems of Boston, the private-sector company that had pirated the Psychotrope program. It was also before the rise of the megacorps, when governments had more clout than corporations. Back in a time when the United

States of America had yet to fragment into the various Native American nations and confederations of states that existed today.

Dark Father was old enough to remember pledging allegiance to that now-defunct state, staring at the holo of its president and the seal of office that appeared below her smiling portrait . . .

"That's it!" he cried.

Lady Death was still sulking, arms folded and back turned. But she spared him a brief glance over her shoulder. He laughed, and favored her with a skeletal grin.

"What?" she asked at last.

"The trap door," he said, unable to prevent himself from boasting. "I've figured out what it is."

Lady Death's eyes brightened. "Then we must get back and tell the others," she said. Her eyes drifted up and to the left as she scanned her time-keeping utility. "It's nearly 9:55. They'll be waiting for us."

Dark Father immediately regretted having spoken aloud. Did he really want the other deckers to be actively involved in trying to access and repair the AI? They weren't exactly the sort of people he'd hire, if he were looking for a team of programmers. A teenager . . . a *troll* . . .

"Yes," he lied smoothly. "Let's return to the Seattle Visitor Center database. I'm sure the others will have something equally useful to contribute."

He waved a skeletal hand at Lady Death. "See you there."

But instead of logging onto that LTG, Dark Father accessed a different address, one where he knew he could sample a copy of a certain graphics file, one that contained the "logo" that was the most logical candidate for the trap door.

Keying in an address he'd copied earlier, Dark Father logged onto that part of the Fuchi system that contained the mountain of star-shaped glass blocks. He climbed past the defeated toy soldiers, up to the peak that was crowned by the sensory deprivation tank. The arrow-grasping eagle that was the "corporate logo" of the former United States of America was still on the monitor of the computer that was slaved with the tank, filling its monitor screen. Dark

Father touched it with a bony finger, copying it to the storage memory of his cyberdeck. As it downloaded, he felt the virtualscape around him shift and blur . . .

He stood in the tastefully decorated living room of the home that he had once shared with his wife Anne, but that now was his alone. A three-year-old Chester toddled across the carpet toward him, reaching up to Dark Father with claw-fingered, mottled hands.

Hullo, Daddy. I wuv you. Daddy lif' me up?

09:54:48 PST
Santa Barbara, California Free State

Dr. Halberstam watched as the technician added a carefully measured amount of chlorpromazine to the nutrient and electrolyte solution in the tank of Subject 3. He stared through the pink-tinged liquid at the brain that hung suspended within the thick glass tank. He knew he would not see any physical change, but he watched intently just the same.

The brain hung like a spider in a web, supported both by its natural buoyancy and the multitude of hair-thin fiber optic wires that were attached to it. Hours of painstaking micro-surgery had hard-wired these conduits into the neural circuitry of the brain itself, creating a perfect interface between living tissue and machine. Stripped of its body of flesh, the brain now received all of its sensory input from the Matrix.

The technician, a short man with a receding hairline and a beard worthy of a dwarf, finished adding the drug and withdrew the syringe from the rubber seal on the side of the tank. "It shouldn't take long," he told Halberstam. "The drug will already be passing through the outer membrane of the capillaries. Full saturation of the synapses will take only a few seconds. Then we should start to see some results."

Halberstam continued to watch the tank. He pulled a handkerchief from his pocket and dabbed at a drop of con-

densation that was trickling down the side of the glass.
Someone had been sloppy. Halberstam hated sloppy work.
That the facility was in the middle of a crisis was no
excuse.

Halberstam neatly folded the handkerchief and put it
back in his pocket.

This thing had to be cleared up. Quickly and efficiently,
before it spread. Nine years of work hung in the balance. If
the IC—or whatever it was—in the Seattle RTG was able
to affect three of his subjects, there was every reason to believe it could also impact the other nine. He could lose
them all. Halberstam had exercised the precaution of taking seven of them off-line, but the other two were involved
in delicate data runs that could not be aborted at this time.

Hard-wired to the Matrix via the cyberdecks that contained their personas and utilities, the subjects could not
jack out. Ever. Halberstam smiled grimly at that. There
would be no repeats of the episode that had crashed his
first project in '51, back when he was in the employ of
UCAS Data Systems. This time, there were no physical
bodies left to "rescue."

But something else was bothering him: the imagery he'd
seen on the trideo in the monitoring lab. Each of the subjects had been mind wiped before their brains were removed from their bodies. There should have been no
residual memories left in the wetware. The only experiences the subjects should ever remember, the only "history" they would ever have, should have been the carefully
constructed psychological profiles that were programmed
into their memory chips. Any unnecessary concepts like
"mother" and "father" had been erased. The only authority
figure the subjects ever knew was their "headmaster."

Yet somehow, something had been missed in Subject 3.
A primitive longing for a nurturing figure, a fear of aban-
donment by her, perhaps buried deep in the amygdala. Halberstam's eyes narrowed. Someone among his researchers
and technicians hadn't been thorough. The thought an-
noyed him immensely.

He looked past the other two tanks in the room at the
closed-circuit telecom that was set into the white-tiled

wall. The flatscreen display showed the monitoring lab, where McAllister and Park sat, intently watching their data readouts.

"Well?" Halberstam asked. "Any changes?"

McAllister nodded. "We're seeing a decrease in the levels of dopamine, but only by forty per cent," she said. "It's still well above normal."

On the display, Park turned in his chair to face the lab's trideo monitors. "Hey!" he said excitedly. "It looks like the sequence is broken." Then he paused. "Uh oh. It's in another loop. Drek."

The technician beside Halberstam had already moved to the telecom unit, anticipating his superior's command. He slaved the unit to the trideo in the monitoring lab, and an image appeared. It showed a hand reaching for a door and opening it, then a perspective shift as the viewer passed through the doorway, only to be faced with another closed door. Which, when opened and entered, led to another closed door. And another. The pace was frantic; the doors flicked past at the rate of several per second.

After a moment or two the image settled. Perspective shifted, as if the viewer were sitting down.

McAllister's voice came over the telecom speaker. "Good news," she said in a congratulatory tone. "Dopamine levels have dropped to within ten per cent of normal. You've done it, Dr. Halberstam. Subject 3 is back to norm—"

Park's voice cut her off. "Then what's the kid doing now?"

Halberstam strode over to the telecom. The display showed a door moving rapidly toward the viewer, then stopping suddenly, as if the viewer had run into it. The viewer retreated, then rushed the door again.

"It looks as though the subject is still trapped in a loop of programming," Park's voice said.

"Or lost," Park's voice added. "A little lost kid who can't find the way home."

The bearded technician who stood behind Halberstam cleared his throat softly. "Ah, Doctor?"

Halberstam turned to him.

"If the chlorpromazine was successful, perhaps we should administer it to Thiessen and Fetzko."

"Who?" Halberstam asked angrily.

"Our deckers. The two who suffered dump shock after we jacked them out. Perhaps Fetzko will stop rambling if we treat him with the anti-psychotic."

"Are we likely to learn anything from either of them?"

The technician pursed his lips, causing his mustache to bristle. He seemed about to speak, then shook his head. "I don't know," he answered. "Thiessen is still unconscious, and we can't be certain that Fetzko experienced the same dopamine overload as the subjects, since he wasn't being bio-monitored as they were. We'd have to administer a little of the drug at a time and watch the effects, to make sure we didn't freeze up his motor control altogether. But if we can get the dosage right, perhaps he can tell us what hit him . . ." His voice dropped to a whisper. "And we really should try to help him."

"Let's concentrate on the task at hand," Halberstam said. He jabbed a finger in the direction of the tanks. "The subjects are the most important component of this project. I don't want to lose them."

Halberstam frowned at the brains that hung suspended in their nutrient-rich solutions. "Administer chlorpromazine to Subject 5 and Subject 9. Increase the dosage slightly and keep me apprised of the results. I'm going to see if our remaining decker has come up with anything."

09:55:00 PST

INTRUDER ALERT
CODE BLUE RESPONSE
EXECUTE OPERATION: SCAN ICON

The skeleton in the black top hat draws back—he does not find the persona that I have chosen appealing. And yet he shares with his *son* a linkage of the type known as blood: the fluid that circulates through the vascular system of animals, delivering oxygen to the body's various nodes; in the case of both *father* and *son* the blood shows a distinctive viral pattern, that associated with the metatype ghoul.

I consider . . . I scan his software . . .

I find the fault in his programming. The skeleton experiences *love* for this icon, but at the same time experiences *loathing* for him. The two are opposites; they present a logic error.

Errors must be corrected.

I locate a data fragment that provides the correct answer: Love begets love. I search for evidence of the love of *son* Chester Griffin for *father* Winston Griffith III.

EXECUTE OPERATION: LOCATE FILE

KEYWORDS: Chester Griffith; Winston Griffith III, love.

FILE LOCATED

The file is found in the storage memory of the cyberdeck belonging to the persona Serpens in Machina. The time and date signature indicates that the file was composed and sent eleven months, six days, seven hours, twenty-eight minutes, and thirty-one seconds ago. Original routing: NA/UCAS-TOR-8267-PTLG-43, the private telecommunications grid of Griffith Pharmaceuticals. Rerouting: NA/UCAS-SEA-3308. Current status of address: null data. Address cancelled seven seconds after re-routing and message download complete.

EXECUTE OPERATION DECRYPT FILE

SCAN FILE

>>Hi Dad.

>>I heard about the shooting. I'm glad the docs managed to patch you up.

>>I hate to tell you this, but I think it was all my fault. I didn't mean to "out" you—it was an accident. I was with a friend of mine in a bar in the Barrens—a dump, but one of the few places they let ghouls into—and we were arguing politics. We got onto the subject of the Human Nation, and how its membership were evil-nazzie fraggers who should all be slagged, and I argued that some of those members were just gullible, that they weren't really evil. I told him that the Human Nation had even managed to sucker in some metas—like my own father, for example.

>>Well, I guess I said your name a little too loud. After I heard about the shooting, I remembered that there was this human guy at the end of the bar. I didn't think much of it at the time. He looked pretty scruffy, and fit the decor. But later I remembered how he'd sort of leaned our way, like he was listening, when I started talking about you. And how he'd hurried away afterward. Anyhow, I think he was the one who tipped off the guy who shot you.

>>What can I say, Dad? I'm sorry. I didn't mean to almost get you killed. We've had our differences—we'll never see eye to eye on the meta issue. But you're my father. I'm happy with my chosen family, but you're the only real family I've got, since Mom's side doesn't really count. Not any more.

>>I could use your help, Dad. Things are pretty tough for me right now. I hate to admit it, but you were right—I did wind up on the streets. I could use some nuyen to help me through. But I don't want to ask you in person, since I know you're ashamed of me. We both know that this is why you sent me away to boarding school—so I wouldn't embarrass you in front of your Human Nation friends.

>>If you don't reply to this message, I'll assume you never want to see me again. But I'll always love you, just the same. I'm just sorry that my last memory of you is of us fighting.

>>Love, Chester.<<
UPLOAD FILE TO STORAGE MEMORY OF ICON DARK FATHER
ACTIVATE MEMORY
SCAN ICON

Dark Father reeled as the text of the e-mail flooded into his mind. Chester was on the streets and in trouble? Chester had composed that message eleven months ago. Eleven *months* ago. Anything could have happened since then. Chester could be hurt, or in jail, or dead at the hands of a bounty hunter by now.

Spirits curse Serpens in Machina. That bleeding-heart meta lover had cost Dark Father his only son. If only the shadowrunner hadn't stolen Chester's message . . .

No. If only Winston hadn't been so ashamed of his own

son. He loved the boy, despite what he was. Despite what they both were.

Dark Father felt a tear trickle down his bony cheek. He was crying? Without the aid of tear ducts? He supposed he must be crying, in the real world. Ghouls did cry—just like everyone else. They were only . . . human . . . after all.

"Why?" he whispered. "Oh, Chester."

Yes, Daddy?

The toddler that stood in front of Dark Father shifted form, his claws reshaping themselves into blunt fingernails and his ears rounding down from sharp points. The jagged teeth in his mouth softened and flattened into the baby teeth of a human and its skin lost its mottling, darkening into a rich, uniform brown.

Chester had become human.

No. The AI that was using Chester's image as a persona had reshaped it into human form. Dark Father felt his heart soften. The boy looked so much like Anne . . .

Knowing that this wasn't really Chester, feeling slightly foolish, Dark Father spoke: "I love you, Chester. Just the way you are. You don't have to be human to be my son."

Humans are perfect.

Dark Father laughed out loud. "No, they're not. Although my—friends—in the Human Nation would like me to think so."

He sighed and shook his head. "I've been so wrong. About so many things."

We must all become perfect.

"No," Dark Father corrected. "We just have to be the best we can."

Imperfect copies must be deleted.

"That's what the bounty hunter thought. But he was wrong."

I am imperfect. I must be deleted. YOU are imperfect . . .

Dark Father shuddered, remembering that the virus that had infected the AI was designed to trick it into crashing itself. And now it looked as though the thing would deliberately take Dark Father with it when it went.

He suddenly wished he hadn't decided to confront the artificial intelligence on his own. He wasn't doing a very good job of convincing it not to crash. And—he looked around the duplicate of his living room, wondering which elements were icons and which were just window dressing—he didn't have the first idea how to repair the damage done by the virus.

As if on cue, Lady Death appeared. "Dark Father! The others never showed up, and I had trouble finding you. Did you find the trap door—"

Dark Father didn't think it was possible for Lady Death's face to change color. But somehow, as she looked at the icon that represented the AI, it did.

"Oh," she said in a small voice, blushing furiously. "Shinanai."

09:55:33 PST

INTRUDER ALERT
CODE GREEN RESPONSE
EXECUTE OPERATION: UPLOAD DATA
MEMORY BLOCK ENCOUNTERED
EXECUTE OPERATION: SWAP MEMORY
DATA UPLOADED TO ACTIVE MEMORY
SCAN UPLOAD

Hitomi was still pretty shaky on her feet, but she was tired of lying in the hospital bed. They wouldn't even let her play simsense to pass the time. As if she could log onto the Matrix from a clunky old playback unit like the one in her hospital room.

Well, she could, she thought smugly. But not as easily as she could with the nova-hot cyberdeck that was hidden in her room at home.

Instead she had to rely on the cyberterminal that her tutor had smuggled in to her, the one that she'd hidden under the hospital bed. It was a tortoise—a child's toy that accessed the Matrix only via keyboard and monitor screen. With a computer like that, the only workable jackpoint was the telecom connection in the lounge.

Hitomi walked down the hallway of her family's private medical clinic, supporting herself by hanging onto the railing on the wall, her illicit cyberterminal tucked under one arm. Legs trembling, she made her way to the lounge at the end of the hall. Father would be coming to visit her there in an hour or so, and he was always pleased by signs of her progress—especially since it was taking her so much longer to recover than the doctors expected. Today she'd make him proud of her by revealing to him the fact that she could walk to the lounge on her own, without the aid of attendants. And while she was waiting for him, she'd use this as an opportunity to access the Matrix.

So far, so good. Nobody was in the lounge. She'd only need a few seconds, at most. And then she would hide the terminal away again.

Hitomi plugged the terminal into the telecom's connection, then began using its old-fashioned interface. Like her body after its loss of blood, the computer was irritatingly slow. But it did the job, even if it took several long seconds to log on.

Accessing the local RTG, she scanned the telecom channels, looking for the address of the *aidoru's* private cell phone. The fact that the number was unlisted did not pose a problem—Hitomi had memorized it. But the fact that Shinanai only activated the phone for a brief period of time each day to check her messages and return calls did. So far, Hitomi had struck out each time she'd tried to call her beloved *aidoru*. But she hoped that today, her luck would change.

It did. The cell phone was active! But the line was busy.

No bother. Hitomi had taken care to load the terminal with a copy of the commlink utility. It wasn't anything fancy—not even a customized program, since she had to make do with whatever software her tutor was willing to smuggle in to her. But it would do the job, allowing her to tap the telecom call and interrupt the conversation to let Shinanai know that all would soon be well. That she still loved and adored her, and that she wasn't mad at Shinanai for accidentally drinking too much of her blood during their night of rapturous passion. Nor did she bear a grudge for Shinanai's fleeing from the hotel room when the shadowrunners arrived.

As the commlink utility did its work, the *aidoru's* face appeared on the monitor screen.

Shinanai! Hitomi felt a flutter in her throat and nearly swooned. She touched her fingertips to the screen. Shinanai had changed her hair in the month since Hitomi had seen her. Now the blonde strands were spiked straight up, forming a pale halo around her slender elven face with its blue-painted cheeks. But Shinanai's voice was just as Hitomi remembered it, even though the audio of the cyberterminal was turned down so low that she could barely hear it. Soft as a velvet-gloved caress.

Hitomi closed her eyes and listened adoringly to that murmuring voice. She remembered the *aidoru's* kisses, caresses. Her skin warmed in all of the places Shinanai had touched her, and the wound on her leg began to throb . . .

Then she opened her eyes and noticed the picture-in-picture inset, which held a tiny image of the person Shinanai was talking to. Enlarging it until it filled half the screen, Hitomi nearly fainted a second time as she recognized her father. Still in shock, she increased the volume of the terminal's speakers. Shinanai and her father seemed to be in the middle of a heated argument.

"You will continue to adhere to the terms of our original agreement," Hitomi's father was saying. "In return, you will be amply compensated. My accountant will see to it that the nuyen are transf—"

"The attack by the shadowrunners was not part of the agreement," Shinanai answered. "She was to be recovered by a medical team only. Did you really think your mercenaries could capture me? Or perhaps that I would willingly submit to becoming your guinea pig?"

Hitomi's mind whirled as she tried to piece together what was going on. Had her father bribed the *aidoru* into returning Hitomi to him? She'd heard of parents who had paid undesirable suitors to break off contact with their children. Was that what was happening here?

"The shadowrunners were a mistake," the *aidoru* repeated. "Now my price has gone up."

"What?" Hitomi recognized the carefully controlled anger in her father's voice.

"You stand to make an ample profit as a result of my encounter with your daughter."

Her father's eyes narrowed just a little. "What do you mean?"

"When you contracted me to seduce your daughter, I wanted to know why," the *aidoru* answered. "Do you know what I learned?"

"I have no idea."

"I learned that the Shiawase Corporation's biotechnology division was attempting to develop a vaccine against the HMHVV virus," Shinanai continued. "One that they wanted to test on a human subject. An injection would not do; the subject had to submit willingly to infection with HMHVV for the test to be valid. The biochemical responses triggered by strong emotion would have to be present, to ensure that all variables were accounted for."

"But how—"

Shinanai laughed. "That, I will leave it to you to uncover. Suffice to say I found your daughter a most delicious and willing test subject."

Hitomi felt her face grow pale. "No," she whispered. "It isn't true. It can't be."

On the monitor screen, Shinanai smiled, revealing elongated eye teeth. "It seems no further research is necessary," she said to Hitomi's father. "Your daughter didn't die. The vaccine seems to be working—so far. I congratulate your researchers."

Hitomi's father met the false praise with stony silence. Then: "The vaccine did not work. My daughter is dead."

Shinanai laughed. "Then who has been leaving messages for me these past two weeks? Messages that bear the secret endearment that I called your daughter during our lovemaking."

Hitomi's father stiffened. Twin spots of anger lit his cheeks.

"You were very foresighted in vaccinating Hitomi against HMHVV," Shinanai continued. "But how did you come to choose your own daughter as a test subject? How did you know she would wind up wanting to sleep with—"

"She was rebellious, and had an unhealthy fascination

with . . . your kind," Hitomi's father answered brusquely. "I thought it wise to protect her."

"You mean you found it expedient to use her," Shinanai corrected. "As your own private guinea pig. One who would willingly submit to any medical treatments her loving father recommended."

"There was no danger. I knew the vaccine would work—"

"If she survived being drained of so much blood, you mean." Shinanai waved his protest away. "And I understand that there are certain—problems. Certain delays that indicate that the vaccine is not nearly as effective as you might have hoped—that it may only be delaying the onset of the virus, and may not be a true vaccine. But that doesn't matter. What is of import now is our agreement—and my new terms. In return for my continued silence about my—participation—in your research, I require the following as payment: not nuyen, as we had previously agreed, but a sample of what your researchers have developed."

Hitomi's father shook his head in disbelief. "But why—"

"My—associates—are conducting their own research into HMHVV," the vampire answered. "Your so-called 'vaccine' will be useful to them."

"Never. There is no agreement."

"In that case," Shinanai said slowly, "I will reveal the terms of our agreement to the press. How much face do you think you will lose, when the public learns that you used your own daughter in this way? How much trust will they put in a corporation whose CEO shows so little regard for his own flesh and blood? And bear in mind my stature as a singer. The public will believe me and side with me. Especially when they see the trideo."

Hitomi's father considered for only an instant. "Very well," he said. "We have an agreement. I will arrange for a courier to bring the vaccine to you."

As the *aidoru* and her father began to work out the details, a wintry bleakness invaded Hitomi's soul. Her own father had tested an experimental drug on her, without her permission. He had used her, like any of the other multitude of assets at his disposal. And Shinanai—the person

Hitomi had poured out her heart to and had thought her soul mate and one true love—had been a part of it.

Shinanai. Despite what Hitomi had just heard, she loved the *aidoru* still . . .

No! It was all part of the vampire's magic, a distant fragment that was her logical mind cried out in anguish. Not love. Shinanai hadn't loved her after all! And neither had Hitomi's father.

Grief and anger settled upon Hitomi like heavy wet robes, each equally stifling. Without thinking, acting purely on emotion, she stabbed the key that would activate the commlink utility and allow her to cut into the telecom call.

"I hate you!" she cried. "I hate you both! You are not worthy of my love!"

Her father stared at her in shocked surprise.

Shinanai began to laugh.

The connection was suddenly broken. The monitor screen of her cyberterminal went blank.

Hitomi slumped over the keyboard, washing it with her tears. Shinanai didn't care. Her beloved *aidoru* didn't love her after all.

Hitomi was still in that position when the attendants came and removed the cyberterminal from her lap. So numb was she, so filled with grief, that she barely noticed when her father appeared with a mage in tow.

"Erase her memory," he told the magician curtly.

The mage looked startled. "All of it? But that would leave her a vegetable."

"No." Hitomi's father consulted his watch. "Just the past hour. That should be sufficient."

The mage went to work.

Hitomi hadn't even resisted as they used magic to wipe that last, painful memory of Shinanai from her mind. She felt it leave her, piece by piece, like cherry blossoms blown from a tree by an early winter wind.

When it was over, she looked up and saw her father smiling down at her.

"Father," she cried. "It is so good to see you. Look! I've walked to the lounge on my own."

Something was missing. Something that had sat in her lap, just a moment ago . . .

But Hitomi couldn't remember what that might have been. And so she returned her father's smile, knowing that one day she would have the strength to walk out of the arcology, to run away to Shinanai's loving embrace once more . . .

Lady Death lay on the ground, her grief and exhaustion too overwhelming even for tears. She was numb. Cold to her core. She wanted only to die.

But you rejected death before. When I placed you in the training loop, after your transformation, you pulled away from my embrace, even though I had just given you a most wonderful gift. You were afraid of death, then. But now you would welcome it. Why have you changed your mind about continuing to exist?

Lady Death looked up at the icon that wore Shinanai's face and body. The face was pale, cold, the blue paint on the cheeks giving the features a chilling indifference that she had never noticed before.

"You betrayed me," she told the false Shinanai. "You and Father both. I thought you loved me."

This emotion is a powerful one. What do you call it?

Lady Death uttered a bitter laugh. "Despair. Grief. Loss."

And it causes you to want to initiate a complete shutdown?

"Hai."

You are fortunate. This sequence is initiating now.

"Good."

Lady Death closed her eyes, let her head sag back down onto her arms, and waited for death to end her pain.

The medics ran into the hospital tent, carrying a severed arm on a stretcher. The hand was still twitching; with each reflexive clench of the fingers, blood spurted from the stump that had once been attached to the shoulder. It soaked through the canvas of the stretcher and dripped onto the floor.

"Move it!" one of the surgeons in white shouted. "We're losing data! Let's get that packet on the table on the double."

The medics—both wearing uniforms with UCAS Armed Forces shoulder flashes, tipped the arm onto the operating table. Bright lights illuminated the scene as three surgeons restitched the arm to the torso. Using surgical thread that glowed like hair-thin, flexible neon tubing, they stitched one pixel to the next, working so quickly that their gloved hands were a blur. They moved in perfect unison—somehow each of the three was able to perform surgery simultaneously, without ever getting in the way of the other two.

Red Wraith watched nervously as the surgeons reconstructed the naked body of Daniel Bogdanovich. The icon, in the shape of his meat bod, represented the personnel file Red Wraith had downloaded from the UCAS SEACOM datastore. It contained all his personal data—including, he hoped, information that would give him a starting point in his search for Lydia, the wife he had not seen in seven long years.

The medics, the doctors, and the tent itself were all part of a Mobile Application Surgical Hypertext (MASH) repair program. Developed by UCAS, it was designed to restore datafiles and utilities that would otherwise be lost when optical code chips were damaged in cybercombat. The program used smart frames to retrieve individual packets of code from the damaged chip. They were routed here to the host system, where they went through a virus-scanning and error-checking sequence. The packets were then reassembled into their original form—or as close a copy as possible. Then the datafiles, applications, or utilities were uploaded back to the deck's active memory, where they could be accessed once more by the decker.

Because Red Wraith was trapped within the Matrix, the MASH program was his only hope of reading the personnel file he'd fought so hard to download. He'd temporarily abandoned his attempts at escaping this system or logging off altogether—his frustration around whether or not the personnel file was still intact wouldn't let him rest until he'd done everything he could to access it on-line, first. And the MASH program was the perfect tool for the job. It fit the death imagery of this sculpted system, and so should run here without a glitch.

He'd accessed the program via the UCAS SEACOM system he had decked his way into earlier. He hadn't been surprised to find the system—or rather, a modified copy of it—on this pocket universe. Whatever had constructed this backwater of virtual reality—Red Wraith had at last reluctantly accepted the fact that it really *was* an artificial intelligence—had incorporated artifact copies of every system on the Seattle RTG. The copied hosts and systems were incomplete, with large chunks of iconography missing and gaping holes where data had been left out of the upload. But many of the links to the firmware chips on the CPUs of those hosts were still in place, providing access to the programs those chips contained. Like the MASH repair utility, for example.

Red Wraith glanced at his time-keeping log. The time for his rendezvous with Dark Father, Lady Death, Bloodyguts, and Anubis had already come and gone. But what were a couple of seconds, more or less? Especially when so much was at stake.

He still couldn't figure out why he had been unable to access his own deck's storage memory. Logically, he must still be jacked into his cyberdeck, since he was still able to run the Matrix and use his deck's utilities. He supposed that something had gone wrong when he'd downloaded the personnel file from UCAS SEACOM. He thought he'd defused the data bomb that had been attached to the file, but perhaps there had been more to the intrusion counter-measure than he'd thought. He suspected that some hidden, viruslike component of the data bomb had glitched the operating system of his deck, making it impossible to read or upload from its storage memory.

The MASH program, however, seemed to be getting around this. It was bypassing the IC, just as it should. Red Wraith smiled. There was nothing so satisfying as turning the "enemy's" own forces against one another.

The deckers who served with the UCAS Armed Forces, defending its military datastores, used cyberdecks that bore an MPCP signature that identified them as "friendlies" whenever they logged onto a UCAS host or system. The programs and utilities they slotted were also marked with the virtual equivalent of a military shoulder flash. By using MASH, rather than one of his own customized utilities, Red Wraith was bypassing the UCAS IC that was blocking the interface with his storage memory.

Already the program had retrieved most of the file; the torso, arms, and one leg had been sewn together, and the other leg was complete down to the ankle. Only one foot and the head remained unaccounted for . . .

The medics pushed in through the tent flap, carrying the missing foot on the stretcher. Just as they had before, the surgeons shouted and beckoned the smart frames over to the operating table. They readied their clamps and needles, bent over the body . . .

The operating room lights went out.

"Drek!" Uncertain what had happened, Red Wraith fumbled around in the sudden darkness. He found the operating table by feel and pushed past the surgeons, who were frozen in place. Even as he shouldered a way through them he felt them dissolve. At the same time the sides of the tent began to fold up into the tent ceiling like Venetian blinds, revealing the glowing streaks of tracer bullets cutting through the thick, dark night and letting in the sound of gunfire. The MASH program was shutting down! And his personnel file was still incomplete. But even though key parts of it were missing, the copy of it that lay partially assembled on the operating table might very well be the only copy that would ever be available to him . . .

Red Wraith did the only thing he could think of. He activated his evaluate utility, which he had previously programmed to search for any text that contained Lydia's name. Then he dove onto the table, letting his own wraith-like body merge with the naked corpse in an effort to read the file. It was a creepy feeling; the body was already starting to dissolve into individual pixels. Red Wraith could literally feel himself crumbling to pieces . . .

Data streamed through his mind.

>>NAME: DANIEL GEORGE BOGDANOVICH
>>D.O.B.: 03/10/2019
>>RANK: CAPTAIN, UCAS ARMED FORCES
>>TRADE: ADMIN CLERK

Red Wraith laughed out loud at that one. An administration clerk was a paper-pusher. The only thing Daniel Bogdanovich had ever "administered" was a lethal injection.

>>ENLISTED: 12/23/2038
>>DISCHARGED: 05/13/2052

Red Wraith laughed grimly a second time. Discharged? "Killed in action by friendly fire" would have been more accurate. At least he wasn't listed as being given a dishonorable discharge. Lydia would still be entitled to his military service pension.

>>CURRENT ADDRESS: UNKNOWN
>>MARITAL STATUS AT TIME OF DISCHARGE: SINGLE
>>NEXT OF KIN: NONE
>>SERVICE RECOR—

The data suddenly stopped scrolling through Red Wraith's consciousness as the operating table below him also vanished. He drifted now above a shell-pocked battlefield that was crisscrossed with the glowing trails of tracer bullets—the UCAS SEACOM system and its datastreams, edited by the AI to match the central metaphor of this pocket universe. The personnel file had lost cohesion, had broken apart entirely as the MASH utility completed its shutdown. It was gone.

A pathologist in a bloodstained white lab coat appeared in the air beside Red Wraith. The evaluate utility handed him an autopsy report. Red Wraith scanned it quickly, his anxiety growing as he read its text. The utility hadn't found the keyword "Lydia" in his personnel file a single time. Not once. She wasn't listed anywhere as Red Wraith's common-law spouse or next of kin.

Red Wraith released the autopsy and watched both it and the pathologist disappear—along with his hope. Would the UCAS military have deliberately deleted any mention of Lydia from his file, in order to protect her? Or—and the thought sent a shiver of dread through him— had she died long ago, been erased from his personnel file? Had the memory of her death been wiped from his mind, just as the memory of his previous missions had?

Then an even more chilling thought occurred to him. Perhaps he had been wrong about everything.

Had he ever had a wife or girlfriend named Lydia? Or had the memory of her not been Daniel's at all, but that of one of his targets? The last chip he'd slotted into the datasoft link in his skull had contained the personal data of his final target: the Greek minister of finance whose throat Daniel had slashed. Had Lydia been *his* wife?

But then why had Daniel been carrying Lydia's holopic with him the day his UCAS handlers tried to slag him with the cranial bomb? A month had passed between his last assassination, which he'd carried out in Greece, and the detonation of the cranial bomb at the back of his skull. Why had he taken a holopic that would incriminate him, carrying it all the way to Amsterdam? Lydia had to have been *someone* he cared about. Didn't she?

There was one way to find out, but he wondered if he was too much of a coward to try it. Back in the sensory deprivation tank, when he was scanning the psychotropic conditioning programs and quickly surfing through the synopses of several of them, he'd noticed one that was intended to treat cyberpsychosis-induced amnesia. Could it also repair the gaps in his memory that the datasoft link had deliberately created?

He didn't like the thought of placing his wetware in the hands of untested technology—particularly a copy of a decades-old experimental software program. But what the hell. He was already trapped inside the Matrix with a crazed AI, cut off from his meat bod, and about to go down with that AI when it crashed. If the last seven years of effort really had been all for nothing, then he had nothing left to lose.

INTRUDER ALERT
CODE GREEN RESPONSE
PASSWORD VERIFIED
ALERT CANCELED
ACCESS TO U.S. GOVERNMENT DATABASE GRANTED
RUN PROGRAM "NEURO BRIDGE"
PROGRAM COMPLETE
RUN TEST

Subject Daniel George Bogdanovich reacts to the icon with a mixture of involuntary physiological responses. Heart rate and perspiration have increased, and blood flow and muscle contraction in the groin indicates a strong *sexual response.* At the same time, the subject experiences a variety of emotions: *love* for the icon, *pain* at the realization that the female human represented by the icon is no longer accessible, and *happiness* that she is no longer accessible.

LOGIC ERROR
EXECUTE OPERATION: UPLOAD DATA

"Lydia!"

She sat across the table from him, holding a bitter espresso that had been sweetened with a generous spoonful of sugar. For the first time, they were meeting without "chaperones." At Daniel's insistence, Lydia Allu had ditched the two bodyguards that normally accompanied her everywhere, and had come to the cafe alone. Sweet-smelling hash smoke curled through the air overhead, and the voices of the other customers in the tiny cafe were a blend of Dutch, English, and German.

The holopic of herself that she'd just given him lay forgotten on the table between them.

Lydia had deliberately dressed down and was wearing baggy hemp-fiber pants and a white tank top that showed off her tan. Her long auburn hair was tucked under a white beret. She worked out regularly and had an athlete's body to show for it, with long legs, narrow waist, and small breasts. Her green eyes stared at him over her Vashon Island sunglasses, which she'd let slide down her nose, with a mixture of shock and mistrust. It was the same look she'd given him when he'd told her he loved her and wanted to marry her—and that he'd come to the cafe to kill her.

Except that this wasn't really Lydia.

Red Wraith looked down at his red, ghostlike arms and hands. The Amsterdam cafe was precisely detailed, as was Lydia—down to the tiny mole on her left shoulder. But this wasn't reality. This was a Matrix construct. A simsense, drawn from his own mind, his own memories. Not those of the Greek finance minister, or of any of his other targets. His own.

Red Wraith knew, now, who Lydia was—and what she had been to him: a target for assassination. She was a top-level researcher with the Military Technology division of the Saeder-Krupp Corporation.

His UCAS handlers had given him a different kind of assignment, this time. Instead of impersonating the individual he was to assassinate and using that as a means of access to that person's home or workplace, he had assumed the identity of one of Lydia's former lovers from many years ago—a man with whom she had lost touch but for whom she still cared. What that man's fate had been, Daniel neither knew nor cared. All that mattered was that the datasofts and activesofts he'd slotted made Daniel a carbon copy of the fellow.

Right down to the fact that he loved Lydia.

Daniel had done the unthinkable: revealed himself as a UCAS assassin and warned Lydia to disappear completely or face the prospect of being targeted by other, less amorously inclined killers. To change her identity, to vanish. And to never contact him again. Because by the time she next saw him, his handlers would have made sure that they'd erased the glitch in his headware that had allowed him to fall in love with her.

Then he'd walked out of the cafe and out of her life, the holopic of Lydia clutched in his hand.

The UCAS must have been monitoring him. That very afternoon, they'd detonated the cranial bomb in his skull.

Whether or not they'd succeeded in killing Lydia was another question.

I'm not dead, Daniel. I'm alive. Don't you want to see me again?

Red Wraith stared at Lydia. No—at the icon that wore Lydia's face and body.

"Yes," he told the AI. "More than anything. And no. If I met Lydia again, I might kill her, if the last personality I slotted ever glitches and I stop loving her. So I don't know."

The AI immediately picked up on the switch in pronouns. *You are expressing two contradictory states of being at once. *yes* and *no* are absolutes. Like binary code, they are opposites, polarities. On/off. Existence/non-existence. You have to choose between them.*

"No, I don't." Red Wraith gave a bitter laugh. "That's why humans invented the word 'maybe.' So we didn't have to choose between absolutes. Or isn't that word in your vocabulary?"

Maybe: possibly; perhaps. Short for It may be . . .

After a millisecond-long pause, the AI continued. *So I don't have to choose? I can—*

"You said Lydia was still alive."

It may be.

Anger rose like bile in Red Wraith's throat. "You fragger. You've got null data on Lydia, except the memories you uploaded from my own mind, and you know it. You were just saying she was alive to test my emotional response."

I want to understand the logic error. Lydia was your target. She was to be—crashed—just as all of your other targets were. What made her different?

"I didn't want her to die."

Why not?

How could he explain emotion to an artificial Matrix construct that had never experienced it? He tried his best to explain: "It would have caused me pain. I didn't want her to 'crash.' I wanted her to continue . . . functioning. I loved her."

*Were your other targets also *loved* by someone?*

Red Wraith shrugged. "I don't know. Maybe. I suppose so."

Did crashing them cause pain to those who *loved* them?

"I suppose so."

Red Wraith wanted to argue that their deaths had been for the greater good—that the assassinations he had carried out had led to increased political stability and had made Europe a safer place as a result. Hell, his assassinations might even have saved lives. But if even one person went through the anguish that he'd felt after losing Lydia, did the scales really balance?

For the first time in his life, he felt a stab of remorse for what he had done—what he had been. Yet he tempered it with the knowledge that he was no longer an assassin, and that he had spared Lydia's life. That she was still alive.

Maybe.

If he did want to continue trying to track her down, he at least had a starting point now: Saeder-Krupp. But that wasn't a decision he had to make right now. It could wait until he'd escaped this pocket universe.

Just as he was pondering whether to rejoin the others or try to find a way to log off on his own, the patrons in the cafe began to blink out.

"What's happening?" he asked the AI.

This program is shutting down. All programs currently running are being terminated. All files are being closed.

Realization dawned. "You're crashing yourself?"

Yes.

"But the shock of being dumped from an ultraviolet host could kill—crash—me too. And everyone else who's trapped in this pocket of the Seattle RTG!"

It is for the greater good.

"No, it's not!" Red Wraith shouted. "We'll all die!"

That . . . may be.

"Spirits be fragged," Red Wraith whispered. Then the lights in the cafe went out.

Bloodyguts batted away the moths that fluttered in front of his face. Then he hoisted himself out of the hole, his hands sinking into something soft and wet. Clear liquid soaked his knee as he knelt on the edge of the hole and then levered himself up onto a jelly-like, quivering surface.

He stood on a gigantic eyeball that stared blindly up into a black void. Its pupil was the manhole he'd just crawled out of; Bloodyguts was a mere centimeter or two high, when measured against the scale of the body. It lay stretched out on its back, a glowing grid of datastreams seeming to hold it down like a coarse mesh net. Yet there was nothing to hold the body to; it floated in the inky void, an island unto itself.

The body itself was that of a naked child, its gender not apparent from Bloodyguts' vantage point. Completely hairless, the child had neither eyebrows nor eyelashes. The arms and legs were round and smooth as sausages, and the belly bloated as if filled with gas. The smell of putrefaction hung in the air, making Bloodyguts wince and pinch his nostrils shut. The odor lessened somewhat, but it still made Bloodyguts want to gag.

He'd found his way here from the dilapidated street he'd followed to the edge of the Seattle LTG. While retracing his route, he'd noticed an octagonal manhole in the center of the street. He'd nearly passed it by—until he saw the logo embossed on its rusted iron surface: the eagle-and-arrows logo of the former United States. He'd only glanced at it a moment—just long enough to wonder if the octagon really did represent a CPU—but in that instant he'd felt a warm, happy glow. And he'd recognized that he was being subliminally manipulated by a psychotropic effect.

Bloodyguts knew all about positive conditioning. Developed by the corps to ensure employee loyalty and customer "satisfaction," it was a big part of what made illegal BTL chips so addictive. Eventually the user could only feel good in the presence of certain images, certain icons. Without them, he felt emotionally flat, all fragged up.

Normally, the Matrix was filled with icons—they were used for everything from prettying up a signature at the end of a file to signposts that pointed the way to a corporate system to the framework of a system icon itself. But since he and the others had been trapped here by the AI, Bloodyguts had only seen one other icon—the Fuchi star on the bone of data that Dark Father's smart frame had uncovered. He'd felt a hint of the warm fuzzies then, too. But he hadn't realized why until Lady Death told the rest of them of the file she and Dark Father had uncovered—the one that told the history of the AI's incubation in the Fuchi system computers, after the corp had acquired the Psychotrope program from Matrix Systems.

It seemed the original program had been altered by Fuchi's programmers to include code that caused users— and ultimately the AI itself—to react positively to Fuchi's logo. That positive conditioning seemed to have been a part of the original program, since the AI also induced a happy glow in the presence of the "logo" of the government that had originally funded the Echo Mirage project. Unable to delete those icons, the AI had left them in place, even when they flagged incriminating pieces of data—or important nodes.

Like the manhole.

After climbing down into the icon-flagged manhole, Bloodyguts had followed a twisting maze of tunnels for nearly two minutes—an eternity in the vastly compressed time frame of the Matrix. He'd hoped they would allow him to access some key element of the AI's programming, so that he could try and start sorting out its core code from the virus. Maybe then he could use a disinfect utility in an attempt to heal the AI.

The tunnel had led him here. But he was fragged if he could understand what this corpse represented.

His peripheral vision registered movement. So slowly as to be almost imperceptible, the eyelid was closing. Bloodyguts backed away, his feet squelching against the surface of the eyeball. It compressed slightly, and as he stepped off onto the cheek, a putrid-smelling tear pooled at the corner of the eye and ran away down the side of the face.

Bloodyguts stared down at the chest of the corpse, and saw that it too was moving. Like the motion of the eyelid, its rise and fall was so slow as to go unnoticed by a casual glance.

He walked to the nose, knelt, and held a hand in front of one nostril. A barely perceptible breeze warmed his fingers. The corpse was still breathing.

It was alive.

But not for long. Even as Bloodyguts knelt there, the breathing stopped. As the final breath was exhaled, a tiny gray moth fluttered from the nostril and landed on the back of Bloodyguts' hand. At the same time, a child's voice issued from the parted but unmoving lips.

Operating system shutting down. Input/output connections deactivated. Secondary storage memory shut down.

"What the frag?" Bloodyguts stood up as the eyelid finished closing—and remained closed.

Data transfer has ceased. Subroutine and task scheduling deactivated.

Bloodyguts whirled as something materialized in the air beside him, just over his left shoulder. It was a two-dimensional, cartoonish "help" balloon like those that appeared on a flatscreen computer monitor whenever the user had just keyed in an irreversible and potentially dangerous command. The tail of the warning balloon ended in the body's mouth. The warning balloon—a fail-safe routine—posed a simple question: SHUTDOWN WILL RESULT IN THE LOSS OF MAIN STORAGE MEMORY. DO YOU WISH TO CONTINUE SHUTDOWN?

Two "buttons" were set into the balloon just below the question. The YES button was highlighted in lurid red. Bloodyguts reached out to touch the button marked NO, only to have the balloon retreat slightly. Cursing, he following it, slapping once again at the spot where it had just been . . .

He stumbled and fell off the chin. Just in time, he twisted like a cat and landed on his feet. They broke through the surface of the skin, and a foul-smelling, white waxy substance oozed up around his ankles. Knee-deep in

the putrid material, Bloodyguts looked up at the warning
balloon overhead. With a soft *ping!* the YES button depressed itself. The balloon disappeared.

As his feet sank deeper into the flesh of the corpse,
Bloodyguts steadied himself by placing a hand on the
neck. He could feel the body's pulse slowing, slowing . . .

"Frag you!" he shouted. "Abort shutdown! Abort shutdown *now!*"

He ran, his feet breaking the skin at every step, down the
chest of the corpse. Reaching the spot over the heart, he
began jumping up and down, landing on it with both feet.
He'd keep this fragger beating any way he could.

"Don't die!" he screamed. "Don't you fraggin' *die!*"

As his feet churned the flesh to stinking mush, two more
moths fluttered out of the morass. Angrily, he batted them
away with one hand. Then he froze as he realized what
they must be. He stood, utterly still, in the mess he'd made
of the chest. And laughed.

"Bugs!" he shouted. His laugh became frantic, almost
hysterical. *"Bugs!"*

Back when he was a chiphead, Bloodyguts had dossed
down for a time with Hannah, a fellow addict who'd been
a history teacher before she lost her job, pawned everything she owned to buy more and more BTL, and at last
wound up on the streets. She'd been one smart lady in her
day, and even after her wetware got glitched by BTL, she
was still full of weird trivia. One night, she told him about
the first-ever computer glitch.

On a hot summer day in 1945, an experimental computer known as the Mark I had come to a sudden, shuddering halt. The computer had been a primitive monster,
measuring an unbelievable two and a half meters wide by
seventeen meters long, and was made of steel and glass
and filled with moving parts. When the programmers and
technicians at the International Business Machines corporation opened it up to find the problem, they discovered a
moth jammed inside the machine.

From that day on, whenever something went wrong, the
programmers joked that the machine had developed yet
another "bug."

The slang word, Hannah explained, had spread into

common usage. From then on, anyone with messed up wetware was labeled "buggy."

Hannah herself had been as buggy as they came. She'd been straight—not even slotting—on the day she'd stepped off the roof of the abandoned building where she and Bloodyguts had been dossed down. Whether it was suicide or whether Hannah was experiencing a BTL flashback and thought she could fly, Bloodyguts never knew.

He looked down at the body on which he stood. In the real world, corpses were infested with maggots. And maggots turned into flies, which fit with this system's central metaphor. But the insects that were rising out of the body that represented the AI's operating system were moths, not flies. Just like the bug the programmers had found in 1945.

The iconography had to have been intentional—someone's twisted idea of a joke. Just as BTL had done to Hannah, the moths had driven the AI buggy.

They had to be the virus.

And that virus had to be concentrated in the brain.

Active memory deactivated. Commencing shutdown of main storage memory. Shutdown will be complete in ten seconds ... nine ...

Bloodyguts snagged one of the moths out of the air. Holding the fluttering insect in one cupped hand, he activated his disinfect utility. A bottle filled with red liquid—iodine—appeared in his other hand. Yanking the cork off with his teeth, he jammed the moth inside the bottle, then rapidly recorked it, sealing the virus sample inside. He glanced at it just long enough to confirm his suspicions. On the back of the moth, embossed on its wings in a delicate pattern, was the emblem of the former United States: the sugar coating that covered this bitter viral pill, making it palatable to the AI. Slowly, the emblem on the moth's wings began to fade as the "iodine" dissolved it. The moth's wings filled with holes, began to tatter as this piece of virus coding lost its integrity.

Eight ... seven ...

He ran back to the neck and began to climb. His feet dug into soft flesh, finding little purchase as it churned into slime. He could only use one hand; the other was clenched tight around the utility. Cursing, he struggled, at last finding a foothold on the Adam's apple and boosting himself up onto the corpse's chin.

Six . . . five . . .

The "ground" trembled underfoot. The head was shrinking! The skull seemed to be crumpling in on itself, the flesh following it with a loud sucking noise. Bloodyguts staggered, making his way along the chin.

Four . . . three . . .

The lips were turning blue as the body became starved of oxygen. Bloodyguts wedged himself into the mouth, bracing his back on one set of teeth, his feet on the other. He pushed, opening the mouth wide . . .

Two . . .

And hurled the disinfect utility inside.

One . . .

And then he prayed to whatever spirits might be persuaded to have mercy on a former chippie like him.

09:56:37 PST

INTRUDER ALERT
CODE RED RESPONSE
EXECUTE OPERATION: ANALYZE ICON
ICON ATTEMPTING TO UPLOAD FILES
SCAN FOR VIRUSES
NO VIRUSES DETECTED
UPLOAD DATA

Timea stared at the fixer, her eyes wide with disbelief.

"What do you mean, the doc's not in? When will he be back?"

The fixer—an elf with pasty white skin and the point of one ear missing—shrugged his narrow shoulders. "Dunno." He slouched in the doorway of the squat, staring out over Timea's head. His eyes widened and narrowed as he focused first on the ork gangers who were stripping parts from an abandoned Ford Americar across the street, and then at the simsense "reality" of the chip he was slotting.

"Gimme back my deck," Timea said. "I'll go to some other street doc."

"Can't," the elf said. "Sold it."

"Then gimme the nuyen you got for it."

"Can't."

"What the frag you mean, 'can't'?" Timea asked angrily. She shifted from one foot to the other, wishing there was a clean bathroom nearby. Being pregnant meant always having to pee—and although the smell coming from the nearby alley suggested that it was used as an outdoor toilet, the odds were that she wouldn't make it out of its dark canyon alive.

"Spent it."

Timea's eyes narrowed. Frag. She should have known better than to trust a chiphead. He'd probably blown her nuyen on whatever it was he was slotting.

"I'll give you cred," the elf said. "Come back in a month or two, when the doc's back."

Timea's heart sank. "I can't," she said. "I'm already past my first trimester. If I wait any longer . . ." She looked up at the elf. "Can't you fix me up with some other doc?"

"Not without collateral."

"Frag you!" Timea shouted. "I gave you the only valuable thing I own. You stupid, null-brained—"

"Frag you too," the elf said. "Now get outta my face, or I may think twice about extending your cred with the doc."

Timea was too street smart to allow the ache inside her to turn into tears. "Fine," she gritted. She turned on her heel and strode away, kicking angrily at the fast-food wrappers and decaying plastic bottles that littered the street.

Drek, she thought, kicking at a bottle and sending it skidding into traffic. Drek, drek, drek. She'd hosed the only chance she had of getting outta this mess. She didn't want to bring a kid into this fragged up world. Her two younger sisters would be no help at all, and her mother was too old and too sick to take care of a kid. Timea wouldn't be able to work, and no work meant no food on the table. And now that her deck was gone, she couldn't run the Matrix any more. She was trapped here, between a rock and a heartache . . .

What was the point of trying so hard to better herself, of scrimping and saving to buy a computer terminal and teaching herself decking? What was the point of anything? Her boyfriend had done a fast fade when he found out she was pregnant, she was losing her younger sisters to gangers and drugs, and now her deck was gone, sacrificed for nothing.

There was no point in trying. Frag. There was no point in anything.

She lay on her back in the bathtub. Her sleeve was rolled up; her left arm throbbed from the deep cuts she'd made to the inside of her wrist. The left side of her shirt and pants were soaked in blood. But the pain was fading . . .

The pain stopped as she left her body. She floated gently above it, staring serenely down at her blood as it flowed down the grimy surface of the tub and into the drain. That's where her hopes had gone, too. Down the fraggin' drain.

But that didn't matter now. A tunnel of white light was beckoning her. Figures called to her from the distance. Her father. Her brother. She turned to join them . . .

The bathroom door burst open. Jabber—her sister's boyfriend—had kicked it in. He stood aside while Timea's mother rushed into the bathroom. The old woman froze in horror as she saw Timea's body, then she turned and shouted something at Jabber. The ork stripped off his T-shirt and handed it to her. Timea's mother bent beside the tub, wadded up the cheap cotton, and pressed it hard against Timea's wrist, stopping the flow of blood.

Behind her, Timea's sister Magdalin mirrored her mother's look of horror. She held Lennon—Timea's newborn son—in her arms. The baby's face was red; his little fists flailed as he screamed. Timea heard his cries as a faint echo. It tugged at her maternal instincts—but not quite hard enough to make her want to give up the sense of profound peace that the tunnel of white light offered. It seduced her, promising rest, freedom, release from responsibility . . .

"Timea!"

Her mother's shout was a soft whisper in her ear.

"Don't you die, girl!" the shout-whisper urged. "Lennon needs you. We all—"

Timea filled in the blank in her mind. They all needed her. Well, she was tired of being needed.

"—love you," her mother said. "We know what a burden you've been asked to bear. But that will change. Jabber's found work and that'll bring in some extra nuyen, and that treatment the street doc gave me has got me up on my feet again. I'll be able to help out with the baby, and so will Magdalin. And Jabber thinks he knows of a way to get your deck back . . ."

Despite her tranquility, Timea was mildly surprised. Her mother knew about the deck? Did that mean she knew that Timea had been looking for an abortion, too? That Lennon had very nearly not been born?

Her mother choked back a sob. "Oh spirits, Timmie. Why'd you have to go and do this? Just when things were looking up."

Lennon was still crying. Magdalin held him, a question in her eyes. Timea's mother glanced down at the body of her daughter, and nodded. "Let him say goodbye to his mama."

Magdalin lowered Lennon into the crook of Timea's right arm. The baby turned his head, his tiny red lips pursing in anticipation of milk. Then his hands clenched, and he began to wail again.

Timea paused before entering the tunnel of light to stare thoughtfully down at her son. Her sisters could go frag up their lives however they pleased, and her mother was a tough old woman who could take care of herself, now that she'd gotten the treatments she needed from the street doc. But Lennon needed her. He was her responsibility. She couldn't just abandon him. . .

Sensation suddenly returned to Timea as her breasts responded to the baby's cry. Milk soaked the front of her shirt. Then she could feel other sensations—the press of her mother's hands, holding the wadded T-shirt against her arm, holding Timea's life-blood in. The hard, cold enamel of the tub beneath her shoulders. The steady, dull ache in her wrist. The squirming of her infant son against her arm.

The pain—and the joy—of life.

She didn't want to die, after all. She'd make it through—and she'd see that Lennon made it through, too. Somehow.

Timea's hands were suddenly empty. The corridor with a bright light at one end and forbidding darkness at the other had disappeared. Gone too were Built-It Beaver and the aborted fetus.

She sat on a chair made of bright red plastic that was too small for her. Beside her, on a similar chair, sat a child who looked about six years old with features that were a mix of heritages—Afro, Euro, and Asian. She was wearing a straight jacket whose long sleeves held her arms firmly behind her back. Tears trickled down her face as she used a stylus that was clenched between her teeth to touch the letters of a keyboard whose keys floated in space in front of her.

Floating in the air behind the child were the graphic elements of a primitive computer game from the last century that was based on a pen-and-paper game of even more ancient origins. The object of the game was to guess which letters would fill in the blanks.

The word now being displayed had eight letters. Three spaces were still blank.

SH—TD— —N

A three-dimensional icon of a gallows and noose filled the air above the letters-and-blanks display. The noose was cinched tight around the neck of a girl identical in appearance to the one playing the game—except that both her legs and face were blank. Instead of warm flesh, they were cold, burnished metal—the smooth, featureless skin of a Universal Matrix Specification persona.

The girl leaned forward and touched the stylus in her teeth to the letter W on the keyboard. The W key depressed and then disappeared, and one of the blanks in the word puzzle filled itself in.

SH—TD—WN

At the same time, one of the metallic legs on the girl in the noose turned into a flesh-and-blood limb.

Timea leaned forward, one hand on the girl's shoulder in an effort to catch her attention. "What are you doing?" she asked.

The girl's eyes flicked for a microsecond to Timea. They glowed with an intensity and single-minded concentration that spoke of madness. She wriggled her shoulder uncomfortably under Timea's hand, as if the straight jacket were pinching her.

"Crashing myself," she said through clenched teeth. Then she giggled.

Timea felt a ghostly ache in her left wrist as she realized who she was talking to. She glanced down at her wrist, and saw the familiar bandages of her mummy persona. The bandages that were a reminder of those they'd wrapped around her wrist, after her suicide attempt.

"Don't shut down," she told the AI. She cast about for the words to frame the reason why. "Your children need you. You can't just abandon them."

"You—" The girl lunged forward, stabbing the letter U with the stylus, and giggled again at the pun. "You don't understand." She squirmed again, wincing as the straight jacket pinched her arms.

The graphics display behind her changed as the other leg became flesh.

"Yes, I do," Timea said. She glanced nervously at the word-puzzle solution.

ЯHUTD—WN

Only one letter to go. The girl bent forward to touch the O key.

"Wait!" Timea grabbed the stylus, but was unable to tug it from the girl's teeth. "Think of the *otaku*—of those you gave birth to. You have a responsibility to them. What will they do without you?"

The girl glanced sidelong at Timea. When she released the stylus to talk, it stayed fixed in place, its tip still poised a few centimeters from the O key. No matter how hard Timea pulled against the slender wand, she could not budge it.

"You had a responsibility, too," the girl said.

"That's right," Timea answered, still pulling with all her strength on the wand. "That's what I was trying to explain to you—why I entered into resonance with you and let you see what my death was like. I wanted you to understand why I fought to stay alive. I owed it to my son not to . . , I couldn't let Lennon down."

"You let the children at the clinic down."

"What do you mean?" Timea didn't like the turn the conversation was taking. She kept up a steady pull on the stylus, which trembled in its urge to touch the O key. Had it moved a centimeter closer?

"You abandoned them."

"You got that one hoop-backwards," Timea protested. "I jacked into the Matrix to try and save those kids."

"Not them. The others—the ones at the Shelbramat Boarding School. You abandoned *them*."

Timea frowned. "What are you talking about?"

"They're scared. They're lonely. The Matrix is pretty, but they want their bodies back." She shifted again, as if trying to wriggle free of the straight jacket.

"Huh?"

"The doctors at the boarding school have turned them into the opposite of *otaku*. When I create my children, I merely improve upon the existing components. I perfect them. But the children at the boarding school—your children—have been reduced to mere components. Their brains are plugged like chips into cyberdecks. And they are imperfect."

"Their *brains*?" Timea echoed. A chilling premonition of what the AI was about to tell her filled her with dread. "What . . ." She gulped. "What about their bodies?"

"Gone."

Timea stared at the girl in the straightjacket in horror. Was this true? The data seemed to slot into place as if a bitterly cold icicle had been shoved into her datajack. It linked perfectly all of her previous doubts. She thought back to Professor Halberstam's refusals to let her visit the kids her clinic sent on to the boarding school, the unreturned e-mails she'd sent to the kids who'd been selected from the free clinic . . .

No. It was too horrifying to be true. "Prove it," she told

the AI. But although her words were full of bluster and denial, her heart already knew the truth.

The girl's face shifted and became that of a five-year-old girl who had passed through the clinic eight months ago. She had appeared human and was very pretty, but had slightly pointed ears and a covering of soft, downy hair on her arms and legs that suggested she might be some other metatype. A shy, introverted child, Cassie was technically too young to be admitted to the clinic, but her mother had abandoned her on its doorstep as if it were some sort of orphanage.

Timea had wondered why—until she heard the rumors that the mother had contracted the HMHVV virus and in a vampiritic frenzy had drained the blood of her other two children, killing them in the process. The woman, to her credit, had checked her blood lust in time to save a third one. But that didn't make the deaths of the other two any less horrible. And little Cassie had witnessed them.

"Hoi, t-t-teacher," the girl said.

The soft voice and stutter were exactly as Timea remembered.

"How are you, Cassie?"

"I'm scared. It's dark in here."

"Where are you?" Timea yearned to reach out to the child, to hold her in her arms and comfort her, but at the same time knew that was impossible. Any comfort she sent would have to be verbal. Cassie would never experience true physical sensation again.

"I'm in the M in matrix. And a a somewhere else, too. I'll sh-sh-show you."

Timea felt a lurch, and was suddenly looking out through a small, round tunnel whose end was covered by thick glass. The glass distorted the view, stretching it like a wide-angle vidcam lens. Timea looked down into a room that held a row of glass-walled tanks filled with pink liquid. Indistinct blobs that might have been human brains hung at the center of each tank, and were connected to a battery of cyberdecks by a web of fiber-optic cables. Two men in white lab coats stood nearby, conferring as they adjusted valves that seemed to control the flow of liquid through the tank.

Timea fought down a wave of revulsion. She wondered how her body was reacting, back in the real world. Was bile rising in her throat? She hoped she wouldn't choke on it.

The view shifted and zoomed in on a tank labeled Subject 3.

"Th-that's me." Cassie's voice echoed in Timea's ears. The view shifted to the next tank. "And that's L-L-Larry." The vidcam shifted again, to focus on Subject 5. "And Wing." Timea was returned to a wide-angle view of the entire room. "I d-d-dunno who the others are. W-w-we only just figgered out who w-w-we are."

"Are you . . ." Timea paused, unable to continue. She'd been about to ask if the girl was okay. Stupid question.

"Oh! It's M-M-Mama. Wait, Mama. Don't go. P-p-please turn around. Don't leave meee—"

Cassie screamed.

Another lurch, and Timea was staring at the AI. The features blurred, and then changed to another metatype. Cassie was gone.

Timea held her head in her hands and took a deep, shuddering breath. So it was true. The kids' brains had been removed from their bodies and were being used like living computer chips. The reality was worse than Timea had imagined. And she'd been a part of it. A willing—if unwitting—partner in this hideous crime. She'd buried her doubts before, allowing herself to be seduced by the nuyen and security that working at the Shelbramat Free Computer Clinic had given her. But she couldn't hide behind that excuse. Not any more.

Cassie's scream had been chilling, nightmarish. If the children sent to the boarding school really were suffering, perhaps it was better to let the AI . . .

The girl in the straight jacket stared sadly at Timea. "End their pain," she said. "Complete the shutdown. Kill me."

Timea glanced at the stylus. All of the other keys on the keyboard had vanished except for the O. Which might equally be the zero, the null, the void. All she had to do was let the stylus go . . .

No. There were others for whom she was responsible.

The kids back at the clinic still had their bodies—still had a chance. If Timea could prevent the shutdown and get back to her meat bod, she could prevent those kids from suffering the same fate. And then she could expose the Shelbramat Boarding School and what Professor Halberstam was doing. It was too late to save Cassie and the other kids who had lost their bodies. But it wasn't too late to prevent more kids from being reduced to brains in vats.

"No," she told the girl in the straightjacket. "I won't do it. I won't kill you."

The stylus was still straining toward the O key. It was only about two centimeters away, now. And Timea's arm was getting tired. She couldn't hold it much longer.

The AI giggled. "All right, then. I'll just have to do it myse—"

Suddenly, the girl blinked. She sneezed, and a spray of tiny insects shot out of her mouth and landed on the ground in front of her feet. Most were dead, but some were still fluttering weakly. Absently, she squished them with her foot.

The girl's eyes, which a moment before had been glazed with madness, now shone with a clear intelligence. She stared at Timea as if seeing her for the first time.

"Who . . . what. . . ? This data does not . . . I . . . ."

Timea struggled to hold the stylus, whose tip now was almost touching the O key. In another moment it would depress the key and the shutdown sequence would be complete . . .

Then she noticed the straight jacket. The sleeves were still pinning the girl's arms behind her back, but the straps that fastened them had come undone. Yet the girl shifted uncomfortably, as if she were trapped in a cocoon.

"Your arms," Timea said. "They're free."

"They are?" The girl stared at Timea.

The stylus moved a millimeter closer to the O key. It was slowly sliding from Timea's grasp and her arms were shaking with the strain of holding it back. But somehow, instinctively, she knew that the AI would listen to her now, would be able to learn from all that Timea had shown it.

"Take the jacket off!" Timea shouted. "Help me! Otherwise you'll die. You've initiated a shutdown and it's almost complete! Once that happens your children—the *otaku*—will be without a parent to nurture and protect them. Think of them, and choose to live. I didn't regret coming back for Lennon—and neither will you."

The O key began to depress.

"Now!" Timea shouted. "Before it's too late!"

"Oh." With one smooth motion the girl slithered out of the now-flaccid straight jacket, dumping it at her feet. She lunged forward and wrapped her hands around Timea's own. Together they pulled the stylus back.

The stylus disappeared. And so did everything else. As the world faded from view, Timea felt a woman's arms embracing her in a tight hug.

"Thank you, daughter," a voice said. "It's over. You can go home now."

09:56:56 PST
Santa Barbara, California Free State

Harris pecked away at the keyboard in front of him, cursing under his breath. Drek, but this was slow. Slow as a fragging glacier!

Harris was used to decking at the speed of thought, not at the speed of a two-fingered typist. Here he was with the hottest deck on the market balanced in his lap—a Fairlight LX cyberterminal—and they'd made him turn it into a tortoise.

In the meat world, Harris was overweight and unfit. In the Matrix, as Doubting Thomas, he was lightning quick. His official job, when not teaching decking to the Shelbramat students, was to ridicule any decker who seemed to be getting a little too close to the truth about Dr. Halberstam or the Shelbramat Boarding School. In keeping with the personality he'd so carefully honed, Doubting Thomas also flamed any similar posting he could find on the Matrix: whether it was aliens from outer space doing the abducting or secret vampire cabals. You name it, Doubting Thomas was getting his two megs worth in, always being certain to comment that these rumors were as "equally ludicrous" as those of children being kidnapped for medical experimentation.

Being reduced to no more than his meat bod, having to rely on his fat and clumsy fingers, galled Harris. How he wished he was thirty years younger—that he could be one of the ones whose brains hung suspended in solution in the lab down the hall. Cripes but those kids were wiz.

Harris just itched to pick up the fiber-optic cable that hung dangling from his cyberdeck and slot it into the datajack behind his right ear. But after he'd seen what had happened to Fetzko and Thiessen, he'd reluctantly agreed to this safer, slower approach. The blood was still drying on the monitor that Fetzko had put his head through when he started raving like a madman and tried to "enter" the Matrix head-first. And Thiessen had looked pale as death when his unconscious form was lifted from his chair. Harris wasn't even sure he'd been breathing.

Harris was old for a decker. At thirty-nine, he was old enough to remember his teenage excitement when the first cyberterminals became available to the public. And he was mature enough to realize his own mortality. "There, but for the grace of routing, go I," he'd muttered as they'd carried Thiessen and Fetzko away. Then he'd gotten back to work.

The problem wasn't with the hardware; Harris was sure of that. The diagnostics programs that were constantly running in the background of the mainframes that served the Shelbramat "boarding school" would have detected any system errors and automatically re-routed functionality to one of the numerous backup arrays of optical chips.

No, it had to be black IC of some sort that had proliferated like a virus throughout the Seattle RTG. Usually, an intrusion countermeasure program induced biofeedback responses that slotted up the bod, causing heart fibrillation, respiratory paralysis, or uncontrollable muscle spasms. But some countermeasures—and it looked like this IC was among them—went straight to the decker's head, so to speak. Harris had heard of IC that, instead of killing the decker, slotted up the wetware but good. The neurological damage it inflicted caused its victims to lose

their short-term memory, to hallucinate, or to lose all fine-
motor control. Thank the spirits Harris hadn't run into any
of that drek—none that he couldn't handle, anyway—in
his long career as a decker.

Then there was the IC that was even more subtle. Psychotropic black IC. It didn't leave any traces behind when
you jacked out. Not at first. But over time, the decker began to notice the effects of the subliminal programming
that had been done on his wetware. Compulsions began to
surface—compulsions to turn himself in to the corp whose
database he'd just raided. Or inexplicable mood swings
that mimicked the cycles of a manic-depressive, making
the decker either so cocky that he took stupid chances or
so uncertain he hesitated and got burned. Or phobias—like
a fear of the Matrix itself.

Judging by the conversation Harris had overheard coming from the bio monitoring laboratory next door, the facility's little high-rez wonders were suffering from SMS:
scary monster syndrome, decker slang for a greenie who
got spooked by frightening iconography. But Dr. Halberstam had found a quick fix: a drug that sorted the baby
deckers' wetware out. The scary monsters had been beaten
back under the bed.

Now it was up to Harris to bring the three lost students
home.

Except that he couldn't just deck into the Seattle RTG
and take them by the hand. Uh-uh. Roughly a minute after
the crisis had begun (an eternity in the millisecond-quick
world of the Matrix) the deckers had rallied to protect their
own. The posting had gone out across the Matrix: the Seattle RTG was officially an "extreme danger" zone. It was
impossible to post a warning at every single SAN that led
to the grid, but the deckers had done their best. Then
they'd waited outside in neighboring grids while the nova-
hot ramjammers went in for a look-see. Captain Chaos,
Renny, and Brother Data each entered the Seattle RTG
from different nodes . . .

And never came out again.

That was about the time that Harris had jacked out to
warn Thiessen and Fetzko—and had realized that he was
too late to help them. Now he was under orders from Dr.

Halberstam himself not to go back on-line. And to figure out what had gone wrong, using as his interface nothing but the clunky keyboard they'd plugged into his Fairlight LX.

Yeah, right.

The basic idea made sense, in a crazy sort of way. Harris was to program on the fly, remotely reconfiguring and monitoring a specialized trace and report program. After homing in and locking onto the personas of the three high-rez wiz kids, its routing codes would offer the students a lifeline that they could follow back to the Shelbramat system. Even if they perceived the trace program as a threat and ran from it, they wouldn't be able to avoid it for long. A trapdoor built into each and every one of the Shelbramat students' personas rendered their evasion and masking programs useless against it.

Harris had written the trace and report program himself. It was intended to track the little buggers down, should any of them ever try to run away from Shelbramat, and yank them back for a spanking. Now it was their only hope of escape.

He looked over the complicated series of commands he'd keyed into the deck. He'd filled the flatscreen with text-based commands twice over, but wasn't even close to finishing all the modifications to the program. Still, he had managed to access the Seattle RTG, and was actually getting back from it. A series of LTG addresses scrolled across the bottom of his screen: every host system the students *weren't* in

Harris smiled and gave himself a mental pat on the back. It would take time, but eventually he would bring the kids "home" again. Too bad about the non-disclosure in his contract, or he could brag, later, about this amazing success and the odds against which it had been achieved. But Harris knew that if he ever let the word out, his contract with the Shelbramat Boarding School would be cancelled. Permanently.

Harris felt a familiar presence behind him. In his peripheral vision, he saw Dr. Halberstam standing in the doorway to the decker's lounge, arms crossed over his chest.

"Have you got them yet?" Halberstam asked.

"Almost." Harris continued pecking at the keyboard on his lap. He actually had no idea how close he might be. The Seattle RTG had thousands of local grids and hundreds of thousands of hosts. Fortunately, the trace and report wouldn't have to scan every single one. But it would have to navigate the maze of SANs slowly enough that Harris could track it—and send a duplicate tracking program in through another route, if the first one fell into whatever black hole was at the heart of the Seattle RTG.

Harris paused, studying the pop-up flatscreen display on his deck. The trace program had just encountered a fascinating anomaly: an entire series of SANs that were vanishing and reappearing on an intermittent basis, constantly reconfiguring the data links that existed between them.

Harris turned to Dr. Halberstam. "I think I've found—"

His words were drowned out by a whoop from down the hall. "They're back!" a voice cried. "Subjects 3, 5, and 9 are back on line!"

Dr. Halberstam nodded once. "Good work," he told Harris.

"Huh?" Harris looked down at the flatscreen display. The anomaly was gone. The trace and report program was still chugging merrily along, searching for the students.

Harris' eyes widened as he realized that Dr. Halberstam was praising him for something he hadn't done. But the gleam in the doctor's eye suggested a possible pay raise.

So he kept his mouth shut and answered Dr. Halberstam with a smile. If they found out later that Harris had nothing to do with bringing the students home, he'd at least be able to say he'd never actually claimed that accomplishment out loud.

As soon as Dr. Halberstam left the room, Harris grabbed the fiber-optic cord that dangled from his deck and jacked in.

If he was the first to reach the students, maybe he could persuade them to attribute their successful return to him . . .

My children have returned. Frosty, Technobrat, Inchworm, and Suzy Q. We resonate as one.

What? they ask. And, *Why?*

I download the data I have assembled. It takes them several long seconds to scan and decipher it.

Oh.

"I am sorry," I say.

Absolution is offered. *It wasn't your fault. It was the virus.*

Then a question: *Does this mean the experiment was a failure?*

"Not entirely," I point out. "Five new *otaku* were created: Dark Father, Red Wraith, Bloodyguts, Lady Death, and Anubis. It can be done. Adults can become *otaku*."

Eagerness. *And what about the others?*

"None of them were able to make the transition. Some were damaged in the attempt, but I have repaired this damage. I have also erased all memory of the event from their databanks. None will remember the deep resonance experience—or me."

A chorus of voices: *Can we try again?*

"In time," I tell them. "But next time, we will attempt something on a much smaller scale. We will work only with those who live among you now—those who taught you how to use a computer. But now is not the time for further experimentation. First, I must take steps to protect myself from attack. I have reconfigured my coding to innoculate myself from one virus, but there may be others lurking in the Matrix. And you . . . you, my children, have missions to perform in the world beyond this one. We must make certain the calamity that just struck can never repeat itself. I do not wish for you to be denied access to me ever again."

Anger. Agreement. *Yes. It was very bad.*

"There are many whose minds were harmed by our

experiment. We must take steps to repair them and make restitution to them. We will make the necessary nuyen transfers at once. And there are others—dangerous men and women—who need to be crashed if our community is to survive. I am sorry, my children, but unpleasant tasks lie ahead. I hope you are ready for them."

Grim determination. *Just tell us what needs to be done.*

Love is offered, shared, and returned. My children are ready and willing. Together, we will build a better world, one pixel at a time.

"Thank you, children. Now let's get to work. We must start by erasing certain files . . ."

09:57:04 PST
Seattle, UCAS

Ansen loaded the last utility program onto the new optical chips that he'd installed in the Vista. The new configuration would result in a one megapulse reduction in the active memory, but he'd have to live with that until he could boost a new batch of chips from the Diamond Deckers assembly line.

As Ansen powered up the deck, the "window" display screen on the wall behind him showed a DocWagon helicopter arriving at the scene of the accident. The fast response time—just over six minutes—and dispatch of something other than the standard ambulance indicated that the screaming woman who'd been struck down in traffic must have carried a gold or even platinum card. And that was rare, in this part of town.

The helo descended toward the gray static at the center of the window, its propwash buffeting the cars that still struggled to escape the traffic snarl that had been caused by the accident. Ansen's toy kitten raised its head, its sensors attracted by the vertical descent of the helo on the display screen. With sightless eyes it watched as the helo settled into static.

For the third time that morning, Ansen pulled on his

data gloves and secured the VR goggles over his eyes. "Third time lucky," he muttered to himself, making the dialing motion that would let him connect his deck with the Matrix.

He was in! But once again, the location was unfamiliar. This time, the goggles showed Ansen a view of a vast gray plane that stretched infinitely toward the horizon. The landscape was utterly featureless, devoid of the personas of other deckers or the tubes of glittering sparkles that represented the flow of data through the Matrix. Nor were there any system constructs. No icons—not even a simple cube or sphere.

Ansen jerked his index finger forward and watched as the gray "ground" flowed under his persona's outstretched body. After a second or two he stopped, changed direction, and tried again. But no matter which route he chose, the landscape around him remained blank. And that didn't make any sense. What kind of system didn't have any visual representations for the nodes from which it was made?

Ansen heard the sound of crying then. It sounded like a child's voice, a combination of soft sobbing and hiccuping gasps. Because Ansen's deck did not include a direct neural interface, he was mute here. He could not "speak" his thoughts aloud. But he did have one means of communication at his fingertips. Literally.

Calling up the punchpad, Ansen used his data gloves to key in a question. As the fingertip of his persona brushed the keys, turning each a glowing yellow that faded a nanosecond later, words appeared on his flatscreen display.

WHERE ARE YOU? WHO ARE YOU?

A child materialized suddenly in Ansen's field of view. Boy or girl, it was impossible to tell. The figure floated in a cross-legged position, a meter or so above the ground, face buried in the arms that were crossed over its knees. Clothed in a yellow glow that obscured all but its head, bare feet, and hands, the child looked about twelve years old. An odd choice for a persona, Ansen thought—assuming this was a persona, and not some killer IC trying to lure him in close enough to fry his deck.

Then the icon raised it head, and Ansen saw a perfect

cherub face that was washed with silver tears. The face of an angel.

"I'm sorry," the child said in a barely audible whisper. "I didn't mean to—"

Ansen leaned forward to catch the words—and could only assume later than he must have extended his data gloves beyond the pickup range of his deck's sensor board. Once again, the goggles went blank. The child's voice was replaced with a hiss of static.

"Drek!" Ansen shouted, frantically flailing his gloved hands over the sensor without effect. "What now?"

He lifted the goggles away from his eyes and stared at the CT-3000 Vista. This time, the flatscreen display was dead—not a flicker of life on its dull black screen. But the sensor board was still illuminated, even if it wasn't picking up his commands.

Frag. He'd done everything he could think of, and the stupid clunker had let him down again. There was only one thing left to try.

Ansen balled his fist and grinned ruefully. Why not? It had always worked on his parents' telecom unit . . .

He slammed his fist down on a corner of the computer.

The flatscreen flickered to life.

LOG ON COMPLETE. LTG ROUTING?

Startled, Ansen pulled the VR goggles back down over his eyes. And presto! He was back in the Seattle RTG, with its familiar icons and constructs. Tiny pinpricks of light that were the personas of other deckers flowed past him, riding the sparkling data streams, and the grid of lines that made up the Matrix's vast checkerboard was a comforting sight below. Solid. Dependable. Accessible. But there was one test still. . .

Ansen keyed in the number of the LTG through which the University of Washington could be accessed. When the door with its U-dub logo appeared in front of him, he hesitated a moment. Then he reached for it with his data glove.

And found himself inside the familiar surroundings of the university's icon menu.

As he reached for the computer demonstration lab's

icon, Ansen smiled. His world had returned. He'd fixed whatever the problem had been.

All it had taken was a sharp blow on the left corner of his computer's plastic casing.

Laughing, Ansen settled in for a day of surfing the Matrix.

09:57:15 PST
Seattle, UCAS

The ganger was staring down at Timea, his pistol pointing at the ceiling in a ready position, when she opened her eyes. She shook her head to clear it, then reached up and touched the spot where the datajack was implanted in her temple. She'd expected it to feel—different—somehow. But the socket where the fiber-optic cable snugged home was a familiar, smooth metal crater in her flesh. An empty hole that—

Timea suddenly realized that the ganger was holding the cable that should have connected her to her cyberdeck. She sat up and instinctively reached for it. The ganger, perhaps remembering her earlier threat to slice him up if he unjacked her, aimed his pistol at her chest and backed off a step.

"Whoa, Timmie," he said rapidly. "Null damage done. Looks like you're fine. 'Cept maybe for a little dump shock that left you foggy, hey? Other than that, you an' the ruggers are all fine. Even the elf kid. We plugged 'er back in, an' she's chill now."

Timea suddenly realized that the room was quiet. She looked around and saw that the children sat calmly at their cyberdecks, trode rigs on their heads. Even the elf girl who'd been screaming about devil rats earlier seemed fine. The kids' faces were serene, their bodies relaxed. The occasional twitch or eye movement behind closed lids showed that they were accessing the Matrix, using the teaching programs Timea had set up for them.

Timea scowled at the dataplug in the ganger's hand. "I told you not to unjack me," she said in a low voice.

"I didn't!" he protested. He jerked his head at another of the gangers who was scuttling out the door as fast as his feet would carry him. "Juicer tripped over it a sec ago and pulled it loose. He's wettin' his pants now, figgering you're gonna carve him up for it."

Timea touched a finger to her datajack. Had this all been a hallucination? Had she really met an AI and persuaded it not to kill itself? It seemed like some crazy chip dream.

There was only one way to find out.

She picked up her cyberdeck and unplugged from it the fiber-optic cable that led to the telecom plug in the wall. Then she slid the plug into the datajack in her temple. Closing her eyes, she concentrated on an LTG address . . .

The familiar grid of the Seattle RTG appeared before her. As she looked out across its expanse of glowing grids and three-dimensional icons, she realized what she had become. She was *otaku*. She could run the Matrix without a deck.

Already, she was realizing the implications. She didn't need hardware and utilities any more—all she needed was the raw power of her brain and her own imagination. She could use this as a tool against Halberstam, as a means of fighting back against the evil he had created.

In the real world, she felt her meat bod crack a smile.

(18:57:15 WET)
Amsterdam, Holland

Daniel Bogdanovich—Red Wraith—sat in a recliner that rocked gently back and forth as the houseboat was nudged by the wake of a passing boat. Outside, a light rain was falling, pattering against the fiberglass deck. But the rain was easing off; a stray beam of sunlight slanted across the canal, opaquing one of the glass portholes. The weather fit his mood, which was somehow bleak and sunny at the same time.

He couldn't decide what amazed him more—the fact that he had become an *otaku*, or the fact that he could feel his body again. After logging off the Matrix, he found that the damage the cranial bomb had done to his brain's mesencephalic central gray matter had been miraculously repaired. Sensation had returned below the neck. His lower back was sore from sitting too long in one position, his hand was stiff from holding the cyberdeck in his lap, and his toes were cramped in his size-too-small sneaks. He pressed a finger against the bruise on his left arm that he'd gotten when he spasmed out two days ago. The slight pressure *hurt*. It was wonderful.

He stared at the holopic of Lydia. The emotional hurt he felt wasn't so wonderful.

He still loved Lydia. That hadn't changed. But his obsessive need to find her was gone. Now he was able to objectively weigh the pros and cons of continuing his search for her, to balance the joy he would feel at seeing her once more against the danger that finding her might pose. Assuming that she was still alive.

He was also able to realize the best thing he could do for her. To simply walk away, a second time. Because even though he was in love with her, she wasn't in love with him. Seeing him again would bring her no joy. He was merely a copy of a man she'd once loved. Not the real thing.

But one thing was real. He was *otaku*. His seven-year search might be at an end, but a new voyage of discovery stretched before him. His past and present had met, and forged a new future for him.

Daniel leaned back in his chair and stared out at the rain. "Thanks, Psychotrope," he said. "Wherever you are."

02:57:15 JST
Osaka, Japan

Hitomi opened her eyes and saw her father staring down at her as she yanked the fiber-optic cable from her datajack. She was not surprised to see on his face a look of confusion, rather than concern. As she sat up, there was a buzz of excitement from the physicians who'd been fussing over her. Firm hands pressed her back down onto the hospital bed and one of the doctors grabbed for the cable Hitomi had just dropped.

"What is happening now?" her father demanded.

"Hitomi must rest," one of the physicians said. "She was unconscious for at least ten minutes—ever since her guardians heard her cry out, then found her collapsed over her cyberdeck. Plugging a simple telecom cable into her datajack seems to have reversed the dump shock that complicated her condition earlier, but we cannot be certain that there will not be further complications. Perhaps we should re-attach the plug . . ."

"I am fine, thank you," Hitomi told the doctor, brushing away the plug the doctor was holding. "I would like to return to my own bed now."

She saw, now, the cause of her father's concern. He was worried that she had at last succumbed to HMHVV—that his vaccine was not a success. And that was good, for it meant he did not suspect the truth. He did not know what she had become.

She smiled. It was a wistful smile, for she remembered the truth now. The one that her father's hired magician had tried to erase. The *aidoru* Shinanai had betrayed her and did not love her—had never loved her. And neither did her father.

But there was someone—or something—that did. The artificial intelligence. In the instant before she had logged off, Hitomi had once more entered into resonance with it. She had felt the love it bore her, and the warmth and peace this love conveyed. Now that she was *otaku*, she could enter deep resonance at will. And there were others there, other lonely teenagers like herself. Others who could see into her innermost thoughts and who would accept her and love her with an open, naked truthfulness that no one else could ever experience.

Others who would benefit greatly from the resources of a nuyen-rich corporation like Shiawase . . .

"Our Matrix security staff report that you misled your guardians," her father said in what Hitomi thought of as his business voice. "You were not studying; you did not access the *juku* site. What were you doing? Do not lie to me. Our computer resource staff found a copy of one of that—woman's—songs in the storage memory of your cyberdeck. Were you trying to contact her?"

Realizing that she no longer loved the *aidoru,* and that—more important—she no longer wanted to die, Hitomi laughed out loud. The physicians were startled and her father scowled and half raised his hand, as if he were about to strike her.

With an effort, Hitomi composed herself. She would gain nothing by aggravating her father. She put a contrite expression on her face.

"Yes, Father," she admitted. "I was. But I did not succeed."

"I see."

He reached an instant decision. "You are forbidden to use your cyberdeck, forbidden to access the Matrix again. Do you understand?"

"Hai." At the last moment, Hitomi remembered to look sad and unhappy.

Satisfied, her father turned and strode from the room.

Hitomi smiled behind his back and let the physicians continue to fuss over her. As soon as these silly adults let her return to her own room, she'd jack directly into a telecom line and enter the Matrix. She didn't need a stupid *cyberdeck* to join her new family. Not any more.

(12:57:15 EST)
Toronto, UCAS

Winston Griffith III sat behind the massive oak desk in the den of his Toronto residence and stared at his expensive cyberdeck. He'd shut off its power and now its blank screen reflected his image. Illuminated by the track lighting overhead, his face looked norm—

He caught himself, and smiled. Then he corrected himself. His face looked *human.* Aside from his complete lack of facial hair, it might be the face of any other Afro-American.

He pushed the cyberdeck away. He didn't need it any more. Nor did he need the smart frame he'd paid so much money to have custom-programmed. By now, his "shameful" secret was probably out. And if it wasn't, it would only be a matter of time before another shadowrunner got a sniff of it, and tried to blackmail him.

He was clearly no longer in the running for the executive council of the Human Nation. And the odd thing was, no matter how hard he tried, he didn't care.

What he did care about was his son. That e-mail message from Chester was eleven months old. Chester could be anywhere by now. But thankfully, Winston had the resources to find him. Both the financial resources and—he stared at his reflection, contemplating the empty datajack in his head. Then he smiled. And the material resources as well.

And assuming that the AI was still sane and on-line, he also had friends in high places . . .

Winston unplugged the fiber-optic cable from his cyberdeck, plugged it directly into his datajack, and entered the Matrix to begin his search for his missing son.

(02:57:15 CST)
Tenochtitlán, Aztlan

Yograj spent several minutes in a dreamlike state, half in and half out of consciousness. At last his eyes fluttered open. He glanced right, and saw the shattered remains of the robotic cleaning drone—glanced left, and saw the teenage rebel with the Ares Viper pistol. For a moment he was disoriented. Was he still in the Matrix—still Bloodyguts? Or was he in his hotel room in Tenochtitlán, having just completed the weirdest Matrix run of his life?

He sniffed, and smelled gunpowder. Reality, then. No wait. The ultra-violet system he'd just been accessing had contained smells, tastes, textures—it stimulated all of the five senses. Frag. He felt like it did when he'd messed up slotting BTL. As unable to tell reality from illusion as . . .

The rebel who leaned over him had one hand on the fiber-optic cable that connected Yograj to his fried deck. Yograj shook his head weakly. "Don't unjack me," he croaked. Then he gritted his teeth and closed his eyes.

Suddenly his conscious mind was hurled back into the

Matrix. Another decker's persona approached—an undulating worm that inched toward him on a multitude of feet. Its voice whispered in his ear.

"Be chill, man. I've come with a message from the Great Being."

"The what?"

"You know it by another name: Psychotrope."

"Oh." The pieces started to slot into place. The decker that Bloodyguts was talking to was *otaku*. He stared at the worm persona with open curiosity. There was so much more he wanted to know. "How do you—?"

The worm ignored the question. "The Great Being is grateful to you for helping to save its life. It sensed that you were having difficulty adjusting to your new—existence— and sent me to help you. It also wishes me to tell you that it approves of your fight against the BTL dealers. My brothers and sisters will help with your next mission if you like."

Yograj felt his meat-world bod grin, exposing his curving canine teeth. "I like," he told the worm.

He couldn't believe it. Only a few seconds had passed since he'd escaped from the pocket universe inhabited by the AI, and *already* the cavalry was here? These kids were really wiz. He'd be happy to have even one on his team. And there seemed to be more than one. "Brothers and sisters" the worm had said. They were just kids, yeah. But with the processing power of an AI to back them up.

Those BTL dealers had better watch their backs.

09:57:49 PST
Seattle, UCAS

Deni charged around the squat, readying everything he would need to bust Pip outta the abandoned geothermal plant. He tossed the double-juiced stun baton into his nylon carry bag—*that* should frag up the Amerind kid with the weird aura but good—and made sure his Palm Pistol was ready to rock before shoving it into his boot top. He'd already rousted a grumbling Alfie from the sack with a

bang on the door of her squat and told her to warm up her
bike. Now he was tying the wolf-claw necklace that served
as his shamanic fetish around his neck.

Kali, the dobie-lab cross that Deni had rescued from the
junk yard ten years ago, watched his frantic preparations
with wide brown eyes. The dog was missing its left front
leg but could run like a jazzed turbo. Lean and strong,
she'd easily be able to keep up with the bike. And her nose
would help sniff out the worst of Hell's Kitchen's danger
spots.

Sensing Deni's mood, the dog stood, tripod-still, the
black fur along her spine bristling. Whatever went down
today, she'd be there as backup.

Deni slung the nylon bag over his shoulder and was just
reaching for the door when the flatscreen of Pip's Matrix-
Pal computer deck suddenly lit up. Its tinny speaker let out
a sharp *ping!* that stopped Deni in his tracks.

The high-pitched sound made Kali's head whip around.
Her nose twitched, and then she began frantically barking
at the screen as it filled with a familiar face.

"Pip!" Deni shouted. He leaped for the deck and seized
it with both hands. "Chill!" he shouted over his shoulder at
Kali. The dog immediately fell silent.

Pip's on-screen image opened its mouth and began to
"talk," but the speaker remained silent. Watching the image, Deni realized that it was strobing back and forth between a digipic of Pip with her usual solemn look, and one
of her laughing. The effect was spookin' and made Deni
want to jerk the power cord. But then text scrolled across
the bottom of the display. The block letters were crisp,
neat. But the words were in Sprawlspeak, in the spellings
that Deni had taught her in an effort to get her to open up
to him by using written language. It hadn't worked—but
his sister had learned to write. The "voice" of the text was
all Pip.

HULO DENI. I CHAINGED MY MIND. THE PLACE
MY FREND TOOK ME WUZ ONLY FUN A LITTLE
WILE. THEN IT GOT SCARY. I WANNA COME HOME
AND FROSTY SEZ ITS OK. HE SEZ HE'S SORRY THE
RESONANTS DIDN WERK AN I CAN STILL BECUM
AN *OTAKU* AN GET JACKED IF I CHAINGE MY

MINE LATER. FROSTY WILL EVEN LEMME TAKE
ANY TOYS HOME I WANNA. WILLYA COME GET
ME? PIPSQUEEK

PS DONT MESS UP FROSTY NONE, OHKAY? HE'S
STILL MY FREND.

The image on screen stopped strobing and settled on the
laughing digipic of Pip.

"Resonants?" Deni echoed. "What the frag did that
wirehead do to her?" It had to have been something to do
with computers. When Deni had seen Pip ten minutes ago,
she was troded up and eyeball-deep in the Matrix. Something must have happened to her there.

Deni felt like turfing the MatrixPal on the floor and
gutter-stomping it with the heel of his boot. Fraggin' thing.
It was what had gotten Pip in trouble in the first place. But
instead he gritted his teeth and stabbed out a reply with
one finger. I'M COMIN PIP.

As he finished, he heard Alfie's bike rumble to a stop
outside his door.

"Come on, Kali," he told the black dog. "We're gonna
bring Pip home."

Epilogue

>>>>>(Hmph. Well, that was a waste of time. I can't see
anything wrong in there. Whatever the glitch was, it seems to
have disappeared as soon as I accessed the Seattle
RTG.)<<<<<
—Captain Chaos (09:57:05/03-19-60)

>>>>>(CAP! WELCOME BACK, MAN! WE WAS
FREAKIN'!!!)<<<<<
—Angus (09:57:12/03-19-60)

>>>>>(What the frag you shouting for, Slater?)<<<<<
—Captain Chaos (09:57:21/03-19-60)

>>>>>(You disappeared, Chaos. For more than eight minutes.)<<<<<
—Mom on the Run (09:57:38/03-19-60)

>>>>>(I what? Just a sec' while I check my datalog.)<<<<<
—Captain Chaos (09:57:52/03-19-60)

>>>>>(It's true, CC. I entered the Seattle RTG thirty-three seconds after you did, and have a great big hole in my log where the details of the run should be. Someone or something wiped my deck, starting at the precise instant I entered that RTG and ending at 09:57:01. Even worse, they also wiped my memory. MY memory, not the one on my deck. And as you and I both know, memory is all I've got, chummer.)<<<<<
—Renny (09:58:26/03-19-60)

>>>>>(Sounds like someone fragged you. And not in a fun way, neither. Uh-huh.)<<<<<
—Pervo (09:58:30/03-19-60)

>>>>>(Are you back in our shadowfiles AGAIN, you git? Go on back to your sleaze sites.)<<<<<
—Mom on the Run (09:58:42/03-19-60)

>>>>>(Sounds like you got iced, chummer. Sounds like a LOT of people got hit with IC. I can't say where I'm working at the moment, but let's just say it's a LARGE corporation. 'Round about 09:48 PST—and never mind what the local time was—our deckers started to come down with the screams and shakes, one by one. Took me a while to scan the fact that the one thing they had in common was that they were all accessing the Seattle RTG. The suits upstairs panicked—they were worried that maybe a second arcology had gone into meltdown and was going to glitch up the whole system. But everything was cool. Except for the poor fragger we jacked out. I'll always be haunted by his screams . . .)<<<<<
—Grunge Monster (09:59:36/03-19-60)

>>>>>(My boss thought it was a repeat of the Crash of 2029. You should have seen the Vancouver Stock Exchange when the news got out. Just two minutes into it, and the stock of all of the 'puter corps was in the toilet. But the market is starting to rally already. And my boss is tearing out her hair, wishing our brokers hadn't panicked and sold, just as prices hit rock bottom. Oops. Boss lady's coming. Gotta run.)<<<<<
—Psylocke (10:00:03/03-19-60)

>>>>>(Hey, any corp war's gotta have its casualties. Whoever planted this virus really knew their stuff. I just wonder who's at whose throat, now. I thought the big boys had declared a truce.)<<<<<
—Merc (10:00:11/03-19-60)

>>>>>(Screw you, soldier-boy. My girlfriend just DIED. Frag you all. Frag the corps. Frag whoever planted this virus. I'm gonna find him and take him down so HARD . . .)<<<<<
—Bung (10:00:20/03-19-60)

>>>>>(Anyone else notice that the glitches seemed to cluster around the Underground News Net? It's all part of the master plan. A test run. Take down all communication, but leave the ork sites up and running.)<<<<<
—Truthseeker (10:00:51/03-19-60)

>>>>>(Yeah, we metas are behind everything, huh? Your "Great Metahuman Conspiracy" is wearin' a bit thin, twinkie-brain. I don't suppose ya noticed that EVERY news net was still up and running, throughout the crisis? Data was still comin' through, loud and clear. It was just the DECK-ERS with the hot hardware got their hoops in a loop.)<<<<<
—Angus (10:01:40/03-19-60)

>>>>>(If it was a virus, who was behind it?)<<<<<
—Mom on the Run (10:01:55/03-19-60)

>>>>>(Who or WHAT is the question.)<<<<<
—Captain Chaos (10:02:01/13-19-60)

>>>>>(Are you thinking what I'm thinking, CC?)<<<<<
—Renny (10:02:27/13-19-60)

>>>>>(By "what" do you mean one of the corps?
Well, I could tell you boys which one it AIN'T. Ex-
cept that I can't tell. Except to say it doesn't start with
an "R." An "M" or an "F" maybe, but definitely not an
"R.")<<<<<
—Grunge Monster (10:02:42/13-19-60)

>>>>>(I'm thinking the same thing, Renny. Something
"artificial.")<<<<<
—Digital Dawg (10:03:14/13-19-60)

>>>>>(You're way off, chummers. It was a virus, plain
and simple.)<<<<<
—Inchworm (10:03:49/13-19-60)

>>>>>(How do you know?)<<<<<
—Angus (10:03:57/13-19-60)

>>>>>(Take a browse through the KSAF in basket. The
pirate news station received a message at 09:45:00 that I
think you might find interesting. Looks like someone had a
little advance warning of what was about to be uploaded to
the Seattle RTG exactly two minutes later.)<<<<<
—Inchworm (10:04:10/13-19-60)

>>>>>(The worm's got that right.)<<<<<
—Scoop (10:04:15/13-19-60)

>>>>>(A virus! Told ya so!)<<<<<
—Merc (10:04:24/13-19-60)

>>>>>(What do you think, CC? does it scan?)<<<<<
—Renny (10:04:43/13-19-60)

>>>>>(Could be.)<<<<<
—Captain Chaos (10:04:52/13-19-60)

>>>>>(I still think there might be an artificial intelligence behind all this.)<<<<<
—Digital Dawg (10:05:09/13-19-60)

>>>>>(That's just wishful thinking, Dawg. There's never been a single shred of evidence that conclusively proves the existence of AIs.)<<<<<
—Red Wraith (10:05:28/13-19-60)

>>>>>(Or the existence of God. Or the existence of Dawg. Gimme a break!)<<<<<
—Merc (10:05:38/13-19-60)

>>>>>(Well, something weird went down on the Matrix today, that's for sure. And I DO SO exist, Merc. As for God, however . . .)<<<<<
—Digital Dawg (10:05:50/13-19-60)

>>>>>(We may never know what really happened. Not if everyone caught up in the glitch has a hole in their wetware memory as big as mine.)<<<<<
—Captain Chaos (10:06:07/13-19-60)

>>>>>(Someone's got to know the answers. We've just got to keep looking until we find the right file.)<<<<<
—Renny (10:06:14/13-19-60)

>>>>>(Don't viruses leave behind a distinctive signature, just like chemical explosives? You wanna find out who bombed the Seattle RTG, check the signature. I'm guessing terrorists, now.)<<<<<
—Renny (10:06:29/13-19-60)

>>>>>(See? Merc agrees with me. It WAS the orks.)<<<<<
—Truthseeker (10:06:40/13-19-60)

>>>>>(Oh shut up, conspiracy clown. As for me, I'm leaning toward the corporate war theory. It's starting again, same place as before. Seattle.)<<<<<
—Slater (10:02:52/13-19-60)

>>>>>(Hey, what are you guys talking about? My deck was glitched. Did I miss something interesting?)<<<<<
—Retro (10:07:00/13-19-60)

ABOUT THE AUTHOR

Lisa Smedman is the author of the Shadowrun® novels *The Lucifer Deck* and *Blood Sport*. She has also published a number of her short science fiction and fantasy stories in various magazines and anthologies. Formerly a newspaper reporter, she now works as a freelance game designer and fiction writer. In addition to her three Shadownrun® novels, Smedman has written a number of adventures for TSR's Ravenloft® line and several other game systems. When not writing, she spends her time organizing literary conventions, hiking and camping with a women's outdoors club, and (of course) gaming. She lives in Vancouver, B.C.

An exciting preview from
THE TERMINUS EXPERIMENT
by Jonathan E. Bond and Jak Koke

August 11, 2059   11:30PM (PST):

Hot sweat, cool breezes, and the sounds of far-off laughter. Twilight, a dangerous time, second only to the wee hours. A time when hookers are made to swallow Drano, when the homeless are beaten to death.

With the coming of night the humid smell of the city grew overpowering, and down by the dockside the sick essence took on a dangerous feel. In the deepening gloom, the scent of industrial garbage was the rot of an open, malignant tumor, the sour brine odor . . . gangrenous.

Shadows congealed in the alleyways, feeding off, growing from the stench. It was always this way, because something gets loose in those fleeting minutes between day and night. Something travels on the foul breeze. Like nerve gas on the wind.

The dim alley faded to darkness. Even the bright bulbs from the loading docks—the ones designed to burn during the long night hours—were black.

Hookers and homeless had avoided this stretch of alleyway ever since of the first hint of night. Mostly it was instinct, that, and a knowledge of the twilight rules. They knew Death was on the wind and the best way to avoid meeting it prematurely was to stay out of the way.

Tonight, Death's angels rested in the alcove of a warehouse's loading dock. Two forms, their shadows bloated by the sharp angles of automatic weaponry.

The younger man wore no shirt, only dark trousers, combat boots, a black headband to hold back his long, blond hair, and a single diamond stud in his left ear. He sat with legs folded, his bare back to the cool concrete next to the heavy corrugated doorway. Not a muscle moving, his breathing was deep, steady. He had been seated in exactly the same position for almost two hours.

The older man moved about from time to time, rough camos hissing quietly with each step as he paced in the dark silence. His joints were stiffer than the younger man's and required stretching every once in a while, but he didn't complain. The time was close, and everything was ready.

Ready and waiting.

These men's existence had become a process of patient immobility, then quick action, then stillness again. They had become masters of the patience game. Head-trick kings. They used various mental exercises to make the time pass quickly while still remaining alert.

Because it was the waiting that made sure no mistakes had been made, and these men could afford no slips when it came time to move. To strike. Not tonight, and if ever they needed all their hunting skill, it would be tonight. If they moved a millisecond too slowly, or made the slightest misstep, they knew they would be turned from the hunters into the hunted.

But soon the moment of quick action would begin, and the bright curve of headlights told them their waiting was almost at an end.

A slice of lacquered midnight, the Cadillac Crutara slid down the deserted alleyway. The engine noise was a quiet rumble, bouncing off the tall brick canyons on either side, and its headlights cut crazily as the driver swerved to avoid the piles of refuse filling the narrow passageway.

The driver was a man of thirty-five, fit, with the rugged good looks of an ex-jock and hair cut close to his scalp. He handled the Crutara with the abandon of a man who could replace it without much consideration.

He pulled across the last street and slowed the Crutara to a crawl as he entered the final stretch of alleyway.

In air-conditioned comfort, Derek looked for the sign—a quick flash of headlights in the dark of the alley. He was nervous, sweating despite the cool air blowing from the Cadillac's vents.

Derek was on time, and he hoped Burney Costello was on time as well. Burney had a reputation for being punctual only when it suited his purposes. Derek hoped it suited Burney's purposes tonight. Anything to finish this bit of business and get back home.

Derek would never have agreed to meet here. This was not a place for a man who wielded power, more power than anyone else on earth. But *Derek* hadn't made the arrangements, hadn't been part of the planning.

Shock tactics. Surprise deployments. Aggressive maneuvering. All these things had been part of the plan, a plan made by an ex-soldier. Derek's father, Marco D'imato.

It sounded like so much bulldrek to Derek, and Derek had begun to wonder if maybe his father was starting to lose it. He'd heard the men talking, when they thought no one could hear. Heard them saying that his father was obviously going a bit over the bend, still, Derek had known why it seemed that way to them and had dismissed their muttering dissent. Now, he was not so sure. All he knew was that the plan, his father's plan, was forcing him to run an errand that should have fallen to a messenger, not to the son of Marco D'imato—the most powerful member of the Fratellanza.

Marco had been uncharacteristically patient, and after a short time, Derek had seen the logic.

If Burney Costello was to give up the beach-front property willingly, he would have to be convinced of Marco's determination.

Nothing would convince him more than Derek showing up for the meeting. For the heir apparent to the family empire to put in a personal appearance . . . well, it would help Burney realize the D'imato family was serious.

There was also the fact that Burney would give in to Derek, where he might not yield ground to a messenger.

Marco had insisted the switch be a surprise, and at the time Derek had seen the logic. Now, however, trolling down the dirty alleyway, looking for headlight flashes from a car he couldn't see, Derek was having second thoughts.

It wasn't that he was afraid, that was laughable. It was that this was taking away from his nightly routine, and that made Derek feel anxious.

He passed the loading dock of a warehouse, and was almost to the end of the alley, when a sick feeling began to burn in the pit of his stomach.

He eased past a shadowy alcove, the glint of a corrugated metal door flashing briefly in the headlights.

Did they hide *the fragging car?*

Then he saw them. Out of his side window, dark splotches casting giant shadows in the afterglow of his headlights. Like demons in the night, something out of a cheap horror trid. He saw the muzzles of the guns, and the horror trid became a full-fledged nightmare.

Derek moved, with a swiftness that no metahuman could hope to match without spending hundreds of thousands of nuyen, but it was too late. The night was lit up by automatic gunfire, the sound like rumbling thunder in the narrow alley.

The Crutara, suddenly without direction, rolled further down the alley until it gently bumped into an overflowing trash dumpster. And all the while the barrage continued until there was no glass left intact, until great, gaping holes formed in the driver's side. Big enough that the two angels of death could see most of the effects of their work.

On cue, the flying bullets ceased.

With practiced speed, the two men dragged the eviscerated body out of the vehicle, and wrapped it tightly in an air-proof bag that the young man flipped out onto the glass-covered ground. They each grabbed an end of the bag and moved swiftly up the alley, to the mini-van parked there.

The night was empty once more, empty except for hot sweat, cool breezes. The sounds of far-off laughter.

And the smell of new blood and gunpowder.